Blazing China

A Novel

R. F. Whong

Disclaimer Notice:

This novel is a work of fiction. Under no circumstances will any blame or legal responsibility be held against the author for any damages, reparation, or monetary loss due to the information contained in this book directly or indirectly.

Content Warning: Although the author follows the "less is more" principle, readers sensitive to sexual situations may find this book unsuitable, as it contains scenes intended to portray characters' attitudes towards sexual morality.

ISBN: 979-8-88904-003-3

Published by Vidasym Publishing
A Division of Vidasym, Inc.
5013 S. Louis Ave., #532
Sioux Falls, SD 57108

Contents

Dedication

I dedicate this book, first and foremost, to my Savior, the Lord Jesus Christ.

Furthermore, I dedicate this book to my brothers and sisters in Christ who have supported us in our ministry over the years.

Last but not least, I dedicate this book to numerous Christians in China who remain steadfast under tremendous pressure and suffering even today. As the writer of Hebrews 11 states, "They were... destitute, afflicted, ill-treated, of whom the world was not worthy."

They are the heroes and heroines in this book and in real life.

Why I Wrote This Book

While my husband and I served together at three churches from 1987 to 2020, many students and visiting scholars from Mainland China attended the Chinese congregation of our church. A majority of them initially identified themselves as atheists, and they came to church out of curiosity. The work of the Holy Spirit was beyond my comprehension. One by one, hundreds of them accepted Christ as their personal Savior. From them, I heard numerous stories about the Cultural Revolution, the most trying period in modern Chinese history. The Lord put an idea in my mind: Someone must write those incidents down. I compiled some of them into a draft and self-published the booklet, "Ninety Degrees of Separation," about twenty years ago.

In 2020, I received another inspiration from the Lord and began to revise my draft into a full-length book. This time, instead of depicting the horror and hopelessness of people at that time, I focused on showing how Christians prevailed under intense suffering and persecution. Many scenes depicted in the book took place in real life.

Discussion questions for book clubs

(1) How does the Communist takeover of China impact the lives of the characters, particularly in relation to their faith and personal relationships?

(2) Discuss the theme of sacrifice in the novel. How do the characters demonstrate selflessness and resilience in the face of adversity?

(3) Examine the pivotal role of decision-making in shaping individuals' lives. Evaluate the transformative impact of each character's choices on their personal odyssey.

(4) Discuss the significance of the setting, from Beijing to Inner Mongolia, Hong Kong, and California. How do these locations shape the characters' experiences and the overall themes of the novel?

Chapter One

"Two roads diverged in a wood, and I—I took the one less traveled
by, and that has made all the difference."

Robert Frost (1874–1963), "The Road Not Taken"

Chungking (Chongqing), China
September 1945

A painting of Christ's crucifixion on the wall loomed over Wang
Leesan. She sat wedged between her parents, her ribs straining
against her dress at the radio's warm hum. The news reporter's loud
voice echoed in their living room. "Japan surrendered after eight
years of war. Let's all celebrate..."

Mama stood up, her long flowery dress draping around her slim
frame. "Finally, we can return to Nanjing. I can't wait to see our old
house again."

"Praise the Lord." Moisture glistened in Papa's eyes, his shiny
black hair bobbing over his forehead. He moved over to draw them
into a three-way hug.

After Papa loosened his hold on them, Leesan crossed her arms
over her stomach. *Will the Lees move back to Peking? I must see my*

beloved Rong!

Was she thirteen when she met him? Smiling over when he moved in next door five years ago, she excused herself and strolled toward their neighbor's house.

Beyond the gate, a tall woman, in the traditional Chinese *qipao* dress with her glossy ebony hair combed into a neat bun, stood under an arbor full of purple blooms.

Leesan quickened her steps. "Mrs. Lee, have you heard about the big news?"

Mrs. Lee's lips curled up. "It's amazing, isn't it?" A slight Peking accent laced her soft-spoken Mandarin. "Rong is waiting for you inside."

Leesan waved and entered the living room. Her heartbeat skittered at Rong's tall profile. Laughter burst from her chest. "How come you're not reading in your study today?"

Both arms extended, he strode forward. "I've been waiting to see you."

"Yes? You must have heard the news." She grinned and sprinted across the tiles to meet him.

"Of course. I foresee today will be earmarked as one of the most memorable days in our history." Grasping her hands, he drew her to sit on the sofa. "I've got something to ask you. We're moving back to Peking. I'll transfer to Peking University, starting my junior year soon. How about you?"

She leaned against him, a tide of tender feelings flooding her. "Peking University has accepted me. I'll go to the same university as you."

"Wonderful." His eyes sparkled. "I can't wait to show you our place in Peking. My family has lived there since my great-grandparents did. Have you seen a Chinese courtyard house before?"

Safe at his side, she shook her head. "I've read about it, a house with a square courtyard in the center surrounded by many rooms on all sides. The main gate always faces south."

He patted her arm. "I'm sure you'll love it."

Her mouth curved up. Oh, she could barely wait to start college life with him and then become Mrs. Lee Rong. She scooted away and pushed to her feet. "I'd better go now."

Grinning, he tapped her nose. "I'll see you tomorrow."

Enveloped in a dreamy excitement, she headed home for dinner.

The air smelled different. The world felt different. Her steps light, she nearly skipped into the dining room to join Papa and Mama at the mahogany dining table. After sinking into her seat and waiting for Papa to give the blessing, she grabbed her chopsticks to pick up a piece of pork and breathed in the tangy garlic scent. Could a day be more perfect?

Her mother gave her a meaningful glance. "We'll move back home soon. National Central University is also relocating back to Nanjing. Didn't you receive an acceptance letter from them?"

I can't hide it anymore. Leesan pushed back her shoulders. "I'm dating Rong. I want to be with him in Peking."

Her parents lapsed into silence.

Wouldn't they say something? She put down the chopsticks and wrung her fingers. "I understand he isn't a Christian yet. Didn't his mother receive her baptism recently? He'll become a Christian soon. I'm sure of it."

Mama let out a long breath. "It's good that the socioeconomic status of our families is similar, and Su-Ann has become my close friend. But you're so young. You've never dated before. Do you understand what love is? Maybe you're just infatuated with Rong?"

As tears dampened Leesan's cheeks, Papa pulled her into his arms. "You're our only child. We'll never prevent you from pursuing your dreams. If you wish to go to Peking University, we won't say no. I urge you to consider your decision carefully. You're barely eighteen. Pray and choose wisely."

She stood up from Papa's embrace and placed a hand over her heart, a heaviness in her chest. "I must be with Rong. I won't be happy without him."

Mama dabbed her forehead with a handkerchief. "I'm afraid we've spoiled you."

Leesan surged forward and sank to her knees at Mama's feet. "I'll be fine. Rong is a decent man."

"It's too bad our small church doesn't have young men suitable for you." Mama cupped Leesan's chin, peered down at her, then smoothed back the hair from her temples. "After you go to Peking, remember to share the gospel with Rong."

Over the next week, although busy packing, Rong came by every morning and often stayed for lunch. And Papa made an effort to talk to him.

Rong also brought along Liang Duan, a tall young man whose long, thick brows and soulful midnight-black eyes added to his habitual melancholy expression. Rong introduced him as his best friend since their elementary school days in Peking. "He came here to help us move. Like me, he'll be a junior at Peking University."

With the same ideology, the two friends often engaged in earnest discussions. Yet, in her father's presence, Duan became less talkative.

Unable to suppress her curiosity, Leesan drew Rong into a corner. "Is Duan afraid of Papa? Why is he so quiet around him?"

Rong made a funny face with crossed eyes. "He doesn't care too much for wealthy folks, especially rich, high-ranking government officials."

She pouted. "Don't joke around. How about me? What does he think about me?"

"Hmm." Rong hesitated with an uneasy laugh. "He learned I'm dating an official's daughter and wanted to check you out. I guess he likes you now. He told me you're a good-looking girl."

She grinned. The more she became acquainted with Duan, the better she liked him. He cared about her feelings more than Rong did and enjoyed reading poems with her.

On this morning, the clock struck ten. Excitement pulsed through her veins as she waited for Rong and Duan. But they didn't show up as expected.

Something must have gone wrong. By lunchtime, she trod to the kitchen. "Mama, please send someone to the Lees."

Her mother set aside the plate in her hands. "Maybe Rong is busy and forgot to send you a message."

Bracing against the countertop stacked with china and supplies ready to be packed, Leesan furrowed her brows.

Mama touched the gold-rimmed edge of a bowl and huffed. "You're really in love, aren't you?"

She dispatched Ah Shan, their servant boy. He didn't return until late in the afternoon.

When he entered the living room, Leesan rushed to him. "Is everything all right?"

"Many men in uniform are in their yard. Mrs. Lee is in custody. Nobody has seen young Master Lee since yesterday. The soldiers are searching for him because he's a member of the Communist party."

Leesan opened her mouth but couldn't utter a word. Beads of sweat slicked her forehead. Then she whispered, "Surely, Rong didn't join the Communist party? He's never mentioned it."

She stayed up late with her parents, awaiting additional news.

Duan came at midnight. Ah Shan led him into their living room. "Rong will leave for America soon. He... might not come back." He stood by the sofa where Leesan sat. His soulful eyes seemed even darker tonight, his voice tight. "He asked me to tell you. Don't wait for him."

Her jaw dropped, a hard knot forming in her stomach. Did Rong expect to end their relationship with one simple sentence?

"Where is he?" Rising from her seat, she pressed a fist against the tightening pain. "How do I get in touch with him? Can I leave with him?"

Incredulity flashed across the faces in front of her.

"You can't." Mama held up a hand. "You two aren't even engaged."

Tears welled up in Leesan's eyes. "He'll marry me if I go with him now."

"You—" Mama's words seemed stuck in her throat.

Papa kneaded his eyebrows. "Doesn't he need to apply to go abroad?"

"Our organization has connections and is in the process of completing his application. Please keep the information confidential. Otherwise, Rong's safety may be jeopardized." Duan's forehead drooped further, and his mouth curved downward before he nodded at Leesan. "I'll contact Rong. I shall be back."

After Duan left, Papa stood and gripped her elbows. "Are you certain you want to enter marriage at such a young age?"

Dabbing her cheek with a handkerchief, she returned his gaze. "I'm one hundred percent sure. I can't live without him."

"If you're so determined, I have nothing else to say." His heavy breath ruffled her hair. "I've felt his political views are on the radical side, but I never suspected he'd join the Communist party."

"Oh, Papa." Tears trickled down once more. "I care about him. I choose to go. If I stay behind, I'll die of a broken heart."

"I'm concerned you two don't share the same values," Papa murmured more to himself than to her. "With the approaching civil war, I do worry about your safety here. This may be God's answer to my prayers. Leaving the country for a year or two doesn't seem bad. I pray you'll come home safely once the political situation stabilizes."

When Leesan was having afternoon tea with Papa and Mama the next day, the doorbell rang, and Ah Shan ushered Duan into the parlor. He stopped in front of them. "Rong has arrived in Shanghai. He's expecting Leesan to join him. They'll get married right away. Their paperwork can be processed together."

Papa stroked his chin, his face suddenly looking much older. "Can you tell us more information?"

Duan ducked his head without replying.

"Why is secrecy so important?" Papa's nervous fingers moved to massage his temples. "At least tell us where in America they're going."

Thrusting his hands into his pockets, Duan rocked back on his heels and met Papa's gaze. "They'll go to Ohio State University in Columbus, Ohio."

"Ohio State University?" Papa's eyes brightened. "Dr. John Sung's alma mater?"

At Duan's puzzled glance, Leesan couldn't help chiming in, "Dr. John Sung was a famous Chinese evangelist. My papa and mama became Christians at one of his evangelistic meetings. Dr. Sung received his PhD in chemistry from OSU but dumped his diploma into the Pacific Ocean during his trip back to China."

"Oh yes." Papa's lips curled up. "Believe it or not, a coffin sat right in front of us during the meeting. Dr. Sung shouted, 'Get rich, get rich, get the coffin!' Subsequently, he laid himself in the coffin."

Her mother nodded. "Dr. Sung was an evangelist full of the Holy Spirit and also an expert in using Chinese words that sound similar but have distinct meanings to convey his messages."

"The words *get rich* and *coffin* sound similar." Papa dipped his head. "Who would have combined such words in the same sentence to demonstrate pursuing money won't lead to eternal life?"

Mama touched her eyes. "His powerful sermon moved us to tears. We answered his altar call and accepted Christ as our Savior right on the spot."

"Doesn't Rong major in chemistry? So, he'll attend the same Department of Chemistry as Dr. Sung. How extraordinary!" Papa's voice dropped. "Too bad Dr. Sung passed away last year." He then took a sip of his tea. "How about you? Have you decided what you want to study?"

"I'll try the Department of Education. I hope they'll accept me."

Papa put down his teacup and forced a smile. "With your good grades, I'm confident you'll have no problem."

That night, during their evening prayer, Leesan prayed for the Lee family and also pleaded for the Lord's protection over her parents as they faced political turmoil.

Afterward, Mama placed a red silk pouch in front of her. "I got these from your grandma. Originally, I planned to give them to you when you became engaged. Since you're leaving tomorrow, I..." She dabbed her eyes. "It's awful. We can't even see you get married. Your papa has dreamed about taking you by the hand to lead you into the wedding ceremony. It seems an impossible wish now."

"Oh, Mama," was all Leesan managed to say.

She opened the bag to pull out several platinum chains, jade pendants, pearl bracelets, and diamond rings. Her fingers brushed over a large transparent green jade carved in the shape of a peach. "Grandma used to wear this."

"Yes, one of her favorite pieces." Mama picked up the pendant. "Give it to your daughter one day."

Her father gave her a Chinese Bible, moisture shimmering in his eyes. "Remember to read your Bible."

Chapter Two

"Truth is stranger than fiction, but it is because fiction is obliged to stick to possibilities; truth isn't."

Mark Twain (1835–1910)

Shanghai, China
September 1945

The train pulled into Shanghai Station. Sighting Rong's tall frame on the platform, Leesan rushed off and fell into his arms. "I was so worried about you. Are you all right?"

"Yeah," he replied in his usual calm tone, then placed a kiss on her forehead.

Her stomach churned, and she leaned against him, tears wetting her cheeks. "How did you get into this trouble? I knew you were involved in some campus activities at your university, but I didn't think it would be so serious."

"No use talking about it now." He frowned. "Let's go to my uncle's place. His friend Pastor Ling will officiate our wedding."

Rong took her to a Western-style house in the city's trendiest district. They were married in a simple ceremony on the same day.

Only the pastor, Uncle Su-Nong, his wife, and their twin boys were present. Different feelings—joy, sorrow, love, and a trace of regret—assailed her. After the wedding, they heeded Liang Duan's directions to hide in a bungalow until further notice.

On their first night as husband and wife, she nestled beside Rong in their dark bedroom. Heat flushed her face. "Do you know what to do?"

"I suppose." His voice sounded thick.

Her fingers curled into the bedsheet. A cold unease climbed the back of her neck. Was he wrestling with this same frantic pulse?

"Do we take off our clothes?" she whispered.

"No need." A sharp, dry cough escaped him. "Just the underwear."

The rustle of shifting fabric rose, and she mimicked the movements.

His mouth crashed onto hers. She pressed back into him, her mind grasping for the velvet prose of her romance novels—the sweeping gestures, the poetic sighs. A wave of heat surged in her chest, a breathless hope for the grand intimacy she'd expected. But no gentle maps traced upon her skin.

"No—" She uttered a gasp of shock at the pain.

Rong ignored her protest, his rhythm driven by blind momentum. The salt of her tears pooled in her mouth as he collapsed against her.

Where was the soul-stirring fire? Nothing like the ink-and-paper dreams of her novels.

A hollow silence settled between them. He didn't touch her in the next few days. She welcomed it with a sense of relief.

The uneasy truce lasted until they boarded the ocean liner a week later. As the ship pushed away from the shore, they stood together on the deck, side-by-side. The coastline dissolved into a thin, gray line.

"Bye, my beloved China, my home, my fatherland. I sincerely want to give myself to you. I don't know if I'll ever see you again," he murmured, his eyes glistening.

She touched his shoulder, then clutched both arms to her chest, unable to lift a heavy dread. When would she see Papa and Mama again?

Soon, the coast vanished from sight. While craning her neck and seeing nothing except water, she swallowed a sigh and grasped his hand. They walked back to their cabin.

Once inside, he pulled her onto the bed and kissed her. She went still, a hard knot forming in her stomach. "Aren't you in a foul mood?"

He nuzzled her neck, his breath hot against her skin. "All the more reason why I need my wife's love."

She turned her head sideways, an ache rising in her throat. "This time, shall we have the light on?"

"No." He turned off the light.

Like last time, she lay beneath him in silence, enduring his full weight on her. Frustration coursed through her veins, and her mind wandered. Was sex between a couple mainly for the purpose of producing children? Mama taught her to be submissive to her husband, no matter what.

Her thoughts returned to the present at the end of his movement. He got up and went to flick on the switch. "I received a letter from Duan before we boarded the ship. He said my mother is still in custody. I don't know what'll happen to her."

She sat up and wiped her cheeks with the back of her hand. How could he mention this now? When had he become so insensitive? "Do you want to pray with me for her safety?"

As he shook his head, she plopped back onto the pillows. Was he always so stubborn?

***

Columbus, Ohio
Fall 1945

When they arrived at Ohio State University, two letters awaited them, one bearing the name Lee Du Su-Ann and the other Wang Jia-Ting and Wang May.

Praise the Lord! Leesan clasped the envelopes to her chest, savoring the news from Rong's mother and her parents. Her heart leaped at the information that Su-Ann had been freed and was already leaving for Peking.

Peking... What would it be like there? She closed her eyes, trying to superimpose the ancient, dusty city over the crisp American air.

The ghosts of home followed her into the following days until the beauty of the Ohio autumn demanded her attention. She accompanied her husband on a walk around the campus. The vibrant display of the changing season acted as a balm for her homesickness. They strolled around Mirror Lake, the jewel of the university, and paused where the water caught the reflection of a world turned to yellow, orange, and fire-red.

"The setting isn't much different from home." Pain and longing contorted Rong's face.

"Oh, Rong." She leaned into him, the fiery gold of the maples fracturing as moisture filled her eyes. The vibrant beauty hollowed, a cruel contrast to the silent question about where her parents might be.

The chilly air followed them back across the threshold of their rented room. Rong pulled her down onto the saggy sofa, the springs groaning under their weight. "We can't eat out anymore."

"I've never cooked anything in my entire life." She placed her hands on her waist, every muscle taut.

"Eating out is too expensive. We can't afford it."

While he glared at her, she pressed her lips together and kept quiet.

The silence in the kitchen stretched until he huffed out a breath. "Okay, I'll do it. Let me go get some groceries."

An hour later, he returned and hurried into the kitchen to prepare their first home meal—spaghetti disguised as Chinese noodles topped with a meat sauce. The savory steam filled the small room, masking the scent of old dust.

The makeshift noodles disappeared as her fork scraped against porcelain. She cleaned her plate and leaned back in her chair with a grin. "I didn't know you were such a superb cook."

Rong shrugged. "Cooking isn't much different from carrying out a chemical reaction." Leaning back in his chair, he folded his arms across his chest. "By the way, I've been washing our clothes since we left Shanghai. You can't expect me to do everything. My study is even busier than yours."

Her smile disappeared, and displeasure came rushing back. "But—"

"No more but." He waved to her. "Cook, or do the laundry. Pick one."

How could he expect her to do so much work? She covered her face to feign crying. Not hearing any movement, she lifted her head.

He still sat there, eyeing her with his arms crossed. She wiped her tears away. "Fine. I'll do the laundry. It's easier."

The rest of the evening passed in silence. She threw herself into the chores. After she'd hung the last of his shirts, the clock struck ten. He reached out and touched her cheek. "Let's go to bed together."

She moved a step away to lean against the wall as a chill gripped her heart. Could she muster up her courage to talk to him, this man she'd loved since thirteen, about such a sensitive subject? The mere thought brought a tightness to her throat. "Should we try different things? Can we take off our clothes and turn on the light?"

Shock distorted his smooth features.

She swallowed hard, resisting the urge to cringe. Had she said anything salacious? No. She kept her chin high. "The Bible teaches Adam and Eve were naked together and didn't feel ashamed."

A sneer further twisted his face, and the Peking accent in his Mandarin became more noticeable. "Your Bible teaches such indecent ideas?"

Her heartbeat slammed against her ribs as she rubbed her forehead. "It's not indecent. We're husband and wife—"

He raised his index finger. "As a Chinese growing up under the teachings of Confucius, you should know well we have our code of conduct. Gentlemen and ladies from good families simply don't spend too much energy on this. Life is full of more important matters."

Maybe she'd been reading too many romance stories? She chewed her lip and went to turn off the light.

***

Columbus, Ohio
Early Winter 1949

At her husband's familiar footsteps, Leesan set down her novel.

Rong entered the living room and shook off the light snow from his boots. "Today, Dr. Boord invited us to have Thanksgiving dinner with his family and other students."

She moved toward him and clapped, excitement bursting through her. "How wonderful. He's so kind."

How she loved their gatherings with friends! Besides school parties, she enjoyed meeting with other Chinese students every week to talk about China's political situation. In their first year at OSU, during one of their parties, someone told her that everyone called Rong Mr. Right. His name sounded like *wrong* in English, and a naughty American classmate nicknamed him.

The only absence was church. She hadn't stepped into a church building during the past four years. Why did studying the Bible or attending church never cross her mind except when she read a letter from her parents asking if she'd found a suitable church? Whisking a tress of hair away from her face, she brushed aside the questions with no answers.

Rong gave her cheek a teasing pat. "Time flies. I'm in debt to Dr. Boord. Without his guidance, I wouldn't have received my master's degree this year. And he also helped me find my first job."

"Your professor has done so much for you. We ought to buy a gift for his family." Perfect timing! The two of them graduated at the same time. With a bachelor's in education, maybe she could find a teaching job in Los Angeles.

Rong waved a piece of paper in the air as he shifted toward the sofa. "I almost forgot to tell you. I received a letter from Mother."

"What does it say?" She smoothed her fingers over her already smooth slacks, her mood plunging. During the past months, every letter from the Far East brought her apprehension. Rong's uncle had moved from Shanghai to Hong Kong to escape the raging civil war. Her parents' last letter described their decision to follow the Nationalist Government to Taiwan.

"Wonderful news." His lips curled up. "Mother mentioned Chairman Mao's speech announcing the founding of the People's Republic of China." His eyes sparkled. "I wish I were there to celebrate with Duan and my friends. I've been waiting for this. It's finally happened. Now we can go home."

"Home?" She grinned, then hitched a long breath. Had Papa and Mama already moved to Taiwan? She touched Rong's shoulder. "Dear Mr. Right, you'd better stay home to help me fill our boxes. We're moving to California right after Thanksgiving, and we're barely ready."

"I..." He scratched his ear. "I've been thinking." He placed the letter on the table. "If we don't go to California, if we go back to Peking—"

She sat, her stomach clenching. As he stared at her, she turned her head away. "How about your job? What'll you do in China?"

"I've also received a letter from Duan. He said the new government is recruiting people with my qualifications. It won't be a problem for me to find a suitable position once we go back. The pay will be decent." He chuckled. "We'll have servants like before. We don't need to cook and do laundry ever again. I'll send a telegram to the California job. Dr. Boord will understand."

He clasped her hands, but she drew away and walked to the window. "I don't know what to say. Papa and Mama plan to go to Taiwan. With the political unrest, if we go back to Peking, can we see them again?"

He came over to hug her. "I won't force you to do anything you don't like. Please consider it. We don't have to decide at this moment."

She tried to smile but couldn't stop her mouth from curving downward. "I must think about it. Please put the remaining books into the boxes. I need to go for a walk."

Her chest heavy, she dragged her feet toward the nearby park. Just an hour ago, their future in California seemed certain. Now everything had changed.

Life might be simpler if they went to California. She furrowed her brows, haziness clouding her mind.

The trees had already gone bare. The scenery remained quiet at first. Then a faint tune teased her ears—a familiar melody, light and merry. One of the hymns, "He Leadeth Me," she used to sing in China.

Could she peer into the future to know which route to pick? She opened her mouth but couldn't utter a word of prayer. As dusk fell, she lifted her gaze toward the lingering blue luster on the western skyline.

I'm tired of cooking and doing the laundry.
Life in China might be more comfortable.

Chapter Three

"I can't go back to yesterday because I was a different person then."

Lewis Carroll (1832–1898), *Alice in Wonderland*

Beijing, China
Spring 1950

Leesan stood in the center of the yard and sucked in the fragrant aroma swirling around the beautiful garden.

I can't believe the peonies are already in full bloom.

She walked toward the main gate to pick up the newspaper. As she passed the exquisite marble pillars framing the door, awe crept into her heart as if she were seeing them for the first time.

Her gaze returned to the paper, and she searched for new information on the civil war.

No, nothing important.

With a heavy sigh, she returned to the lush yard surrounded by bushes, trees, and odd-shaped stones.

Had they arrived in Peking, now called Beijing, only two months ago? On that February day, a thin layer of snow helped the magical scenery cast a spell on her. Yet concern about Papa and Mama's safety had broken her enchantment.

Moisture gathered behind her eyelids. Did they reach Taiwan? Were they safe?

A faint, consistent voice floated into her ears, rousing her from her thoughts.

Mother must be praying in her room.

Leesan drifted toward the north section of the main hall, her gaze tracing the rooflines of the adjacent houses where Rong's mother resided. A familiar weight pressed against her ribs. Had they made the right decision to leave the US? Could she see Papa and Mama again?

Sitting by the pond, she dipped a finger into the glass-like surface. The water broke into lazy circles against the mossy bank. Such a sprawling, silent luxury, a world away from the cramped, saggy sofa in Ohio!

The tension in her shoulders gave way to an appreciation as her mind turned toward Su-Ann. Her mother-in-law was a unique woman who commanded any room with an unexpected energy that Leesan had come to rely on.

A sharp creak of a hinge snapped the thread of her thoughts.

"Ms. Leesan, breakfast is ready." Ah Tian, who had shadowed Su-Ann since the woman's first breath, beckoned from the kitchen door.

"Ms. Leesan, breakfast is ready." Ah Tian, Su-Ann's nanny since birth, beckoned from the kitchen door.

Leesan strolled into the dining room and sat by her mother-in-law.

Like always, Su-Ann wore a traditional Chinese qipao dress. Leesan couldn't remember ever seeing her wear anything else. At forty-nine, her mother-in-law still maintained a well-kept, youthful look, maybe because she had a household of servants working for her.

Yet she appeared changed in a certain way. She used to play mahjong with some aunties late into the night and wouldn't get up until noon. Nowadays, she rose before dawn every day to read the Bible.

The scent of ginger pulled Leesan back to the present, the steam from the central tureen rising between them. She reached for a bowl of congee. "How early did you wake up today?"

Getting ready for work nearby, Rong chimed in. "I know why Mother gets up so early every morning. She tries to practice—" He paused. "What's that phrase you told me?"

Su-Ann lifted her face. "No B No B."

"Yeah." He laughed. "Bye. See you tonight."

Leesan waved at her husband and grinned. "Rong seems quite satisfied with his government position."

"It's great he's landed this job so fast. Duan's assistance was invaluable. What a blessing to have your childhood friend as a colleague!" Su-Ann peeled apart an orange and examined the pulp.

Leesan stood up to take a piece of bread. "What's No B No B?"

"No Bible No Breakfast. I learned it from missionaries at my Chungking church where your mama led me to Christ...."

Mother stopped because of a concern for me.

Moisture clouded Leesan's vision. After they returned to China, she heard from Su-Ann that her parents were among the first groups of people to go to Taiwan, and that was the last piece of news about them.

Su-Ann handed over a handkerchief. "Are you all right?"

"I'm fine." Leesan dabbed away her tears. "Thank you."

"Do you know I majored in English? I didn't have any occasion to speak English for many years. So, I was pleasantly surprised when the missionaries organized an English Bible study class in Chungking. I learned No B No B there." Su-Ann set aside her orange pieces and cleaned her fingers. "Why don't you come to worship with me this Sunday?"

Leesan ducked her head and shifted in her chair. She hadn't been in a church since she'd left home. "I can't. It'll cause Rong trouble. And we've already promised Duan to go hiking together."

Her mother-in-law placed the uneaten orange into a bowl. "I see." She rang a bell for the servants to take away the breakfast. "Rong mentioned gossip spread among his associates that I'm a Christian. I wonder how they found out."

I have no clue, either. Leesan shrugged and excused herself.

The afternoon shadows lengthened, the day's quiet monotony deepening as the sun dipped below the walls. After dinner, the house settled into its evening hush, and Leesan retreated to the bedroom. When familiar footsteps approached, she dropped her romance novel on the sofa. Rong leaned against the doorpost, a somber look dragging down his thin lips.

Her gaze held his. "What's the matter?"

"I heard some news." He shifted forward. "The People's Liberation Army has taken over most of China. The Nationalist Government has retreated."

Tears warmed her cheeks. "Are Papa and Mama safe in Taiwan?"

"Oh, Leesan." He pulled her up into his arms. "I believe they're well. I'm sure we can see them again soon."

She snuggled against his broad chest. Listening to his even heartbeat calmed her frayed nerves.

"That's not the only troublesome news." He released her and took a step away. "New campaigns are unfolding to combat corruption. Unscrupulous officials have been chipping away at the coffers for so long. It's about time to crack down on them." He tugged on an ear. "But I worry the new campaigns will also aim at eliminating the capitalist class, including the landlords in Beijing. Mother is one of them."

With the dread in his eyes so visible, something heavy pressed down on her shoulders. "Anything we can do?"

His mouth curved downward even more. "Maybe. We'll see."

An uncomfortable hush stretched across the room. *Time to change the subject.* She ducked her head and nudged a slipper along the wood floor with gold stripes. "Do you think Mother has changed?"

"Not her appearance—" His fingers ironed out the lines crinkling his forehead. "Her speech and behavior haven't altered either. She always speaks softly and calmly, giving the impression of confidence and solemnity."

She placed a palm on her heart. "Her character?"

"No." As he lowered his hand, he wrinkled his eyebrows. "It's more than that. She's always been educated, prudent, and well-mannered, although sometimes she came across as too proper. I should say she used to be too much in control, cold, like a stone wall."

"How about now?" Her chest swelling, she touched his arm.

He moved aside her novel and motioned for her to sit next to him on the sofa. "Mother is still proper, polite. Yet I sense the barrier has disappeared. She has a new kindness and an unselfish concern for others. Do you know what our driver told me this morning? Old Zhang said his daughter had a baby last year. Mother gave him a fat red envelope. She also visited his daughter and baby in person."

"Is that why all servants listen to her?" She crooked up a corner of her mouth.

Rong flipped through her novel, using it to fan himself. "If her Christian faith did such wonders for her, I should say being a Christian isn't too bad."

Her heartbeat quickened. Dare she hope...? "How come you don't want me to go to church with her?"

He slammed the book down, then shot to his feet. "Don't you understand? I'm a Communist. I believe in communism. Religion is the people's opium. We don't need it. Communism will soon build a utopia in this world. Everyone will live well, no need to commit crimes, no need for Christian redemption."

He was so stubborn. She stifled a sigh and focused on the magnificent painting on the wall—a pomegranate tree laden with red flowers and fruit nestled against huge, oddly shaped boulders. Subtle. Mother wanted them to produce as many seeds as the pomegranate. "In one aspect, Mother hasn't changed a bit."

He followed her gaze. "Yeah, she always tries to give us hints. No doubt she wants to have many grandsons like the pomegranates." He gave her a wink. "Mrs. Right, let's continue our mass-production project tonight."

"You're insufferable." With reluctance, she flicked off the light switch.

***

Three months fled away. Leesan strolled to the main gate to pick up the newspaper. News about the new campaign to redistribute land ownership occupied the front page.

Oh no. It's happening. But what could they do?

Sparrows flitted over the pond as she read in her favorite corner of the yard. Shaking her head, she dropped the paper and mused over a more pleasant idea. Her menstrual period was regular. Now she'd missed her period for two months.

Mama's words whispered in her head. "Your mother-in-law looks forward to having a grandson inherit the vast family fortune.

In the past four generations, each generation produced only one son. If possible..." Mama didn't elaborate. Topics about bedroom activities leading to children were always difficult for her parents to broach.

Mother and Rong would welcome the baby's arrival.

Her glee evaporated as images of her parents overshadowed her. Uncontrollable tears welled up. Would she see Papa and Mama again?

The morning passed in a blur of forced composure, each hour marked only by the leaden weight in her chest. By the time the late afternoon sunrays stretched across the courtyard, the routine of the house took over. Rong returned at his regular hour, his expression grave.

After dinner, they sat together to enjoy tea as usual. Su-Ann asked the servants to bring out a special set of utensils that had been with the Lees for four generations. The pot and its six matching cups, a gift from the emperor to Rong's great-grandfather, were carved from high-quality green jade.

Rong picked up his cup. "Mother, how much land do we own?"

Su-Ann's head jerked up. "Don't be concerned. All our family properties will be yours one day."

"No, that's not what I meant." He took a sip, choked, and started coughing. When he ceased wheezing, he walked to the window, his steps soft against the wood floor.

Outside, night had fallen. The chirp of crickets rang in the stillness. The room felt tranquil in comparison.

He turned from the window. "A reliable source warned me a large-scale land reform campaign will take effect soon. I worry about our situation."

While Su-Ann remained silent, Leesan fidgeted. Unable to keep still, she excused herself to step out. But she didn't go far and leaned against the wall beyond the door.

Her husband's words drifted out. "This new campaign will target the city landlords. We're one of them."

Su-Ann didn't reply. Insects chirping in the background created the only sound. After the clock struck eight, she spoke in a voice lower than usual. "The tea is cold."

Mother must have just sipped her tea. Leesan lifted her gaze toward the crescent of the new moon, pale in the dusk sky.

Rong heaved an audible sigh. "We need to take action soon."

"What are you trying to say?"

"We have to get rid of our land—quickly."

"What? Get rid of it?" Su-Ann nearly screeched before adjusting her tone. "The land has been in the family for generations. Your great-grandfather gave specific instructions that it should not be divided even if there's more than one son."

"I know it all."

"Our ancestors won't forgive the offspring who squanders the property. Do you want me to be that person?"

Leesan touched her forehead, then massaged her temples. As she prepared to return to the room, Rong's bass voice sounded once more. "Mother, forgive me, please forgive me."

Her husband didn't bring up the topic again that evening. Yet as the week progressed, he talked to his mother about it nonstop. Leesan couldn't help asking, "How come you push her so hard?"

"Because it's a serious matter." He paced around their bedroom. "I understand communism. The land reform campaign is bound to happen. Sooner or later, she'll lose the land. Sooner is better than later, especially if she volunteers to give it up."

Her gaze followed him. "What can the government do if we refuse?"

His steps halted by the sofa. "The government can do a lot, including prison sentences and capital punishment. The current goal is clear—eliminate the landlord class."

A shiver ran up her spine. She rubbed the back of her neck. "Do you regret coming back?"

He gave her a stern stare. "Why do you ask such a question?"

"I'm just wondering." She turned her head sideways. "You don't look happy."

"I have no regrets." He snapped his fingers, making her jump. "The government is doing the right thing for China, including the land reform campaign. I'll convince Mother, although I do understand her sentiments. She dreads to bring shame to the family."

After two quick strides, he sat beside her and tucked her hair back from her cheeks. "And you? Do you have regrets? It must be tough for you, especially not knowing how Papa and Mama are."

"I miss them a great deal. I'm grateful I have you and Mother." Giving him a forced smile, she patted her belly. "Soon we may have a fresh addition."

He clutched her shoulders. "What did you say?"

"I think I'm pregnant."

"Truly?" He pressed a palm against her abdomen, and his lips crinkled up. "How wonderful. I can't believe it. I'm going to be a father. Let's go tell Mother."

His excitement scarcely matched her mother-in-law's response. Upon hearing the news, she looked into the distance, an enormous grin rounding up her cheeks. "Praise the Lord."

The relief in her voice brought warmth to Leesan's heart. The Lee family line would continue.

Although disturbing information about the new campaigns continued to reach her, nothing could diminish the jubilant feelings when the doctor said she was pregnant with two babies.

After one regular checkup, Su-Ann gestured at Leesan's protruding belly. "It must run in our family. My younger brother also has twins. *Twin boys.*"

"I remember Ming-Ming and Tong-Tong, two active naughty boys. We saw them a few years back. Auntie Shu-Fang always yelled at them." Leesan chuckled at her recollection of meeting them before her wedding.

"Yes, two fine, healthy boys." Then Su-Ann's smiling expression stiffened into seriousness. "Do you know what Pastor Fu taught us on Sunday? He cited Matthew chapter thirteen."

"The parable about a farmer who went out to sow his seed?" Leesan tilted back her head.

"Yes." Su-Ann clenched her hands together. "Pastor Fu emphasized the seed that fell among thorns. It's like a person who hears the truth, but the worries of this life and the deceitfulness of wealth choke it, making it unfruitful. The Lord is giving me a message. I used to think all the wealth was mine. In reality, everything, including my life, is just entrusted to me temporarily. I'm willing to give it all back to the Lord. Tomorrow, I'll give the land to the government to set an example for other landlords in the city."

Strands of white hair shimmered on her mother-in-law's head. Noticing them for the first time, Leesan couldn't help rubbing her temples.

With nonstop political campaigns, what would happen next?

Chapter Four

"Every man must do two things alone; he must do his own believing and his own dying."

Martin Luther (1483–1546)

Beijing, China
Chinese New Year 1951

Leesan sat in a chair with both hands on her swollen belly and watched her mother-in-law examine a fish on the countertop.

"Tomorrow is Chinese New Year's Eve." Su-Ann put away the fish. "It'll be nice if we have dumplings. Most servants have already gone home. Although Ah Tian, Old Zhang, and his wife are still here, they'll be busy with other preparations."

"I know how to make them." Leesan twitched her body with a grunt. Her stiffness gave way as a sudden memory of the brick walkways at Ohio State flickered in her mind. Her lips crinkled up. "In Columbus, Rong and I used to meet with other Chinese students to make dumplings together."

Her mother-in-law cocked her head. "Are you sure you can handle it in your condition?"

"Yeah. I—"

Her husband entered the kitchen, his brows knotted and lips pressed into a thin line.

"Leesan, I heard some troublesome rumors. The government will enforce the campaign to eradicate opposition elements, especially those who have connections with the Kuomintang."

"The KMT? The political party of the Nationalist Government?" She slumped back against her chair, something pinching her chest. "Why are you worried? Does it concern us?"

"Yes and no." He shifted from one foot to the other. "Your parents went with the KMT to Taiwan. So far, only Duan knows. Most people think I'm a member of the Communist Party and work for the government. They assume you're also a Communist. Anyhow, unless necessary, don't go out by yourself."

She patted her abdomen. "Don't worry. I can hardly move with this."

His slippers whispering against the floor, he crossed to her side and crouched to her eye level. "I just don't want anything bad to happen to you."

Leesan shook off the warning and threw herself into the company of Ah Tian. They spent the next day making a massive batch of dumplings, fueled by Ah Tian's stories about Rong's childhood. By the third day, they were still eating the leftovers. At lunch, while Leesan reached for the soy sauce, a sharp pain pierced her, and water gushed between her legs. She grabbed the dining table. "My water broke. The babies are coming."

"Now?" Rong clattered his chopsticks against his plate. "We've not packed the bag yet."

She frowned, the pain getting worse. "Not now, but soon."

He stood up. "Let's get you to the hospital."

As the pain intensified, she screeched like an injured animal all the way to the Union Hospital. In the delivery room, Rong sat by her side until the nurse asked him to leave.

How much time had gone by? Her voice turned hoarse. Then the torture started again.

"Keep pushing," the doctor urged.

At last, a baby's cry sounded. Minutes later, another baby wailed. But the pain didn't subside. Why did it still hurt so much?

Confusion, dread, hope, joy, and irritation stirred inside of her.

When her husband entered the room, she raised her battered body with her elbows. "Girls or boys?"

"Two girls." He kissed her forehead. "Mother suggested we name them Ann-Ann and May-May. Ann is after my mother, and May is after yours."

She slumped back in bed. What a disappointment to Mother. She wanted twin boys.

As if reading her mind, Su-Ann came to her side. "The Lord has blessed us with two beautiful girls. I'm sure they'll have brothers soon."

Although Su-Ann followed an age-old Chinese tradition for well-to-do families and hired two wet nurses to take care of the twins, Leesan checked on her babies around the clock. A mix of tears and smiles came over her every time she examined their angelic faces.

Shouldn't I be happy? Why do I have so much sorrow, fear, and doubt? Was it because her life became hectic even with servants surrounding her?

She soon found a rhythm within the chaos. Six months passed in the blink of an eye as the twins grew. The Mid-Autumn Festival arrived. She helped Su-Ann compile their shopping list: moon cakes, Chinese grapefruits, crabs, and pork. "Mother, don't you think it's comforting to see the full moon shine brightly regardless of the many changes around us?" She feigned a grin, yet she couldn't prevent herself from chewing the inside of her cheek. "I'm worried. Rong has been feeling ill during the past few days."

"Yes, he looks exhausted. I've been praying for him." Su-Ann rubbed her chin. "Maybe his work stresses him out."

On the festival night, they sat together to enjoy a sumptuous feast.

Leesan tore apart a crab leg. "Rong, how do you feel?"

He flashed a forced smile. "Don't fret over me. I'm fine. I just need more sleep."

Yet come morning, he failed to get up. Their family doctor declared he had acute hepatitis and sent him to the hospital right away.

"Why did Rong get so sick?" Moisture gathered behind Leesan's eyelids, and then warm droplets slipped down her cheeks.

His health deteriorated. He lost so much weight in two weeks that he appeared like a skeleton covered with a thin layer of skin.

Su-Ann pulled Leesan aside. "He's getting worse. Let's take him home. Let's try Chinese herbal medicine."

Back at home, his mother kneeled by him every morning, pleading for God's healing power. But when his condition didn't improve, her prayers changed, and she asked God for his salvation.

The shift in her mother-in-law's plea chilled Leesan. Why didn't Mother ask God to heal Rong anymore?

That afternoon, as her mother-in-law left the bedside with a bowl of leftover herbal brew, Leesan cornered her. "You don't think he'll get better?"

Su-Ann put down the bowl and squeezed her in a tight hug, her former jasmine scent now overpowered by the tangy smell from the Chinese medicine. "You have dark circles under your eyes. Please rest more."

"I'm okay." Leesan scooted back and drew a series of quick breaths, trying to unclog her throat and lungs from the reminders of sickness. "Recently, Rong has been having nightmares, often involving ghosts and deceased people. He said his father visited him last night. What can we do to help him?"

"Evil spirits are disturbing him." Su-Ann coughed. "If you don't mind, I'll send for my pastor."

Leesan nodded. She would have welcomed a ghost if it meant peace for Rong.

Pastor Fu arrived later that evening, his presence bringing a quiet authority to the room. He kneeled by the bed and prayed with a steady fervor. Afterward, the tension left Rong's face, and he fell into a peaceful slumber.

Su-Ann approached after he awakened. "Will you accept Jesus Christ as your Savior?"

He dipped his head.

"Heavenly Father, I have sinned against You and men...." She prayed one sentence, and he repeated it.

Later, Pastor Fu baptized Rong at his bedside.

The days that followed became a blur of cold compresses and hushed prayers, the household suspended in a state of agonizing uncertainty. By the following week, the high fever broke. When he opened his eyes and searched for his mother, Leesan hurried to find Su-Ann. As the nannies with the twins entered, an eerie hush befell the room.

He turned his head on the pillow, his gaze hovering over the twins. Leesan reached to grasp his bony fingers, her shoulders trembling.

"Promise me..." He spoke in a low voice like in a whisper. "Promise... you'll live a fulfilling life without me."

"No, don't say that." Her entire body aching, she brought his hand to her face and wept into his palm.

"Don't cry." He stroked her forehead. "When you encounter difficulties, go to Duan."

The twins wailed. Su-Ann patted the two little girls, yet tears shimmered down her cheeks.

Rong closed his eyes, then talked with his lips barely moving. "Mother, I'm sorry."

His mouth wriggled, but no sound came out. As the light of life grew dimmer, his body went motionless.

When his mouth stirred again, Leesan had to lean over to hear him. "Mother... She's young. Help her."

Before midnight, he drew his last breath.

Leesan clenched her fists, screaming. "How could You take Rong away from us? Do You even care?"

On the morning of the funeral, she followed the Chinese custom and donned a gown made of white sackcloth with another piece of white cloth covering her face. She'd cried so much. Now she stared at the ground with dry eyes.

A baritone echoed around her. "Auntie Lee, Leesan, if you have any needs, please let me know."

She jerked up her head. Duan stood in front of her with her mother-in-law.

The guests were leaving.

"You—" She struggled to find her breath, but she could only think of the poem she and Rong used to recite. "The campaigns have not been fulfilled. The body is gone."

Duan strolled away while Pastor Fu and his wife lingered. Once home, Su-Ann led the group toward her room. "Leesan, do you want to pray with us?"

She clutched the windowsill, pressed her fingers against the cold wood so hard they bent backward, and didn't bother to respond.

"The twins want you."

The glass windowpane reflected the nanny's moving lips. Two

small hands grabbed Leesan's leg. She lowered her head to May-May in silence. *My daughter needs me, but I have nothing left to give.*

An invisible cocoon trapped her, blurring her surroundings.

Different people from the church visited their house every day. They invited her to pray, but she waved her arms and wandered away. What was the use?

When Pastor Fu and his wife stopped by again one afternoon, Mrs. Fu asked like before, "Will you pray with us?"

Leesan burst into crying. "Why bother? If God exists, how come He let Rong die?"

"You—" Su-Ann began.

Mrs. Fu tugged at Su-Ann's sleeve. "It's okay. Let her."

Leesan's weeping fractured into a jagged howl. When her mother-in-law reached out, Leesan collapsed against her. "Not fair... barely twenty-six!"

Then she slumped to the ground.

The next morning, she woke up in her own room. The first undisturbed sleep since Rong's passing rejuvenated her. She dressed and went to the living room.

Su-Ann was conversing with a visitor. "I'm worried about Leesan's mental state. She doesn't eat much or function well. Luckily, the wet nurses take good care of..."

Leesan stifled a sigh. Had she caused Su-Ann concern? How about the twins?

After the guest left, May-May pulled herself up and tottered toward her twin. Leesan gasped. The last time she'd truly looked at them, they were learning to sit up. How the world had moved on without her! She rushed to her mother-in-law. "When did they start to walk?"

"Oh, not that long ago." Su-Ann bent to pat the toddler.

Leesan's nails bit into her palms, guilt crowding her heart. She squatted to examine her daughters. They were identical in their appearance, except May-May had a mole on the end of her left eyebrow.

As though reading her thoughts, Su-Ann stooped beside her. "They look the same, right? Don't be deceived. Their personalities are quite distinct."

Rising from her crouch, Leesan frowned at something odd.

"What happened?" She tugged at her mother-in-law's cotton jacket. "How come you're not wearing your qipao dress? Why did you cut your hair short?"

Su-Ann ran one hand through her ear-length hair. "Duan told me to make some changes. He said short hair is easier to manage. He also told me gray or blue Mao suits are in fashion."

Leesan twisted the material between her fingers. "Duan is like your second son."

"Yes, I've known him since he was seven years old." A small smile curled up Su-Ann's lips.

Leesan went to bed that night with the ghost of a long-haired Su-Ann in her mind, but the morning brought a reality she didn't recognize. On Sunday, her confusion only deepened. She stood at the gate, eyes wide, as a stranger pulled a rickshaw to the curb. "Why isn't Old Zhang driving you to church? What's wrong with him?"

Su-Ann tucked her handbag under her elbow. "Old Zhang has retired."

Leesan heaved a long breath. "So, the servants are leaving us."

"Dictated by the new policy to liberate the working class, all of them are taking up other jobs." Su-Ann switched her handbag to her other hand. "The wet nurses are leaving soon. We'll have to take care of the twins ourselves."

How would her mother-in-law handle the chores? In her entire life, Su-Ann had never touched dirty dishes. *At least in my OSU days, I've learned domestic skills.* She'd have to shoulder most of the house tasks now.

The last servant to leave was Ah Tian. At the gate, she dabbed her eyes. "Su-Ann." Unlike other maids, Ah Tian always called her by name directly. "You take care of yourself."

Su-Ann handed her a red envelope, but Ah Tian declined. "Don't worry about me. You need the money."

Robbed of Ah Tian's help, Leesan and her mother-in-law took turns playing with the children during the daytime. At night, Ann-Ann slept with Leesan in one room while May-May stayed with Su-Ann in another.

At first, Su-Ann went to the restaurant every day to buy prepared food. After eating six Peking ducks in ten days, Leesan stopped her mother-in-law on her way out. "Please buy a piece of pork and a bunch of spinach from the wet market. I can cook. I know how."

How she valued the mundane duties! They kept her occupied and alleviated her misery. Every task, no matter how small, became a form of therapy. While busying herself in the kitchen, she couldn't retreat into her cocoon.

Duan visited them one afternoon when she was playing with Ann-Ann. He made a face with a cross between a smile and a frown to tease her. "Your black dress is ugly. Try the dark-blue Mao suit."

"Yes." Su-Ann chimed in. "You like to wear clothes in the American style because of your upbringing. It may take you some time to get used to wearing a shirt and a pair of pants. Like me, you'll adapt. The new fashion isn't bad at all."

He gave out a small laugh. His expression changed as he moved toward Su-Ann. "Auntie Lee, have you considered offering your house to the government to ease the housing shortage in Beijing?"

At his question, Leesan's shoulders stiffened. "We lost our land not that long ago. Do you mean we will lose this house?"

The muscle in his chin twitched. He ducked his head and spoke without making eye contact. "It's going to happen sooner or later. Taking the initiative has some advantages. You'll be able to stay in this place."

Leesan lifted her chin. "What can the government do if we refuse?"

"You must understand. Under communism, private property ownership is not allowed. The government owns everything and allocates a portion to each person based on their need." He brought a palm to his forehead. "The consequence could be dire. The government will do whatever it takes to achieve the goal, including exile, prison sentences, and the death penalty."

A chill ran up Leesan's spine as her gaze fell on her daughters playing nearby.

Su-Ann cleared her throat. "I thought I'd learned my lesson well. Whatever I have is just entrusted to me temporarily." Her voice was as low as a whisper. "Why does the idea of losing this place hurt so much?"

"Auntie—"

"It's okay." She raised a hand, tears shining on her cheeks. "You're right. We need to do it soon."

Mother, this is beyond your control. The Lee ancestors wouldn't blame you. Leesan longed to comfort her mother-in-law. Instead, she shifted one step toward Duan. "Do you know how many families are moving in?"

"Two or maybe three." He turned away to avoid her gaze.

She shook her head. "It'll be very inconvenient. We only have one kitchen. Does it mean I have to cook with total strangers?"

While Duan stood in stony silence and Su-Ann's composure shattered into weeping, Leesan pulled her mother-in-law into her bosom. "It's not your fault. Don't think you're bringing shame to the family."

Once Duan departed, a cold weight settled. Together, they packed their lives into a few trunks and moved to the rooms on the east side, freeing up the remaining space for other families.

Chapter Five

"I do not understand what I do. For what I want to do I do not do,
but what I hate I do... What a wretched man I am! Who will rescue
me from this body of death?"

Romans 7:15, 24

Beijing, China
Spring 1953

What an unusually warm spring day! Leesan took the twins to the
yard to enjoy the glorious sunshine. When three figures walked in,
she dropped the ball in her hand.

Is this the Dong family Duan told us about?

The man approached her in long strides. "I'm Dong Guang.
They're my mother and wife."

Before she responded, Su-Ann rushed over from the kitchen.

The wife stepped forward. "My name is Shen Jia. You can call
me Ah Jia." She lifted her chin. "I used to work for Dr. Ding, a well-
known surgeon in Union Hospital."

Su-Ann smiled. "We're familiar with Dr. Ding."

Ah Jia nodded and thrust out her chest.

Leesan glanced at her. Judging from the husband's age, she guessed the wife was likely in her twenties. Yet with a skinny frame and dark-brown skin, she looked worn out, like a flower that wilted without reaching the peak of its bloom.

Life hadn't been kind to her.

In sharp contrast to his wife, Dong Guang was short and muscular. His hands appeared rugged with large knuckles. He must be a laborer, but he kept his nails clean.

His gaze danced on the opening of Leesan's blouse. "I'm an expert at all kinds of maintenance work, including electricity, plumbing, and carpentry. Need anything fixed around the house? Just call Ah Guang." He walked closer, his voice loud, obnoxious. "I'm also the best cook among my friends."

At the man's moving lips, Leesan shivered, shifted a step away from him, and tucked her clothes firmly into place.

She avoided the common areas as much as possible for the next few days, but the house didn't stay quiet for long. One week later, the second family moved in—Chen Kang, a lanky man, and his little boy, Yao.

Upon meeting Leesan, Yao stared at her with large eyes. "My ma died. I saw her in a coffin."

"Oh, poor thing." She gave his head a gentle pat.

The boy's words hung heavy in the air, leaving Leesan at a loss for what else to say. Later, Su-Ann told her Mrs. Chen had passed away three months earlier.

Yao stayed in the government-run childcare center during the week and came home for the weekend. Being in a similar situation, Leesan showed extra kindness to the new family and often invited the Chens to dine with them.

At their dinners together, Yao fought with Ann-Ann all the time but got along well with May-May. Leesan couldn't help commenting to her mother-in-law. "Yao seems to favor May-May. Her gentle temperament fits well with his. Ann-Ann is like a competitor, not a playmate."

Su-Ann pulled May-May to her bosom. "You're right."

One night, Yao finished his bowl of rice and spoke in an earnest tone. "Pa, when I grow up, I want to marry May-May."

His solemn expression brought a smile to Leesan's face. Yet Ann-Ann began to wail. "No, me marry Yao."

A playful mood getting the best of her, Leesan scrunched her nose to tease her daughters. "Hey, how about you both marry Yao?"

May-May walked over to wrap an arm around her sister's shoulder. "Yes, we marry Yao."

"No, no." Ann-Ann pushed her twin away, crying even louder.

The playfulness dissolving, Leesan frowned. "Ann-Ann, stop right now. Be good."

At her reproach, the little girl lay down on the floor and howled.

"It's all right. They're just children. Don't take their words seriously." Su-Ann strode over to pick up Ann-Ann. "Why don't you come with Nana tonight? I have candies for you."

A classic Su-Ann move. Of course, Su-Ann had treats. She always had something for everyone and often bought extra food for the other two families. Tucking Ann-Ann onto one hip, she smoothed back the girl's askew hair, then faced Leesan. "This morning, I picked up something for the elder Mrs. Dong. The poor woman doesn't have good health." Su-Ann drew her brows tight. "Mrs. Dong said her daughter-in-law treats her badly. Ah Jia doesn't look like a mean girl. Some misunderstandings might have occurred between them."

No doubt. Ah Jia liked Su-Ann since she came by to gossip every day. Leesan once overheard Ah Jia's whisper. "My husband spends a great deal of money on clothes. He's so wasteful. His ma doesn't help with housework at all."

Why didn't Ah Jia treat her the same? Instead, all Leesan received from her new neighbor was a mixture of civility and contempt, as if the woman wanted to remind her that they, the laborers, were now in charge.

Worse than the wife's dislike of her, Dong Guang's unscrupulous gaze always fell on the opening of her blouse when they met. This afternoon as Leesan ran into him in the bathhouse, he walked up to her. "You've got a moth on your blouse."

He raised a hand. Before she dodged away, he wrapped an arm around her waist.

"What're you doing?" She pushed him away and dashed out.

In the evening, she halted before the kitchen door and peeked inside. Great. Nobody was there. She stepped in to wash dishes. At the sound of someone entering, she whirled around, and her nose almost bumped Dong Guang's.

"You—"

Before she said more, he grabbed her shoulders and covered her mouth with his. She shoved him in the chest with both hands, but he didn't move. His kiss deepened, and her mind blanked out, All rational thought ceased. Then she came to her senses and stomped on his foot.

"Ouch." He released his hold, and she ran out with an unstable gait.

As she entered their room, Su-Ann frowned at her. "You don't look well. Are you sick?"

Leesan rubbed her forehead, her chest so tight she could scarcely draw breath. "I feel tired. Can the twins sleep with you tonight?"

Back in her room, she touched her lips, a languorous, delectable sensation rising in her lower abdomen. *Rong never kissed me like that. I must avoid Dong Guang.*

Yet he didn't allow her to shun him. The next day, he cornered her behind a tree in the yard. While his fingers cradled her face, she raised a hand to slap him.

He caught her arm with ease. "Don't even try."

"Let go of me," she ordered. "If you don't stop harassing me, I'll go to the police to file a report."

"He-he-he." He leered. "Do you think the police will listen to you? Don't forget we laborers are in control now."

Noises rose from the other side of the yard, and he retreated.

Why does Dong Guang always find opportunities to trap me?

Leaving her room became torture. Her stomach churned and her heart palpitated whenever she ventured out. As she took each step away from her haven, her muscles tensed, and a knot tightened in her chest.

Yet she couldn't avoid the man. With each encounter, he grew bolder. Soon, his actions went beyond kissing. He molested her while whispering indecent words. "Ha, I recognize your type. You can't hide the hunger in your eyes from me. I have quite a few tricks. You'll like what I do to you."

She fought him hard but also responded in a way she couldn't comprehend. He was a scoundrel, and she despised him. Still, when the pair of rough hands caressed her, a burning desire flamed up, and her knees trembled.

That part of herself seemed so foreign, unreal.

Am I an adulteress?

At dusk this day, she passed through the hallway with a pounding heart. Her eyes darted around her. Then she relaxed her shoulders at the tranquility of the yard. *Dong Guang must be at work.* She rushed into the kitchen and dumped vegetables into the sink. At a click, she turned, and he stood before her with the door locked behind him.

"What do you want?" Her voice quivered, a chill gushing through her veins.

He chuckled. "You know very well what *we* want."

He stepped forward to embrace her. She fled to a corner, but he moved to pin her against the wall.

She jerked her head sideways. "Please leave me alone. Please respect me."

"Don't play coy using those empty words. Your body is sending different signals. Trust me. I'll make you happy, beyond anything you've ever dreamed." He tightened his arms to kiss her.

She pounded his chest. He didn't budge. When he fused his lips with hers, her fists relaxed into open palms.

As if receiving a cue, he loosened his hold and briskly unbuttoned her clothes.

"Beautiful." He grinned. "Better than I've imagined."

His lips brushed over her bare skin. Her breath grew heavy, and an unfamiliar spasm zapped through her abdomen. She couldn't help clasping him tightly, pulling him even closer.

"Easy, easy." He chortled. "Don't lie. You want it bad—"

The turning of the door handles clattered.

"Why is this locked?" Ah Jia's voice sounded. "Ah Guang, come open it."

He remained silent.

"I know you're inside." Ah Jia spoke again.

"D... it." His hands fell away, and he walked out.

Like a robot, Leesan put her clothes back on and finished her chores.

Night fell. She forced herself to act as before. They sat down to dine, and Su-Ann eyed her from time to time but said nothing.

After dinner, Leesan took Ann-Ann back to their room. While she tucked her daughter into bed, the child pointed to her neck. "Mama, dirty."

A cold prickle of dread raced down Leesan's spine as she pulled up her collar. After Ann-Ann fell asleep, she hurried to look in the mirror. A cluster of kiss marks marred the pale line of her throat. A wave of nausea rolled through her, and she rubbed at the skin, a vain attempt to scrub away the memory of his touch.

No wonder Mother kept giving me strange looks.

Her mind attempted to conjure up Rong's portrait, but his face overlapped with Dong Guang's. She'd never bared her chest in front of her husband. Today, she was almost naked in broad daylight.

How shameful.

She began to pace. Was sexual enjoyment unrelated to love? Dong Guang brought her a pleasure she'd never tasted before.

"Heavenly Father—"

No, there's no God. Even if God exists, He won't accept me anymore. I'm a whore.

She lay down and shut her eyes. Slowly, she arrived on a ship with Rong by her side. One moment they stood together on the deck. The next, they fell into the ocean. She moved her arms through the warm water in a lazy motion. Rong grasped her legs from behind and whispered, "I want you happy."

Her body twisted in a convulsion. Gasping for air, she woke up. *I'm no match for Dong Guang. I have to leave this place. I must leave China.*

Chapter Six

"Perhaps the reason he was separated from you for a little while was
that you might have him back for good."

Philemon 1:15

At breakfast, Leesan left her bowl of congee untouched. "I plan to
leave Beijing."

"What did you say?" Su-Ann jerked up her head, her eyebrows
furrowed.

"I want to leave Beijing."

Su-Ann rubbed her temples, then dropped her arms. "Why?"

Too ashamed to meet her mother-in-law's gaze, Leesan ducked,
letting her hair shield her.

"Is Dong Guang harassing you?"

When Su-Ann reached out to touch her, Leesan buried her face
in her hands. She kept her weeping quiet, hoping not to distress the
twins playing nearby.

"Did you—did he—?"

"No." Somehow, she squeezed out a syllable.

Su-Ann flopped back in her seat. "How come?"

"Please." Leesan's shoulders tightened. "I can't stay here

anymore."

"What about the twins?"

"I plan to take them with me." She clutched her chest, apprehension tightening her heart. "I want you to leave as well. There's no future here."

Su-Ann moved to the window, the wrinkles on her forehead sagging downward. She'd aged a great deal in the past months. Her hair had turned grayish-white.

Outside, the early morning sun shone on the blooming peonies.

"My roots are too deep in Peking," Su-Ann spoke more softly than usual, as if talking to herself. "This is the burial place of my ancestors. My husband is buried here. Now my son is also buried here."

She returned to her chair, her face contorted. "I agree. You must leave with the twins. Where do you plan to go?"

"Hong Kong or America if possible." Leesan clenched her fists, fighting the anguish pulsing through her. If only her life hadn't come to such a point!

Su-Ann loosened Leesan's fists, squeezing her fingers. "You'd better discuss it with Duan. He can help."

Duan... Right, he'd help. "I'll go at once."

She drew a steadying breath. Before venturing out, she tied a silk scarf around her neck. The bright sun shone, warming her cheeks as she hailed a rickshaw.

By the time she reached the quiet of Duan's street, her pulse had slowed.

At the sight of her, Duan started to smile, then stopped, his eyes widening. "You came by yourself? Is everything okay at home?"

She covered the distance between them. Then, oddly startled at finding him so close by, she scuttled back a step. "I want to leave Beijing. Do you know how?"

"You—" His smile disappeared. "Why?"

"There's no future here." She shook her head. "I would like to go to Hong Kong or America."

"Yes. The situation is bleak for you in Beijing. Someone will discover your parents' connection with Taiwan. You'll be labeled a counterrevolutionary. The consequence is dire." He heaved a long breath. "Do you plan to go alone?"

"I want to take the twins with me." She held her chin high. "I've asked Rong's mother to leave too, but she said no."

The animation drained from Duan's features, leaving his face unreadable. "Under the current political environment with the anti-Western sentiment, America isn't possible. It has to be Hong Kong. The best way is to take the train. I may be able to get hold of two passes, one for you and the other for one of your daughters. You have a long journey. It'll be difficult to travel with two toddlers. Besides, identical twins attract attention. Safety should be your top concern. You must not arouse any suspicion."

Her heart sank. How was it possible to leave one daughter behind? She curled up her fingers, her whole body shaking. No, it wouldn't do.

"You don't have to decide now." His baritone, gentler than usual, soothed her. "Think about it. Once you reach a decision, let me know right away."

Why was he so attentive? Did he sense her despair?

His questions echoed in her mind over the rhythmic clatter of the rickshaw wheels on the cobblestones. Back at home, Leesan recounted his words to Su-Ann. "I can't do it. Either the twins come with me, or I stay."

The decision lingered long after the conversation ended. With her muscles tense, Leesan prepared to take a bath for relaxation. After pouring water into the wooden tub, she removed her clothes. Just then, familiar footsteps echoed from the hallway and halted at the door.

"Let me in." Dong Guang's words pierced through the thin door.

She stood frozen, goosebumps covering her arms.

He turned the knob. "Come on. Unlock the door. You love what we did the other day. Let's do more."

Her legs trembled. The cold spring air engulfed her nakedness.

"I promise to bring you up to heaven, beyond anything you've ever experienced." He launched into details about the different tricks he would use on her.

She plugged her ears with both hands but couldn't stop a pool of heat rushing into her loins.

A woman called his name from the yard, and he took leave.

Leesan put her clothes back on and hurried back to her room. *He won't give up. I'm ripe for his plucking.*

No. She had no choice.

Yet how her heart ached at the mere thought of leaving a daughter behind. All night, she paced in her room, occasionally pausing to examine Ann-Ann in her sleep.

She must leave. There was no alternative. None.

The days that followed her decision blurred into a haze of quiet grief. A week after she told Duan she planned to leave with one child, he brought over two permits.

Su-Ann stood by the gate, and her mouth dropped open at the sight of his car. "What a surprise! You no longer ride your bicycle?"

Leesan answered for him. "Duan got a promotion. The government gave him a car."

With a look of deep concern, he gave her the passes. "Do you have any friends or relatives in Hong Kong?"

Su-Ann guided them back to their room. "My brother is in Hong Kong. I've already informed him."

Duan sat on the sofa. "Is he the one who used to live in Shanghai? Leesan, you and Rong visited him on your way to America, right?"

"Yes." A tightness seized her throat at the image of her wedding in that Western-style mansion. Was it only eight years ago?

Did her curt reply add to Duan's discomfort? He stood and spread out his hands, his eyebrows drawn together. "Auntie, if you have valuables, give them to Leesan. We'll have more campaigns ahead of us. Eventually, most of your possessions will be confiscated. Besides, Hong Kong is a foreign place to her. It'll be easier if she doesn't have to worry about money."

Upon seeing Su-Ann's teary eyes, Leesan struggled to find her breath. Rong used the same tone when he told his mother to donate the land. Unlike before, her mother-in-law didn't argue.

As a stifling stillness fell over the room, Duan spun on his heel and headed out of the door. Su-Ann beckoned Leesan to follow her to her room and dragged a trunk from under the bed. She brought out their collection of treasures and ran her fingers over them, tears trickling down her cheeks. "These have been with our family for so many generations."

"It won't be that bad. The government can't take everything away from people." Leesan stepped forward to give her a gentle hug.

Su-Ann shook her head at the pile of antiques, gold, and jewelry. Her shoulders slumped and her lips wobbled.

What went through her mind with the simple waggle of her head?

Did she feel the disapproval from the Lee ancestors? Leesan squeezed her mother-in-law into a tight embrace. "I'm confident I'll find a job to support Ann-Ann and myself. Plus, it's dangerous to travel with a lot of valuables."

Su-Ann stood up from her. "Duan isn't a person to exaggerate. Another wave of political campaigns is approaching. You mentioned Ann-Ann and you. You've decided Ann-Ann will leave with you? It makes sense. May-May is attached to me." She grabbed a brooch and traced a finger along the huge piece of translucent green jade forming the body of a crab. "This is also a gift from the emperor to Rong's great-grandfather." Her body sagged with her sigh. "We can sew this and other pieces into your coats."

At Su-Ann's determination, Leesan squinted. "I suppose I can take some jewelry with me." She picked up the jade teapot. "I don't know how we can pack these. Antiques aren't suitable for the trip. We'll have to travel light. I plan to bring only two suitcases. Otherwise, I can't handle Ann-Ann."

"You've got a good point." Su-Ann lifted her chin. "We must make your travel arrangements in secrecy. Let me take over the housework. You'll have more time with May-May."

Leesan lowered her gaze. *Good. I can avoid being alone with Dong Guang.*

Still, the next day, on her way to the bathroom with Ann-Ann, the scoundrel stopped her. "Remember our tryst in the kitchen? Don't deny it. You enjoyed what I did to you. I have unbelievable tricks to drive you wild. Take your daughter to her grandma. I'll wait for you here."

When he attempted to grab her arm, Leesan stepped back, disgust flooding her. Ann-Ann scowled at him and howled. Her wailing broke the tranquility of the yard. Then he cursed and retreated.

The disgust of the encounter soon gave way to a hollow dread. With only days remaining in Beijing, Leesan focused on May-May. She bathed her, fed her, and kept telling her, "May-May, remember how much Mama loves you."

Yet Ann-Ann got hysterical. "Mama, me hold." She pushed away her twin and glared at Su-Ann's offer to hold her. Stealing a peek at her nana, May-May slipped off Leesan's lap to vacate the spot for her sister.

Tenderness flooding her heart, Leesan couldn't help but shake

43

her head. "They have such distinct personalities."

It was a sweetness she memorized, a shield against the looming shadow of the calendar. On the morning of their departure, she hustled around May-May. With her usual good temper, the child smiled and accepted Leesan's nonstop kisses.

Before lunch, Leesan handed Su-Ann a small silk pouch. "This jade pendant used to belong to my grandmother. If I don't get to see May-May again, please give it to her before her wedding." Warm, salty droplets rained down her cheeks into her mouth.

In return, Su-Ann placed a thick envelope on the table. "It's yours."

Leesan opened the flap to slide out the Bible Papa gave her before she left home. "I thought I lost it during our move. You've been keeping this?"

Su-Ann nodded. "Take it with you."

"Oh, Mother." Leesan directed her gaze toward the ceiling, a deep sorrow washing over her. "You prayed by Rong's bedside, pleading for his cure. God didn't answer your prayer. Why do you still believe in Him?"

"Are you familiar with the story of Daniel's three young friends in the Old Testament?"

"Yeah." She massaged her throbbing temples. "I studied the book of Daniel in Chungking, but I don't remember their names."

As her mind turned toward how Mama led Su-Ann to Christ, Leesan's muscles relaxed somewhat. Her mother-in-law, so serious about her faith, had even invited Chen Kang and his boy to church.

"Difficult names indeed." Su-Ann's mouth curled up into a half-smile. "They were thrown into the furnace because they obeyed the Almighty and disobeyed the king. They declared that, even if God didn't save them, they would continue to worship Him."

Leesan's jaw tightened again, her hands fisting. "They had a happy ending. The three men walked out alive."

"They did. Rong didn't." Su-Ann slid cold fingers up and down Leesan's arm. "Still, the message is clear. Even though they didn't know if God would save them, they remained faithful."

"Isn't that foolish?" Leesan jerked away from her mother-in-law, a hardness in her tone. "Maybe there's no God, or He doesn't care at all."

"God exists, and He cares. In the story, the Almighty was with them amid the flame." Something blazed in Su-Ann's eyes, her faith aglow, both beautiful and frightening. "I don't understand why tragedies happen. On this earth, the Lord braved intense sufferings, including crucifixion, the most terrible form of death. He's aware of the pain I'm experiencing. He's promised to walk with me regardless of my circumstances."

"Did He walk with you then?"

"Yes." Su-Ann fixed her impassioned eyes on Leesan, peering into her as if wanting to spark the same fire within her. "You fell into a deep depression following Rong's death, and so did I. Even when my husband died, I didn't run into such agony. But this time, there's always a gentle voice from the Holy Spirit comforting me. Besides, you may remember Pastor Fu and others from my church came to pray with me often. They were by my side while darkness swallowed me."

Leesan dipped her chin and nudged one slippered foot along the wooden floor. "Is He walking with you now?"

"Yes, He is with me." Su-Ann pulled out a chair and sat.

He is with me. He is with me. He is with me. The words whispered through Leesan's heart like a foreign promise. Heat burned her eyelids, and her throat hurt.

"What does it feel like?" She lifted her face.

Su-Ann clasped her hands together as though in prayer. "I get to know Him a bit more every day, which transforms my entire person. My assignment from Him provides me with a larger perspective on life. I wouldn't trade it for anything else in this world."

What was that supposed to mean? Leesan knitted her brows. "You say 'my assignment'?"

"To love people around me, seek their spiritual growth, and help them enter His family so they can enjoy a relationship with Him." Su-Ann tugged at Leesan's jacket sleeve, her mouth curving up again. "Chen Kang has accepted Christ as his Savior. My brother is also attending worship every Sunday. Go to church with him. Bring your brokenness to the Lord."

Leesan remained silent. *Too late. I'm sinful, rotten. God will not accept me.*

She swallowed the bitter thought, tucking her guilt away behind a mask of forced composure. Shortly after lunch, Duan drove up in his car. Leesan forced her mother-in-law to sit down. "To avoid arousing unnecessary attention from neighbors, please stay in your room. Don't come out with us."

She placed one last kiss on May-May's forehead and left with Ann-Ann. On the way to the station, tears flooded Leesan's cheeks. Duan didn't disturb her. Even Ann-Ann was quiet, directing her gaze at the street scenes.

With his habitual frown, Duan helped them stow their two large bags and watched them settle in their seats. "I'll take care of May-May and Rong's mother for you. Don't worry about them. Look toward the future. Have hope." He patted the toddler's head and strode away.

"Thank you." Leesan couldn't help expressing her gratitude once more.

He turned slightly to wave. Then he was gone.

"Mama, where did Uncle Duan go?" Ann-Ann lifted her head. "Where are Nana and May-May?"

Leesan dabbed her face with a handkerchief. "Uncle Duan needs to go to work. Nana and May-May are home. We're going to a different place. Be Mama's good girl, okay?"

The train moved. While the scenery attracted Ann-Ann's attention, Leesan held her daughter close, each long breath a silent release of anguish over the daughter she couldn't hold.

Chapter Seven

"There are two ways of seeing: with the body and with the soul. The body's sight can sometimes forget, but the soul remembers forever."

Alexandre Dumas (1802–1870)

Hong Kong
May 1953

The train chugged into Kowloon Station.

"I'm finally safe," Leesan murmured while stepping off the train with her luggage, Ann-Ann gripping her jacket hem.

Tears stung her eyes when Uncle Su-Nong and Auntie Shu-Fang waved from the platform.

Auntie surged forward. "Leesan, you haven't changed a bit." She bent down and cupped Ann-Ann's cheeks between her palms. "Wow, what a beautiful little girl."

Uncle picked up their bags. "Let's call a taxi."

They might think her the same, but she felt nothing like the girl she'd been as a young bride. And both of them had changed a lot. When she met them in Shanghai, Su-Nong gave her the impression of a man who loved to talk. Now he seemed quiet. Auntie, who used

47

to dress in high fashion, was clad in a cheap floral-print dress.

Disturbed by the shadow of their past, Leesan swallowed a sigh as a car stopped before them. Shu-Fang slid into the taxi's backseat with Leesan and took Ann-Ann onto her lap. "She's such a pretty child. I wonder how she feels without her twin. I cannot imagine my boys ever being separated."

The tightness in Leesan's chest increased. She swallowed hard and watched the traffic until they arrived at an old six-story building.

Shu-Fang frowned. "Our flat is on the fourth floor. There's no elevator."

"Why don't you let me bring up one suitcase first?" Uncle pulled out his keys. "I'll come down for the second one, and we can climb the stairs together."

The group waited in the cramped entryway, the silence between them filled only by the thud of Su-Nong's footsteps retreating upward.

After he came back down, Leesan held Ann-Ann in her arms and went up the narrow staircase. As she entered the flat, her heart sank. She pressed her lips tight while surveying the living room, bathroom, kitchen, and two bedrooms. Each room was less than a hundred square feet. From anywhere in the apartment, through the thin walls came the sounds of people screaming at one another in a foreign dialect.

Auntie sighed, then scooped Ann-Ann from her again, bouncing her on her hip. "Wait till evening. You'll hear the neighbors playing mahjong all night long."

"I know what you're thinking." Uncle waved at the space. "It's the only thing we could afford."

Leesan scratched her cheek. Okay, time to change the subject. "Where are Ming-Ming and Tong-Tong?"

A corner of Su-Nong's mouth crinkled up until he almost resembled the man she remembered. "They went camping with the church youth group."

Ann-Ann tugged at her sleeve. "Mama, hungry."

"Yes, you must all be hungry." He strode into the kitchen and brought out three cold Shanghainese dishes. "Shu-Fang prepared these earlier today. Let's eat."

Following dinner, Ann-Ann fell asleep. Leesan tucked her into bed and returned to Uncle and Auntie.

As Auntie poured them tea, Uncle folded his hands into his lap. "We're disturbed by the political turmoil in China. I hoped my sister and May-May would have come to Hong Kong with you."

"Mother didn't want to leave Beijing. Also, we got only two permits." Leesan scuffed her feet beneath her chair, the thin slipper soles scarcely cushioning her from the laminated floor. "Leaving them behind was... so..." Her throat closed over, but would any word express what she needed to say? "Punishing."

Anguish burned in her heart like wildfire, and moisture gathered behind her eyelids. Uncle shouldered a hefty burden to keep their family fed. Now they had two more to feed. Maybe they should be grateful Mother and May-May hadn't come.

"Uncle." Leesan cradled a plain teacup between her palms. An uncensored question escaped her. "You used to own many properties like Rong's family. What happened?"

"I don't know how others handled it. We fled Shanghai in haste and didn't get opportunities to convert our possessions into cash or gold bars." He wiped his nose, his body twitching. "It's difficult to make a living here. We don't speak Cantonese. I tried various plans but failed. Now we operate a small store in the wet market in Waterloo, selling household items."

She sipped her tea, then let out a light cough. "Is Cantonese very different from Mandarin?"

"Just as Chinese is distinct from Japanese. You'll find it out for yourself." Shu-Fang's face scrunched, and her voice wobbled. "It's a difficult dialect to master. Since our arrival, we've been attending our church's Cantonese class. We still can't converse freely with the locals."

Leesan set down her cup. "How are Ming-Ming and Tong-Tong doing?"

"As children, they picked up Cantonese fast. They'll soon graduate from high school and start working." Su-Nong clasped his hands as though in prayer. "Thank heavens. Otherwise, I'm not sure what to do."

When Leesan last saw them in Shanghai, they were two naughty boys. Yet what a blow to such a highly educated family that the twins couldn't go to college.

"It's late. Let's go to bed." Auntie placed the teacups on a tray. "We're going to church tomorrow. Will you come with us?"

"Maybe not." Leesan headed to the kitchen. "I'm tired from the train trip."

She excused herself after bidding them goodnight.

Following a restless night, in the morning she waited for Uncle and Auntie to leave, then stepped out with Ann-Ann to pick up a local newspaper. Back at home, she made herself a cup of tea and went through the For Rent ads one by one.

Nothing suitable.

She dropped the newspaper and cried aloud. "It's impossible to find a rental within my budget."

Ann-Ann, who played nearby, jerked her head and wailed.

Leesan went over to pick her up. "I'm sorry. I shouldn't have raised my voice."

The child pointed to her right side. "Hurt."

A bruise on Ann-Ann's leg looked like she'd hit a hard object. "Did you bump against the desk again? Oh, Ann-Ann, try not to run around so much."

Misery flooded her heart as Leesan surveyed the tiny space. How she missed their house in Beijing with its sumptuous yard.

After Su-Nong came home, he shook his head at the newspaper. "Don't worry about moving to your place. You can stay with us. We're blood relatives."

She sank into the sofa, weighed down by an invisible load. "Thank you, Uncle. I feel bad. Because of us, Tong-Tong and Ming-Ming will have to sleep in the living room."

The saggy cushion groaned under her weight like the lamentation grinding her heart. Would she ever adjust to the new life?

In a haze of homesickness, the calendar turned. By the end of the second month, life had fallen into a routine. Uncle's family left the flat early every day. Staying back with Ann-Ann, Leesan worked hard to finish the household chores but paused from time to time when her mind drifted back to her encounters with Dong Guang in Beijing.

Why couldn't she leave behind her shameful past? What was wrong with her?

On this day, she brushed aside unwanted images and focused on preparing noodles with meat sauce for her daughter's lunch. When she attempted to place a bib on Ann-Ann, the girl pushed her hands away.

Leesan stooped to touch the child's face. "Isn't this your favorite dish? But you need to put on the bib first."

"I don't want this." Ann-Ann threw the bib on the floor. "I want the one with kittens."

Ann-Ann had never been this defiant. Or had Leesan forgotten the struggle? A sharp, physical longing tightened her chest. How she ached to have Mother and May-May by her side!

She picked up the bib. "I washed the other one. It's still wet. This one with the puppies is just as cute."

"I don't want it. I want the one with kittens." Ann-Ann flung the plate off the table. The noodles with sauce flew around the room.

"What have you done?" Leesan's pent-up frustration surged free. She slapped Ann-Ann's arm hard.

Ann-Ann stared at her, then dropped from the high chair to the ground with ear-piercing cries.

"Darling." Leesan rushed over. "Are you all right?"

The child appeared fine, apart from a bump on the forehead. Still, Leesan wept. "Sorry. I shouldn't have hit you."

"Mama, don't cry." Ann-Ann stopped her tears and stretched out a hand to wipe Leesan's face.

"Oh, Ann-Ann." She pulled her girl to her lap, sensing the arrival of a headache.

Even with a fan, the oppressive summer warmth in their small space echoed the gloom in her mind.

The weight of the day's frustrations followed her into the dark. That night, for the first time since their arrival in Hong Kong, Leesan dreamed of the Beijing courtyard house.

The two sisters sat together inside a wooden tub, splashing water on each other. The bathhouse door opened, and Rong strolled in. An inexplicable joy overtook her. She trod away from her children. "Rong, you look so well. You're not sick anymore."

Her husband hugged her shoulders and kissed her. When his hands fondled her, she giggled. "You've learned to play like a bad boy. You're no longer a gentleman."

Just then, the twins cried. She lifted her gaze. The man in front of her turned into Dong Guang, and she staggered back. The scoundrel didn't pursue her. He grabbed a child from the bathtub and ran outside.

Leesan chased after him but halted at the sound behind her.

"Mama, Mama."

She glanced at the girl in the tub and shrieked, "Rong, bring May-May back to me!"

A crescendo of noises leaked through the walls. She woke with her nightgown soaked in a cold sweat. Lying in the darkness, she listened to Ann-Ann's even breathing and let tears wet her pillow.

Rong, why did you have to die? Why did I leave May-May behind? Will I ever see her again?

At breakfast, Auntie sat next to her. "We'll have a visitor today."

Leesan gave Shu-Fang a questioning glance. Auntie flashed a grin and picked up a boiled egg from the plate. "Did I tell you our church has two worship services, one in Mandarin and the other in Cantonese? A sister in the Cantonese group, also a widow, learned about you and wanted to visit you. Su-Nong can't get away from the shop. I'll be home."

Following lunch, while Ann-Ann slept in their room, a large woman in her forties arrived.

"I'm Wong Kam-Chu. Nice to meet you." She spoke Mandarin with a heavy accent.

Heat rushed to Leesan's cheeks. She didn't even catch the visitor's name. "Sorry, I didn't get your name in Cantonese."

The woman grabbed a pen to write on a piece of paper—Wong Kam-Chu.

"Huang Jin-Zhu." Leesan pronounced her name in Mandarin. "What a beautiful name, a yellow-gold pearl."

"Isn't it odd that we Chinese don't understand each other's speech? But we can when it's jotted down." Shu-Fang laughed.

Leesan let out a breath and smiled. "Indeed, it's the fault of our first emperor, Qin Shihuang. He unified the written language. Unfortunately, he couldn't enter each home to force everyone to speak Mandarin."

Kam-Chu spoke and wrote simultaneously. Her only daughter got married the year before, and she lived in a building two blocks away from Uncle's.

"Mama?" Ann-Ann's voice from the other room interrupted them.

"Excuse me." Leesan hurried away.

After she brought Ann-Ann back to the living room, Kam-Chu's face lit up. "Such a beautiful girl. Too bad my daughter doesn't want children yet. She told me she needs to establish her career first. Nothing I said would change her mind."

As if struck by a sudden idea, Kam-Chu clapped. "I have an empty room since my daughter moved out." She spread out her hands. "Maybe you and Ann-Ann can come to live with me? It'll give me a chance to practice being a grandma with your little girl."

The offer seemed like a lifeline. Within a week, Leesan became Kam-Chu's tenant.

***

Beijing, China
May 1953

Does Ann-Ann experience the emotion of separation as acutely as May-May? Su-Ann placed her clean dishes into the storage bin, her heart weighed down by misery. *Why does the pain seem more intense for the ones who stay behind?*

In the hours after Leesan and Ann-Ann left, May-May appeared not to notice any difference. But when only the two of them sat together at the dining table for dinner, May-May wailed. "I want Mama. I want Ann-Ann."

"My baby. Don't cry. Nana is here. I'll take care of you." Weariness warred with the moisture gathering behind Su-Ann's eyes. She held back her tears, afraid of causing May-May unnecessary distress.

Her soothing words didn't bring the expected effect. May-May scrambled down from the high chair and ran to the room her mother and sister shared.

Su-Ann trekked after her. The sight nearly broke her heart. Her precious girl had squeezed into one corner of the bed and curled herself into a tiny ball.

She hurried away to get the last piece of chocolate from the black market. "Nana has your favorite candy. Come, eat it."

"No. Not candy. I want Mama. I want Ann-Ann." May-May buried her face in her arms, her words muffled.

At last, she quieted. Su-Ann checked on her. She'd fallen asleep. With a sigh, Su-Ann carried her back to their room. After pacing around for a while, she kneeled beside May-May's bed. *Lord, please shine Your mercy and goodness on us.*

The night passed in a restless silence. The next morning, May-May woke and called for her mama. Su-Ann hurried to the kitchen and brought milk in her favorite cup, but May-May pushed it away, howling. "No. Not milk. I want Mama. I want Ann-Ann."

Coaxing her granddaughter with no effect, Su-Ann raised her voice. "Stop crying and drink your milk. You make Nana unhappy."

May-May clawed at her cheek, lapsing into silence. Then she lifted her chin and spoke in a broken voice. "Are Mama and Ann-Ann in heaven like Papa?"

Su-Ann's mouth went dry, heat swelling her chest. In one day, May-May's world shattered. How could her good-natured girl not fall into despair?

A lump lodged in her throat, and Su-Ann forced calmness into her tone. "Mama and Ann-Ann went to Hong Kong. They have to leave us for a while."

May-May shook her head and kept begging for Mama and Ann-Ann.

Lord, please grant me wisdom. What can I do to help my precious girl?

The morning stretched into a long ordeal of tears and pleas. Liang Duan visited them that afternoon and placed a stuffed puppy dog in front of the child. It didn't help. May-May pushed it to the ground and ran to the other room.

Su-Ann huffed a heavy breath. "I don't know what to do. I can only pray."

"Pray?" He gave her a stern glance. "Auntie, do you still go to church?"

She jerked up her gaze. "Why do you ask?"

"Unless absolutely necessary, don't go anymore." He scooped up the puppy and pulled out a chair to sit on. "The government is starting a new campaign called Withdraw from the Sects Movements."

She rubbed her temples, sensing the beginning of a headache. "What is this campaign for?"

"To denounce secret societies and religious organizations deemed potential threats to the authority."

"But..." She raised her eyebrows. "Christianity isn't a secret religious organization."

"It doesn't matter." He twiddled with the puppy's floppy ears, his shoulders hunching. "In the ongoing campaign to suppress counterrevolutionaries, the government sets a quota for the executions of Kuomintang remnants per local population. Some provinces couldn't find enough previous KMT members to meet the quota and randomly arrested people to satisfy the requirement. Many were executed for no particular reason. I'm afraid it's the same in this new campaign."

She chewed the inside of her cheek. "Thank you for letting me know. I'll be more careful."

The warning left a bitter taste in her mouth. After he left, she went to look for May-May. Her granddaughter stood in a corner with a broken doll placed against her face.

Wasn't that a toy Ann-Ann dumped in the closet a while ago?

"Give it to Nana." Su-Ann tugged at the doll. "It's dusty. You'll get sick."

May-May wouldn't let go and hugged it more tightly.

Su-Ann's heart hollowed out. *My girl's suffering.*

The following Friday, a letter arrived, ordering her to report to a textile factory in their neighborhood within a week. Her chest tightened. Now she must send May-May to the childcare center.

Would a change in the environment help May-May?

Lord, please let this be a temporary arrangement. I need time with May-May to teach her Your ways so she'll become Your disciple.

Chapter Eight

"It was the best of times, it was the worst of times."

Charles Dickens (1812–1870)

Hong Kong
May 1953

When Leesan and her daughter moved into their new place, her landlady invited them to a sumptuous dinner.

As she cut grilled beef into small pieces for Ann-Ann, Kam-Chu gave her a meaningful glance. "My husband was a kind man. He left me with enough money. I could concentrate on my daughter's needs. She turned out well and earned a finance degree from the University of Hong Kong."

She poured tea for Leesan. "I usually have dim sum with her and her husband every week following our worship. If you're available, will you come to church with me this Sunday? You can join us for lunch afterward."

While Leesan remained quiet, Kam-Chu spoke again. "Our church has a Cantonese class for new immigrants from Mainland China. Your uncle and auntie said it helped them a lot." She squinted, a smile rounding up her wide cheeks. "I think that's why they understand my Mandarin. You're welcome to come."

Why was she so persistent? Leesan let out a silent sigh. "Sure. Thank you."

The class met at the same time as the Cantonese worship. After her first lesson, a classmate stopped her at the door. "Wang Leesan, my name is Han Tao. Are you free for lunch with me today?"

Standing in front of her was a short, muscular man. Dong Guang's profile popped up. She shook her head and dashed away.

The following weeks settled into a rhythm of repetitive drills. By the time two months had passed, she could communicate with Kam-Chu well enough without a need for them to write down the speech. When Kam-Chu invited her to attend the church's Mandarin worship, Leesan ducked her gaze. "At this point, I'm more concerned about my financial situation. I must find a job soon."

She wasn't entirely truthful. Yet how could she tell Kam-Chu what tormented her? During her sleepless nights, fire flamed up in her core at the memory of Dong Guang's mouth on her body. She tossed and turned, weeping and cursing her fate. *I'm filthy. God won't accept me.*

"I see." Kam-Chu gave her arm a gentle pat. "If there's a need, I can watch Ann-Ann while you go to your interview. It'll let me practice being a grandma."

It was useless. She'd gone to so many interviews without being offered a job. Leesan lowered her head and ground her teeth. Should she sell her jewelry?

Standing on a street corner later that afternoon, she stared at the huge Chinese character *Pawn* written on the curtain-like banner. After she double-checked no one was around, she clutched her purse to her chest and rushed inside.

A strange, high-pitched singing voice echoed in the room. *Must be Cantonese Opera.*

The white-haired man sitting behind the counter shot her a brief grin but remained quiet. She spoke in Mandarin. "I'm here to pawn something."

The old man yawned. "What do you have?"

She slid over her brooch, a crab with its body made of a huge translucent green jade set in yellow gold.

He held up the jewelry against the light on the wall to examine it with a magnifying glass. At last, he put down the item.

"How much?" She lifted her chin.

He still fixed his attention on the piece. "Thirty-five."

"No." She stretched out her hand to take back the brooch.

He raised a palm to stop her. "What number do you have in mind?"

"Two hundred."

"Are you crazy?" he shrieked. "A trained worker's daily wage is about ten Hong Kong dollars. My son is an elementary school teacher. He makes four hundred dollars a month." His tiny bright eyes glared at her with such intensity that she lowered her gaze.

"Fine. I'll go to another shop." She grabbed the crab.

"Wait. I'll give you fifty."

After two more rounds of bargaining, she walked out with one hundred and twenty dollars. The brooch—a piece of their family legacy—was gone.

If her mother-in-law found out, what would she say? Would she understand Leesan had fallen into a desperate pit where day-to-day survival loomed larger than anything else?

With her second, third, and numerous more visits to the pawnshop, her aptitude in the art of negotiation improved. Even so, she curled her arms across her chest, holding on tight every time she examined her diminishing pile of valuables.

After another failed interview at an elementary school, she complained to Kam-Chu. "So, a degree from the US is worth less in Hong Kong than one from Australia, Canada, or the UK?"

Her landlady nodded. "Hong Kong is a British colony. There's subtle discrimination against people who obtain degrees from non-Commonwealth countries. The biggest problem is your Cantonese. You need to be proficient in the local dialect to be a teacher."

Leesan stared down at her feet. *I'll never find a job.*

But helplessness was a luxury she couldn't afford. Again, she scoured the newspaper for potential jobs. Like before, nothing was suitable. She couldn't help throwing up her hands in despair. Then an advertisement caught her eye. The publisher was holding its annual story contest. The top three winners would win two hundred, one hundred, or fifty dollars.

Wow, that was a lot of money for an article.

One week later, she mailed out her manuscript. Then she checked the mailbox every day. Three months passed before a thin letter arrived from the publisher.

She didn't win. Her heart sank. Nothing she could do other than pay the pawnshop another visit.

The world seemed indifferent to her loss. When she returned home, Kam-Chu was reading a martial arts novel in the living room, and Ann-Ann was playing with wood blocks by her side.

The sight pulled her back to Chungking, to a conversation with Rong many years ago.

Was she fourteen that year?

Leesan stood transfixed, sinking into the memories.

With her eyes closed, she heard her childish voice, high-pitched with eager inquiry...

"Rong, do you read martial arts novels?"

"What a question." He'd laughed. How vivid the sound remained in her heart. "Have you met any Chinese who doesn't?" He took down a bunch of books from the shelf in the study. "See?"

"You're lucky. Mama said they're trash and will pollute my soul." Leesan had hitched a quick breath. "She threw mine away."

"I understand. She's partially right." He'd dropped the books on a nearby table. "Most martial arts novels running in series in the newspapers are poorly written. They follow the same plot. Scoundrels slaughter a boy's parents, but a grandmaster rescues him. The boy grows up to be a master and strikes out to find his enemies. Along the way, he meets a beautiful girl. Together they learn of secret activities plotted against the emperor. It turns out those are the very same people who killed his parents. They save the emperor, and he has his revenge."

He'd extracted a book from the stack. "Some are well written, like this one. I'm certain it'll become a classic in the future." He gave her a sly gaze. "Want to borrow it? I won't tell."

She'd grabbed the novel and hugged it to her chest. She hugged her arms there now as if she could still feel it, her voice from that day resounding in her head. "Why do you know so much? You're merely two years older than I am."

"Mama?" Ann-Ann's voice interrupted her contemplation, and Rong's youthful image vanished.

"Ah, you're back." Kam-Chu raised her head. "How did it go?"

"The usual." Leesan stifled a sigh and took her daughter to their room.

But what if...? She almost laughed. *I can do it.*

She completed a martial arts novella within a month and submitted it to a local newspaper. A few weeks later, a letter with an enclosed check for eighty dollars arrived. She whisked Ann-Ann off her feet and twirled around the cramped living room. "Mama doesn't have to go to the pawnshops anymore."

While Ann-Ann looked at her with wide eyes, Leesan grinned. "Let's go shopping. Now I can buy supplies to send to Nana and May-May."

***

Six months later, her novels occupied spaces in the art and literature section of four newspapers. Kam-Chu, Uncle, and Auntie became her loyal readers. To celebrate, Kam-Chu invited all of them to have dinner together at her flat. After placing the steamed crabs on the table, Kam-Chu gripped Leesan's shoulder. "You should let the second female character die."

Smiling, she shook her head. "I plan to keep her active until the end. It'll add extra suspense to the relationship between the young man and the heroine."

Kam-Chu settled into her chair and changed the subject. "Have you considered sending Ann-Ann to preschool? She needs to learn more Cantonese to prepare for elementary school."

Uncle and Auntie also inclined their heads.

They're right. Why didn't I think of it? Leesan's chest swelled. She scooted forward to tuck wisps of hair away from her daughter's cheeks. "You're becoming such a big girl. You'd like to go to school, wouldn't you?"

Ann-Ann beamed.

Leesan gave her girl's arm a gentle squeeze. "I'll sign you up for the five-day-a-week program."

The following weeks, she spent the extra time writing but declined Kam-Chu's invite to worship services, choosing instead only to attend the Cantonese class at church. On a Sunday, as she gathered up her purse after class, Gu Hua, a classmate, approached her. "Wang Leesan, want to go out together to a movie? The nearby theater is showing *Gone with the Wind*. Would you be interested?"

Gu Hua had been paying her attention for a while. This time, she took a closer look at him—a tall man with a delicate face. Maybe in his early thirties?

She intended to decline but said instead, "I'm only available on the days my daughter goes to school."

"That's great. Let's go to the afternoon show tomorrow."

Back at home, she couldn't help asking herself, "What's wrong with me? Why did I agree to go out with a stranger?"

Did she crave a man's touch? *It's worse than physical hunger.*

The next day, Gu Hua treated her to a delicious seafood rice bowl before they went to the Astor Theater. While Scarlett was dancing with Rhett, Gu Hua placed a hand on her leg. She refrained from speaking at first. Then his fingers moved along her thigh. A fire ignited in her loins, sending heat to her abdomen. Ashamed, she stood up. "Excuse me. I must leave."

She walked out without looking back. As she entered the living room and saw her landlady, she expressed her rage about what had happened.

"How horrible." Kam-Chu flapped her hands. "You're young and attractive. Watch out for wolves who prey on widows."

Her words threw Leesan into turmoil. That night, the courtyard house in Beijing came into her dream again. She lay in bed, and a man came to her side. "Rong, you're back." She clasped his hand, anticipation pulsing through her veins. The man caressed her hips, and she came to her senses. "You're not Rong. Who are you? No..." She woke up screaming. It turned into another sleepless night.

Exhausted, she slogged into the kitchen when light glimmered outside.

"You look tired." Kam-Chu set down her teacup. "Did you sleep well?"

Leesan lowered her head, mortified.

Kam-Chu didn't wait for her response. "The Chinese New Year is approaching fast. A relative of mine needs a temporary place. Would you mind if he comes to live with us? He'll stay in the living room."

"Not at all." Stifling a yawn, Leesan poured her own tea without raising her gaze.

In the evening, Kam-Chu introduced Zhao Shin-Yan, her husband's nephew. Heat crept up to Leesan's cheeks as she surveyed the handsome, rather bookish-looking young man.

"Call me Danny. Like other folks in Hong Kong, I've adopted an English name to make myself more memorable to the surrounding British." With one finely sculpted brow lifted, his eyes sparkled. He spoke Mandarin with no accent. "My aunt told me she has a tenant. I didn't expect to see such a beautiful lady."

"Danny is a sweet talker." Kam-Chu smiled. "He came to Hong Kong from the mainland about eight years ago. His parents sent him here when he was seventeen because of the political unrest in their village."

Kam-Chu rubbed his arm. "Too bad the restaurant closed recently. Hope you'll find another job after the New Year."

The young man seldom stayed at home during the day, piquing Leesan's curiosity. "Is Danny very busy?"

"He's attending school." Kam-Chu let out a sigh. "He's an ambitious, hardworking young man. I tried to invite him to church. He declined. He doesn't seem interested in spiritual matters."

Right. Kam-Chu tried to invite everyone to church.

"That's too bad." Leesan made a sympathetic sound, tucked her handbag under an elbow, then kneeled beside her daughter, winking at the girl. "You need a new outfit for school. We've got some shopping to do."

At Wing-On, the largest department store in her area, she selected two identical sets of shirts and pants, one for Ann-Ann and the other for May-May.

But Ann-Ann grabbed a red velvet dress. "Mama, buy this."

Leesan checked the price tag. "We can't. It's too expensive."

When she tugged at the garment, the child held it tight against her chest, crying aloud. "I want it."

"Be a good girl. Give it to Mama." She snatched the dress away from Ann-Ann's grip.

"I want it. You have money. You just don't want to buy it for me. You only want to buy stuff for May-May, not for me." Ann-Ann howled and threw herself on the ground.

As people stopped to indulge in the drama, Leesan's face burned. Swallowing hard, she squatted to her daughter's level.

Then a pair of arms reached down to scoop up Ann-Ann, and Leesan lifted her head. "Danny?"

He patted the child. "Good girl, don't cry. Uncle Danny will buy you the dress."

Ann-Ann's wailing ceased.

Leesan squeezed out a few words. "Thank you very much for your help."

"It's nothing." He chuckled.

They walked to the cashier together. She tried to pry Ann-Ann from his arms, but the girl pushed her hands away.

As Leesan placed the dress on the counter, he gestured to her. "I'll pay for this. I've already promised Ann-Ann."

Unable to find her tongue, she followed him out of the store in silence.

When they reached the bus stop, he glanced at her. "Are you going home? I can continue to hold Ann-Ann for you." By then, the child had fallen asleep on his shoulder.

"Yes." She smoothed down her hair. "You don't have school today?"

He grinned. "I've graduated. I hope to find a better job soon."

"Congratulations." She stepped closer as they boarded the bus. "I didn't know you graduated."

"Only a technical diploma." He shrugged and moved to a seat. "I didn't want to bother anyone with such a trivial thing."

Back at their flat, to express her gratitude, Leesan cooked fried chicken, steamed fish, and spinach with minced garlic for Danny and Kam-Chu. After dinner, Ann-Ann, clad in her new dress, sang and danced to music flowing from the radio.

Kam-Chu applauded. "Ann-Ann, you're so cute in the red dress. And you sing and dance well." She shook a finger at Leesan. "You always buy those practical garments for your daughter. Sometimes a girl deserves a bit of dress-up. See how beautiful she is in this attire."

"I–I—" Leesan bit her lip, stifling her response.

Yes, she could afford to buy a few luxurious outfits for Ann-Ann. But how about Nana and May-May? Every day, Hong Kong newspapers reported horrid political movements in China. *How can we enjoy unnecessary items while they suffer?*

Danny touched her hand. "I understand your concerns. I don't mind buying this dress for Ann-Ann at all."

A gentle warmth rose in her heart. *He's such a kind man.*

That warmth stayed with her through the weekend, a quiet comfort that hadn't faded by the following Monday. While Kam-

Chu went out to visit her daughter, Leesan dropped Ann-Ann off at school, then returned to her room to write.

A knock interrupted her. When she opened the door, Danny flashed a broad grin. "Have you done your shopping for the New Year?"

She ran a hand through her newly permed hair. "Not yet. Why?"

"I plan to do it today. I must buy gifts for my parents back home and remember you need to do the same. Will you come along?"

A knot cinched up her stomach. What would happen if she went out with him alone?

He leaned forward. "We can go to the flower market afterward. I doubt you've had a chance to visit the market. Let's go. It'll be fun."

Right. Hong Kong people liked to buy a tree full of tiny oranges from the flower market for the Chinese New Year, very much like Americans having a pine tree during Christmas. She did need to buy gifts for Nana and May-May. "Okay. I can't go out for too long, though. I still have some pages to write."

The holiday bustle replaced the quiet of her room. At the Wing-On store, Danny jammed his hands on his hips. "So many people. Maybe we shouldn't buy anything just yet. Let's go to the flower market."

She followed him toward Mongkok, a major shopping area for locals on the Kowloon side. The entire place came alive with the festive spirit. Bright sunshine cast its rays on festivalgoers. Merchants shouted to attract passersby's attention.

He wrapped an arm around her waist. "People are bumping against you."

She tried to pull away. When he persisted, she gave out a faint sigh and let him hold her tight.

They didn't return home until almost noon.

That sense of being held followed her across the threshold of their door. Once inside, the walls seemed to pull them closer together. She became conscious of his presence in a way she hadn't been before.

And, unlike before, he was home all the time.

One afternoon after a shower, he slouched on the sofa with only a towel wrapped around him. The scene ignited the simmering heat in her loins into a flame of hunger. She averted her eyes yet couldn't help questioning what was wrong with her. Why couldn't she tame the fire inside of her?

***

Beijing, China
Summer 1953

Su-Ann entered their yard and passed Chen Kang sitting on the tree stump. He stood and followed her. "Mrs. Lee, bad news."

Fear seized her. Her mouth dropped open. "What's wrong? Something happened to May-May or Yao at the daycare center?"

He shook his head. "Let's talk inside. Let's go to your house."

As they entered the room, he halted his steps. "Pastor Fu was arrested."

"What?" Her legs grew weak. She pulled out a chair to sit on. "Because he refused to join the Three-Self?"

Chen Kang raked through his hair. "I don't understand why the Three-Self has such an impact on our church. Could you explain, please?"

"Atheism remains at the core of communism, which clashes with our Christian belief. Our government uses various tactics to suppress Christianity. The Three-Self is one of them." She moved to her bookshelf to retrieve a piece of paper. "Here is the information Pastor Fu gave us a while back."

Chen Kang walked to stand by her. "Yes, I remember. When there was a debate at church over whether to join the Three-Self, Pastor Fu prepared this. He asked each of us to seek guidance from the Lord and obey the voice of the Holy Spirit, because the church wouldn't have an official stand."

She read from a paragraph on the sheet. "'Not long after the government gained solid control of the country, the Preparatory Committee of the Three-Self Patriotic Movement proposed a campaign against imperialism and scum within the church and encouraged churches to hold accusation meetings with the assistance of the local government.'"

Kang raised his gaze toward the ceiling. "That's why the famous preacher Watchman Nee was jailed."

She rubbed at the shivers puckering her arms. "After the formation of the committee, accusation meetings were held all over the country. Nee's church, the Small Group Meeting House in

Nanjing, accused him of conspiracy activities. He was put into prison. Nobody knows whether he's still alive."

Su-Ann returned to her chair and recited another paragraph. "'The Three-Self has made the following purposes clear to the churches: Unite Christians across the country; promote the Chinese church to achieve complete autonomy, self-support, and self-denial; actively participate in the patriotic, anti-imperialist movement; defend world peace. Believers across the country must join the Three-Self. It is unpatriotic not to participate.'"

Still standing, he tapped the table. "Some of our church members did take part in the Three-Self, although Pastor Fu refused."

"Since the Nee incident, Pastor Fu knew eventually all church leaders would face similar treatments. He thought we could gain time by lying low." Closing her eyes, she let out a long breath. "But the government used the Suppression of Counterrevolution Movement to label the church leaders who did not support the Three-Self as counterrevolutionaries and arrested them one by one."

Kang rubbed the back of his neck. "Recently, Pastor Fu talked about the jailing of another famous preacher, Wang Mingdao. He probably didn't expect he would face the same outcome so soon."

"Yes, very bad." She flexed her hands, yet couldn't fight an inexplicable sadness. "Is Mrs. Fu all right?"

He shifted from one foot to the other. "Mrs. Fu is fine. She joined the Three-Self early on, likely a stopgap solution."

Kang is nervous. I understand how he feels. Su-Ann scratched her cheek, then tucked the offending wisps of hair behind her ears. "Although Mrs. Fu is more flexible, she loves the Lord."

"I wonder..." He began in a small voice. "I wonder if we should visit Pastor Fu?"

"Uh, let's discuss it..." A movement from outside startled her, and Su-Ann pressed a palm against her chest. Liang Duan stood leaning against the doorframe. "Duan, what a surprise."

"Auntie Lee, I happened to be in the area." He gave Chen Kang a sharp gaze. "I'm glad you're also here. It'll save me some trouble. A friend mentioned that Pastor Fu from your church was locked up. You must understand it's not appropriate to visit him now."

While she exchanged a glance with Kang, Duan stepped closer. "Sometimes it's better to save your strength for the future than to do something impulsive. Those activities usually don't help." He gripped the back of her chair, bent down, and made eye contact. "You can give supplies to Mrs. Fu for her to take to her husband."

"Thank you for reminding me." She ducked her head.

The weight of his gaze remained even after the door closed behind him and Kang. Only when the house fell quiet again did she feel she could breathe. Taking a bag of canned food from her stash, she sought out Mrs. Fu. "How is the pastor?"

"Let's go to my bedroom. It's safer." Mrs. Fu guided her into a small room. "Like what they've done to other preachers, he's facing a barrage of physical and mental torture, threats, and brainwashing." Mrs. Fu gave a pained stare as they sat on the bed. "Nothing we can do, anyway. We must remain steadfast in our faith." She touched her forehead. "I thought about it at length. Watchman Nee's small group meeting mode is worth considering. Without a church building, we'll have to meet in private homes."

Folding her hands on her lap, Su-Ann kept her back stiff. "Pastor Fu mentioned that the Greek word for church means 'gathering of a set of people called by the Lord.' Whenever we believers meet, we can be God's house without an actual structure."

"Let's pray." Mrs. Fu put her palms together. "Lord, please give us wisdom so we know how to break up the congregation into small groups."

Chapter Nine

"If anyone is in Christ, he is a new creation; the old has gone, the new has come!"

II Corinthians 5:17

The Chinese New Year came. Leesan and her housemates enjoyed a feast of traditional Cantonese dishes that Kam-Chu prepared. One week later, Danny moved out. Then Leesan ran into him the next Tuesday after she dropped off Ann-Ann at school.

"Hi." Hands in his pockets, he flashed an easy smile.

Her mouth slid open, unease creeping up. "Danny? You don't have to work today?"

"It's my day off." He stepped closer. "Do you have time? I know a decent dim sum place nearby. Shall we have brunch together? My treat."

She glanced at her watch, her stomach churning. "Sure."

Against excessive noise from diners and the clatter of plates in the crowded restaurant, Leesan raised her voice a tad higher. "This is the most delicious dim sum I've had since I arrived in Hong Kong."

He pointed his chopsticks her way. "I told you it's good."

She chewed on a BBQ pork bun with deep satisfaction. "It's better than good. It's excellent."

When he bought another order of the pork bun for her to take home, a pleasing warmth swooshed into her chest. *He's so generous.*

As she entered the flat, Kam-Chu was sorting mail at the table. "You came back late."

"I did some shopping." She turned her eyes away.

"I see." Kam-Chu handed her two letters. "For you. Somehow, I forgot to check the mailbox yesterday."

Leesan opened the one from her mother-in-law. As usual, Su-Ann wrote they were well and told her not to worry.

The second one came from Liang Duan.

> *Your mother-in-law may have mentioned it to you already. After the arrest of a famous preacher Watchman Nee, the government began a nationwide sweep targeting leaders in the local churches. Pastor Fu was arrested recently. Auntie Lee intended to visit him in prison. I told her not to go, and she took my advice. But she's been giving supplies to Mrs. Fu. If possible, please send her more...*

She frowned at the disturbing news. Su-Ann mentioned Watchman Nee in one of her previous letters. Around that time, the *South China Morning Post* in Hong Kong also ran an article about Nee, detailing the twelve days of accusation meetings and how Nee's coworkers were forced to renounce him.

Since Kam-Chu had left the living room, Leesan walked over to the kitchen to find her. "I've just read Duan's letter. He mentioned my mother-in-law constantly gives away food I send her and doesn't have much left for her and May-May. Duan said I should buy her more stuff. It irks me."

"What your mother-in-law does is a kind act. I'm sure it's pleasing to God." Kam-Chu set down a skillet. "If you're worried about not having enough money to buy her provisions, I'll chip in."

Tears welled up in Leesan's eyes. "How can I let you do that? You've helped me so much already."

"Allow me the honor." Kam-Chu grinned and raised a finger in the air. "I'm doing it for the Lord."

Thinking of her earlier lie, Leesan ducked her head. "Kam-Chu, thank you." Still, no way she would tell her landlady about her chance meeting with Danny.

Yet she ran into him again the next Tuesday, and they enjoyed brunch together. Was it a date? It certainly felt like one to her.

On their fifth date, Leesan let him hold her hand. In the same Cantonese restaurant, they made small talk about the weather, shopping, food, and other trivial matters.

Afterward, he clutched her arm. "Do you have time? I'd like to take you to a special place."

She twisted her watch into view. Okay, still early. She didn't need to pick up Ann-Ann until three. "Let's go."

By bus and ferry, they went to the affluent Mid-Levels area on Hong Kong Island.

With her hand in his, Danny leaned his body toward her. "Have you been here before?"

She surveyed the incredible view of Hong Kong Harbor and the mansions across the road. "I heard about the lifestyle of wealthy people in Hong Kong but had no idea it's so different from mine."

He chuckled. "Now you know."

They strolled into a quiet alley lined with shrubs full of pink flowers.

"So beautiful. What are they?" She withdrew her hand from his to press down her skirt that flew up in the wind.

"The flowers? Hong Kong camellia." He pointed at the road. "Do you know what this alley is called?"

As she gave him a questioning glance, he edged closer. "The Lover's Lane. In the evening, you'll see many couples make out with no restrictions." Then he drew her into the bushes and planted his lips on hers.

Her breath grew heavy. They sank to the loamy ground together and kissed with such intensity that flames crept up from her toes to her head, melting her, boiling her. Nothing, not even the public surroundings, mattered anymore.

As his hand reached under her skirt, she regained her senses and pushed him away. "We shouldn't."

"How come?" He frowned. "You don't have a husband. I'm single. You're lonely. So am I. Why can't we have some fun?"

"It's a *sin*." She averted her face.

"A *crime*? We aren't doing anything illegal." He snorted. "You're concerned about the passersby. Don't worry. No one comes here during the daytime."

Mama's words from long ago whispered through her mind. "Sin and crime are distinct words, but the Chinese language has one single expression for the two divergent concepts. That's why most folks mix them up."

She shot to her feet, her heart full of self-loathing. "It's late. I'd better go."

Yet back in her room, her thoughts kept shifting toward their tryst—their kisses, his fingers on her body.

It's not right. But why do I enjoy it so much? Am I a hopeless whore?

The following Tuesday, they went to Lover's Lane and concealed themselves in the thickets like last time. Still, she broke their embrace when his fingers reached into her underwear.

"What's wrong with you?" He huffed.

She cringed at his annoyance, even as she lowered her gaze, shame bowing her head. "I can't. It—"

"You're shy. Haven't you seen dogs do it on the street side? They don't mind the presence of others. It's just a part of animal instinct."

She struggled to move away from his arms. "We're not animals."

"Whatever you say." He released her.

The next week, after they had dim sum together, he locked his eyes with hers. "Let's go to a nice secluded place today."

Her heart skipped a beat. *Does he love me? Will it matter if we go one step further?*

They strolled hand in hand to a narrow street in Mongkok lined with cheap small hotels. When he stopped by a building with Mayflower written in poor penmanship on its sign, he flashed an opaque smile. "Let's take a break here."

"I'm fine. I–I"—her voice trembled—"I need to go home now."

"No. You have time." With an arm around her waist, he guided her through shabby doors. Inside, he loosened his hold.

She hid behind him to peer at the skinny woman by the counter, who stared at a bunch of fake flowers in a chipped vase.

Danny seemed to know what to do and gave the woman some cash. "Rest. Two hours."

Without any comment, the woman took the money and handed him a numbered key.

They climbed the steep, narrow stairs. He opened their room and turned on the light, and her gaze fell on the only furniture, a bed against the wall.

While strolling toward the mattress, he shed his shirt, pants, and underwear with a toothy grin. "You're right. The Lover's Lane is too exposed. This place suits our needs better."

Leesan stared at the male form on the only furniture in the cramped space, and her mouth went dry. She moistened her lips. The anticipation of his body on top of hers brought a shudder.

"Take off your clothes."

At his urgent tone, she stretched out her hand toward the switch, but then his husky voice stopped her.

"No, keep the light on. Let me see you strip. Don't be shy. Show me your beautiful body. I've wanted to see you naked since the first day I laid my eyes on you."

She dropped the purse and began to unbutton her blouse.

Then a familiar tune formed in the air, and she perked up her ears. Oh, one of her favorite hymns in Chungking.

> *Earnestly, tenderly, Jesus is calling,*
> *Calling, O sinner, come home!*

The flaring fire receded as if someone dumped a bucket of icy water over her head, and shame rushed in. Without a word, she picked up her purse, unlocked the door, and stepped out.

In the following days, she couldn't concentrate on her writing. Her mind kept shifting back to Danny's muscular body in that small room. She wanted to call him but didn't have his phone number.

During the sleepless nights, she sat up to look at Ann-Ann in her sleep. Would Danny love her like his own daughter?

Her thoughts focused in and out, along with uncertain questions. Did he love her? Did she love him? After they were married, they could make love all they wanted. Why couldn't he wait?

Next Tuesday, Danny waited for her as usual, and she followed him to the dim sum restaurant.

"Hey, what happened to you last week? I wasted ten dollars for nothing." He furrowed her brows as the waiter placed a tray of shrimp dumplings on their table.

She gripped her chopsticks, the slim pieces clattering with her trembling. Beneath his gaze, she swallowed hard, searching for the proper words. "Danny, have you considered marriage? We can't go on like this. I want to know your plan."

His upper lip curled into a sneer. "I don't understand."

"Do you care for me enough to—?" Her throat seized up.

"To marry you?"

The chopsticks slipped free. She wrung her fingers, still harboring a hope he was interested in her as a woman suitable to be his wife.

"I thought we had the same idea. We both need spice in our lives. What's wrong with giving each other some pleasure?"

Dumbfounded, she became mute. Fury burned within her, propelling her to scream at him, but she could only say, "I..."

He raised a hand. "Please don't tell me you dislike it. Your problem is you think a marriage certificate will sanctify it. Don't be ridiculous."

Her jaw tightened. Disgust, more at herself than at him, rose from the bottom of her stomach. She'd rendered him a kind, loving person. What a joke! *I know nothing about this man. He's never told me anything personal about himself, not even where he lives.*

She pushed against the table to stand up. "Don't bother to come next week. I don't want to see you ever again."

On her way home, ignoring glances from passersby, she let tears tumble down her face.

When she entered the flat, her landlady was reading in the living room. At the sight of her, Kam-Chu shot to her feet. "Are you all right?"

As if finding a haven, Leesan threw herself into Kam-Chu's arms. She cried aloud, oblivious to time. The clock struck eleven. She moved away to get a piece of facial paper. "I'm sorry."

"It's okay." Kam-Chu pulled her to sit together. "Are you suffering from a toxic relationship? Unscrupulous men often prey on young widows. I understand the hardship."

Leesan lowered her head to avoid her friend's searching gaze.

"For years, I struggled to control the excessive destructive force inside of me." Kam-Chu paused with an audible sigh. "I–I was involved with a married man. He brought me temporary relief. But every encounter plunged me further into despair."

Kam-Chu must care very much about me to broach this taboo subject. Leesan tipped her head back and squinted, warmth tingling in her limbs.

"Then I became a Christian." Kam-Chu wiped her face with a handkerchief. "My faith freed me from the shackle of lust. After I accepted Christ as my Savior, my focus shifted from my selfish wants to a larger perspective. I found a calling from God and desired to live a life worthy of that calling."

While Leesan remained quiet, Kam-Chu went to get her Bible. "Ephesians chapter four says we ought to put off our old corrupted self and put on the new self, created to be like God in true righteousness and holiness."

Tears welling up again, Leesan bared her secrets—her childhood in a Christian home, her marriage to Rong, her reason to leave Beijing, and her recent liaison with Danny. "I loved Rong since I was a kid. Although the erotic scenes in novels never occurred in my marriage, Rong's behavior was consistent with his being a decent gentleman. I also behaved like a lady." She murmured in between sobs. "After my encounter with Dong Guang, the lust inside of me spun out of control. I'm a wanton woman."

She grabbed a fistful of hair to relieve her pent-up tension. "I despise myself. But I can't control my mind, no matter how hard I try. God can't accept me. I'm too far away from Him."

Kam-Chu flipped through the Bible pages. "According to Ephesians chapter two, it is by grace we're saved. It is the gift of God, not by works. We're all sinners. Through Christ, no one is beyond the reach of God's love."

Leesan stopped her hand from twisting around her tresses and looked up at the ceiling. A ray of bright light dawned on her soul. She blurted out, "It's by God's grace, not by my own struggle. I grew up in church. How come I never understood this until now?"

"I can see God's protection over you. If not because of your upbringing, you might have already fallen victim to seduction and become the sex toy of a scoundrel." Kam-Chu stared into her eyes. "Will you come back to God's family today? Shall we pray?"

They fell to their knees. As Kam-Chu prayed, Leesan's shoulders loosened up, peace engulfing her whole person. *Lord, thank You for Your unconditional love.*

Afterward, her landlady invited her to study the Bible together every day. Four months later, after the Bible study, Kam-Chu gave Leesan's arm a gentle squeeze. "Danny is getting married. His fiancée is his boss's daughter. I heard she's a nice girl from a rich family. To an ambitious young man, the shortest route to obtain success and wealth is to get a rich wife."

"Thank you." She forced a smile and searched her heart for anger and resentment, but she didn't find any. "I'm okay."

"Our society is full of men like Danny." Closing her Bible, Kam-Chu sighed. "May I ask you a personal question?"

"Sure." She glanced at her friend.

Kam-Chu placed a palm over her forehead. "How have you been handling the unwanted images that invade your brain?"

Heat crept up Leesan's cheeks. "A bit better. Still, it's difficult to cleanse my mind of filthy thoughts."

"Thank you for being so candid." Kam-Chu edged the Bible aside and drummed her fingers on the table. "We often have unreal expectations. In reality, being a Christian doesn't mean we'll not sin. On the contrary, our inner struggle seems worse than before. We become more sensitive toward sin because of the Holy Spirit's help."

Leesan took a deep breath to subdue her jitters. "I certainly feel that way. It makes me wonder if I've really been born again."

"Satan likes to use our environment to accuse us. My own experience told me the faith journey is an ascending line with many ups and downs. Time and again, I found myself falling so low, making me question my salvation." Kam-Chu took a pen to draw an upward zigzag on the paper.

"How do I minimize the frequency of falling?" Leesan examined the sketch. "I can't shun men who pay me attention."

"No, avoidance isn't the solution. Accept the fact that believers can and will sin. It takes effort for our lives to be transformed." Kam-Chu dropped her pen.

Bracing an elbow on the table and her chin on her palm, Leesan lifted her gaze. "How?"

"To me, the transformation of my life is a long process. I'm still working on it. At least I learn to ask myself in everything I do, 'If this is pleasing to God and helpful to others?'" Kam-Chu leaned over to hug her. "Give yourself time. The most important thing is to make sure that the Lord occupies the center of your life."

While Leesan pondered those words, Kam-Chu rubbed her hands together. "Yesterday, I heard a sister at church talk about her relatives from Taiwan. Your parents are in Taiwan, right? Maybe she can help you get in touch with them."

"Truly?" Leesan jerked up her head, an inexplicable hope pulsing through her veins. "That would be wonderful."

Through that sister, Leesan met Mrs. Kuhn, a missionary with the China Inland Mission, who was forced to leave China in 1949 and now served in Hong Kong. With Mrs. Kuhn's assistance, she sent out a letter to her parents. Soon, a thick envelope with her father's name reached her. Her hands trembling, she tore it open. At her father's familiar handwriting, tears rushed to her eyes.

> *Leesan,*
>
> *We received your letter with much joy. Mama and I cried several times. We have been praying for you but never expected to hear from you. It's a special blessing from God. We are glad you have become a mother... sad to learn Rong passed away. With the nonstop political campaigns in China, it's disheartening to learn Su-Ann and May-May are still in Beijing.*

He mentioned he still worked for the Nationalist Government. Because of the martial law enforced in Taiwan, he couldn't send letters to China or leave Taiwan unless he retired from his job.

That's why they didn't write to me, even though they knew back in 1950 that Rong and I had returned to Beijing.

She let out a heavy sigh. How she longed to see them right away. *I have so many things to tell them.*

But, no, she couldn't afford to travel.

With an aching heart, she kneeled and poured out her misery to God. "Lord, I'm so helpless about my situation. Oh, please protect Papa, Mama, Mother, and May-May."

When could she reunite with her family?

Chapter Ten

"Later, Joseph of Arimathea asked Pilate for the body of Jesus. Now Joseph was a disciple of Jesus, but secretly because he feared the Jews."

John 19:38

Beijing, China
May 1959

"May-May." Su-Ann picked up her sweet girl from school. "Tell Nana what you've learned today."

"Not much." May-May swung the bag over her back. "I played with my classmates. Xiao-Hung was mean to me. Yao told her to leave me alone, and she did."

Su-Ann curled up her lips at a picture of Yao rescuing her granddaughter from a mean-spirited kid. *What a typical eight-year-old.*

"That's great. Did you thank Yao for his help?" She held May-May's hand in hers, thankful that, unlike some kids who stayed at school during weekdays, May-May came home after classes every day.

Lord, thank You for Your mercy and Duan's help. I have time with May-May in the evening to teach her the biblical principles.

Skipping forward, May-May shook her head. "Yao is my best friend. He doesn't need me to thank him. He understands."

"He knows, doesn't he?" Su-Ann chided with a smile. "I still think you ought to thank him. It's good manners, right?"

"Yes, Nana." Her girl glanced up. "Yesterday, our teacher took us to a field to kill sparrows. She said they harm our farmers. Why are the birds bad? They look cute."

Su-Ann's chest tightened as she rubbed her nose. New campaigns were unfolding before them—the Great Leap Forward to prohibit private farming and the Four Pests Campaign to eradicate rats, flies, mosquitoes, and sparrows.

Her textile factory had also shut down for three days to participate in the sparrow-destroying activity. She'd gone with her team to a nearby park, taking with them different utensils like tin cans.

Their supervisor had commanded, "Make noises as loud as you can to scare the birds into the sky to prevent them from landing. The sparrows will fly nonstop, become exhausted, and eventually drop dead."

The idea was so absurd that she wanted to laugh. Yet she didn't dare to chuckle. Instead, she banged her tool with feigned enthusiasm, like all her associates.

How could she explain the political aspect of such a ridiculous incident to an eight-year-old?

She scratched her nose again. "Sometimes we don't understand our leaders' instructions. They have good reasons. We may not agree, but if we don't follow, we'll run into trouble. May-May, promise Nana one thing. No matter how strange school events are, don't bring up your questions to anyone other than me. Okay?"

"Yes, Nana." May-May inclined her head. "We're home."

As their house came into view, Su-Ann let out a silent breath. So many years had passed since she gave the deed to the government. *Why does my heart still ache every time I enter the main gate?*

The door went missing. Most of the brick walls were hauled away for other purposes. The magnificent estate that used to be the envy of her friends had deteriorated into a "big mixed yard," a term Beijing folks dubbed their peculiar living arrangements with several families from different social circles sharing the space.

Since Leesan and Ann-Ann departed, one additional family had moved in. The Shaos comprised a couple with two daughters, Hui and Li. Shao Hui was a bit older than May-May, while Shao Li was two or three years younger. Meanwhile, Dong Guang's wife had left him. Rumors circulated that Dong Guang engaged in lewd activities with other women.

The four families had converted the yard into a small farm. They filled the pond and turned it into a vegetable patch. Tomatoes, cucumbers, and beans replaced peonies, which were deemed useless. They all raised chickens to supplement the meat shortage.

Weighed down by the memory of their old days, Su-Ann huffed another sigh. "I forgot to tell you. We received something from Hong Kong." Yes, she did it on purpose, keeping the good news until the last minute to give her girl a surprise.

May-May's eyes brightened. "Mama? Mama sent us a package?"

"You're right." Su-Ann loosened her hold to let the child run ahead.

As she entered their room, May-May, with her palm on the opened box, gave her a questioning glance. "Nana, did you open it?"

"No. I received it like that." Su-Ann waved in a vain attempt to brush aside her apprehension. Why did the government have to check every package from outside of China? "Not much we can do. Let's sort through it."

Inside the box lay children's Bible storybooks and provisions, including canned bamboo shoots, dried mushrooms, and a bag of rice.

A broad smile crinkled up May-May's lips when they unearthed Leesan's letter and a picture. She valued them more than anything else.

In the black-and-white photo stood a young woman and a girl. Both had shoulder-length hair and were clad in beautiful dresses.

"Nana, read it to me."

While she read, May-May's eyes sparkled at Leesan's description of her recent publications, Ann-Ann's school activities, and the world news.

At the end, a sentence appeared to be added at the last minute. "Wait. There's a postscript."

"Yeah?" May-May leaned closer.

Su-Ann grinned. "She's found your grandpa and grandma."

"How wonderful." May-May clapped. "Where are they?"

"Um... No, she didn't say. It's not important. Remember to keep it a secret between us." At her granddaughter's solemn nod, Su-Ann clenched her jaw, the stiffness returning to her shoulders. Why did political situations beyond anyone's comprehension keep loved ones separated? How long would the separation last? Could May-May ever see her mother and sister again?

Bowed down, Su-Ann stowed the supplies in their storage bin. She forced calmness into her tone. "Tonight, we'll have visitors. Will you have dinner with us?"

"I won't." May-May picked up the picture. "I'll eat with Yao."

"Okay." Su-Ann took out a few boxes of cookies. "Give them to our neighbors, two boxes for each family."

After May-May left, Su-Ann hurried to the kitchen to cook rice and prepare a dish of sautéed cabbage with eggs. Mrs. Fu had asked her to host a fellowship meeting.

Since the government shut down their church building, they'd been meeting in small groups. Her cell group consisted of five individuals: Old Zhang, his wife and daughter, Chen Kang, and herself. Mrs. Fu, who took over the church's leadership responsibility, joined them occasionally. Everyone also participated in other fellowship gatherings according to their needs. The key consideration was safety.

The sound of a light knock interrupted her thoughts.

"Hi, Mrs. Lee." Kang arrived first.

Other visitors soon appeared one by one. After their simple dinner, Su-Ann led them in prayers. Then they recited Bible verses to one another. Following Mrs. Fu's advice, each of them memorized different Bible books in case the government confiscated their Bible. Last but not least, they broke a piece of unleavened bread that Old Zhang's wife had made and drank water as a remembrance of Jesus' sacrificial love. Not wanting to rouse suspicions from the neighbors, Su-Ann didn't allow them to sing hymns but asked everyone to recite the lyrics.

* * *

May-May visited the other two families before skipping to Yao's room. When he opened the door, she whispered, "I've got something to show you."

The corners of his mouth lifted as he drew her to sit under the window. "Must be a package from your mother."

She squeezed her legs into her chest and braced a piece of paper on them. Then she moved her index finger along with the words. "Mama mentioned they went to a concert at church...."

After she finished, Yao gaped. "How did you recognize all the words? I'm one year older than you are. I've not learned some of the characters your mama wrote."

"Easy." She held back her shoulders. "After Nana read it to me, I've memorized the letter."

"I forgot you have an excellent memory. Your nana has to teach me many times before I can memorize a hymn. Unlike me, you pick it up right away." He heaved a long breath, his tone dreamy. "I wish I lived in Hong Kong. It must be a fun city."

"Yeah, sometimes I wish I were with Mama and Ann-Ann, but I can't leave Nana alone." She handed him the picture, bouncing where she sat. "Ann-Ann is almost up to Mama's chest. Do you think she's taller than I am?"

"Maybe, hard to tell." Yao examined the photo.

She pursed her lips. Did Yao think her not as tall as Ann-Ann?

He gave her a glance. "You're just as cute."

At his praise, she smiled, her chest swelling. "Mama also sent us many books. Let's read them together tomorrow."

After saying good night, she hurried back to their room. But she couldn't sleep. Lacing her fingers behind her head, she pictured Mama and Ann-Ann in their pretty dresses in Hong Kong. Was Hong Kong very far away? Why couldn't Mama and Ann-Ann come to see her in Beijing? Oh, how she longed to see them face-to-face.

When the moon shadows faded on the ceiling and the sun rose, she scrambled from bed, had a simple breakfast with Nana, then joined Yao on their favorite tree stump in the yard to read together.

"Hey, what're you two doing?" Shao Hui stood in front of them.

Yawning, May-May lifted her head to their neighbor and hid the book behind her, uneasiness washing over her. "Nothing."

"Come on." Shao Hui tugged at May-May's sleeve. "Show it to me."

Tears blurred her vision. "I can't."

"Why not?" Shao Hui stomped a foot. "You read it with Yao.

Why can't I see it?" She reached out to yank the item.

"No." May-May grabbed it at the same time.

The book ruptured into two pieces. They remained transfixed, gaping at the torn pages. Then May-May cried out, her heart broken like the book. "Oh no!"

"See what you've done." Yao stood up to shove Shao Hui.

"I didn't do it on purpose." Shao Hui raised her hands, her lower lip protruding. "I'm sorry."

"I'll fix it myself." May-May wiped her cheeks and gave Yao a quick peek. Would he approve of her response?

Yao crossed his arms in front of him and jutted up his chin. "May-May is too kind. I want you"—he jerked his thumb toward Shao Hui—"to go get your glue. We'll patch the book back together."

"Okay." Shao Hui hurried away, her pigtails bouncing. She sprinted back with her peace offering. While they were working, she touched the three figures on a page. "Nice pictures. What does it say? What language is it in?"

Remembering Nana's instructions, May-May remained quiet.

"It's in English." Yao thrust out his chest. "A story about a father and his two sons, one good, the other bad."

"Wow." Envy shone in Shao Hui's eyes. "You two can read English?"

"You..." May-May almost blurted out that Shao Hui could join them, but stopped at Yao's warning glare.

Hui scratched her ear. "How come you two always glance at each other as if you have lots of secrets?"

Yao gave her a sharp gaze. "You're imagining things."

A clatter of footsteps reverberated from the entrance.

"Uncle Duan." May-May scrambled to her feet, brushed bark from her knees, and ran toward him.

Duan stooped to kiss her forehead. "May-May, you look terrific. Where's your nana?"

"In our room."

Before they walked away, Yao rushed over. "Let's go swimming after lunch."

***

Su-Ann frowned at the sight of Duan. What brought him here when he'd visited two days ago?

He pulled out a chair, the metal legs squeaking against the patched-up wood floor as he sat. "Auntie, I heard you had visitors last night."

She jerked up her head. "How did you find out? I didn't know the news spread so fast."

"It doesn't matter how I learned about it." He waved in a circle. "I'm afraid the walls have ears, as the saying goes. You've got to be more cautious."

She lapsed into silence, searching for the right words.

He nodded at May-May. "Consider her well-being. Your activities will impact her."

The child's dear face pinched tight with a puzzled expression.

Su-Ann stifled a sigh and eased into the chair across from him, her muscles aching. "May-May, why don't you go to the other room to read? I have something to discuss with Uncle Duan."

She waited for her granddaughter to leave. "I've never talked to you about this. Do you believe in God?"

Seeming unsurprised by her question, he braced his elbows on the table. "I've known you since I was a little boy."

"Were you seven when you first came to our house?" She curled up her mouth into a half-smile at their shared memories. "Rong asked you to stay the night with us. We were concerned your parents would be worried. You told me they were dead, and you lived with your grandma, so we sent a maid to ask your grandmother's permission for you to sleep over."

"I forgot about that." He drew a deep breath. "But I remember your mournful eyes after Rong's father passed away. We were in the sixth grade. Following the funeral, whenever I went to your house, I only saw the maids."

She blinked away hot tears. "My husband's death hit me hard. During those days, to forget my pain, I played mahjong day after day."

With the way he tipped his head, his thick brows overshadowed his soulful eyes. "For many years, Rong and I were together like two orphans. Fortunately, your servants treated us well."

"I still feel guilty about being addicted to the game for such a long time. By God's mercy, Rong didn't go astray." She touched her forehead, cringing over those lost years.

"You changed a lot since becoming a Christian." He cleared his throat. "I didn't understand why. Back then, both Rong and I were so into communism. We didn't want to believe in the existence of God."

She studied his expression for clues to carry on their conversation. Although Rong's death was still painful to all of them, maybe it was okay to talk about his passing now. "Rong's stubbornness led Leesan to leave the faith. I'm grateful he was baptized on his deathbed. Leesan has also returned to God's family."

His chin trembled as his face twisted and blotched. "I saw how you grieved his death. Because of your Christian belief and the care from your church, you shone an inner peace you didn't have when your husband passed away. I also knew about the beatings, threats, and brainwashing Pastor Fu endured after his arrest. Yet he didn't give in. I couldn't help asking myself what force gave you both your strength."

She kept quiet, waiting for him to continue.

His deep-set eyes narrowed. "I've been reading the Bible that you gave me some time ago. I'm amazed to learn Jesus didn't just pop up in history. The Old Testament prophesied His coming. The descendants of the Jews who compiled the Old Testament are still with us today."

He scooted to the edge of his chair and clamped his hands on his knees. "The book of Isaiah, written seven hundred years before Jesus, clearly states, 'For to us a child is born, to us a son is given, and the government will be on his shoulders. And he will be called Wonderful Counselor, Mighty God, Everlasting Father, Prince of Peace.' Can anything be more explicit than this? The Almighty God, the Everlasting Father, would be born as a baby into the world."

She blurted out, "You memorized Isaiah chapter nine, verse six?"

He didn't reply but stood to pace. "Jesus knew His teachings were against the Jewish tradition. The outcome would be His death. He might be crazy because only a madman would insist on doing what He did. Yet, unlike a lunatic, His words are so full of authority."

His pacing came to a halt. "When I studied the Sermon on the Mount in the book of Matthew, I realized even our great Confucius failed to give us such lessons. There's no way to explain the Bible other than that God had indeed become flesh and born into human history. Even more astounding, as Jesus had prophesied, He rose again from death, proving that He is the Almighty God."

Su-Ann moved to embrace him. "Welcome to the family, my brother." She eased back and gripped his shoulders. "Then you understand why we continue to meet."

"I do." Beneath her hands, his shoulders relaxed. "I often feel I'm another Joseph of Arimathea who secretly followed Jesus. He did step up at the right moment to bury Jesus' body in his new tomb. Sometimes I think my current position may be useful to others. Or perhaps it's just an excuse because I'm a coward. Only time will tell."

"I appreciate how you've tried hard to assist us through the various campaigns." She stepped away and crossed her arms over her chest, shielding herself. "I sense more campaigns are coming. Remember Jesus' teachings in the Sermon on the Mount? Many of us are ready to receive the blessing."

His face twisted again. "Are you referring to the verses 'Blessed are those who are persecuted because of righteousness, for theirs is the kingdom of heaven'?" Something hollow echoed in his words. "I don't know what to say other than to ask you to be vigilant. You may be well prepared, but how about May-May? If possible, don't hold meetings at your place."

"I'll try my best." She couldn't help hugging the dear young man once more. "Thank you again for all your help."

Chapter Eleven

"My name is Peter; my name is Peter. I've denied my Lord."

Wang Mingdao (Chinese pastor and evangelist, 1900–1991)

Hong Kong
July 1960

Leesan sat by the coffee table and looked up from her travel brochure. "I'm planning a trip to Taiwan to see your grandpa and grandma."

Ann-Ann, standing nearby, rolled her eyes. "Why can't we go to Europe instead? Most of my friends visit Paris or London during summer vacation."

"Be reasonable. Your grandparents are in Taiwan, not in Europe." Leesan let out a hard breath.

Ann-Ann wasn't even ten but already acted like a teenager. Was her twin as difficult as she?

A twinge pinched Leesan's chest, and her shoulders stiffened for another inevitable confrontation.

Surprise! The girl didn't yell, merely crooking her mouth to one side. "Make sure the trip is fun."

Leesan dropped the brochure onto the coffee table with a hollow thud. "I'll try." When would Ann-Ann become more conscientious about their budget constraint?

Resigned to being the responsible one, Leesan fell back on habit and booked the cheapest possible fare across the Taiwan Strait.

The reality of that thrift didn't hit until they stepped onto the ship. Their "cabin" was nothing more than a crowded deck where passengers lay sprawled within three-by-six-foot rectangles chalked onto the floor.

At the sight of their two assigned spots, Ann-Ann wrinkled her nose. "Is one of them my bed?"

Leesan ignored her terse comment, then snapped open a sheet she'd brought and let it settle in its place.

Still frowning, Ann-Ann threw her bag on the floor. "Mama, let's go to the dining room. I'm hungry." In the onboard restaurant, she rushed forward to examine each plate. "Wow, the food is better than I thought. Look at the chicken, fish, and pork."

"It's awesome, isn't it?" The old woman nearby commented in Mandarin. "They even provide an afternoon tea. You ought to try it."

The steamer blew its whistle. Leesan crossed to the window. The ship was pulling away from the dock. Soon, the vessel rolled and rocked.

Ann-Ann's face lost its color. Beads of sweat speckled her forehead. "I don't feel well."

Leesan set down her chopsticks to grab a nylon bag. "You need to lie down."

Back at their spots on the deck, she hustled around Ann-Ann. Losing her energy, her girl slumped on the makeshift bed.

On the third morning, the steamer docked at Keelung Port in Taiwan. Shading her eyes with a hand, Leesan faced eight enormous Chinese characters carved on a cliff: "Return to the mainland. Take back our homeland."

How incredible it would be if the KMT government could succeed. Was it going to happen? If only she could see May-May and Mother.

As they stepped onto the solid ground, she exhaled her relief, then covered her nose. The subtropical sunshine reflected off the sea, and the summer wind whisked dirt, wafting a pungent fishy smell.

Passengers and their relatives crammed the dock, jostling her and her daughter. A familiar voice called her name, and she hurried over to fall into Papa's arms.

While Mama pulled Ann-Ann into a long embrace, Papa examined Leesan's face. "We haven't seen you for so many years. You look a bit heavier." He then smiled at the child. "Ann-Ann, you're prettier than your pictures."

Even as Leesan's chest swelled, something weighed on her shoulders. At thirty-three, her appearance hadn't altered much. Yet fifteen years had left visible marks on her parents. Papa was going bald. His remaining hair, although carefully combed, had gone gray. The changes in Mama were even more evident. She'd gained weight, and her back became hunched. With her throat closing over, no words could come. Leesan couldn't help but stretch a hand to touch Mama's wrinkled face.

"Let's go to the station." Papa herded them away. "It'll take hours by train to reach home."

She dabbed her wet cheeks. "Papa, you mentioned in your letters Chia-Yi is close to Ah-Li Mountain. Is it a famous tourist site?"

"Yes." He led the way.

She wrapped an arm around her mother's shoulders. Why did political situations beyond their control tear their family apart? Yet, because the sorrow of separation was so deep, the reunion was extra sweet.

On the train, she settled into her assigned seat beside Papa, then described to him and Mama her life during the past years. As she came to Rong's deathbed baptism, tears welled up again. Then she turned the subject to May-May and retrieved a picture from her bag. "I received this before we left Hong Kong."

In it stood a tall woman and a girl. Both had ear-length hair and were clad in simple blouses and pants.

Papa glanced at Ann-Ann in her sleep, her head resting on Mama's lap. "May-May looks identical to Ann-Ann."

"Yes, except May-May has a mole on the end of her left eyebrow." And May-May was thinner. Leesan stifled that comment. The comparison again ignited a deep ache within the marrow of her bones. Oh, if only she could have kept her girls together. She'd tried, but failed. Was she ready to give up? No way.

Her attention returned to the daughter with her, and she stretched across the compartment to cover Ann-Ann with a billowy scarf. "Ann-Ann must be exhausted. She was motion sick all the time."

Mama, sitting across from her, tipped the photo to catch light from the window. Her lips pressed tight. Then she blurted, "Su-Ann looks older than her age."

Papa laughed. "I'm sure she'd say the same about us if she saw us. We've all grown old. At least her back remains erect."

Her father's joke brought Leesan a twinge. Time to change the subject. She sat up straighter. "Do you remember Liang Duan, Rong's friend?"

"Yes." Papa's eyes sparkled. "How's he? Is he married?"

"He continues to work for the government. My mother-in-law said he's doing well. The last time he visited her, he drove a sleek black car. I don't think he's married. Otherwise, Mother would have told me." She took back the picture. "We also write to each other regularly. Duan informed me of Pastor Fu's arrest. He's still in prison."

"You mentioned it in one of your letters. Our newspapers seldom provide information on China, but I did hear about the persecution of Wang Mingdao. He was already a very popular preacher when we were in China. At one point, your mama and I loved to read his newspaper, *Spiritual Food Quarterly*." Papa placed a hand on his forehead. "What did the Hong Kong newspapers say about his persecution? Please tell us."

After stowing the picture back into her purse, she hooked her arm through Papa's. "He was persecuted because he declined to join the Three-Self Patriotic Movement."

He tilted his head. "The state-controlled religious organization in China?"

She hugged his arm tight, breathing in the familiar woody and spicy smell of his aftershave. "The newspaper said he, his wife, and other fellow believers were imprisoned. The church building was shut down. Following fourteen months of torture, they forced him to sign a confession put together by some officials before releasing him."

"What happened next?" Papa furrowed his eyebrows.

A shiver running up her spine, she lowered her voice. "He lost his mind afterward. For days, he walked up and down the street alone at night, talking to himself repeatedly. 'My name is Peter. I have denied my Lord.'"

"How horrid." Mama covered her mouth.

Terrible indeed. Leesan shuddered. Yet it didn't end there. "He eventually recovered from the nervous breakdown and recanted his confession. They locked him up again." She shifted her feet, repositioning herself against the swaying motion. "To this day, he refuses to give in, no matter how they beat him, threaten him. He sings the hymn 'All the Way My Savior Leads Me' by Fanny Crosby every morning in his cell. In the beginning, the guards tried to stop him, but he continued. As time went by, they asked him to teach them the lyrics."

The three of them quieted down. As the train rattled along, she rested her head against Papa's shoulder.

Then Mama formed her fingers into a steeple. "It's so challenging to be a believer in China. We must pray for Su-Ann. I'm glad she remains steadfast in her faith. I hope we'll see her again soon."

Sitting upright again, Leesan loosened her grip on her father and relayed her conversation with Su-Ann before she left Beijing. "Mother has a close relationship with the Lord. No matter what happens, she's full of peace and joy." She narrowed her eyes. "As long as Duan is in power, she'll be fine. He's a guardian angel our heavenly Father places by her side."

"How is your spiritual life?" Papa shifted toward her. "In your letters from America, you never mentioned church. We're pleased you attend Sunday worship every week now."

Leesan shook her head, heat creeping up her neck. "I don't know why I didn't understand Christianity when I was growing up. It was—" Even though her relationship with Danny faded a while ago, she still had trouble facing it.

Seeming not to notice her unease, Papa straightened his shirt where she'd rumpled it up. "I'm afraid many kids growing up in Christian families are like you. The Bible stories become too familiar. They don't realize they aren't just stories, but a part of the salvation plan from God. Christ paid a heavy price for this saving grace." He touched her arm. "What led you back to church?"

"Ann-Ann and I rent a room in an apartment. Our landlady, Wong Kam-Chu, is a devout Christian." The uncomfortable heat moved to her ears. "Through her, I recognized my sins and repented.

Since then, I've established a personal relationship with God. He is not only my Savior but also my heavenly Father."

"Ah, I remember you mentioned it before." Papa beamed. "You still live there, don't you?"

She stifled a sigh of relief, glad that Papa didn't ask her the details of her conversion. "Kam-Chu and I are close friends. She's also a widow. We pray and read the Bible together. We also belong to the same fellowship group."

"Great." Papa patted her hand. "On our spiritual journey in this world, it's necessary to get together with brothers and sisters. That's why the Bible teaches us not to give up fellowship with one another. I'm glad you have a good support system."

Mama wagged a finger. "How could you leave May-May behind with her grandmother? How come they didn't go to Hong Kong with you?"

Leesan's chest constricted. Hadn't she already explained? Dear May-May... Duan said her classmates often taunted her. Yet Su-Ann and she never mentioned any hardship and suffering in their letters. Their words were always full of gratitude and cheerfulness. Her timid, kindhearted May-May was like an angel. *Oh, Lord, please don't let the angel fall. Please protect her from the evil ones.*

The lump remained lodged in Leesan's throat. She swallowed hard. "I had no choice. We got only two permits. And traveling with a pair of identical twins would have aroused suspicion. During our first few years in Hong Kong, I barely found enough money to keep us from starving."

The memories associated with her last few days in Beijing were still raw, so she took their conversation in a different direction. "Writing fiction brings me sufficient income. I mail supplies to May-May and Su-Ann regularly."

A gleam lit Papa's eyes. "I didn't expect you to become a famous writer."

"When you were a kid, you loved to read martial arts novels." Mama gave her a toothy grin. "I never thought you would make it a profession."

Leesan crooked up one corner of her mouth. "In Chungking, you said they were trash. You scolded me if you caught me reading them."

The weight of the old grievance hung between them until a rustle broke the silence.

"I'm hungry." Ann-Ann peeled away the scarf to sit up.

When had she awakened?

Papa reached for his wallet. "Let's have the railway lunch boxes. They have spareribs and marinated eggs, very delicious."

After dinner, they reached Chia-Yi. From the station, Papa hailed two rickshaws to ride home. "I don't know what kind of transportation you have in Hong Kong. Cars and taxis aren't common here. The three-wheeled cart pedaled by a man is more popular."

They soon approached a Japanese-style house. Perhaps sensing her curiosity, Papa pointed at the door. "We have many *minkas* like this because Taiwan used to be Japan's colony before World War II."

As Leesan followed Papa into the house, she stretched her eyes wide. Except for the kitchen and bathroom, every room had rectangular mats made of straw called *tatami*. Mama opened the sliding closet doors in their room to retrieve two sets of blankets. "Here, we use one set to sleep on and one to cover up with. I hope you will find it comfortable."

When they were alone in their room, Ann-Ann plopped down on the tatami. "Why don't Grandpa and Grandma have beds?"

In a jolly mood, Leesan waved, grinning. "They save money not having to buy beds. Or maybe they want to follow the local customs."

Who cared about the trivial differences in the living style? All she wanted was to immerse herself in her parents' pampering. For a long time, she'd been the one taking care of others. Being taken care of felt so good.

At the wet market the next morning, she and Mama bought vegetables, meat, and fish. Back at home, Mama's eyes flew wide open at the sight of her skill in cleaning the fish. "You'd never done any housework before leaving us. How did you learn to cook?"

Leesan placed the fish into the steamer. "There's this Cantonese expression, 'If the horse dies, you learn to walk.'"

"You're right." Mama's laugh shook her shoulders. "How about Su-Ann? She used to be surrounded by maids. How does she handle her daily life without servants?"

"She still dislikes chores but does them, anyway. Duan told me she's good at many tasks, including raising chickens in the yard and even sewing clothes." Leesan added soy sauce to the fish. Soon, an appetizing aroma swirled around the kitchen. "Duan also said May-May is a wonderful cook. She has shouldered most of the housework from Nana."

"That's incredible. Both Su-Ann and May-May are smart for sure." Mama dropped the snow pea pods into the skillet. "You mentioned in your letters three families moved into their courtyard. How do they share the same kitchen?"

After placing the pork on the chopping board, Leesan ran a knife through it. "From Duan's description, although quarrels are common in living arrangements like theirs, my mother-in-law is wise to avoid conflict. Plus, she's kind toward others and often shares supplies I send her."

While busy with her hands, she lifted a silent prayer. *How nice to cook together with Mama. Lord, thank You so much for my parents.*

Yet, unlike her, Ann-Ann was miserable. As soon as the novelty of a new place wore off, she grumbled, "Nothing interesting here. I miss my friends in Hong Kong."

Papa offered to take them to Taipei, the largest city in Taiwan. "We can take the train, seven or eight hours from here. You still have plenty of time to have an enjoyable trip."

Leesan shook her head. "No, don't worry about Ann-Ann. She'll be fine. I don't want to be a tourist. I plan to stay home with you and pretend to be your young, unmarried daughter again."

At lunch, when Ann-Ann learned they wouldn't go to Taipei, she put down her tofu soup and ran out. Leesan trekked after her to their bedroom.

Ann-Ann dropped her full length onto the floor and hit the tatami with her fists. "You only care about your happiness. I'm bored to death here."

Luckily, we're alone in our room. After twenty minutes of coaxing, she brought Ann-Ann back to the dining room.

"Why is my bowl empty?" Ann-Ann sat and glared. "Who ate my soup?"

Papa and Mama gaped at each other. Mama spoke in a low tone. "It was getting cold. I ate it for you. We have more in the pot." She stood up to reach for the bowl. "I'll fill it for you."

Ann-Ann flung away her hand. "I don't want another one. I want *my* soup back." She kicked the table with both feet.

"Ann-Ann, stop it." Leesan gasped and pressed against her tightening chest. "Be reasonable. There's more in the pot."

"No, no, not the same." Ann-Ann's shoulder-length hair was spilling free of its pins.

Leesan massaged the back of her neck, suppressing the urge to slap the child.

Papa scratched his ear. "Ann-Ann, do you want to see a movie? I heard the town theater is showing *Snow White* today. Let's go watch it."

Ann-Ann stopped her fret, and Papa whisked her away.

As the door clicked behind them, Mama cleared her throat, her eyes still wider than usual. "Um... Does Ann-Ann usually behave like that?"

Leesan stifled a sigh and stood to collect the empty plates. "She's strong-willed. I suppose it's not easy growing up without a father. And she always thinks I care more about May-May."

"Does she go to church with you?" Mama scraped the leftovers together.

"Yes, when she's in a good mood. If she's angry, she refuses to go." Leesan plopped back down on the chair and lowered her chin to her chest. "Nothing I can do to make her change her mind."

"It must be tough." Mama leaned over her. "Still, you'll need to teach her biblical principles. With a solid value system, she's less likely to wander astray in the future."

As if thinking of something more important, Mama grasped her hand. "Have you considered finding her a father?"

Leesan stared down at their intertwined fingers. "Oh, please, let's not talk about that."

"I'm serious." Mama loosened her grip, tipped up Leesan's chin, and stared into her eyes. "You're young, not even thirty-four. You have a long life ahead of you. Once Ann-Ann goes to college, you'll be alone."

Danny's image popped into her head. Although she didn't harbor bitterness toward him, she couldn't help turning away from Mama's searching gaze. "I will if the right man comes along. Who wants a widow with children? Besides, I have my criteria. He must be a Christian and love me and my daughters. We have to be..."

She stopped mid-sentence at the memories. Quite a few guys had pursued her, and she'd also ventured out with some. She didn't conceal anything from Kam-Chu.

During one conversation, Kam-Chu had said, "If the first marriage is difficult, the second time around is even more challenging. We all understand passion fades quickly and beauty disappears over time. Many people pay great attention to sex, but the simple fact is that having sex with the same person becomes boring after a while."

How well Leesan knew that. She'd been quick to respond, saying, "I know what you mean."

Kam-Chu nodded. "If a man and a woman focus only on their selfish needs, the relationship will fall apart."

"What's your idea of a perfect marriage?" She'd prodded.

Her friend had waved as if to encompass all those around them. "Is there such a thing? To me, a happy marriage means that husband and wife are in harmony in three aspects: body, mind, and soul." Then Kam-Chu asked her how she'd been handling her need for physical intimacy.

No subjects were off-limits between them. She'd admitted she still struggled. "As we've discussed before, Genesis portrayed Joseph as a well-built man in his prime, likely with a strong need for sex. His master's wife tried to seduce him more than once. But he resisted the temptation, saying, 'How could I do such a wicked thing and sin against God?' My situation is easier than Joseph's."

Heat tingled in Leesan's cheeks as Mama's heavy sigh jolted her out of her thoughts. "You still love Rong even after so many years, don't you?"

Leesan didn't answer, thinking again of Kam-Chu's words. What did it mean to be harmonious in body, mind, and soul? Wasn't that asking a lot?

After they washed the dirty dishes, Mama made them a pot of green tea. Sitting together at the dining table, Leesan placed a palm on Mama's shoulder. "We've never talked about this before. Are you happy in your marriage?"

Mama's muscles stiffened under her touch. "We belong to the old-fashioned generation. Marriages were often arranged by parents between families with similar economic or educational backgrounds."

"But are you and Papa happy together?" Leesan drew her hand back.

Mama sipped her tea, then rubbed her chin. "We didn't go through the courting process. The notion of 'falling in love' was never in our vocabularies. Our personalities are distinct. Our views on key issues aren't the same. You can imagine how difficult it was for us to have a harmonious time. We had many conflicts in the beginning."

Words rolled off Leesan's tongue. "How about physical intimacy?"

Mama wiped her forehead with a handkerchief, the flowery cotton drooping over her face. "We both grew up in good, well-educated families. Confucianism took firm root in us. We were taught that a certain code of conduct must be followed. By those rules, women in the bedroom should be compliant."

Leesan peeled her mother's handkerchief away to look into her eyes. "Mama, you still haven't answered my question."

"Is it important to you?" Mama blinked.

When Leesan nodded, Mama stared back at her. "Okay, I hope my sharing will help you solve some issues in your heart. I was passive in the first few years. We'd never seen each other's naked bodies. We always did it in the dark with clothes on. Later..."

"What happened?"

"After we became Christians, we learned sex was created by God, a beautiful act between a husband and his wife. Adam and Eve were naked together and didn't feel ashamed." Mama spread out her handkerchief on the table as if ironing it before folding the cotton into a tidy square. "Understanding is one thing. It's another matter to put into practice. After many attempts, we finally let go of the restraints of teachings instilled in us since childhood to reach a state of harmony."

Leesan pressed a palm on her chest. "Did you and Papa become one in body, soul, and mind?"

"Yes, we're lucky. The influence of our Christian faith is comprehensive. In comparison, we've witnessed many of our friends' marriages going through a slow dying process."

Springing from her chair, Leesan couldn't help but hug her mother. "Thank you for sharing this with me. So, it's possible to have a relationship that is harmonious in body, mind, and soul."

Mama patted her back. "I'll continue to pray for you. If the Lord is willing, I hope you'll find a suitable match soon."

The door opened. Papa and Ann-Ann strolled in. Had she spent two hours alone with Mama already?

Ann-Ann, carrying a stack of books, dashed away toward their bedroom.

Papa sat down by them. "I hope you don't mind that I bought some comic books for Ann-Ann to keep her busy."

"Papa, sure." Leesan bit back a sigh. "Ann-Ann loves them."

Yet when Sunday came, the child refused to go to church with them, insisting that she must read her books.

Pulse quickening, Leesan glared at her. In return, the girl lifted her chin.

Leesan sucked in a deep breath to put away her annoyance. *Our vacation will be over soon.* She was going to enjoy every minute of her remaining days here. *I'll deal with Ann-Ann later.*

The day before their departure, Mama brought up a subject they'd been talking about on and off since their arrival. "Why don't you move here? It'll be easier for us to take care of one another."

"It won't work." Leesan wrung her fingers, a knot forming in her stomach. "If I come to Taiwan, I won't be able to send provisions to May-May and Nana. They count on me. I can tend to their needs better in Hong Kong."

The wrinkles on her mother's forehead sagged downward. "Can you get them out of China?"

"If it were so easy, I'd have done it long ago. We were lucky Duan helped obtain two permits. Since then, the policy has tightened so much that even he can't do it anymore." She swallowed hard but couldn't rid herself of the painful lump in her throat. "My mother-in-law would never agree to leave Beijing, anyway. She still considers herself a guardian of the Lee family tradition."

"Leesan is right." Papa gave Mama's back a gentle touch. "Until our government changes the China policy, she must stay in Hong Kong. I understand how you feel. I want them here too. But she must do the right thing. I often think the Lord sent her to Hong Kong with a special purpose. If she'd remained in China, she would be under severe persecution because we're in Taiwan. Remember Joseph's words in Genesis? 'God sent me to save you alive by a great deliverance.' Su-Ann and May-May's situation is easier because of Leesan."

Lord, thank You for Papa. Her chest swelled. Then the air rushed from her lungs. *Oh, Lord, when can my family reunite?*

The next day, they took the train back to the port. Papa pulled them into a circle. "Let's look to the Lord together."

Like his other prayers, he offered his praise to the Almighty God, followed by confessing their sins and thanking Christ for His sacrificial death on the cross. He then asked the Lord for His continuous protection over everyone, including Su-Ann and May-May.

Leesan let her tears flow, overwhelmed by sorrow with a trace of joy. *Lord, thank You for Your mercy.* At least her parents were well, a part of her life she didn't have to worry about.

Chapter Twelve

"He is completely God, completely human... Although He is God and human, yet Christ is not two, but one."

Athanasian Creed, AD 500

Beijing, China
May 1963

May-May glanced at the clock. Forty minutes until school started. Maybe she should go right now to avoid running into others?

She put on the yellow blouse that Nana sewed from an old dress, a gift for her twelfth birthday. Her head buzzed with chaotic visions of her schoolmates. Why wouldn't they leave her alone?

The answer, like a solved jigsaw puzzle, stared back at her. She fell into the wrong categories of landlords, rich peasants, counterrevolutionaries, bad elements, and rightists. Her schoolmates viewed her as equivalent to a criminal.

How she wished to belong to the right categories—poor and lower-middle peasants, workers, revolutionary soldiers, revolutionary cadres, and revolutionary martyrs.

But no. Nana used to be a big landlord, and Mama lived in Hong Kong.

When she sneaked past the main gate at school, Qiao Chong, together with his gang, was leaning against the wall. He stepped forward and pointed to her shirt. "Look at her."

Xiao-Hung, a girl with two thick braids, narrowed her eyes. Then she raised a hand and led the group to sing a made-up impromptu song. "Rich landlord's granddaughter wears a yellow blouse. The bad element acts like a princess."

As the mob laughed aloud, slapping one another on the back, she darted her glance around. Was there an escape route? Yet the group formed a circle around her. She sat on the ground, tears streaming down her cheeks.

A boy handed Qiao Chong a pair of scissors. With a toothy grin, he cut her sleeve. "Let me do some alterations for you."

May-May buried her face between her knees, a hard knot forming in her stomach. How would they punish her today? What had she done wrong?

"You leave her alone."

At the familiar voice, she looked up. Yao? When did he arrive?

Yao pushed Qiao Chong to the ground. "What did she do to deserve this? You should be ashamed of yourself."

Shocked gasps rose from the entourage, but Yao didn't back down and glared at them one by one.

"She's a landlord's granddaughter!" a girl yelled back.

"Lang, you shut up. If I hear you say it one more time, I'll slap you." He shook his clenched fist.

Oh, Yao. Would he get into trouble for her again? Her classmates usually stayed out of his way, likely because of his height. Or maybe because he belonged to the right category since Uncle Chen was a laborer?

Qiao Chong regained his position. "Who do you think you are? She's a bad element. That's enough reason for us to do whatever we want."

Yao swung his fist at him. Qiao Chong staggered back, then launched forward. Soon, fists and elbows rained down blows on the foe. Kicks and stomps followed.

Did someone inform the teacher? Her large figure rushed into the circle. Dragging Yao and Chong by the arms into the hallway, she ordered them to stand outside the classroom.

When May-May returned home, Yao was sitting alone on the tree stump in the yard.

"Yao." Tears blurred her vision, and she managed to say his name before rushing over to sit beside him.

Like before, he grasped her hand to play with her fingers. His gesture cast a soothing effect on her, and she calmed. "I'm sorry you got beaten because of me."

"I'm fine." He crooked up his mouth into a forced smile. "It doesn't hurt at all."

"Thank you for your help." She eyed the cucumber vine nearby. "Please don't tell my nana."

"Not to worry. I won't. She'll learn about it, anyway. Did she say anything when she noticed your damaged blouse?" He pulled her closer.

She lowered her head, hair tickling her cheeks. "Nana thought the color was subdued enough not to attract attention."

"See? Your nana found out by herself." He patted her arm. "Now tell me. Why don't you ever defend yourself?"

Why didn't she? She whisked her hair behind her ears. "I don't know how."

Yao sighed. "Can you hold your tears? They love to see you cry."

"I–I can't help it." She frowned, fixing her focus on the ground.

"Learn to grit your teeth. If you refuse to let them see your tears, maybe they won't taunt you so much."

She bit her lip and glanced up, her chest tightening. "Don't be angry with me. Remember what Nana said last week? Jesus taught us not to resist evil. If someone strikes you on the right cheek, turn the other cheek."

He drew his eyebrows tight. "Jesus is God. He could come back to life after being crucified. We're human. We can't."

"You confused me." She raised her gaze toward the blue sky dotted with puppylike white clouds, then returned it to him. "Have dinner with us. I'll prepare something special today."

He brightened. "What's it?"

She flashed a faint smile. "Care to guess? It's your favorite dish."

"Ah, you're going to use the canned bamboo shoots your mama sent?" Yao licked his lips.

"I'd better go now." She stood up. "See you and your pa soon."

Trudging away and sensing his eyes on her, she turned and gave him a wave.

Tonight, she'd make two dishes. First, she sautéed ginger threads and stirred in fresh green soybeans, white bamboo shoots, and red carrots. For the other dish, she soaked potato slices in vinegar and stir-fried them with lard, green onions, and chopped chili peppers.

In their room, a delightful aroma greeted their guests.

Uncle Chen gave her a thumbs-up. "You're such an outstanding cook."

"So delicious." Yao gobbled down three bowls of rice with vegetables.

***

After dinner, the children went to the other room to read while her guest helped Su-Ann stack the empty plates together and clucked his tongue. "May-May amazes me. She's so capable."

"She's a blessing from the Lord." Su-Ann twined her fingers into a steeple. *Lord, thank You for May-May.*

How did May-May develop all her domestic skills? Since eight, her girl had taken over most of the housework. Oil and meat were scarce, but the child found ways to toss in different ingredients to make them last as long as possible. If they had leftovers, she threw in rice to create a tasty rice soup.

But why didn't she learn to protect herself?

Su-Ann stood up to pour tea for Kang. "I worry about her. She's too timid. Her classmates like to torment her."

"Yao told me what happened today at school." He rubbed his chin. "He also said some kids envy her because she has excellent grades."

"She does. It may be useless. We fall into the wrong categories. It has always been my sincere wish to send May-May to college. I don't know whether it's possible anymore." She let out a long breath, her mind drifting toward the recent news. "Ah Kang, have you heard the rumor? Beijing will soon set up its first commune center."

"Yes." He lowered his hand from his chin. "But I don't understand why. The news leaked out that people in the rural communes lack incentives to work hard because everything belongs to the government. Now they want to expand it. It makes no sense."

"Worse, personal freedom vanishes once the militia arrives to enforce the system." Shivers tingled up Su-Ann's spine. "The Four Pests Campaign was a disaster—locusts everywhere after the sparrows were gone. The Great Leap Forward fared no better."

He blinked. "No. A severe famine followed."

"Duan said more campaigns are coming." A tightness gripped her chest. "I worry about the remaining antiques in my possession. They've been with the Lee family for generations. Once a mark of prestige, the family wealth had become a heavy burden and a cause for fear."

Moisture gathered behind her eyes. She pressed against her heart. *The Lee ancestors will never forgive me if I lose them.*

"Don't do anything for now. Let's pray about it." Chen Kang gave her a sympathetic glance. Then he pushed to his feet and went to fetch his son.

The door clicked shut, leaving the room heavy with the scent of tea and the echoes of Kang's warnings. While Su-Ann remained at the table, May-May came to sit by her. "Nana, did Jesus feel pain when He was crucified?"

Unease swirled in Su-Ann's belly. Had school today made the girl doubt her faith? *Lord, please give me wisdom.* "How come you ask such a question?"

"I just think..." May-May scrunched her forehead. "Jesus is God. He came back to life from death. Yao said Jesus was different from us. Maybe He didn't feel pain at all."

Su-Ann turned her teacup, peering into the steamy liquid. "Do you remember the Bible verses about Jesus praying in the Garden of Gethsemane?"

"Of course. Luke chapter twenty-two says Jesus prayed so hard that He sweated drops of blood."

"My good girl." Su-Ann managed a smile. "Jesus was already in distress at Gethsemane. As God, He foresaw the torture. But his most unbearable agony was knowing the eternal fellowship of the Trinity would temporarily shatter while all sins were laid on Him. That is why He cried out, 'My God, my God, why have you forsaken me?'"

May-May listened with an intense gaze, head tilted.

Su-Ann brushed a stray hair back from the girl's thin cheek. "I've taught you the Trinity doctrine. Could you recite it?"

May-May bobbed her head. "There is but one God. The Father is God, the Son is God, and the Holy Spirit is God. The Father is not the Son, the Son is not the Holy Spirit, the Holy Spirit is not the Father."

"Excellent." Su-Ann patted her shoulder. "You once asked how three persons could be one God. I told you I didn't fully understand it myself. The Bible teaches the concept, just as it teaches the hypostatic union. Jesus is fully God and fully human. When you asked whether Jesus could feel pain, you considered Him God but didn't think Him human. Am I right?"

May-May moved her chair closer.

"As God, He possessed supernatural power. Yet as a man, He was like any of us. He also felt hunger, exhaustion, sorrow, happiness, and pain."

May-May frowned. "So, was He like the monkey king in our fairy tale who could turn himself into seventy-two copies?"

Chuckling, Su-Ann put down her teacup. "Not quite. The seventy-two monkey kings were all identical. Jesus' manhood and godhood were distinct."

The girl's eyebrows drew tighter. "Was He part God, part man?"

"No." Su-Ann wrote *100* on a piece of paper. "He is one hundred percent God and one hundred percent human, simultaneously."

May-May shook her head. "How? One hundred plus one hundred should be two hundred."

Su-Ann gave May-May's fingers a gentle squeeze. "As humans, we can never truly grasp the mystery. We're limited by time and space. God isn't. You often dream of being in Hong Kong with your mama and Ann-Ann, yet you're here. Why can't you be in Hong Kong and Beijing at the same time? Because you're limited by space."

"I'm still confused."

Maybe she needed a new approach? "The space issue has two distinct aspects. None of us can go to two different places simultaneously. Also, we can't exist as two separate persons. So, May-May is May-May and can never become Ann-Ann, even though you two are identical twins." Su-Ann paused to search for the suitable words. "God isn't limited by space. He can appear at two locations and exist in three persons concurrently. Trinity and hypostatic union reveal to us an important attribute of God. He is far beyond us, beyond time and space. This teaching is so different from our experience that it must be a revelation from God."

May-May propped her chin up with one hand. "I seem to understand it a bit more. God is far beyond us. If we use our limited mind to explain God, we'll make mistakes."

Su-Ann grinned, warmth filling her heart. Could a child grasp such a mystery?

"Nana, we've been talking for too long. It's late." May-May stood.

"You're right." Su-Ann glanced at her darling granddaughter. "Whenever you run into trouble at school, remember to tell me. I may not be able to help, but we can ask the Lord to protect you."

May-May leaned her head on Su-Ann's shoulder. "I'm sorry for making you worry. Nana, I love you so much."

Moisture gathered in Su-Ann's eyes. *My precious girl, you're more important than anything else in this world to me.* "Let's prepare for bed. You have class tomorrow."

***

Early in the morning, they left home at the same time. When Su-Ann returned from work in the afternoon, May-May was playing Chinese chess with Yao in the yard. Su-Ann strolled over to watch.

May-May scrunched her forehead, paying great attention. Although Su-Ann didn't know much about the game, May-May seemed struggling. She had only a few key pieces left, while Yao still had almost a full set.

As he drove his rook to chase her remaining pawn, May-May shouted, "Checkmate!"

Her knight aimed right at his king. With a complete set surrounding the monarch, his king had no place to go but to surrender.

Yao pushed the board aside. "Not fair. You tricked me."

"It's your fault." May-May giggled. "You shouldn't go after my pawn and neglect the important king."

"I must admit, you're getting quite good." He shot to his feet, an indulgent smile spreading across his wide face.

He'd lost on purpose. Did a boy his age already harbor such deep feelings for her?

Familiar footsteps sounded at the entrance. Su-Ann jerked up her gaze.

"Uncle Duan is here!" May-May raised her arms.

Duan walked toward them with an easy grin. "May-May, you grow more beautiful every time I see you."

"Here you go again." Su-Ann laughed, shaking a finger at him, though her chest warmed. "Don't put the wrong idea into her head. I've been teaching her appearance isn't important. The inside is."

Yet who could argue with Duan? May-May had a perfect oval face with clear, smooth skin, almond eyes, and a high, straight nose. She was still short for her age, but she'd had a growth spurt during the past months. Her girl would grow tall like herself. Her beauty might be a curse. Their only protection lay with God and Duan.

"I'm sure her inside is just as beautiful." Duan patted May-May's arm. "How is your cooking? What delicious dishes have you made for your nana recently?"

At his praises, May-May's cheeks reddened.

"Okay, that's enough." Su-Ann waved them on. Would May-May become less timid? "Let's go inside. I'm sure you didn't come here only to flatter her."

Yao came over and whispered something to May-May. Her girl beamed. "Okay. Go. I'll see you later."

After entering their room, Duan grabbed a chair to sit on. "Auntie, I bring you good news. The government has decided not to set up communes in Beijing."

"Praise the Lord." Su-Ann clutched her hands together. "We've been praying about it."

If only they could have no more campaigns. She choked back a sigh. For sure, more political movements were coming.

Chapter Thirteen

"Prayers outlive the lives of those who uttered them; outlive a
generation, outlive an age, outlive a world."

E. M. Bounds (1835–1913)

Beijing, China
October 1965

May-May looked out the window and pressed her palm to the cool
glass. More than its invisible barrier stopped her from reaching out.
I haven't heard from Mama for two months. What's going on?

"May-May."

At the gentle voice, she turned toward the door. "You're back."

"Did you receive anything from Hong Kong today?" Nana
walked to the table to check the pile of paper.

"No, nothing." May-May squeezed her hands together. "I hope
Mama and Ann-Ann are well."

"Maybe the problem is more on our end than theirs." Nana pulled
out a chair and sat. "I heard at work today the government has been
confiscating materials sent from outside."

"Something must be happening." May-May stifled a heavy breath, yet the oppressiveness in her chest wouldn't lift. "Yesterday I tried to listen to the English program on the radio like before, but the channel has disappeared."

"Not much we can do other than count on God's mercy."

At Nana's whisper tone, May-May shivered. "Yes." Stiffening her back, she strolled toward their storage bin to pick up three potatoes. "I'd better prepare dinner before the neighbors show up."

Tonight, she'd recreate the crunchy grated potatoes, Nana's favorite. Stepping into the kitchen, she tied her apron and cleared the counter.

"May-May."

She spun around at the sound. "Shao Li. Is it your turn to cook again? Where is your mother? Where is Shao Hui?" She crinkled up her mouth into a smile. Shao Li favored her over all others in the courtyard, even more than her own older sister.

"Mom went to a rally meeting. Hui stepped out. She said she was going to her classmate's house to do homework." Shao Li lifted her chin as if aware of something no one else knew. "Ha, I know better. She has a date with her boyfriend."

Hui's serious expression brought a chuckle to May-May. "How could you say that?"

"I saw her with Zhang Tao holding hands behind the house. That was a while ago. She has a different boyfriend now." Shao Li made a disgusted face with crossed eyes.

"Who's Zhang Tao?" May-May chewed on her fingers to keep from laughing aloud. The vision of Shao Hui, a lovely figure with a narrow waist, came to mind. Hui was only one year older, but her behaviors were much more mature. Even when Hui was Li's age, she wasn't afraid to kiss Uncle Dong in exchange for cookies.

Shao Li didn't reply. Instead, she jammed her hands on her hips. "Hui said Yao *likes* you, right?"

May-May started grating potatoes. "I don't know what you're talking about. Yao and I grew up together. We're good friends. That's all."

But had her relationship with Yao changed? She still had to tell him everything—school, Nana, Uncle Duan, her concern over Mama and Ann-Ann. Yet, recently, she often felt awkward in his presence, especially when he gave her such strange looks as if she was someone unfamiliar.

She shook her head to brush aside her tangled emotions and renewed her repetitive motions. "Let me go back to my cooking. My nana is waiting for our dinner."

Shao Li let out a sigh and picked away tiny pebbles from the rice. Then she lifted her chin. "The teachers at school encourage us to serve the people with all our hearts. Who are the people?"

May-May's fingers slowed, her gaze drifting to the wall. "I suppose everyone is a member of the people." She put the threaded potatoes into her skillet, added seasoning, and began to stir-fry. "Don't bring it up to adults. They won't appreciate this type of question."

"I understand. I'm just curious." Shao Li tilted her head up again. "Do you think Chairman Mao is a member of the people?"

May-May dropped the spatula. Covering Shao Li's mouth with her palm, she chided in a whisper, "Are you crazy? You and your parents can be in big trouble. Be careful of what you say."

Li's eyes widened with dread, her lips quivering. "I mentioned it only to you. You won't tell others, will you?"

"I won't. You must be more cautious not to ask questions like that." Weighed down, May-May rushed to the door and peeked into the hallway. Good. Nobody was around. She went back to pick up her pan with the potatoes. "I'm done."

Back in their room, she served the crispy potatoes while they were still steamy. Yet tonight, their favorite dish lost its appeal, and an uncomfortable sour taste lingered in her mouth. *Oh, Lord, why do we have to look over our shoulders all the time? Do Mama and Ann-Ann live like this in Hong Kong? Why don't they write anymore?*

After dinner, she pushed aside her trepidation and stepped into the dark yard to see her good friend. "Yao, do you know what's going on?"

She sat in their favorite corner and raised her gaze toward the sky. Moonlight filtered through the tree branches, casting strange shadows on his face.

He drew his thick black eyebrows together into a deep frown. "I notice some changes as well. Nothing we can do. Just lie low and try not to cause trouble."

She plucked a remaining leaf from the wilted cucumber vine next to her. "And pray. I pray together with my nana every day, asking for God's mercy upon us."

"My pa also prays nonstop." He scratched his cheek, scrunching up his nose. "I'm not sure whether God answers our prayers."

"For sure He does." She jerked up her head. "How could you doubt it?"

"All along we've been praying for a better world around us." He kneaded his brows. "See what's happened? Even though the Great Leap Forward campaign has ended, terrible communes still exist in the countryside. Luckily, we didn't get it."

She freed the leaf from her palm, goosebumps crawling up her arms. "Nana told me God always responds to prayers, although the responses may not be according to our wishes. God's answer may be yes or no. Often, He wants us to wait." While Yao remained silent, she nudged his shoulder with hers. "At least during the past years, the regulations have eased."

He let out a long breath. "Restrictions are tightening up. Last week, the teachers commanded us to get away from being controlled by the bourgeoisie."

"I'm scared to death people at school will taunt me again." As a chill spread through her heart, she wrapped her arms around herself.

"See?" He slashed a hand through the air. "We used to pray about it. They continued to torment you."

The corners of her mouth twitched upward into a faint smile. "I don't know why God's answer was negative back then. But going through it, I've become stronger."

"You wept when they abused you."

"I used to cry easily. I couldn't help it." She stood to reach for another dry leaf from the cucumber vine. "Yet I always had a sense of peace in my mind, even in tears. Nana told me it's from the Holy Spirit."

Yao tapped his foot. "Sit back down next to me. You're making me nervous."

"In the presence of the Holy Spirit, no matter what happens, no one can take away our inner peace." Ignoring him, she crumpled the leaf. "Nana mentioned that, although anguish gripped her whole person after my papa died, a remarkable peace flooded her heart in her most dejected state, as if the light from the Lord shone even more brightly in the darkest situation."

He cocked his head. "What do you think about the evolution theory we learn at school? Do you think humans evolved from monkeys?"

Why did he change the subject? Did he doubt God's words? She scooted back to sit by him. "Evolution isn't a theory, merely a hypothesis."

He stretched an arm out on the tree behind them, a pungent garlic aroma coming closer. "Creation is also a hypothesis, right?"

Did his pa cook something with garlic? She moved away and dropped the broken leaf. "Nana said the debate between creation and evolution is unnecessary because they've both overlooked an important factor. God transcends time and space."

"What does that mean?"

She brushed off the leaf debris from her pants. "Creation and evolution both involve the element of time, but God is beyond time. God created time and can't be confined by time."

"The Bible teaches God created the world in six days."

Her gaze followed his uplifted hand toward the full moon beyond the ginkgo tree. "That's correct. God had to reveal Himself using a method we could understand. Thus, the Bible was compiled in human languages with the constraint of time and space." She grinned. "The only verse in the Bible not written in our languages is the writing on the wall in the book of Daniel. Even so, nobody could comprehend. With God's guidance, Daniel translated for them."

"What do you believe? Evolution or creation?"

She sniffed her palm. An autumn scent drifted into her nostrils. "For sure, I believe in creation. The Bible uses human terms to convey the message that God created the universe. It doesn't matter whether it's six days or six million years because God transcends time. To Him, there is no difference."

They sank into quietness. Like before, Yao grasped her fingers. Heat rushed to her cheeks, and she drew back.

"What's wrong?"

She ducked to dodge his penetrating stare. "Nothing."

He pulled her closer. "With moonlight on your face, you look like a fairy in the storybooks, an enchanting fairy."

Heat spread to her ears.

He murmured, "May-May."

"Ha, I caught you." A voice rang out from behind the tree.

Cringing, she stepped away from Yao.

"See?" Shao Li jumped out. "Hui was right. You and Yao were holding hands."

"Hush." May-May touched Li's lips with a finger. "If you promise me not to tell anyone what you've seen, I won't tell others what you mentioned to me this afternoon. Do we have a deal?"

Shao Li lost her smile. "You've already given me your word of honor. I thought you were my friend."

"Don't worry. I'm your friend. You're also my friend. So, we help each other. Okay?" She patted Li's arm.

"Sure." Shao Li glanced up at her. "Why are you so concerned? Everyone knows you and Yao are a pair."

At Li's words, Yao shifted to her, his eyes boring into hers.

May-May turned away from him.

Shao Li waved at them. "It's late. I'm going home."

With the moon high above in the clear sky, May-May scooted around him. "I'd better go too. My nana is home alone."

Chapter Fourteen

"God be with you till we meet again; By His counsel's guide, uphold you..."

Jeremiah Rankin (1828–1904),
"God Be With You Till We Meet Again"

Beijing, China
September 1966

May-May dropped her chopsticks and placed a hand on her chest, but the heaviness still weighed hard on her exhausted body. Outside the window, the early September sunshine lit up the yard, bringing out some of its original beauty.

"What's wrong?" Nana picked up another piece of sliced cucumber marinated with a creamy herb dressing. "Why don't you eat your breakfast?"

May-May dragged her fingers through her hair. "Yao showed me his red armband yesterday."

"So, he's joined." Nana laid down her chopsticks.

"He's now a Red Guard." May-May thrust both hands into her armpits. A persistent chill had claimed the room, a sharp contrast to the warm autumn sun streaming through the glass.

The recent news kept citing the rallies held in the city during the past month. Thousands of students from different districts gathered in Tiananmen Square. She didn't go, but Yao said Shao Hui was there, as were many of their classmates. Chairman Mao's speech galvanized the crowd. Their voices rose in a unified pledge to the man they revered as their Eastern Rising Sun.

A deep sense of dread clogged her throat and tears welled up.

"Don't cry." Nana hugged her. "Yao has no choice. He belongs to the Red Five Categories and has leadership skills. If he refuses to join, he'll be in trouble."

May-May leaned her head against Nana's shoulder and shuddered. Fear gripped her like invisible hands tightening around her neck, choking out the air in her lungs. How could she possibly eat? What would happen to them?

Like a robot, she left Nana, plodded to the yard to pick green beans, and ran into Yao on his way out. Hitching her basket against a hip, she couldn't help the tartness in her tone. "Will you attack the 'Four Olds' like others?"

"I can only talk for a few minutes." His eyebrows furrowed. "I'm going to school."

She brushed aside a fly from her arm. "We don't have class anymore." Her heart ached at the thought of school. *Nana is crushed. She always harbors a wish that one day I'll go to college.*

He scratched his cheek. "We have assemblies."

She hugged her vegetable basket to her chest, wrapping her fingers tight around the handle. "You mean the struggle meetings where you have to criticize everyone's family history?"

"I'm presiding over the meeting today. I'd better hurry."

As soon as he stepped out, she dropped her basket and massaged her temples, trying to soothe a headache that had no physical cause. Nana was the personification of the "Four Olds"—a relic of old ideas, culture, customs, and habits.

Would this new campaign sweep Nana away with it?

The gnawing anxiety plunged her mood into a downward spiral, a gloom that only deepened as the days passed without a sign of Yao. The silence was broken by Uncle Chen's visit. "Yao must be losing his mind. He's been running with a pack of youths, plastering the community with slogans to attack everyone in sight. Now, even Mr. Liang Duan is in trouble."

"The Red Guards are everywhere. We can't avoid them. But they're just boys and girls." Flicking aside her white hair, Nana rubbed her neck. "I've been praying for Duan. I hope he'll be all right."

What could they do? Nothing other than to pray. May-May swallowed her sigh and went to dig in the vegetable patch.

As she unearthed a fat worm and nudged it aside, Shao Hui walked by. "May-May, where is your red armband?"

Feeling like the squirming worm, she raised her gaze. "I don't have one."

"What?" Hui jammed a hand on her waist. "Don't tell me you aren't a Red Guard."

May-May didn't reply and returned to digging.

Hui should know I'm not qualified to join. After a brief silence, she looked up. Shao Hui was gone.

Hui must be up to something.

She set down the hoe to pluck beans from the low-lying bush. Tonight, she'd make stir-fried beans for Nana.

After dinner, she tidied up their dining table and bid Nana good night. Yet the weight on her heart refused to lift, and she tossed and turned.

A violent *thump* jolted her up from the bed. How long had she dozed off?

Her gaze darted around the dark surroundings. Did someone break into their room?

The sound source was more distant. She scrambled from her bed and shifted to the window. Under the gleaming moon, a light came from across the yard.

Oh no. They'd broken into Uncle Dong's home.

Shao Hui's high-pitched voice cut through the heavy stillness. "See? I told you, Dong Guang is a poisonous weed. Look at what we've found. All these pornographic magazines."

Loud shouts reverberated in unison, filling the entire courtyard with slogans.

"Uproot the poisonous weed!"

"Topple the womanizer!"

"Down with the counterrevolutionary!"

May-May squatted under the window. *Lord, please let the Red Guards be satisfied with their finds. Let them leave others in peace, at least for a short while.*

When the clock struck two, the intruders retreated. She couldn't move. Her legs and arms were as stiff as the windowsill.

Nana's voice sounded behind her. "Are you all right?"

May-May nodded.

"Let's pray for Dong Guang." Nana kneeled next to her and pleaded for God's mercy on Uncle Dong and his mother.

Three days later, the denunciation meeting against Dong Guang was held in their community high school's gym. May-May went with her nana and joined others to form a circle.

Two Red Guards dragged Dong Guang forward. He stumbled, but they pulled him back up, yanked him to the center, then forced him to his knees. A placard hung around his neck with his name written upside down and a description, "Lewd, filthy counterrevolutionary Dong Guang."

Shao Hui stood, retrieved a piece of paper, and spelled out Dong Guang's crimes in a stern tone. "He bought pornographic magazines from the capitalist enemies. He engaged in lewd acts, often with girls young enough to be his daughters. He dares to criticize our great leader, Chairman Mao."

After her every sentence came the ear-piercing shouts of anticapitalism slogans.

Stunned, May-May shoved her shaking hands beneath her armpits. *I didn't know Uncle Dong was such a terrible person.*

"Tell us. Have you criticized Chairman Mao?" Shao Hui's voice turned venomous.

Dong Guang didn't raise his head.

After a brief wait, she waved to the crowd. "Look. He's confessed his crimes."

The teenagers morphed into savages. Yao ran in formation with others to Uncle Dong. Merciless fists and feet slammed into his body. A girl attached a burning cigarette to his face. Another girl shaved off half of his hair with a razor.

Someone in the audience fainted. *Uncle Dong's mother!* May-May gasped, then brought a palm to cover her mouth. She scanned around her. Good. Nobody paid her any attention.

Two boys slapped Mrs. Dong hard to revive her. They hauled her by the ears into the circle and beat her until she kneeled next to her son.

Shao Hui screeched, "How dare you show sympathy to a criminal? Bad element! Petty bourgeois rubbish!"

The chant of revolutionary slogans dragged on until late in the afternoon. At the end, Shao Hui sniggered. "A labor reform in a Shaanxi rural commune center is perfect for you. Go home to fetch your personal items. Report back to us tomorrow morning."

After the assembly dissolved, Nana tugged at May-May's arm. She followed Nana to Dong Guang. They helped him and his mother to their feet and half-lugged, half-carried them back to the courtyard.

Nana fetched alcohol to clean their wounds, starting with the elderly woman. "Sorry, but it's the only thing we have."

When she moved to treat Uncle Dong's injuries, he cried out, "Mrs. Lee, I don't deserve your kindness. Please forgive me."

May-May gave her nana a questioning glance.

Nana soaked a piece of cloth with alcohol and laid it on his burned face. "We've all sinned one way or another. Let bygones be bygones. Please remember not to make the same mistake."

"You know, then?" He gaped at her.

She didn't answer but continued to work on his wounds. Tears trickled down his cheeks.

"Ah Guang, don't worry about your mother. If we remain in Beijing, we'll help take care of her." Nana spoke in a gentle tone while dropping the bloodstained cloth into a basin.

"Mrs. Lee, please forgive me." He sobbed so hard that he hiccupped.

She picked up another piece of clean cloth. "I've already forgiven you. You must learn to forgive yourself."

Mrs. Dong waved a hand. "I've been telling him all the while he would get into trouble one day. He told me he just wanted fun. He often boasted nobody dared to challenge him since he belongs to the Red Five Categories. See what happened today?" She clasped Nana's hand. "Mrs. Lee, please ask your god to protect Ah Guang."

Nana hugged the woman. "You can pray to God as well."

"Can I?" Mrs. Dong lifted her head. "You're always so kind to us. I want to be like you and believe in God."

Nana explained the gospel. "Will you accept Jesus Christ as your Savior today? You can establish a relationship with God right now and pray to Him directly."

"I do," they replied in unison.

At her request, the four of them kneeled together. Uncle Dong and his mother repeated after Nana, sentence by sentence.

Poor Uncle Dong. May-May stifled a hard sigh. But he was lucky.

In one denunciation meeting, Red Guards beat an old man into unconsciousness. Her math teacher couldn't face the humiliation brought on by the false public accusation and chose to jump to his death.

***

The courtyard grew quieter. Like others, Su-Ann began tiptoeing about. Soon, carefulness turned into a habit. She dared not utter any unnecessary words to strangers for fear of being eavesdropped on, wrongly interpreted.

Chen Kang stopped by one morning. "Mr. Liang Duan was indicted. He'll be sent down to Yunnan in a few days."

It finally happened. She cupped her mouth with a hand, a painful tightness gripping her chest. *Oh, Duan, I'll miss you so much.*

After dinner, she relayed the bad news to May-May. "I'll go to see him tonight."

"How awful." Her girl's shoulders slumped. "Can I go with you?"

Su-Ann shook her head, her chest constricting again. "I'd better go alone. It's safer."

At nine, she crossed the city. With dread in her mind, she dragged her feet across the small yard leading to Duan's apartment and knocked.

Opening the door, he stretched his eyes wide and flexed his lips. "Auntie, how did you find out? We live in different divisions."

"The walls have ears." Her throat hurt, and a hard knot formed within. "What crime did they accuse you of?"

His soulful eyes peered out beneath his thick brows. "I've been cautious and discarded all potentially offensive materials. But they got hold of the last letter I wrote to Leesan and used it to accuse me of being a spy and providing information to capitalist enemies."

"We also haven't received anything from Hong Kong for a while. I hope the confiscated items won't be used to punish us." She stepped into his bachelor's simple living room, then wrinkled her nose. "How many times did they ransack your place?"

His usually calm face contorted. He pointed at the graffiti-filled walls and pulled out two battered chairs for them to sit on. "Only once, but it's more than enough."

She hesitated, then took one seat. "Are you leaving for Yunnan this week? It must be God's mercy that they allowed you to grab a few personal items from home."

"Yeah. God's grace is sufficient." He slumped into the other chair. "Be mentally prepared, although your situation is different. Leesan is your relative."

"Anything can be used against us." She ran her fingers over the broken armrest. "These Red Guards... they're just teenagers and easily manipulated."

"They're young and strong, more capable than any of us to condemn, destroy, and kill. Have you noticed even the traffic lights are reversed? It's crazy. China is moving in the wrong direction." He let out a long breath. "You shouldn't have taken the unnecessary risk to come, but I'm glad you're here. I need you to do me a favor."

He reached into his shirt to retrieve an object. "If you get a chance, please give this to Leesan. Otherwise, give it to May-May." He handed her a piece of green jade in the shape of an ox on a silk cord. "I was born in the year of the ox. It's a gift from my grandma, the only valuable thing I still have."

Eyeing the object in her palm, Su-Ann grasped its meaning. "You..." She couldn't find the words to finish her sentence.

He lowered his head. "I don't think I'll have a chance to see her again in my lifetime."

She had to ask. "You never married because of Leesan?"

He didn't answer. Instead, he spoke in a low whisper. "Goodbye, Auntie. I won't be around to help you anymore. People come and go due to altered circumstances. Our Lord will continue to be with you."

"I'm sure He will." She offered an assuring smile. "Leesan is still single. With God's help, we'll meet again soon."

After she bid him good night and trudged into the yard, Duan's singing arose behind her. "With His sheep securely fold you; God be with you till we meet..."

Back at home, she tugged her girl into their bedroom. "We have to act right away."

May-May's eyes opened wide. "What's wrong?"

"Last week, we burned our books, including the Bible. It's not enough." Su-Ann dragged a trunk out from underneath the bed. As her gaze caressed the remaining antiques in their possession, moisture rushed into her eyes. "These have been with the Lee family for so many generations. I know they're problems but continue to hang on to them. Every time I want to get rid of them, guilt floods my heart. I'm afraid our ancestors won't forgive me."

"Please don't think that way." May-May embraced her, pressing her soft cheek to hers. "Our ancestors will understand. They probably would do the same if they were here today."

Su-Ann remained silent, tears pooling up and then warm droplets streaming down her face.

"Nana, we no longer have a choice." May-May patted her back. "We're not getting rid of them. We simply follow the Lord's command to store them in heaven."

"Thank you." Su-Ann wiped her face with the back of a hand. "What shall we do?"

May-May moved away to sit on the bed. "Maybe bury them in the yard?"

"It won't work." Su-Ann tapped her foot. The heavy guilt and helplessness refused to lift. "We can bury a few small items when our neighbors aren't paying attention. But all these? It takes time to dig. There'll be digging marks."

May-May stooped to pick up their favorite jade teapot and one of its matching cups. "Can we break them into pieces and throw them into the garbage?"

"Not good enough. They may be able to trace the stuff in the trash to us." Su-Ann grabbed a snuff bottle and shook her head, a stubborn chill lingering in her bones. "How about this one made of gold? It's not breakable."

"Nana?" May-May gripped the teapot, her fingers whitening around the spout and handle. "Remember that river where Yao and I used to go for a swim? Could we dump them there?"

"Hmm." Air whooshed from Su-Ann's chest, and her heartbeat kicked up speed. "The Yongding River? Not a bad idea."

They made several trips the next day and brought a few items every time. She packed the jade teapot and the six cups in a large scarf for their last trip. Standing by the riverbank, she drew a quick breath and tossed the bag into the deep end of the water. The heavy object pushed water out of its way. A ripple formed from where it landed, and soon it disappeared.

"It's gone." May-May clutched her arm. "No need to worry anymore."

Gone. Gone. Gone. The word gonged in her head. Su-Ann started to frown, but a wave of relief washed over her as the anxieties brought on by those materials vanished.

How strange, I sense... joy.

She raised her eyes toward the puffy white clouds and lifted a prayer. "I was foolish to think I could guard the Lee family treasure. Lord, thank You for releasing me from the bondage of tradition."

By evening, the only remaining valuables were the two jade pendants.

"This peach was passed down from your mama's grandma. Your mama wanted me to keep it for you until you're engaged. It was originally on a gold chain. I just kept the pendant." She placed the object in May-May's palm. "The ox belongs to your uncle Duan. He said to give it to your mama if possible. If we don't see her again, he wants you to have it."

They dug in the yard to bury them. After dinner, Su-Ann pulled her girl to a corner. "Listen carefully. If I'm indicted in a meeting, you have to come forward to criticize me. You must declare you've drawn a line between us. Do you understand?"

"I..." May-May wept. "I can't do it."

Su-Ann dabbed her darling girl's face with a handkerchief. Why were family members forced to war against one another? "Think about it as a play. If you do it well, it'll help us. Promise me. Be courageous."

Her granddaughter's tears continued to trickle.

"My good girl. Don't cry." Su-Ann patted May-May's cheek, her voice thick. *Lord, please grant me and May-May strength for whatever is approaching.* "Now, I hope we've taken care of everything."

Chapter Fifteen

"Does Jesus care when my heart is pained... Oh, yes, He cares... I
know my Savior cares."

Frank E. Graeff (1860–1919), "Does Jesus Care?"

Beijing, China
May 1968

May-May rested her chopsticks on the plate and stifled a sigh. How
could the sun still shine as if nothing had happened while the world
around them stopped its normal rotations?

"Is this the first batch of cucumbers for the season?" Nana wiped
her mouth with a handkerchief. "It's nice to have homegrown
veggies for breakfast."

"We—" May-May jerked her head as someone pounded the door
open.

Red Guards thundered in, crowding the room.

"You two, stand up!" a youth of fifteen or sixteen yelled. "Go to
the corner."

The same teen reached into his pocket to retrieve a small red book.
Then he flipped to a page and read Chairman Mao's sayings.

May-May tried to listen. Yet her legs trembled. Her mind refused to cooperate.

When he finished reciting, he waved, and the gang went into action. With force, they shoved the table, flipped the chair, beat the closet door ajar, and wrecked the contents inside with clunky iron bars. Glass and ceramic shards flew in all directions.

The leader raised his arm again. "Nothing here. Let's go."

After they left, May-May plopped down on the floor and sobbed, dread grabbing her heart.

Nana gave her shoulder a gentle pat. "Take courage. More is coming. They'll be back."

"Oh, Nana." May-May wrapped both arms around her head.

"Let's pray." Nana kneeled beside her. "Lord, I pray for the Red Guards who stopped by today. Teenagers are easily misled. Please forgive them. Lord, please help us remain faithful to You, no matter what our situations are."

The prayer brought more tears. *Lord, could You please let them not come back?*

Yet, as Nana predicted, three additional groups of Red Guards ransacked their home within the same week. Following each of their visits, May-May's spirit plunged further into despair. She lost her desire to cook and couldn't sleep.

Lord, what will I do if Nana is indicted?

Nana sat her down for a talk. "Things are beyond our control, and the best way is to face them with courage. It's not easy. With the help of the Holy Spirit, we can claim the promise from the Lord, 'In this world, you will have trouble. But take heart! I have overcome the world.'"

Tears welled up in May-May's eyes. "Nana, if something ever happens to you, how can I bear living?"

Nana touched her hair with tender fingers. "When the time comes, you'll receive strength from the Lord. I'm sure you will."

Lord, please let that time never come.

But in the following week, the fifth ransacking occurred. While eight Red Guards were searching, one of them pulled out a piece of paper and flashed it in front of the others. "Look at this, Lee May-May in a Western dress."

A teenage girl with two braids chided, "She stands by a woman also in a Western dress."

On the arrival of a familiar figure, May-May's jaw dropped.

The leading boy's eyes opened wide. "Chen Yao? I thought you were in a different home-ransacking team."

"We're done early." With hands on his hips, Yao halted before him.

The leader raised his picture. "See what we've found."

Rocking back on his heels, Yao took a peek and shook his head. "This can't be Lee May-May. She has short hair. The girl in the photo has long hair."

The youth in command frowned. "How could it be?"

"Lee May-May has an identical twin in Hong Kong." Yao turned away his gaze.

The Red Guards glanced at one another.

The boy stepped up and held his picture against May-May's face. "Identical twins? How interesting." Then he stomped toward Nana. "Relatives in Hong Kong, huh? We know you also have an Anglo-American imperialist brother named Du Su-Nong over there. You write to him often."

He lifted his iron bar. "Unite the people! Overthrow Imperialism!"

Yao added his voice to the raucous chorus of slogans.

The leader waved. Two girls dragged Nana from the corner and forced her to walk out with them.

A deafening silence shrouded the room. Captured in a sudden aloneness, May-May stared at the blank wall. As she regained her senses, a deep hollowness bored out of her heart. She was all by herself, alone in this terrifying world. She tried to move, yet her legs seemed cemented to the ground.

"May-May," someone called from outside the broken windows. Yao trudged in.

She gawked at her traitor friend as if she had never known him before.

***

"May-May." Yao rushed to her side. He tried to pick up her hand, but she flung him away.

He dropped his chin and clenched his fists at his side. How could he explain? Wouldn't she understand? "I'm sorry." He pressed the words past his tight throat. "Please understand. I needed to do what I did."

As he spoke, a knot formed in his belly. The vision of a family he and his gang had ransacked earlier flashed across his mind. They'd found two hundred yuan—a huge sum of money—hidden in a jar under the bed. After they confiscated it, the old woman gawked at them in silence, resonating with the expression on May-May's face now.

At last, May-May spoke. "They hauled Nana away. I don't know where she is."

Devoid of its usual warmth, her voice chilled him.

"Oh, May-May." He clutched her arm. This time, she didn't resist. Yet she didn't utter another word and just frowned with glazed eyes.

Gripping her elbow, he forced her to walk with him to his room. She sat at the dining table, her expression blank, her gaze unfixed.

While he was pouring her a glass of water, his father came home. "Pa, Red Guards took away Lee Nana today."

Pa nodded. "It's only a matter of time."

Yao placed the water before May-May. "Let's go to Lee Nana's place to fix the broken windows."

At dinnertime, he followed his father to the kitchen to cook rice and a simple dish of stir-fried cabbage. "It's enough. I don't have an appetite, anyway."

They put two plates on the table. May-May began to gobble up rice with cabbage.

Yao gaped at her. He'd never seen her behave like that before. "What're you doing? Slow down. You'll choke yourself."

"Let her." Pa waved at him. "It's her way of dealing with the ordeal she's gone through." He let out a long breath. "Luckily, they didn't find out we're Christians."

"She'll get choked. She'll..." Yao didn't finish his sentence.

May-May plopped her forehead on the table and wailed.

He shifted over to hug her shoulders, tenderness mingling with empathy. "Oh, May-May."

In the morning, he fetched some old party newspapers. "May-May, they scheduled Lee Nana to be indicted in two days. These are for your reference."

Her miserable eyes brought a heaviness to his heart. He swallowed hard. "They'll help you write articles about your nana's crimes. Be specific. Otherwise, your paper may get rejected."

Tears trickled down her cheeks, but she took the newspapers and started writing. For two days, she remained mute. Yet so strong was the sound of her silence, akin to that old woman's expression during his last home-ransacking escapade, that May-May's misery and tribulation appeared to him like an immense, invisible wheel circling in emptiness.

The day of the denunciation meeting arrived. Banners bearing the words *Great Proletarian Cultural Revolution* strung up high across their communities.

Three people kneeled together within the circle. Like the other two, Lee Nana's hands were bound behind her back. She wore a pointed cap like a wizard's hat, except it was made of paper with no brim. Around her neck hung a placard that read: Du Su-Ann, Counterrevolutionary.

Lee Nana's head bent low. A girl moved up and grabbed her white hair to force her face up. May-May averted her eyes. The dread and love in her gaze, sustaining and desperate, called blood to Yao's face. Moisture gathered behind his eyelids, and he blinked hard to subdue his turmoil.

One by one, the criminals were condemned, criticized, and punished. When Lee Nana's turn came, a Red Guard, Jiang Xiao-Hung, Yao's classmate, advanced and screeched, "Du Su-Ann used to be a big landlord. Her husband and brother had close ties with the rebelled government. They utilized their power to exploit the tenants. They abused, deprived, and persecuted the poor. Until recently, Du Su-Ann continued to write to her relatives in Hong Kong who work for the rebels. She's very wicked. In 1950, she even pretended to support the land reform and offered her land to our great party...."

With the announcement of each of Su-Ann's crimes, slogans rose like thunder. The Red Guards swarmed up to spit on her. Cruel, powerful fists and feet pummeled her. Soon, blood oozed from the corner of her mouth.

Xiao-Hung waved to May-May. "Do you have anything to say?"

May-May stumbled toward Lee Nana. She pulled out a piece of paper from her pocket and read in a monotone. "This stinking old woman is rebellious toward our great leader Chairman Mao. She needs to repent."

She thrust a foot out to kick her nana.

Yao winced.

Su-Ann sank to the ground.

The crowd applauded.

Xiao-Hung strutted forward again, and the group called out more slogans.

"Long Live Chairman Mao!"

"Long Live the Cultural Revolution!"

After the assembly dissolved, May-May wobbled away. Yao walked behind her, wanting to make sure she reached home safely. Along the way, as the image of how he and his classmates cropping half of their teacher's hair flashed across his mind, tightness seized his chest.

What had their world become?

***

How had she come home? May-May had no idea. The scenes from the denunciation meeting kept replaying in her mind—Nana's disheveled white hair, the blood tracing her lips, the shouts, the kicks, and the slaps.

Night fell. She sat in darkness and wailed.

"May-May." A faint voice sounded from outside. Yao entered. "Are you all right?"

She cried against his chest, letting her tears wet his shirt. "I can't forgive myself. How could I violate Nana? She's everything to me. She asked me to do it. She told me to do it like in a play."

"I know." He patted her back. "Lee Nana understands."

Warmth soothed her chest, the chills receding. She calmed and found his arms around her waist. Instead of drawing back, she snuggled closer. Following the ordeal, she needed to be held, to feel safe. Was it a mere illusion? Could anyone own real safety anywhere? Yet, for this moment, she wanted to pretend all was still okay.

Then his lips fell on her forehead, and Nana's teachings popped into her mind. "Oh no." She pushed him away and shifted to a corner.

"I'm sorry." He took a few steps toward her and stopped. "Tomorrow, I'll find out what happened to Lee Nana."

"Please do." Guilt swept her, and fresh tears stung her cheeks. "Why did I kick her?"

He stood next to her. "Take courage. We have no time to feel sorry. More hardship will come." He clasped her hand. "I don't think you've eaten dinner. Have you? Let's go. Pa has cooked noodles for us."

Oh, Lord, have mercy on Nana. Yet Yao's words became an omen. Over the next five days, Nana went through two additional denunciation meetings. May-May watched in silence, the horror and helplessness rushing back. *Lord, please let Nana live.*

Nana survived. After the final accusation, they ordered her to walk around the block, beat a gong, and announce, "I'm a landlord. I'm a counterrevolutionary."

The Red Guards delivered the verdict—guilty. Lee Du Su-Ann needed reeducation in the Inner Mongolia Autonomous Region.

The night before Nana's departure, she got permission to come home to pick up personal items for the trip. Yao and Uncle Chen came to say farewell.

Nana spread out her hands. "Let's pray together."

With his head bowed low, Yao didn't respond. When he lifted his gaze, May-May gasped at his tears. She'd never seen him cry.

He roared, "Does God even care about us? Why does He allow this to happen? Why does Lee Nana have to go away? Why can't we live like people in other parts of the world?"

"Hush." Uncle Chen walked over and clamped a thick hand over his son's mouth. "Don't be so loud."

Yao wept against his father's chest as Uncle Chen stroked his back. "Why do we have the class struggle meetings?" Low and taut, his voice echoed in the hollow places opening up in May-May. "If God exists, why doesn't He intervene? Why should a kind person like Lee Nana be punished unjustly?"

May-May stared at her feet, fighting her turbulent emotions. "I also don't understand. Do these events around us have any meaning? Is there any purpose? Why am I here? What would it be like if I lived in Hong Kong with Mama and Ann-Ann?"

Tears tickled her cheeks. "Amid helplessness, God seems distant. I've learned not to rely on feelings but to count on the promises in the Bible. Nana told me that when Papa died, she brought many questions to God. God reminded her Jesus experienced all sorts of sufferings in life, including crucifixion. At the most painful moment, Nana experienced the fellowship from the Holy Spirit." Her mouth crinkled up into a half-smile. "Yes, our heavenly Father does care about us. He is here with us now."

"Oh, May-May." Nana came over to hug her. "Let's ask for the Lord's mercy. We'll see one another again soon."

This time, Yao didn't resist. They kneeled together to seek God's guidance.

After the guests left, Nana sat by her. "I'm unsure what will happen next. The Cultural Revolution may end soon. If so, you shall stay in Beijing to wait out this wave of uncertainty. With the Lord's blessings, you may be able to go to college. On the other hand, if the turmoil continues, then it's better to leave Beijing."

"Nana." May-May sobbed, a tightness grabbing her heart. "I don't care about going to college. I want to be with you."

"The Lord has entrusted you in my care. I'll consider it a big failure on my part if you don't attend college. It's beyond our control. I don't even know if we'll see each other again." Nana let out a long breath. "During the time you're alone here, remember to ask this question in everything you do. 'Is it pleasing to God?' Let's learn to trust and obey."

May-May kept swiping fresh tears from her cheeks, most grieved by Nana's words that they might never see each other again.

After Nana left, loss and restlessness engrossed May-May. Her wretchedness grew acute at finding herself alone at night in their room. Alone, alone... Would she see Nana again?

Lord, please give me strength to live through every day. Please let me see my nana again soon.

Time crawled without Nana by her side. To keep herself occupied, May-May worked around the courtyard, wrote to her nana, and sat as a model for Yao to draw her portraits. Uncle Chen treated her like his own daughter. She had dinner with them every day, and they recited Bible verses to one another before each meal.

Then the government began another campaign—educated youth had to leave the cities to be retrained in rural areas. In December, May-May received a notice. The officials had approved her application to go to Bada Village in the northwestern corner of Inner Mongolia where her nana was.

Oh, Lord, thank You for answering my prayers.

After she told Uncle Chen and Yao the news, Yao's face contorted. "May-May, please don't go. Please stay here with us. I..."

Uncle Chen patted Yao's arm. "She needs to do what is right for her family."

The day before her trip, May-May dug out the two jade pendants. Sitting alone in the room she used to share with Nana, she traced along their smoothly carved forms. *What shall I do with them? Give them to Yao?*

Her index finger stilled over the peach, Mama's peach. Then she closed her hand over it. She'd keep the peach.

She gave Yao the ox pendant during dinner. "This is from Uncle Duan for my mama. I don't know when I'll be back. If you stay in Beijing, you may see my mama first. Please give this to her."

Yao clutched her hand. "May-May, write to me."

Uncle Chen gave her a gentle glance. "Let's pray."

They fell to their knees. All three of them wept.

Chapter Sixteen

"There are two worlds: The world we can measure with line and rule, and the world that we feel with our hearts and imagination."

James Henry Leigh Hunt (1784–1859)

Hong Kong
May 1968

"Ann-Ann, hurry up. We're late." Leesan called from the living room while clicking her fingernails against the coffee table.

No response.

She waited, then heaved a heavy sigh.

Ann-Ann must be busy with one of her favorite activities—putting on her makeup. Why did she become so engrossed with her appearance?

"Did you hear me? We'd better leave." Leesan yelled again.

At least the girl's idea of buying this flat was good. Ann-Ann, at thirteen, had demanded to have her own room, claiming she didn't want to stay in the same room with her mother anymore. "Buy an apartment. I need my privacy."

When Leesan consulted Kam-Chu, her friend replied that Ann-Ann was right. "She's at an age she needs to try her independence. Having privacy is an important step. And owning property makes sense. With the way this city is developing, the home price will only go up, not down."

Back then, Leesan was dating Hsieh Henry, a surgeon from her church. She'd expected to move into his house once they married. But it didn't work out. After their relationship ended, she bought the current apartment.

Not hearing any movement, she trod over to check on her daughter. A shudder went through her as she squinted at the scene.

Empty yogurt drink bottles lurked amid the dirty clothes and crumpled papers on the floor. Sitting on the unmade bed, Ann-Ann held up a mirror with a tube of lipstick in hand.

"Lee Ann-Ann, didn't you hear me?" Leesan drew her eyebrows tight in an attempt to restrain her irritation. "We should have left twenty minutes ago. We'll be late for your granduncle's sixtieth birthday party."

"I'm almost done. Give me one sec." Ann-Ann didn't look up.

Have I spoiled her? Maybe I should have disciplined her more.

Yet Ann-Ann was all Leesan had in Hong Kong. And the girl flourished into an adorable young lady.

Even seething, Leesan marveled at her daughter's good looks. Fully grown with long, shapely legs, the teenager boasted a flawless oval face with shiny black hair in dramatic contrast.

"You don't need any makeup." Leesan's shoulders relaxed a bit. "Youth is your best asset."

Not receiving a response, she stifled another sigh. They'd clashed over this issue three years ago when Ann-Ann demanded ten dollars to buy a piece of lipstick. Leesan had refused, but the child threw a tantrum, yelling, "You never love me. You love only May-May."

Before going to school the next day, Ann-Ann tossed a sentence over her shoulder at the door, saying she'd taken ten dollars from her purse.

How could Ann-Ann take money without asking? When did she become so difficult to handle?

But that was three years ago. Leesan had consoled herself then by rereading Duan's letters, taking relief in knowing May-May had grown tall and healthy and no one at school tormented her anymore.

Were Su-Ann, May-May, and Duan well? During the past two years, she no longer received letters from Beijing. And the daily newspapers detailed the horrid events in China.

"Okay. Let's go." Ann-Ann's voice pulled Leesan back to focus.

As they walked toward the elevator, she ground her teeth over her run-ins with Ann-Ann. Everyone in her daughter's circle wore makeup. Her girl didn't want to be left out.

The unpleasant thought brought tension to Leesan's shoulders once more. Nothing was wrong with her daughter's companions, except that a majority of them hailed from affluent households located in the upscale Mid-Levels region of Hong Kong Island. Although Ann-Ann had never invited any of them home, she often visited their magnificent mansions.

How did Ann-Ann break into the group of those wealthy, spoiled young ladies?

Yet Leesan must give her daughter credit for doing well at school.

Ann-Ann attended the Diocesan Girls' School, one of the best Christian schools in Hong Kong. Having excellent grades to garner others' respect and admiration was important to Ann-Ann. Since childhood, she became angry if she felt neglected, overlooked, or slighted.

Breathing past the lingering dissatisfaction, Leesan dropped her keys into the purse and quickened her steps to catch up.

***

Ann-Ann walked down the hallway and habitually peered into her neighbors' interiors through the opened door. By now, she knew who lived where, although she'd never spoken to any of them.

Were their lives more exciting than hers?

"I've checked the mailbox." Mama spoke behind her. "We still didn't receive anything from Nana and May-May. It's been a long time without any news. I'm worried. This morning, I prayed for their safety again."

"You say this every day for the past two years. Aren't you tired?" Ann-Ann halted, a burned smell drifting into her nostrils. A family must have overcooked their pork chops.

Mama came to her side, her face distorted in anguish. "How could you say that? Don't you care about your nana and sister?"

Ann-Ann resumed her steps. "Does it make any difference whether I care or not?"

One of her earliest memories was about a trip to the local store. She'd wanted a red dress, but Mama had refused her. She still remembered Mama's excuse. "We can't. It's too expensive." Even then, she'd known Mama had money but was saving it to spend on May-May and Nana.

Inside the elevator, Mama spoke again. "Terrible news from China floods the newspaper every day. I've also written to Uncle Duan. He didn't reply either. So unlike him."

Why should I bother?

Ann-Ann had no recollection of those people in Beijing. Since childhood, her days revolved around a few individuals—Mama, Auntie Kam-Chu, and her granduncle's family. Oh, yes. The two phantomlike figures from Beijing. And occasionally some uncles from church who tried to date her mother.

One of those men, Uncle Hsieh, almost became her stepfather.

An amused grunt of derision escaped her over the recollection of a particular afternoon. Was she twelve or thirteen? Mama hurried into the kitchen to prepare dinner because a friend from church would dine with them.

Auntie Kam-Chu had shooed Mama away. "Leesan, go put on makeup. I'll steam the fish for you."

Ann-Ann's stomach had fluttered about this mysterious guest as she watched Mama apply glossy red lipstick on her pursed lips.

Just before six, Uncle Hsieh showed up, handed her a box of chocolate, and introduced himself as Amy's dad. "You and Amy are in the same youth group, right?"

When she nodded without accepting the gift, red flashed across his cheeks. He waved away a fly and asked about her school. She frowned. They stared at each other in silence before she dashed away. "Mama, I don't feel well. I'll eat in our room."

Auntie Kam-Chu sat her down for a chat the next day. "I know you always wonder how it feels to have a father. What do you think about Uncle Hsieh? Will you like him to be your daddy? He's a kind man and a wealthy doctor. If he becomes your daddy, you'll have your own room in a big house."

Ann-Ann had scowled. "Amy will live in the same house. I don't like her. She's the most snobbish girl at church. I'd rather share a small room with Mama than live in a big house with Amy."

Auntie Kam-Chu let out a hard sigh.

On Sunday, as her mother laughed with Uncle Hsieh at church, anger and jealousy surged inside of Ann-Ann. She rushed over and screeched, "I hate you. I hate your daughter. Stop harassing us. Leave my mama alone." Her throat seized up, and she burst into tears.

Passersby stopped to watch the commotion.

"Ann-Ann." Mama covered her mouth with a palm, seemingly in shock.

Uncle Hsieh's face fell. He gave her a stern glare and trudged away. People in her circle never mentioned him again.

The elevator door opened, jolting Ann-Ann back to the present.

I wish I could get rid of the two individuals in Beijing as easily. If it weren't for them, life would be so much better.

Whenever she asked for anything, she heard the same odious response. "Too expensive. We need to save money to send food to May-May and Nana."

Why was it always about them? She'd seen the pictures from Beijing. The old woman looked awful—battered and weak, like a bag lady. Her sister appeared decent. *She has to. After all, we're identical twins. But May-May looks plainer.*

"Tomorrow is Sunday. Are you coming to church with me?" Mama patted her arm.

Ann-Ann led the way out. "I'm going to Maggie's house to celebrate her birthday."

Mama walked behind her. "Keep away from alcohol. Remember the verses in Second Timothy. 'If a man cleanses himself'—"

"'Flee the evil desires of youth, and pursue righteousness, faith, love.'" Ann-Ann threw up her hands. "Don't forget. I have a near-photographic memory."

"You do." Mama sighed. "Besides the Bible teachings, I hope you remember what I've told you. Men in our society like their wives inexperienced on the wedding night."

Mama had talked about it many times. *Of course, I know. I'm not stupid.*

Perhaps not hearing a response from her, Mama tapped her shoulder. "Will you go to the church's youth camp next week? This is your last summer."

Ann-Ann strode out of the gate in big strides. "I haven't decided yet."

They hailed a taxi to the restaurant in Tsim Sha Tsui. As soon as they entered, Grandaunt Shu-Fang came forward. "Wow, Ann-Ann, every time I see you, you're more beautiful."

"Not only pretty but smart," Granduncle chimed in. "Are you excited about attending the University of Hong Kong in September?"

She kept her silence, trying to find something of interest. No, nothing. Just the same group of people.

They squeezed into a large round table. Mama asked right away, "Uncle, did you receive any news from Mother?"

"No." He shook his head. "Did you see today's newspaper?" He placed the *South China Morning Post* in front of them.

The front page displayed pictures of mutilated bodies floating in Hong Kong waters. Most of the corpses were bound up, some with visible broken bones. Her mother's face turned ashen. She examined the pictures as if trying to identify whether any of them might be Nana or May-May.

"Too many dead people. They don't bury corpses anymore and throw them into the Pearl River." Uncle Tong-Tong tapped the table. "With all the terrible things happening in China, Christians encounter the worst. A friend of mine told me a family was charged with fake evidence. The couple and their four children kneeled before the Red Guards. One teenage guard questioned them one by one about whether they believed in Jesus or communism. When they replied they believed in Jesus, the fellow beat them with a hammer repeatedly. Their youngest child died in front of them."

Boring, boring... Why did their family's conversations always focus on the Cultural Revolution in China? Weren't there other more pleasing topics?

Mama placed an elbow on the table. "How did your friend learn about it?"

"Their eldest son escaped to Hong Kong. My friend participates in his church's program to help the freedom swimmers. You know the term? That's what we call those escapees from Mainland China. The young man was placed under my friend's care for a week."

Uncle Tong-Tong took a sip of tea. "I'm afraid the rest of that family will face an outcome even worse than before because of him."

Her mother's eyes became moist. "Which town are they from? Maybe Beijing won't be so bad."

Uncle Tong-Tong let out a sigh. "The family is in Guangzhou. He mentioned it's the same everywhere. He said Watchman Nee's wife in Shanghai has suffered horrific abuse."

A distressing silence followed. Then Auntie Kam-Chu stood up. "Our church ought to put a program in place to help the freedom swimmers as well. I'll talk to Pastor Mang tomorrow. Today is Su-Nong's birthday. Let's pretend everything is all right in China."

"Kam-Chu, since you're standing, why don't you say grace for us?" Granduncle raised a finger.

Auntie Kam-Chu bowed her head. She thanked God for food on the table and launched into a lengthy prayer, earnestly pleading for God's protection over Nana and May-May.

After the amen, they feasted on the Shanghainese dishes, but the conversation soon drifted back to the two individuals in Beijing. Mama resurrected May-May's letter from two years ago and gave it a second life by passing it around once more. Ann-Ann had committed the contents to memory. Her twin wrote about her vegetable patch, Nana, her friend Chen Yao, and Uncle Duan.

Everyone praised May-May's penmanship again. Ann-Ann's jaw tightened. A scorching fury burned away her frustrated sadness. *I'm right here. But they don't care. They love only May-May, not me.*

Chapter Seventeen

"But for many, it is prosperity of life that constitutes the greatest trial."

St. Basil the Great (329–379)

"Wow, so many luxury cars." The taxi driver navigated up the private road to a mansion at Mid-Levels.

A stream of Jaguar, Mercedes-Benz, and Rolls-Royce cars glided through the open gate to drop off stylishly dressed passengers. When her turn came, Ann-Ann stepped out to a warm welcome provided by a jolly melody. Once she strolled inside, pleasure from the brilliant balloons overwhelmed her.

She weaved through the crowds with a group of waitresses serving elegant hors d'oeuvres and found her target. "Maggie, happy birthday." She grasped her friend's fingers. "You're so beautiful today."

In the ambient lighting, a string of pearls glowed around Maggie's neck, slithering against her pink gown as she moved.

Each pearl is at least 10 mm in size. Must be super expensive.

"Thank you. You look great too." Maggie withdrew her hand and hurried away to greet a newcomer.

Ann-Ann touched her bare neck. Heat crept up to her cheeks. How her simple red dress differed from others! Her poverty must be on full display among the guests.

No one will dance with me tonight.

She stifled a sigh and walked to the buffet table to nibble on sashimi, crab cake, caviar, and other delicacies.

Okay, enough. I can't gain weight. Or I'd be a wallflower for life. She drifted to the floor-to-ceiling windows overlooking the gorgeous Victoria Harbour.

"You're frowning." A stranger's voice reached her. "What's bothering you?"

She glanced at the man to her left and shook her head. "Nothing."

The guy shifted one step toward her. "Are you a new friend of Maggie? I don't think I've seen you before."

One more peek brought a smirk to her lips. The fellow had a funny face. His jaw was square, masculine, but his nose was ridiculously round, almost like a little ball. The attractive part of his face was his full, sensual mouth. "Oh no. I've known Maggie for some time. You're right. We haven't met before."

He covered the distance between them. "Well, allow me to introduce myself. I'm Maggie's older brother. My name is Vincent."

"You're Vincent?" Her jaw dropped. "Maggie has been telling us all about you. You're the one who's just graduated from Oxford University? Wow, I've never thought..." She halted. *Don't behave like an enthusiastic idiot.*

"Eh?" Vincent grinned. "Did you say something?"

She ran one hand through her hair, flicking loose strands over her shoulder. "You and Maggie don't look alike."

"She takes after my mother." He chuckled. "I look like nobody."

She couldn't help smiling back. "I heard you have another sister?"

"Yes, Gloria. She's over there." He pointed across the room. In a gorgeous blue gown, the girl reigned over those around her. "How about you? Do you have any siblings?"

"A younger sister. She's not in Hong Kong." Ann-Ann touched her left eyebrow where May-May had the mole that reportedly made them stand apart, not wanting him to know about her twin in Mainland China.

The live band played a waltz. He stretched out his palm, and they glided onto the dance floor. When the music changed into a tune for "Shake and Shimmy," they shook their bodies in a wild rhythm.

All night, he danced only with her.

Her chest swelled. An Oxford graduate was interested in *her*.

He called her the next day. "I thought about you all night. Are you free today? Want to go out with me?"

She crinkled up her lips. Oh, how her friends would envy her if she had a boyfriend like him. "I'd love to." She brushed a fly away from the receiver. "Where shall we meet?"

"Let's meet at the Tsim Sha Tsui Pier."

As she tried to slip away, her mother stopped her. "Where are you going?"

She drew her eyebrows together. "Mama, I'm just going to a classmate's house. I'm almost eighteen. Shouldn't you give me some freedom?" Before leaving the door, she tossed a sentence over her shoulder. "Don't wait on me for dinner."

Mama yelled behind her. "Come home earlier. Kam-Chu wants to have dim sum with us tomorrow."

Who wants to go out with you and Auntie Kam-Chu? All your conversations focus on May-May. You never care about me.

Such a typical summer day, hot and humid. She took a bus to Tsim Sha Tsui. Vincent was already standing underneath the Five Flagpoles, a popular meeting point for young people.

"You came from home to meet me here?" She grinned. "Thank you. You're so thoughtful."

Vincent laughed aloud and jammed his hands into the pockets of his tapered slacks. "It's my honor. Shall we go to the Hong Kong Island side?"

As they took the Star Ferry across Victoria Harbour, she surveyed her miniskirt with a tiny flower print. Everywhere girls and women alike wore super short skirts, but miniskirts showed off her long legs nicely, giving her an advantage over the others.

From the pier, she followed him to pick up his tan Jag. He drove to the Repulse Bay Hotel, overlooking a beautiful white-sand beach.

After he led her out of the low-slung vehicle, she tucked a tress behind her ear. "Come, let's go to the ocean."

They took off their shoes and played with the gentle waves.

"Interested in going to the Peak?" He patted her shoulder.

R. F. Whong

Startled at finding him so close, she took a step away. "Sure."

"Shall we drive or take the tram?"

"Let's pretend to be tourists." She smoothed her hair again.

They trekked behind foreigners to Victoria Peak, stopping to take in the panoramic view that extended from Victoria Harbour to Kai-Tak Airport to sites beyond Kowloon.

Vincent brought out a small box. "For you."

With a coy grin, she raised the clamshell lid to reveal a silver-tone bracelet. Tiny heart beads shimmered in the sunlight. She stretched her eyes open. "How nice of you." A silent sigh caught in her throat. She'd asked Mama to buy her a bracelet before. Even though it didn't cost much, Mama refused.

"Let me put it on for you." He grasped her fingers. "You have the most beautiful hands I've ever seen."

She lowered her face to hide her blush. "It fits well. The length is perfect. Thank you very much."

"You're welcome." He didn't release his hold of her. "Where do you want to go for dinner?"

Delight bubbled up in a giddy laugh. "How about right here at the Peak Lookout?"

Since her youth, she often wondered how it felt to dine in that restaurant. She'd asked Mama a few times but always received the same reply. "That place is for foreigners. Local people don't eat there."

He tickled her wrist. "Your wish is my command."

Once seated by the floor-to-ceiling window, she flipped through the menu. Maybe she'd try the filet mignon. She'd never had it before. *It's one of the most expensive items. Hope he doesn't mind.*

Her order came. As she struggled to cut the steak with a knife and a fork, her neck burned.

His eyes sparkling like their red wine, he raised his glass as if in a toast. "You're quite a charming girl."

She chewed on a piece of beef. *Is he laughing at me?* The tender meat melted in her mouth. *Who cares?*

After dinner, he wrapped an arm around her waist. "I know an awesome place for dancing. Let's go."

She didn't get home until midnight. As usual, Mama waited for her in the living room. Ignoring Mama's anxious inquiries, she walked straight to her room.

141

In the following days, as promised, Vincent took her out to roam the countryside and outlying islands. He always remembered to bring her gifts—a pair of pearl earrings, a gold ring with tiny rubies, and a silver bangle.

I love, love them even though they aren't that expensive.

She knew the price well, for she often went to the Wing-On store to check on accessories. Mama never allowed her to buy any jewelry and always reminded her they shouldn't own unnecessary items because Nana and May-May didn't even have their basic needs met.

On this balmy Friday, she met Vincent at the Central Pier on Hong Kong Island.

He clasped her hand. "I'll take you to Lantau Island today."

They took the ferry. Upon arrival, they rented a bicycle. He helped her sit in the back seat and pedaled until they reached a beach house, a handsome bungalow surrounded by white fences full of climbing purple flowers. Once inside, he brought out a drink from the refrigerator. She sat with him on the plush sofa and sipped cold fruit juice.

"Nice to drink this on a hot day." She let out a soft breath. "Whose house is this?"

"My parents'. Cute, right?" He retrieved a jewelry box from his pocket. "For you." Inside lay a string of cultured pearls. "Maggie told me you wanted a pearl necklace."

The beads weren't large, but she'd never owned any pearl necklace. She pressed the gift against her heart. "I love it. Thank you."

"Come closer." He gestured to her. "Let me put it on for you."

She shifted toward him and turned her back. As he nuzzled his face at her nape, her body shivered.

"Do you know you have the most beautiful neck? How do poets describe it? Ah, yes, swanlike." He turned her around and placed his mouth on hers.

He tasted fruity, like the drink they'd just sipped.

She tried to return his favor, heat creeping up to her cheeks at her clumsiness.

He drew back and smiled. "An attractive girl who's never been touched? Incredible." He teased her lips again. "Let's learn together."

She shoved him away and smoothed down her hair. "How many women have you kissed?"

"Come on. I swear to you. There's only one other girl before you, and that was when I was a kindergartener." He pulled her into his arms to kiss her again.

When his hands molded her hips, shock washed over her. As her mouth dropped open, their tongues met in a close exchange. Then his fingers reached beneath her miniskirt.

Alarm emerged. She pushed him in the chest. "Vincent, stop."

Ignoring her protest, he continued his caresses. Her fear faded. She shut her eyes and let waves of unfamiliar pleasure crash over her.

"No." A pained whimper escaped her lips at the prick of discomfort.

Not long after, he moved away from her.

Mama's words popped into her mind. "Ann-Ann, keep yourself pure."

Moisture gathered in her eyes.

He put his shorts back on. "Nothing wrong with what we did. We're in love. Our love is now more complete."

"But—" She winced at the red stain on the sofa, tears trickling down her cheeks.

He brushed her face with the tips of his fingers. "Everyone is doing it. If you don't believe me, ask your friends."

She clutched a fist to her chest. "How do you know? You must have other women."

"You're my only girlfriend." He raised his right hand. "I swear Tang Vincent loves only Lee Ann-Ann."

Unlike before, his comical gesture didn't make her laugh. She frowned and straightened her clothes. "I'd better go."

That night, she didn't sleep well, battling divergent ideas. *Why does our church teach us sex is bad?* She'd never experienced so much pleasure in her life. *It's so enjoyable. No wonder everyone is doing it.*

The next afternoon, she followed him to the beach house again.

Then, one morning in midsummer, Ann-Ann strolled into the living room, and queasiness washed over her. She heaved a few deep breaths. When the sensation refused to lift, she dialed Vincent's number. "I don't feel well today and plan to stay home. See you tomorrow. Same place, same time."

As soon as she dropped the receiver, another surge of nausea hit her. She dashed for the kitchen sink. *Did I catch the flu? Something is seriously wrong with me.*

Her mother saw her vomiting and rushed her to the hospital.

Dread and disbelief flooded her as the doctor's words echoed in her ears. "Your daughter is in good health. She's pregnant."

Pregnant? I can't go to college anymore?

Back at home, Mama wagged a finger at her. "How did it happen? All those lessons our church has been teaching you. All the things I've been telling you. You..."

Mama's body shook as if in violent epilepsy. Throughout the years, Ann-Ann had never seen her mother so angry.

I have to stay home, get huge, and birth a baby? Her gut twisted up.

Tears stung her cheeks. *My friends will sneer.*

Mama stopped her rants and spoke in a calmer tone. "You should tell me who the father is. Maybe he'll marry you, an acceptable outcome."

Yes, that's it. We'll get married. All will be fine. Ann-Ann wiped her tears away. *We can move to the UK or the US. His family is rich. They can afford it.*

She told Mama about Vincent.

Mama gestured at the phone. "You'd better call him right away."

After she told Vincent the news, he lapsed into a long silence.

"Hello?" Ann-Ann couldn't help asking. "Are you there?"

"I need to discuss it with my parents." His tight voice rang in her ears. "I'll find an open spot on their calendar. I'll call you tomorrow."

A week went by with no information. Her heart kept tightening. Why didn't he call? Was he waiting to see his parents?

She dialed his number again. This time, a servant answered. He didn't go to fetch Vincent. Instead, he said, "Vincent isn't in town."

"Where is he?" Her hands and feet grew cold.

"He's in Europe. I don't know when he'll be back."

Ann-Ann dropped the receiver to the floor, her vision blurring. "Mama, I'm a fool. He's tricked me."

Chapter Eighteen

"Your eyes saw my unformed body. All the days ordained for me
were written in your book before one of them came to be."

Psalms 139:16

A lump lodged in Leesan's throat as she dialed Vincent's number.

Lord, please let Mr. Tang be my fan and agree to see me.

After she told the servant her pen name, he exclaimed, "Are you
really Jin Yue? We're all your fans. Mr. Tang would love to meet
with you. Let me check on when he's available." Soon, the servant
returned. "He's planning an afternoon at home on Wednesday if the
time works for you."

She hailed a taxi to Mid-Levels Wednesday afternoon. As a
magnificent iron gate blocked the way, she let out a hard breath. *If
Vincent lives here, he'll never be allowed to marry Ann-Ann.*

From what she had read in newspapers about Hong Kong's super
wealthy, Ann-Ann had no chance to become a daughter-in-law of
such a family. She had neither money nor fame and only possessed
youth and beauty, two useless attributes to Vincent's parents.

I must try, for my girl's sake.

She approached the guardhouse. After the man confirmed her appointment, he brought her into the house and left her in a spacious hall adorned with lavish furniture and elaborate paintings. A middle-aged man walked in. "Please come with me. Mr. Tang is waiting for you in the study."

Following him into a room lined with tall bookcases, Leesan sat in a chair before a gorgeous mahogany desk and eyed the man behind it.

Mr. Tang smiled and spoke in Cantonese. "I appreciate your call. I'm so glad to have met you. I've read every one of your novels. Please let me know how I can be of any assistance."

She replied in Mandarin. "Mr. Tang, I'm here for my daughter, Lee Ann-Ann."

The warmth disappeared from his face. "Lee Ann-Ann?" He picked up his teacup. "Sorry. I don't recognize the name."

He isn't pretending. She narrowed her eyes as heat surged through her heart. Vincent had never mentioned Ann-Ann to his father.

She explained the situation.

Mr. Tang's expression went blank. He sipped his tea. When he opened his mouth again, his tone came across as cold. "Thank you for the information. Please forgive me if I sound unkind. I wish I could help you solve your daughter's problem. What I must do next is to hear the other side of the story. I need to check with my son."

He appeared courteous, very much a gentleman. Yet his politeness turned into a brick wall, preventing her from going further. Still, she pressed on. "He's in Europe, isn't he? He won't be back for months, right?"

Mr. Tang looked steadfastly at her. Then he stood, a clear dismissal signal. "As much as I admire you and your books, I can do nothing at this point."

Lord, what did I do wrong with my girl? Her chin dropped to her chest. *I've tried to teach her biblical principles. Why did she turn out this way?*

As she entered their flat, her daughter was standing in front of the coffee table. Ann-Ann stared at her face, then walked into her room without a word.

Stifling a sigh, Leesan strolled to the kitchen. *Ann-Ann probably needs some privacy now.* She stir-fried beef with onion for dinner. Once done, she went to knock on the door. "Dinner is ready."

Not a single sound.

She yelled again. "Time to eat."

Still only silence.

She tried the doorknob. It was locked. A frightful idea taunted her. She pounded on the door with trembling hands. "Ann-Ann, come out. Please."

Absolute quiet, no movement, not a murmur.

With an unsteady gait, she ran to dial Kam-Chu's phone number. "Ann-Ann locked herself in the room. I can't get in. She may have... killed herself." Her throat seized up, and she burst into tears.

"I'll call the emergency hotline right away." Kam-Chu spoke in placid tones.

Within minutes, paramedics broke into Ann-Ann's room. At the sight of her daughter lying lifelessly on the floor with blood all over her blouse, Leesan stumbled back and screamed.

Ann-Ann had slit her wrist. They saved her life and kept her in the hospital for further monitoring. Leesan went with Kam-Chu to see her every day. A week later, a doctor approached them. "Ann-Ann asked me last night for an abortion. Since she's a minor, we need her legal guardian to sign the paperwork. Which of you is her guardian?"

Leesan's shoulders tightened. She scraped a palm against her dress as a scene from her OSU days flashed across her mind.

She'd missed her period for two months and uttered a plea to God, her first in more than a year, begging for it not to be a pregnancy. Stories she overheard in China about jumping rope to induce miscarriage tempted her and propelled her to enter a vigorous exercise routine. Rong had eyed her and questioned why she suddenly started exercising. After her period resumed, she lifted another silent prayer, this one of thanks, and stowed the rope away.

"Mrs. Lee is the legal guardian." Kam-Chu's voice interrupted her contemplation. "It's a major decision. We'll need to discuss it. Can we give you a reply tomorrow?"

On their walk home, Leesan confessed what had happened in Columbus, Ohio. "It must be God's punishment. Back then, I considered only my convenience. I didn't acknowledge there might be a life growing in me."

Kam-Chu patted her shoulder. "It's a myth that jumping rope may induce miscarriage. It won't hurt a healthy pregnancy. Likely, you weren't pregnant at all. After you accepted Christ, God has forgiven your sins. He'll not use Ann-Ann to punish you."

Leesan sighed out her agitation as she stepped around a parked bicycle. "Regardless, my thought wasn't pleasing to God."

"Abortion is a complicated issue." Kam-Chu linked their arms. "Unfortunately, we rarely study this subject at church."

Briefly closing her eyes and letting her friend guide her, Leesan brought her free hand to her forehead. "You're right. It seems ambiguous to many Christians. Most people don't think the Bible has clear teaching."

A group of teenage boys approached them, laughing and yelling profanity. Kam-Chu pulled her into a convenience store by the road. "The message from the Bible is unequivocal. God formed us in the womb. Even in Genesis, before the twins Esau and Jacob were born, God recognized them as two individuals who would eventually become the founding fathers of two nations."

Leesan nodded, but her anxiety refused to lift. "The Bible teaches a fetus in the womb is already life. God sees its existence."

"I once read a book about children who die young. The author, whose daughter passed away shortly following birth, asked, 'The Bible tells us suffering refines us like fine gold, making us closer to God. But for my daughter and others in similar situations, what does the pain of death mean?'" Kam-Chu led her back into the walkway.

As they turned into her street, Leesan's steps slowed. "I would ask the same question."

"Not easy to find a satisfactory answer. That book mentioned if there were only the material world, the lives of many like her daughter would be utterly meaningless. The author concluded that in the spiritual realm, God, together with thousands of angels, has seen the existence of her daughter." Kam-Chu unhooked their arms. "In eternity, suffering, no matter in what form, is always meaningful, even though we can't comprehend it from our limited human perspective."

Leesan stopped in front of her apartment building, her heart heavy. "I'll need to talk to her about putting up the baby for adoption."

When she broached the subject of adoption the next morning, Ann-Ann grew hysterical and pounded her fists on the bed. "You don't love me at all. You've never loved me. You just care about your stupid faith."

At Ann-Ann's outburst, Kam-Chu shook her head. "Sometimes love is used to justify cruelty."

While leaving the hospital, Leesan wiped the tears away with a handkerchief. "I have to talk to her again. The doctor plans to release her tomorrow. Kam-Chu, I'm stressed out. Please pray for me."

Kam-Chu lifted a prayer at the street corner, bringing a trace of peace into Leesan's heart, something she hadn't felt since sending Ann-Ann to the hospital. Back at her flat, she had her daughter's bedroom door taken down.

After Ann-Ann came home, Kam-Chu stopped by, yet the girl refused to see her.

"I've been monitoring Ann-Ann closely. She stays in her room all day long." Leesan heaved a hard breath as she sank into the chair across the table from her friend. "With a scar on her wrist and a wound in her heart, she's no longer that active, outgoing, fun-loving girl."

Kam-Chu flattened her palms on the smooth yellow tablecloth, frowning at them. "The emotional scar may be invisible, but deeper, more difficult to heal." She slid from her chair and beckoned Leesan to the thin area rug. "Let's pray for her."

Leesan kneeled and cried out to God. "Lord, I'm weary and burdened. So many things have happened in my life. I still haven't received any news from May-May. And now this. Oh, Lord, please give me wisdom so I can help Ann-Ann."

Following her morning devotion four days later, Leesan dashed out to the neighborhood market to buy toilet paper. When she returned home, Ann-Ann was gone. She dialed Kam-Chu's number, who rushed over right away.

They called the police. The man advised them to wait since Ann-Ann was missing for less than an hour.

Leesan paced around the apartment, weeping, praying out loud. "Lord, where could she go? Please keep Ann-Ann safe."

Kam-Chu forced her to sit down. "Don't panic. Look to the Lord for strength."

Two hours went by before a nearby hospital called. Ann-Ann was there. When they ran over, she was sleeping peacefully with tubes attached to her body, her face as white as snow.

Leesan uttered a plea to the nurse, her voice quivering. "Please, please tell me what happened to my daughter."

"Is she your daughter?" The woman gave her a sympathetic glance. "She tried to have an abortion in one of those places. They couldn't stop her bleeding and sent her to the emergency room. She almost died. We had to operate on her."

Having passed by the cheap abortion clinics before, Leesan understood what the nurse meant.

Kam-Chu stepped forward. "Is Ann-Ann all right?"

"She should be fine. Except she may not be able to have children in the future."

Her heart breaking, Leesan plopped down on Ann-Ann's bed, crying aloud. "Foolish, selfish child, what have you done? Have you no concern for others?"

Her friend came over to hug her. "No use saying this now."

Oh, Lord, what would become of Ann-Ann? Please have mercy on us.

When the hospital released her a week later, school was about to start. As Leesan mentioned the University of Hong Kong, her daughter scowled. "How many times do I have to tell you? I won't go there. If you want me to go to college, send me to the UK or the US."

"But..."

Before she could say more, Ann-Ann walked away.

Kam-Chu visited in the afternoon, and Leesan drew her to the kitchen. "What shall I do? I can't afford to send her abroad. Ann-Ann is so stubborn. Nothing I said would change her mind. I'm so worried she'll do more foolish things."

"Have you considered Taiwan?" Kam-Chu pulled out a stool to sit on. "Taiwan has a program designed specifically for Overseas Chinese students. The cost is low. Plus, your parents can help take care of her."

She rubbed her throbbing temples. "It won't do. Ann-Ann insists on going to Europe or America."

Kam-Chu tapped her fingers on the countertop. "Maybe we ought to talk to Mrs. Kuhn, the missionary in our church. She's from the States."

With Mrs. Kuhn's help, Ann-Ann applied to four universities in the States. After an acceptance letter from a school in California reached them, Leesan shared the good news with her friend. "Praise the Lord. It's Ann-Ann's top choice. After some careful calculations, I can give her only one semester's tuition, plus room and board."

"Did you tell her? How did she take it?"

She sighed. "She wasn't happy but seemed to take it well. Mrs. Kuhn mentioned that most college students in the States work at least part-time to support themselves."

Kam-Chu nodded. "We can just pray and hope she learns something from this ordeal to become more mature, more responsible."

Chapter Nineteen

"I have seen all the things that are done under the sun; all of them are meaningless, a chasing after the wind."

Ecclesiastes 1:14

Beijing, China
January 1969

Dark clouds gathered in the sky. Was it about to snow? Had she forgotten to pack her gloves?

May-May followed Yao and Uncle Chen to Tiananmen Square. Several buses awaited there. Amid the cold weather, a mass of people filled the space, making conversation difficult.

Yao grasped her fingers, his own shaking slightly. In front of her bus, he spoke in a cracked voice. "Take care. I'll go to see you soon."

Simmering with mixed emotions, she threw a glance in his direction, then climbed into the coach.

After she took her seat, a girl with a pair of thick, myopic glasses sat next to her. "My name is Song Mei-Hua."

"I'm Lee May-May."

Mei-Hua tilted her head. "Where are you going?"

"Bada Village." May-May glimpsed at her. "And you?"

"Bada Village as well. What a coincidence." Mei-Hua clapped. "I'm a student in the high school affiliated with the Academy of Fine Arts. How about you?"

"I used to attend the high school in our community." May-May gave her seatmate another look. Her mood lightened a bit at Mei-Hua's radiant smile. "You must be an outstanding artist?"

"I've loved painting since childhood and can't wait to get to Bada Village." Mei-Hua waved her arms. "I heard Mongolia has vast, beautiful grasslands and more freedom. It'll be an ideal spot for artists."

May-May turned up the corners of her mouth, warmth bubbling up. "My good friend, Yao, loves drawing too."

"What does he usually draw?"

"Lots of things, mainly portraits." She shifted her body. Memories of her countless sketches in Yao's notebooks stirred rippling unease with a resurgent heat in her heart.

As she remained muted, their conversation faltered, and Mei-Hua soon succumbed to slumber.

May-May jammed her knees into the seat in front. As her emotions spilled forth, she shut her eyes tight. *Lord, please watch over Uncle Duan, Mama, Ann-Ann, and my friends in Beijing.*

Then she sat up straighter and gazed out the window at the houses along the road. *I'll see Nana in a few days.*

Around her, people were laughing, talking, and singing popular revolutionary tunes. One of them, "The East Is Red" compared Chairman Mao to the sun and described him as the people's savior.

The jubilant mood waned. Someone snored behind her. The bus stopped several times for people to disembark, but none of those places was her destination.

The view changed. Fewer and fewer buildings dotted the landscape, replaced by patches of dirt, sharp-edged rocks, and wilted plants. The desolate field stretched away into the horizon. *A harsh, unfriendly region. How can people survive here?*

Soon they drove on a bumpy dirt road, and the bus swayed. A combination of fatigue and motion sickness overtook her. Her surroundings faded into the background.

"Lee May-May, wake up."

The call awoke her. The bus had pulled up to a station again. Like a sleepwalker, she followed Mei-Hua to the restroom. Everything seemed unreal, dreamlike.

Two days later, the bus stopped at the Baolige Ranch in Mandula, the terminus for most of the youth. May-May transferred with a dozen others to the waiting carriages. They traveled on the prairie for one more day. She tried to survey the area, yet the motion lulled her into another slumber.

"May-May."

She opened her eyes. Slender hands clasped hers. She traced the arms to the person and stood to fall into her nana's embrace.

"Nana." She laughed through her tears.

A smile crinkled up Nana's wrinkled face while tears traced their way past the crevices. "May-May, my good girl."

She followed Nana off the carriage and down a gravel path, toward earthen huts and brick houses. But no yurts. As if understanding her thoughts, Nana directed her gaze toward the vast grasslands. "The cadres live in the houses. We stay in yurts."

"Which one is yours?" Straining her eyes, May-May located the round, tentlike structures rising from the sea of grass.

"One of those." Nana pointed toward the west side. "I asked for us to stay together. With the Lord's blessings, I hope my request will be granted."

"I've never lived in a yurt before." May-May clapped. "I'll get to stay in one this evening."

"Not yet." Nana patted her cheek. "Tonight, you'll stay in one of the houses here. Tomorrow, we'll know which yurt you're assigned to."

Early the next morning, May-May trailed the other newcomers to the orientation meeting. Three officials showed up, but none was the regional chief. Before the scheduled starting time, the person in charge arrived. May-May opened her eyes wide at the profile of their regional Communist party secretary, who looked not much older than she was.

"My name is Ying Jie." The man spoke in a calm baritone. He gave the group a brief description of the region. After he assigned yurts and tasks, he challenged them to work hard to prove they were worthy of participating in the revolutionary cause.

"He's *so* handsome!" A murmured exclamation reverberated from the back.

May-May surveyed his profile. He was indeed an exceptionally good-looking man: a chiseled face complemented by wavy jet-black hair, a straight nose, and a sensual mouth. His eyes, accentuated by lush eyelashes, were the most unusual—large, luminous in a peculiar light golden-brown hue. The dark-blue Mao uniform couldn't hide his tall, sculpted physique.

When Jie's eyes connected with hers, he smiled, revealing his even white teeth. She dipped her chin, sensing a quiver in her stomach.

Following the meeting, the young people dispersed. She entered her tent and grinned at the sight of her nana. *Thank You, Lord, thank You.*

Nana nudged her toward a stout woman in her early forties. "Big Sister Liu, this is my granddaughter, Lee May-May."

Like many Mongolian women, Big Sister Liu featured a round face with red puffy cheeks.

Nana took a step back. "Big Sister Liu is one of the few locals who speaks fluent Mandarin. She lives in a nearby yurt and is responsible for supervising outsiders."

"You're such a good-looking girl." Big Sister Liu grasped May-May's hand and explained what needed to be done. "Except for officials, we all take turns completing our assignments. You'll need to fetch water from the river, prepare meals, harvest wool, and milk the yaks."

May-May nodded along with her words. Oh, for sure they'd have endless chores both indoors and outdoors.

"I made this myself." Big Sister Liu touched her large scarf. "We all work on the wool we collect from our sheep."

Nana patted a piece of cloth-like material on the wall. "In winter, we use wool from our cashmere goats—we don't have sheep—to make felt for many purposes, especially for covering the yurt."

After their chitchat, Big Sister Liu took leave. Nana guided May-May to the beds lined up on the entrance's left side. "The second one is yours."

The furnishings included a small table and some utensils, but no stove. As if reading her mind, Nana pointed to the furnace in the middle. "That's where we cook and how we keep warm in winter."

May-May fingered through her hair, dirty from the long trip. "Um... How do we take a shower?"

"In the summer, we jump into the creek. If it's cold like now, we have to haul water from the river, warm it, and then bathe in the wooden tub."

That didn't sound too promising. Well, she'd get used to it in time, right? Then she frowned at another missing necessity. "Where's the toilet?"

"Outside." Nana clasped her arm. "Come with me."

They walked behind the yurt. A primal thatched hut lurked quite some distance away. "They didn't even have this before. It was built one or two years ago. In the past, everyone just did it directly on the ground."

As May-May drew her brows even tighter, Nana stared into her eyes. "Life in this village is tough. And everyone is assigned many tasks. Remember what the Bible teaches about work?"

An immediate reply rolled off her tongue. "Yes, Nana. 'Whatever you do, work at it with all your heart, like working for the Lord, not for men.'"

"My good girl." Nana inclined her head. "Youngsters from Beijing find life here too challenging. A majority of them complain constantly and seek excuses to skimp. Don't join them. You have to work harder. Besides your duties, try to help others. Do everything as if you're doing it for our Lord."

Lord, I need Your help. May-May let out a long breath and followed Nana back to the yurt.

No matter what was in store, she was sure of one thing—Through the Lord's mercy, she and Nana were reunited.

Except for the inconvenience, May-May soon savored the freedom this place offered, so different from Beijing. They didn't have too many political events to attend. The only review meeting every Sunday morning usually ended at ten. After that, they had a few hours of free time.

She and Nana always left the cadre area immediately. To worship God on their way back to the yurt, she sang hymns with a joyful heart and recited Bible verses to Nana. If the weather permitted, they walked to the prairie to praise God amid nature. Sometimes, Ying Jie rode a black horse and galloped past them, disappearing into the far horizon.

As a custom, Big Sister Liu often invited them over for lunch. Nana made sure they brought food to share.

Two months after she arrived, May-May ducked into Big Sister Liu's yurt after Nana, placed her bowl on the low dining table, and sat on the wool area rug.

During their chitchat, Big Sister Liu waved at another rug hanging on the wall. "We Mongols are peoples of the Gobi. For centuries, we led a nomadic lifestyle. Now we also grow crops, mainly soybeans and corn." Her forehead creased. "Our difficulty is that very few of us speak Mandarin."

May-May leaned forward with interest. "What's your written language? What does it look like?"

"Our spoken and written language is Mongolian." With a faint smile, Big Sister Liu retrieved a letter from a nearby wooden desk to show her. "This is how it looks."

Wow. May-May traced a character in the row. *It looks like a string of lines.*

After settling back on the floor, Big Sister Liu sampled the spicy potatoes. "May-May, you prepare such delicious food. I notice, no matter what your assignment is, you work hard to complete it."

May-May fidgeted, sensing the heat on her face. "I was idle for a while in Beijing. I'm glad I have something to do."

"The chief is looking for someone to prepare meals for the officials. I mentioned to him you're an excellent cook." Big Sister Liu dipped her chopsticks into the bowl again. "I think he'll transfer you there soon."

A gasp almost slipped free as May-May's chest tightened. "What about my nana? I don't want to—"

"Don't worry." Big Sister Liu gestured with the chopsticks. "I've already told Ying Jie that Mrs. Lee has to go with you. He likes my suggestion. It's an outstanding opportunity. You'll have better living conditions."

On the way back to their yurt, May-May gave Nana a questioning glance. "Don't you consider it a wonderful thing? How come you don't look happy?"

Nana hitched a hard breath. "I don't know if you've heard about it. The year before, news about the Inner Mongolia incident gradually leaked to us."

May-May shook her head.

"It was an inhumane purge event, almost a campaign of genocide. Many people were tortured and slaughtered. Thousands of Mongolians were killed. It's still going on in some parts of Inner Mongolia." Nana covered her eyes. "I thank God for His mercy. Our small village hasn't been affected too much, maybe because of our remote location or because Ying Jie seems determined to maintain order here."

"I'm sorry. I don't understand." May-May tugged at Nana's sleeve. "What does that have to do with our job transfer?"

"Well, some reports say officials took opportunities to persecute innocents. Many women were—"

"Raped?" A shudder crept up May-May's spine. The hair on her nape stood up. She rubbed her arms, forcing goosebumps to subside.

"God forbid it should ever happen." Nana's face contorted. "In any case, be vigilant. Stay away from the offices. So far, God has been merciful to us."

Within one week, they got transferred.

***

The sun just peeked over the horizon, yet sounds already took over the streets of Beijing.

"Long Live Cultural Revolution!"

"We will defend Chairman Mao's revolutionary line!"

From afar, Yao could hear the other Red Guards echo his chants. As he drew closer to Tiananmen Square, the shouts hurt his ears.

Are you all right, May-May? A soothing warmth spread throughout his chest at the thought of his beloved.

He received a letter from her a week ago. In it, she described helping the local people make cheese from yak milk. She seemed happy.

Still, since her departure, he couldn't shake the fear that one day a letter would arrive, informing him she was dead.

The march came to a stop. They'd arrived at Tiananmen Square. Since nobody knew when Chairman Mao would appear, the officials organized them into different groups to sing revolutionary songs to maintain high spirits. Yao imitated others and waved the small red book in the air.

I shall go to Inner Mongolia.

Like a robot, he followed every command without missing a beat. When the other teams sang, he sat in silence and focused on his plan to visit May-May.

Eight hours later, Chairman Mao showed up for less than ten minutes. Yao smiled. It didn't matter. He'd see May-May soon.

Back at home, he told Pa his plan, and Pa shook his head. "It's not a good time to go to Inner Mongolia. I've just received a letter from Mrs. Lee. She mentioned it's cold there."

Yao paced around their room. Feeling imprisoned brought a tightness to his throat. "I'm tired of the nonstop rally meetings here. I need to get away. Otherwise, I'll go crazy."

What he couldn't tell Pa was that he detested the home-ransacking activities. After Lee Nana's incident, they disgusted him even more than before. He couldn't forget the desperation and dread on May-May's face when the Red Guards abused Lee Nana.

Pa's eyes softened. Then he gave a nod, even as his shoulders slumped. "Take care of yourself. Give my regards to Mrs. Lee and May-May."

By morning, Yao stood underneath the enormous portrait of Chairman Mao at Beijing Railway Station. All around him were young people who traveled across the country for fun.

He curled up his lips into a grin with the anticipation of the coming reunion with May-May. In just a few days...

Despite no direct train to Bada Village, he could get to a nearby station and transfer to a bus. As he walked over to board his train, someone stopped him at the door. "Where are you going? Do you have a ticket and a passport? Only domestic trains are free to Red Guards. This train goes to the Mongolian People's Republic."

"I'm sorry. I made a mistake." He stepped away. *Idiot. Don't you know you can't go to a different country?*

Across the platform, he jumped into a train waiting to depart.

As he moved inward, someone shoved him away.

His mood plunged further. He glared at the girl. "Why did you push me for no reason?"

She swung her thick braid over her shoulder. "Because you touched me first."

"He didn't do it on purpose. Can't you see the entire place is crowded?" A boy nearby spoke up. He then shifted his body backward. "Come on. Let's make room for..."

A whistle blast drowned out his words. Yao spread out his legs against the sudden rocking motion. "Where's this train going?"

"Are you serious?" The boy thumped a fist into Yao's chest. "You don't know where you're going?"

He feigned a casual smile. "I was supposed to take another train. They wouldn't let me in. It doesn't matter. I just need to leave Beijing for a change."

"You're traveling all over the country for fun like other Red Guards, huh?" The boy nodded. "This train is heading to Qufu, Shandong." He lifted his chin. "We took part in the anti-Confucius campaign about two years ago and want to check how things are now."

He detailed how more than two hundred people followed Tan Houlan, the leader of the Red Guards of the Normal University, to Qufu in late 1966 to denounce everything related to Confucius.

"My name is Zhang Hong." He jerked his thumb toward the girl. "She's Lin Xiao-dong. What's your name?"

"I'm Chen Yao."

Zhang Hong grinned. "If you have nothing to do, come to Qufu with us. I can show you the Three Kong Sites."

Why not? Some delay wouldn't make any difference to his plan.

For three days, Yao toured Qufu with his new friends.

At Kong Mansion and Confucius Temple, smashed relics marked the sites. Kong Lin, the graveyard where Confucius and his descendants were buried, didn't fare any better. Many toppled stone stelae with defaced characters desecrated the area. Once symbols of glory, reign, and power, yet now they symbolized defeat, abandonment, and flight.

"We first targeted the tomb of one of Confucius's descendants. Inside a large coffin lay a bunch of red, silky blankets. We yanked them away and found a body along with some gold and jewelry. With my stick, I poked at it." Zhang Hong thrust his hand forward, and his face contorted. "The garments on the corpse came off piece by piece, exposing grayish, lifeless flesh. Some strange fluid oozed from the cuts. So horrid. I almost vomited."

Yao rubbed shivers from his arms. "In Confucius's tomb, did you guys find anything?"

"We dug and dug but found nothing. We were all fooled by the old jerk." Zhang Hong pointed to a hole. "That's it."

As the empty pit drew him closer, somber thoughts hollowed Yao's mind. *Only earth, emptiness, nothingness. Is everything in this world perishable?* Confucius, China's greatest teacher, didn't even have a trace remaining at his burial site.

He let out a heavy sigh. *Time to leave for Inner Mongolia.*

After thanking his friends, he hurried to the station. While he queued in front of the information counter, someone called his name.

He spun around. "Shao Hui? What are you doing here?"

She blinked. "Let's find a quiet place. I need to talk to you." She pulled him toward an empty corner. "You can't return to Beijing. You'll run into trouble. They're looking for you."

For him? That made no sense. Still, his heartbeat quickened. "What did you say?" He jerked backward, shaking free of her grip. "Who's looking for me?"

"Your pa is dead."

Pa—dead? He drew his brows even tighter. "What nonsense are you talking about?"

"Your pa died in a denunciation meeting two days ago."

His heavy heartbeat thudded in his ears. He grabbed her arms, almost shaking her. "What do you mean? Whose denunciation meeting?"

"He and five others were arrested for attending a Christian gathering." She slid free from him, keeping her voice in a whisper. "Now they're looking for you. You can't go back to Beijing."

"No, you lie!" He uttered a piercing cry, his voice reverberating around them. "It can't be. It can't be."

Passersby eyed them.

"Shush." She yanked at his jacket. "Calm down. I saw it myself. I was there. They beat him with a hammer and hit him on the neck. Mrs. Dong from our courtyard asked permission and buried him on the same day."

"No, you lie. You lie." He pushed her away and dashed out of the station.

Bolting toward an open field, he screeched, "Why? Pa? Why are you so stupid? Why do you believe in a God who doesn't even care?"

No one answered.

"Are You there? If You're powerful, wise, and loving like they say, why can't You prevent this from happening?"

Silence prevailed.

He fell to the ground. Anger, hatred, and sorrow mingled and burned inside of him. He raised a fist to hit the ground with wilted grass until his hand bled. As blood oozed out, he halted and burst out crying.

Chapter Twenty

"There is a God-shaped vacuum in the heart of each man which cannot be satisfied by any created thing but only by God the Creator, made known through Jesus Christ."

Blaise Pascal (1623–1662)

Hong Kong
January 1969

Surrounded by her family at Kai-Tak Airport, Ann-Ann fumbled with the chunky watch on her wrist.

"I'll wait for your call." Mama dabbed her eyes with a handkerchief. "Call me when you reach California."

Auntie Kam-Chu hugged her tight. "Take good care of yourself."

Ann-Ann nodded without saying a word and hurried past the Passenger Only sign. Once settled in her window seat, she gazed at the scenery. The plane took off and flew over one skyscraper after another. Gradually, the islands below appeared like black dots on a blue canvas.

I've left Hong Kong.

She laughed while tears rolled down her cheeks. As all her buried emotions surged to the surface, Vincent's image intruded. She shook her head hard. *From now on, I'll never allow any man to take advantage of me. Not ever again.*

California and a new life awaited just hours away. She tried to smile. Instead, her lips curved downward. *I should be excited. Why do I feel empty?* Finding no simple answer, she drifted off to sleep.

At the San Francisco airport hours later, Mrs. Kuhn's friend, Pastor Montgomery, came to take her to the dormitory. The old gentleman helped her stow her luggage in a corner. "Call me if you need anything."

She leaned against the plain white hall to watch him leave, but her mind shifted toward the days to come. What should she do to find a job? Was Mary Anderson, her roommate, agreeable? *At least I don't have to listen to Mama talking about those two individuals in China anymore.*

After school started, she hurried to the Student Career Center and handed in a job application form. While she walked out, a man in torn jeans stopped her.

"Are you new here?" he asked in English and then switched to Mandarin. "Do you speak Chinese?"

What on earth had torn his jeans like that? "I arrived recently."

"My name is Jonathan Peng, a sophomore in chemical engineering." He inserted a hand into his pocket. "What's your name?"

"Lee Ann-Ann, studying finance." She turned to leave.

"Wait." He held his arm across her path. "Do you like pizza? Let's have lunch together. My treat."

She tilted up her head. With high cheekbones and a cleft chin, he'd probably be handsome, if not for his unkempt, long hair that obscured part of his face. And pizza? She might as well try it. "All right. I have no class, anyway."

They strolled to Telegraph Avenue, and she stretched her eyes wide at the scene of men with scruffy beards playing guitar on the sidewalk.

My dress is too formal. Jonathan's long hair matches the surroundings better.

They stopped in front of a pizzeria called Pepe's. He guided her through the door. "This restaurant is superb."

Fifteen minutes later, the pizza came. She took a bite. With a thick layer of cheese inside, it tasted unpalatable. She forced herself to finish the piece on her plate. In contrast, Jonathan had a healthy appetite and gobbled down the rest.

He wiped his mouth. "You don't eat much."

"This is my first time trying pizza." She wrinkled her nose. "It's not tasty at all. I don't like it."

His eyes sparkled. "You're quite amusing."

She averted her gaze. *Yeah, sure. I've heard that before.*

"You probably prefer Chinese food?"

As her interest swelled, she inclined her head.

He grinned. "Tomorrow, let's go to Oakland Chinatown for dim sum."

Inside Wong Kee the next day, Ann-Ann devoured the tripe steamed with ginger, then leaned back in her chair with a satisfied sigh. "Quite authentic. As good as what I used to eat in Hong Kong."

He laughed aloud. "I'm glad you like it." Setting down his chopsticks, he switched to a serious tone. "Many of us participate in various movements on campus aiming at different racial and social issues. I'm a member of the Asian-American Political Alliance." He gave her more information about their organization. "Are you interested in joining?"

She drummed her fingers on her leg. "I'm afraid I can't. My mother gave me only one semester's tuition and living expenses. I need to find a job soon."

"Are you always so straightforward?" He chuckled. "I understand. My family just came here from Taiwan four years ago. My parents run a Laundromat. So, I rely on loans. Unfortunately, you're not a US citizen. You can't apply for a loan."

Okay, I got the point. No loans.

Despite her need to find a job, she squandered more time with him. How many dates had they had? She lost count. On this Friday, they went to his home in Oakland, a bungalow with a cute backyard full of vegetables.

He picked a pod from a vine. "Have you eaten raw snow peas?" He clamped a pea between his lips, then fused his mouth to hers to pass it along. She chewed it slowly. It tasted sweet, grassy.

"Want to see my room?" He caressed her face.

"Where are your parents?" She swallowed hard, anticipation flooding her.

He clutched her hand. "They're busy in the shop."

She followed him into a small bedroom. After he shut the door, they didn't make it to bed but coiled up together on the carpet. *Ahhhh, divine!* She couldn't help moaning. *I forgot how much I enjoyed sex.*

Two hours later, humming the hit song "Hey Jude," Ann-Ann strolled into her dorm room.

Mary raised her head from her book. "Great. You're back. Do you have any plans for Easter?" She placed the book on the plain wood table. "I'm going home. Will you come with me?"

Was it Easter already? Where did the time go?

Ann-Ann dipped her chin. "I wanted to meet up with Jonathan. But we've been hanging out almost every weekend. He probably won't mind if I go with you this time."

Mary's family lived near San Francisco Airport. When they approached a luxurious mansion on Good Friday, Ann-Ann opened her eyes wide. "You live here?"

"Yeah." Mary frowned. "Anything wrong?"

"No, nothing." But something *was* wrong. Very wrong. Plain Mary lived in a house with five bedrooms and five bathrooms. The bungalow Jonathan's family owned seemed shabby.

Why did she have to worry about finding a job to pay for her tuition while others enjoyed luxury?

Mr. and Mrs. Anderson inquired about life in Hong Kong. When they discovered she grew up in a Christian family, a look of delight crossed their faces. "Wonderful. We weren't sure whether to invite you to church because we've heard most Chinese aren't Christians. Please celebrate Easter with us on Sunday."

Sunday morning, she tagged along with the Andersons to attend service, her first since her arrival in California. The church building looked magnificent, the music touching. Yet she fidgeted during the sermon. *Just as boring as before.*

After the worship, Mr. Anderson trekked to the backyard to grill steaks. Mrs. Anderson handed Ann-Ann a cup of apple juice. "We've invited our neighbors, the Kengs. They're also Chinese."

The doorbell rang. Mrs. Anderson introduced her to a middle-aged couple and their son, Charlie, who had recently graduated from an out-of-state university. From their chitchat, Ann-Ann learned that the town formed an exclusive region occupied solely by rich white people until recently. The Kengs were the first non-whites to purchase a house there.

Back in the dorm on Monday, Ann-Ann was holed up in her room with books. One of her housemates came to summon her, saying a Charlie was on the phone. She tucked the receiver to her ear, sank against the cold wall, and pictured the lanky guy as she said hello.

"Ann-Ann, this is Charlie Keng. We met yesterday. Have you been to a drive-in cinema? Are you interested? I'll pick you up tonight."

She twirled the phone cord around her finger. "An outdoor movie theater? You're right—I've never been to one before. Do you have a car?"

"Of course. How about I pick you up at eight?"

On their way to the theater, he revealed that his parents operated an international trade company. Cocooned in his sleek sports car, they watched *The Sound of Music*. During the dance scene between Colonel von Trapp and Maria, he slid her into his arms to kiss her. When he tried to reach into her blouse, she pushed him away. *He's a spoiled brat from a wealthy family, very much like Tang Vincent.*

Yet she couldn't deny she enjoyed Charlie's attention. He came to her dorm every day. Sometimes she ignored him and let him wait in his Chevy Camaro. Other times she went out with him to eat, drink, and dance. The more she played coy, the more he fell for her.

This afternoon, he sat in his car like before. "I know an excellent French restaurant. Let's go to dinner together."

She leaned against the window. "I have a date with someone else tonight."

While she was speaking, Jonathan rushed over. "Who is that?"

Charlie got out. The two men glowered at each other like raging bulls, prepared to battle to the death. With the mounting tension, pride buoyed Ann-Ann. "You two figure it out. I'm going back to my room." She left without glancing back.

The next morning, Jonathan found her and drew her to sit on the grass. "I've taken care of that guy for you. He won't bother you anymore."

"Oh no." She cupped a hand over her mouth. "What did you do to him?"

"Don't worry. I didn't punch him." He chuckled. "I told him we adore each other and make love often. He glared at me and then left."

She kneaded her brows. "How could you tell another person such an intimate thing?"

He caught her arm, tugging her hand from her head. "Isn't it true? I love you and you love me."

What was love? She shook her head and trod away.

After her last class of the day, Jonathan waited outside the classroom. Seeing her, he sported a sheepish grin. "I've signed up to help clean and improve a space close to Telegraph Avenue. Are you interested?"

As she shifted away, he grabbed her shoulder. "Don't be angry with me." He pulled her closer. "Ann-Ann, I love you very much."

At his earnest expression, her anger dissipated. *Maybe we do love each other.* She stifled a sigh. "Okay, tell me more about it."

He slipped a hand into his pocket. "The university owns a piece of land that has been idle for a while. Sometimes, students use it for gathering. Now we plan to convert it into a park."

"Interesting. Sure. I'll go." She touched his cleft chin. "Come to pick me up on Sunday morning."

Accompanied by him, she visited the empty lot. They joined others to level the ground and plant flowers. The People's Park took its form.

Nice to have different activities in my daily routine.

Afterward, she strolled with Jonathan to the park every evening and ran into his friends, most of them student activists like him. Then one morning, he came to her with a glint in his eyes. "The school plans to shut down the park. We'll organize a protest."

On Thursday, students assembled near campus to talk about the Arab-Israeli conflict. Someone shouted, "Let's take the park." The purpose of the assembly took a dramatic change. They marched along Telegraph Avenue, chanting, "We want the park."

She and others soon came face-to-face with police officers assigned to guard the place. Her gang in thousands appeared to reign supreme, as they hurled bottles, bricks, and rocks. But the police force in full riot gear fought back. When tear gas canisters failed to disperse them, officers pumped bullets into the crowd. She bolted with Jonathan, scurrying for shelter.

After they reached safety, he plopped down on the ground, his eyes narrowed and lips tight. A muscle jerked in his jaw even as his skin mottled red. "They can't do this to us. It's wrong. We shall—"

"Forget it." She waved to stop him. "We're still alive. Not much we can do."

"Yes, we can."

When he ranted about his ideas, she rolled her eyes and trudged away. *I don't need this. It's stressful even to think about it.*

One week later, her work permit application came back— rejected. She could work only on campus or take an illegal job in Chinatown.

Defeat swept over her. How she hated San Francisco Chinatown! Since President Johnson signed a new immigration act to allow more Chinese to immigrate to the US, Chinatown had grown. Many of her friends loved to go there for dim sum. Every time she visited, she gaped at the dirty streets crowded with uneducated peasants.

Yet the sole job available to her was as a waitress in Chinatown. She wouldn't make enough to pay tuition. But what else could she do? Would she have to quit school?

When the summer vacation started, she moved to temporary housing for restaurant workers.

During a break, she stood in front of their bathroom mirror to put on her earrings. The phone rang. As she answered, Mary Anderson's gentle voice sounded. "Jonathan asked me for your new phone number. Shall I give it to him?"

"Please don't." Annoyance crept into her heart.

She hung up and made a last check of her appearance. *He's become such a bore.* On their last date, all night long, he rambled about helping organize another strike.

Tonight, the local Chinese businessmen were holding a banquet at her restaurant. The gratuity would be better but not quite sufficient. She drew a deep breath. Yeah, she had a long way to go to achieve her financial goals.

Inside the ballroom, she stood by the kitchen to scrutinize the crowd. As usual, many guests chattered at the mahjong tables in one corner to enjoy the game before dinner. Peering around the room, she couldn't spot anyone she knew apart from her coworkers.

Just as well...

The hair on her nape tingled.

Someone was watching her. She raised her head and met the gaze of a man leaning against the main entrance's doorframe.

In his early forties, he looked tanned, as if from a tropical place. A tailor-made gray suit hugged his tall, muscular body. He raised a hand to rub his clean-shaven chin, and a gigantic diamond sparkled on his middle finger.

Why did he look familiar? When she smiled, the corners of his mouth curled into an answering grin. He waved at the restaurant's owner, and Mr. Chung walked over.

Both kept glancing in her direction.

Ah, now she knew who he was.

She'd seen his picture in a recent article about the influx of capital into the Bay Area from the Far East. Because of Mainland China's unstable political environment, wealthy industrialists of Chinese descent in Malaysia, Indonesia, and Hong Kong diversified into the American market.

The Bay Area became one of the top choices for investors because California had a long history of attracting Asian immigrants. This brought powerful men into San Francisco. The report had shown four tycoons. The man staring at her was one of them.

At the recognition, she twirled the ends of her hair and wrapped tendrils around her fingers.

The banquet began, and she brought out the dishes. Whenever she set a plate on that man's table, his gaze shifted to her.

After dinner, the light dimmed, and the dance began. While she cleaned the tables, the man whirled around with different girls in his arms. Yet he smiled at her every time he moved in her direction.

He must dance often. *He's interested in me.*

She had an inkling something might happen and, sure enough, a call came through the next morning. The man identified himself as J. T. Poon. "We met last night. Sorry I didn't have a chance to introduce myself. Mr. Chung told me you're off today. Will you do me the honor of accompanying me to lunch?"

He took her to a seafood restaurant. As she feasted on the tender lobster meat, its unique flavor tickled her taste buds. *It's a joy to eat this from time to time.*

He retrieved a box from his pocket. "For you."

Inside lay a sheet of paper and a ring with a gleaming pigeon-blood-red stone surrounded by multiple accent diamonds. She unfolded the paper—a certificate depicting the eight-carat natural Burmese ruby. How much did it cost? Was it enough to pay her next semester's tuition? What was he up to?

"Do you like it? Try it on your middle finger." He spoke with a twinkle in his eye.

Should I? Or should I not? Her mind raced. She traced a fingertip over the halo of diamonds. *I'm damaged goods. Nothing to lose. I need the money.*

She slid it on, a perfect fit.

During their eleventh outing, JT gave her a diamond ring, and she agreed to live with him. Before her move, she verified that the flat was legally registered in her name. In addition, sufficient funds had been deposited into her bank account to cover her tuition and the cost of living for the next three years.

On the night she moved in, he took her out to a classy Italian restaurant. After returning home, she lingered in the living room with a terseness in her stomach, mentally preparing to go to bed with the man in front of her.

He's as old as Mama. But it was too late to back out.

JT sauntered over, his eyes gleaming, and presented a gold-embossed black box. "A gift to celebrate our new life together."

Her fingers trembled as she fumbled to open it. An 18-karat gold Cartier watch glistened against a black velvet cushion, shining as she tipped it to the light.

"Come here." He patted the place beside him on the new sofa. "Let me put it on for you. Hope it'll fit."

She hesitated, sank onto the stiff seat, and stretched out her left arm.

He removed the clunky watch from her wrist, paused at the sight of the scar, and then covered it with the new watch. "The length is just right."

"Thank you." She lowered her gaze. *Is it because of his dark skin or something else? I can't tell what he's thinking.*

He cradled her face and placed a soft kiss on her forehead. "Go to sleep early. You must be tired. Tomorrow is Sunday. I'll take you to a special place."

That night, she didn't sleep well. What had become of her? Was she doing the right thing? What would Mama say if she found out?

Mama wouldn't care. She loved only May-May. With a sigh, Ann-Ann drifted off.

A pleasant aroma awakened her. She walked into the kitchen. JT lounged at the table, clad in a blue robe, with two cups of coffee and a stack of freshly prepared pancakes.

He smiled. "Come eat. It's still hot."

While she chewed on a piece of fluffy flapjack, her eyes became misted. *No one has ever treated me so well. What kind of man is this?*

Later, they drove to a town in East Bay, near an area where a river merged into the sea. He parked and went around to open the door for her. "Have you searched for clams before?"

She shook her head and followed him to a beach. After removing his shoes, he dug his toes into the wet sand to show her. "Use your feet to explore the clams buried inside the sand."

When she found her first one, she couldn't help giggling. Soon, they had a whole bucket of harvest. He stooped to examine the littlenecks. "Let's go home. I'll make spaghetti with clams and garlic sauce."

Following dinner, they sat on the sofa to watch TV. She leaned on his shoulder. He lowered his mouth to meet hers. As their kiss deepened, she reached to unbuckle his belt.

He uttered a short laugh and moved her hand away. "No need to rush. We have time." He stood up. "Good night. Tomorrow is your first day of school."

When she ran into Jonathan on campus between classes, he grasped her by the shoulders. "Why don't you tell me your new phone number?"

Her stomach tightened, an ache stirring deep inside. "Jon, you and I are vastly different in so many ways. Our relationship won't last." She took a step away. "You're a nice guy. You'll find someone more suitable for you."

He shifted his legs, a hollowness in his eyes. "How about our love?"

What's love? She shrugged and left.

That evening, JT splurged on a steakhouse dinner for her. Back in her room, she changed into a pink silk robe and strolled over to knock on his door. He pulled her in as if expecting her. Her robe fell to the carpet to expose all of her. He rested his mouth on her nakedness, not missing any small parts. She moaned and pleaded, "Hurry. I can't stand it anymore."

Ignoring her plea, he took his time. Her body jerked, ready to explode. Just then, he gave her what she desired. Afterward, she lay in his arms and giggled. "I never knew it could be this good."

She called Mama two weeks later. "I found a better part-time job and have a new phone number."

"Ann-Ann, be careful. Don't..."

She pushed the receiver away from her ear and leaned against JT's chest. Without a doubt, a smart decision to live with him. No one had ever treasured her so much. Not even Mama. She only cared about May-May.

JT bought her surprising gifts all the time and converted their bedroom into a magical place for wild adventures. The age gap between them became an advantage. When she threw a tantrum over trivial matters, he simply chuckled. "Come here. Sit on my lap."

Her vision became blurred at his gentle words. *He makes me feel secure. I've never felt this way before.*

As they relished their soup in a French restaurant one evening, she divulged some of her innermost thoughts. "When I was nine or ten, I went with Mama to see my grandparents in Taiwan. An indelible part of that trip remains in my mind. Grandma ate my soup. I became upset and screamed at her. They kept saying the pot had more, but they had no idea how I felt. My soup vanished forever. An irreversible loss. I was afraid something would happen, something awful, impossible to mend or replace. My mama scolded me for being headstrong, obstinate."

"Yeah." His muscular hand covered hers. "Sometimes a trivial thing like a bowl of soup can trigger the hidden fear in us, the fear about the unpredictability of life."

"You understand how I felt?" She twisted her fingers to grasp his. He nodded.

Moisture gathered behind her eyelids. "My mother never bought me anything because we had to save money to send food to my nana and twin sister in China."

JT inclined his head. "You didn't know your nana and twin. They're strangers to you. Even though you can't see them, they're always present, like some phantoms who keep stealing from you. You have no way to fight back."

She dabbed her eyes, something akin to love cascading through her being. "You don't think me selfish? Whenever I complained to Mama about my nana and sister, she responded by saying I was selfish, unreasonable."

How odd. She didn't feel the need to hide her true self from him.

The next day, when he caught her peering at half-open apartments in their building and asked why, she shared how, since a child, she always felt something amiss. "I like to look into people's windows to see how they live their lives."

Still, she didn't tell him about her abortion.

And she couldn't tell anyone about him.

As she ran into Mary on campus, her former roommate pulled her to sit on the grass. "Jonathan said you two broke up."

"Yeah." Ann-Ann yanked up a dandelion.

"What happened?" Mary nudged her with an elbow, grinning. "You have a new boyfriend?"

Ann-Ann examined the weed. What could she tell her good friend? JT had a wife and two teenage sons? His conglomerate resulted from a merger between two large family firms? She hitched a silent sigh. No, she couldn't tell anyone about him.

"Is he a student here?"

"He isn't." She blew the fuzzy ball in one breath. "He's like my soulmate. He understands everything I share with him."

"Really?" Mary snagged a tuft of dandelion fluff as it drifted away. "It's not easy to find someone like that. You're so lucky."

Ann-Ann's spirit sank at the sight of the remaining seeds on the stem. *The legend may have its merits. Maybe JT doesn't love me as much as I love him.*

Months ago, she thought she'd learned to manipulate men. But no. *I'm the same foolish girl.* "I'd better leave. My boyfriend is waiting for me."

A week before Chinese New Year, JT held her tightly after they made love. "I'll return to Malaysia next Tuesday."

Her body stiffened, and she gave him her back.

"Come on, baby." He turned her around and placed small kisses on her cheeks. "You know I must go."

"Who cares?" She couldn't stop the frigidity in her tone. Not hearing a response from him, she sat up. "When will you come back?"

"According to my original plan, August..."

August! She attacked the bedsheet with a fist. "Six months from now? That long?"

"Shush." He drew her to lie down beside him. "I told you from the beginning. Once the subsidiary is established, I'll go back to Malaysia. The branch is doing well. I don't have much to do in San Fran anymore. Now, I only need to come here once or twice a year to audit."

"But I'm..." She couldn't finish her sentence.

"I appreciate what you're about to say." He heaved a sigh and traced the line of her cheek. "Love always complicates things. You surprise me. You're much more than I thought you were."

Her heart jolted, hope surging.

But he pressed a finger to her lips, silencing her and her fragile hope. "I can't get a divorce. My wife's family is too powerful. They'll destroy me."

No matter how much I need him, he isn't mine. Her eyes fogged, an internal void expanding, consuming her, devouring her. *Just like Mama. She belongs to May-May, not me.*

"Baby, don't cry." He wiped her tears away. "Tell you what. I'll arrange to get you a position at the subsidiary. They'll also sponsor you for the application of a green card. You're a finance major, aren't you? You can keep a watch on their numbers for me."

While she kept on crying, he sighed again. "I need to make a trip to Europe in late June. Isn't your school off at that time? Will you join me in London? I'll arrange to have you flown there."

"Europe? London?" She'd never been there before. Traveling around Europe with JT would be fun, wouldn't it?

"Yes, Europe, London. Now be a good girl. Let's have some sleep. I need to go to the office tomorrow."

Chapter Twenty-One

"Be faithful, even to the point of death, and I will give you the crown of life."

Revelation 2:10

At her new job, May-May ran into Song Mei-Hua almost every day. Youth flocked to the cadre area to mingle, and girls, including Mei-Hua, sought opportunities to linger in Ying Jie's office until he shooed them away.

Whenever they met, Mei-Hua praised Ying Jie. "He'll make a great model for my paintings." She removed her eyeglasses, revealing a pair of large, dreamy eyes. "Look at his tall, muscular body, his handsome face with a deep dimple on each cheek. He's a strange combination of masculinity and femininity. I guess he isn't of pure Chinese blood."

"Have you asked him?" May-May couldn't help giggling at the idea of Ying Jie as a model.

"I tried." Mei-Hua placed her glasses back on. "I told him I wanted to draw him on his black horse, but he declined."

As May-May recounted her conversation with Mei-Hua, Nana shook her head. "Don't go to Ying Jie's office. Don't ever be alone with any official or cadre." She let out a hard sigh. "The youngsters don't recognize the danger they're in."

Three weeks later, four carriages arrived with more teenagers from Beijing. Before the welcome meeting, May-May's jaw dropped at the sight of Qiao Chong, her former classmate.

Shuffling closer, Qiao Chong shoved his hands in his pockets. "I didn't know you were here."

She bobbed her head. "I came to this village not long ago. Why did you sign up? I thought you were doing well as one of the Red Guard leaders."

Qiao Chong didn't weep, but his misery appeared so great that his hands trembled and his lips turned white. "My father committed suicide following a denunciation meeting. He was hanging a picture of Chairman Mao in his office and dropped it. The image ripped apart. They labeled him an anti-revolutionist."

She slapped a palm on her mouth. "How terrible. I'm so sorry. Did they give you trouble?"

"Things like this happen often." His expression gloomy, he ducked his head and scuffed his feet across the scratchy cement floor. "I'm lucky. They didn't bother me."

Her arms relaxed a bit. "Do you have news about our classmates? Where are Chen Yao and Shao Hui?"

"They both left Beijing. Maybe they went *Chuanlian*—you know the revolutionary tours many Red Guards take."

She cleared her throat. "That can't be. The large-scale revolutionary tours ended two years ago."

"Yes, the large scale is over, but some Red Guards still travel around the country for fun."

Was that so? She hugged her shoulders, a sudden concern chilling her. "Is Chen Yao's pa well?"

Qiao Chong's face contorted. "He died. It's another terrible event in our neighborhood. He and five other people were arrested during a secret Christian gathering. A Red Guard hit Chen Kang's neck with a hammer and killed him."

She jerked up her gaze. Moisture clouded her vision, but she forced herself to remain calm. "Did it happen recently?" She blinked to subdue the dread weighing her down. "Was Yao present at the scene?"

"Not that long ago. I can't remember the exact time." Qiao Chong's jaw tightened. "Yao wasn't there. I believe Mrs. Dong, the elderly woman who lives in the same courtyard with them, asked permission to bury his body."

She wanted to ask more, yet the welcome meeting started.

In the evening, her pent-up tears broke free as she relayed the incident to Nana. "When I was alone in Beijing, Uncle Chen treated me like his own daughter. Why did this tragedy fall on a good Christian like him? How does Yao handle it? He must be crushed."

Nana's eyebrows furrowed into a deep frown. "I have no answers. I know you care deeply for them. We can only pray for Yao." She shook her head. "No wonder I haven't received any letters from Chen Kang. In his last one, he seemed to have a bad feeling about something."

She stepped away to find the letter, then waved it before May-May. "In this, he mentioned Yao was coming to see us. He asked us to tell Yao not to worry about him, no matter what. He'd already received words from the Lord. 'Be faithful, even to the point of death, and I will give you the crown of life.'"

The letter fell to the ground. Nana held her hands together, tears tracing along her wrinkled cheeks.

***

Yao shifted his gaze from the ground toward the sky. A black cloud gathered above him.

If they want to arrest me, will my arrival in Inner Mongolia threaten May-May's safety?

What if...?

Yes, he'd do it.

In the afternoon, instead of going north, he boarded a train toward the province of Guangdong in the south. A week later, equipped with information and maps of the nearby areas, he left the busy streets of Guangzhou at dusk to wait for the cover of night in a thicket near Pearl River.

He shut his eyes in a vain attempt to sleep.

Why didn't he spend more time with Pa in Beijing? Would it make a difference if he'd stayed?

In his mind's vision, Pa kneeled with others in the middle, surrounded by everyone from his community. Agony pulsed through his veins at a vivid image of blood spurting out of Pa's ruptured artery, caused by the crushing force of a Red Guard's hammer.

Pa, what a terrible way to end your life. Why am I left alone in this world?

And what about May-May? A gentle warmth swamped his heart. *I still have May-May. One day, I'll get her out of Inner Mongolia to be with me.*

He lifted his head. Amid the branches, the Milky Way with millions of stars blinked at him. Must be two or three in the morning. Time for action.

With a deep breath, he wrapped the jacket around his shoulders. Guided by the dim torch beam, he trod toward the trail he'd visited in the past few days.

"You, stop. Don't move." Commands came from nowhere.

Yao turned off his flashlight, reviewed a mental picture of his surroundings, and ran in darkness. Fallen leaves crunched underfoot. Sharp tree limbs cut through his exposed skin. The pain drove him to push harder. He lost track of time until a wave of weakness brought him down.

He perked up his ears. No sounds. No commands.

Safe! For the moment.

A rustle rose from behind him. A new vigor charged through him. He shot to his feet, and his jacket slipped from his shoulders. He flung away the light coat and didn't know how long he'd run until, overtaken by exhaustion, he dropped to the ground.

A gasp escaped his mouth as his hand's outline leaped into view. *Dawn is approaching. I can't wait any longer.*

But he'd lost his sense of direction. *Orient yourself.*

Just ahead of him perched a silhouette of a trail, indistinct yet certain. He grabbed a bush to steady himself and stood up. Placing one wobbly step in front of the other, he clawed his way forward.

He exhaled when the edge of the wood opened up. The riverbank spread before him. Only an empty field separated him from his target.

The guards patrol this area. Maybe I shall wait till tonight.

He hadn't eaten anything since lunch. His stomach rumbled as he reached into his pocket. "Oh no."

Idiot. Why did I cast off my jacket?

The sweet buns he'd stowed in his coat pockets were no more.

I can't go for one more day without food. His body wouldn't handle the long swim ahead then. He brought a palm to his forehead. *There's no choice.*

He left the haven of the thicket and sprinted toward the river.

"Hey, you, stop!" Shouts came from his right.

Gunshots roared. He bolted ahead. His foot pushed off the riverbank, and he hurtled himself into the water. A sharp pain ripped into his side.

He'd been hit

Chapter Twenty-Two

"His left arm is under my head and his right arm embraces me.
Daughters of Jerusalem, I charge you: Do not arouse or awaken love
until it so desires."

Song of Songs 8:3–4

Inner Mongolia, China
Spring 1969

May-May paced around the kitchen but couldn't block out the news
of Uncle Chen's death. *Yao, how do you manage this tragic loss?*
Are you well?

Nana went to Big Sister Liu's yurt to get onions and left her alone
to prepare lunch. Yao's question about whether God cared kept
intruding.

A hymn nudged her, and she sang out loud, "'Does Jesus care
when my heart is pained, too deeply for mirth and song?'"

At the approaching footsteps, she whirled around and came face-
to-face with Ying Jie.

"You..." Her courage failed her to ask if he'd heard her.

"Are you interested in learning how to handle a horse?" He spoke in his usual tone. "It may help if you need to get supplies from different yurts. I can coach you. I'll have time tomorrow morning."

Good. He hadn't seemed to notice her unease. She lowered her gaze. Why did he offer to teach her to ride?

"I..." She swallowed hard and forced out her response. "Thank you. I need to check with my nana."

He nodded and strolled away.

Upon her nana's return, May-May rushed over to tell her. "I'm worried he's heard my song."

Nana's eyes clouded. "I've been dreading this day. It's come."

"You think he'll..." May-May couldn't finish her sentence. A chill ran down her spine as she contemplated the frightful visuals in her head. Goosebumps prickled her skin. She couldn't help wrapping her arms around herself.

"Let's ask the Lord to protect you. Ying Jie seems disciplined in managing this village. I haven't heard of anything bad." Nana rubbed her eyes. "Maybe he sincerely wants to help. If he has other intentions, there's nothing we can do."

Still, May-May's heart thudded when she met Ying Jie by the stables the next day.

He introduced her to a brown horse with a white mane. "This mare is docile. She suits you well. Her name is Orange." For himself, he chose the black stallion he often rode.

May-May's lips curled up as Orange's warm breath huffed on her face, blowing her hair aside.

Jie guided them toward the edge of the prairie, then commanded, "Give me your hand."

At his word, she slapped a palm against her stomach, and her knees almost buckled.

Was there a way out?

Impossible.

She stood frozen.

"Don't worry." He spoke in a clipped, haughty tone. "I won't bite. Do you know how to get on a horse by yourself?"

I've misunderstood him. Her body relaxed a bit. She shook her head hard, heat creeping up her neck.

Jie assisted her to get on Orange and led her into the prairie.

The grassland's earthy scent wafted around them. Spring had arrived and awakened the field from winter hibernation. Among the vast green, patches of purple, red, violet, white, and yellow wildflowers danced across the field.

Then he crooned. "'Does Jesus care when I've tried and failed, to resist some temptation strong...'"

Her heart skipped a beat. She must have jolted because the mare skittered as well. "You know this song? Where did you learn it?"

A smile tugged at one corner of his mouth, his dimples deepening. "My mother taught me. Oddly, we never forget the things we've learned at a young age."

After they returned to the stable, he helped her get off Orange. "You'll feel muscle soreness tonight. It's normal. Tomorrow is Sunday. Let's skip the lesson and meet here again on Monday morning. You shall get better by then."

Back in the kitchen, Nana sat her down, concern dimming her normally bright eyes. "How did it go?"

"It went well. Ying Jie is a good teacher." May-May fidgeted in her chair. "He knows the hymn 'Does Jesus Care' and sang it to me."

"Really?" Nana sat by her. "Is he a Christian?"

"He didn't say. He only mentioned his mother used to teach him to sing hymns."

Nana hugged her. "I'm glad everything went well. Still, be vigilant."

May-May's heart sank as she clung to Nana. If he wanted to do something bad, how could she fight him off?

But Jie behaved like a true gentleman in their subsequent outings. As the lessons continued day after day, she grew better at handling Orange, albeit still not as skillful as Ying Jie.

Sometimes they got off their horses to walk around the grassland and chitchatted.

"I love Mongolia. Nothing compares to the serenity that comes with watching the sun fade away while the shepherd tends their sheep on the prairie." He directed his gaze toward the vast land. "The disappearance of the far, far horizon always mesmerizes me."

Initially, he did most of the talking, and she just listened and smiled.

"I was born in Beijing. My family stayed there during the war against the Japanese."

He told her his background, his thoughts on books he read, and his concerns about the village. She calculated he was roughly ten years her senior.

A few weeks later, she became bolder about speaking. "Are your parents still in Beijing?"

"Yes, my dad is." He stooped to pluck a red flower. "My mother passed away shortly after my fourteenth birthday."

"Oh, Ying Jie." She meant to express her sympathy but decided against it. "My papa died when I was a baby."

"Yeah." He took a step closer to her. "I also know your mother and twin sister live in Hong Kong."

She stretched her eyes wide.

He chuckled, revealing dimples in his cheeks. "Our government is aware of many things about each of us." He pulled a picture from his wallet. Inside stood a woman and a boy. "My mother and I."

May-May leaned over to look at it. "She's gorgeous, but she doesn't look Chinese."

"She's half Chinese, half Russian."

No wonder your eyes look so strangely beautiful. She wished to praise him yet couldn't say it out loud as heat flushed her cheeks. Sensing a need to respond, she asked, "Do you have siblings? What does your father do?"

"I'm an only child." He stowed the picture away. "My dad joined the Party in the thirties. He did well in the government until the Red Guards invaded Beijing. He's under house arrest like other officials. I'm sure he'll be fine. His contribution to the Party is too important."

After learning that he joined the Communist Party in his teens and graduated from Peking University, she couldn't help asking, "Why did you move to this remote place? Was it your choice? Or was it an assignment?"

"I applied for it. Since nobody else wanted to come, it was relatively easy." He resumed walking. "I'm happy with my decision. Look at all the turmoil in the big cities. I left before the Red Guards invaded Beijing. Otherwise, I don't know what would've happened to me."

"Yes, our village is peaceful." At a brisk neigh, she turned. Their horses followed them.

"Besides, one more advantage. Since our locale is so remote, I don't have to worry about my boss watching me all the time. I can do whatever I desire." He glanced at her.

The implication brought a shudder to her spine. She took a step back and trailed him in silence. When they reached the hilltop, he sat on the grass and motioned for her to join him. "Let's make a stop here."

She darted her eyes around the grassland and went to sit opposite him.

As if sensing her unease, he changed the topic. "You and your grandma passed by my office on Saturday. Where did you go?"

"Big Sister Liu invited us to her yurt to have tea." She picked a piece of grass to wrap around her finger, dread chilling her anew.

He moved to sit next to her. "Big Sister Liu dislikes city girls. She adores you, though. She mentioned you're different. Youth from Beijing often grumble nonstop. You work and never complain. You also help others with their tasks."

At his praise, she tipped her head away. Heat crept up from her neck to her face.

Oh, if only she didn't blush so easily.

Catching her off-guard, he cradled her onto the grass and planted his lips on hers. Fear flooded her whole being. Her body became rigid. She opened her eyes wide and shut her mouth.

He released her. "I have yet to force myself on any woman." Then he mounted his horse and galloped away.

She sat up. He and his black horse were already at a distance.

What had happened?

A tumult of feelings surged through her. As her gaze fell on the wildflowers, her voice cracked and rose to a loud lament.

She didn't know how she rode back. Everything around her seemed blurred. When she entered the kitchen, her puffy eyes must have caused deep concern, for Nana grasped her shoulders. "What happened?"

"Ying Jie... He..." May-May's muscles tensed even more under Nana's trembling hands. "He kissed me."

"Did he do anything else?"

She shook her head, and Nana let out a long breath.

Still shaking, May-May pulled out a chair to sit on. "I compressed my lips. He let go of me and said, 'I have yet to force myself on any woman.' Then he left me alone on the prairie. What did it mean?"

"He's a proud man. Obviously, he's never been turned down before." Smiling, Nana picked up May-May's hand. "He isn't what I thought. He's courting you."

Courting her? She lowered her head.

Nana lifted May-May's chin to stare into her eyes. "May-May, do you find him attractive?"

She tipped her face sideways to avoid Nana's intense gaze. "I don't know. He confuses me."

Nana dropped her arm. "In comparison, do you prefer Yao over Ying Jie?"

What a question! May-May rubbed shivers from her arms. "Yao is like a brother to me. I feel comfortable with him. Ying Jie makes me feel—"

"Yes?"

"I feel uneasy but excited." That was it. Hidden emotions started to break through. "I'm not sure why. I've never felt this way before."

She passed the day in a haze, then met Jie at the stable like before the next morning. They rode to the field together.

He slowed their pace, coming alongside her. "Have you read Jane Austen's books?"

Why did Jie act as if nothing happened? Grateful he didn't mention anything about yesterday, she touched Orange's mane. "Only *Pride and Prejudice* and just the Chinese translation."

"You ought to read the English version. Her wits are often lost in translation. I have all her novels. Will you be interested?"

She nodded. Later that day, she stepped into his office by herself for the first time to pick up *Emma*.

Autumn arrived. The weather turned cold, and their lessons ended.

Missing his company, she debated seeking him out.

After a few sleepless nights, she initiated a new routine of bringing snacks to his office in the afternoon.

Maybe noticing her changed behavior, Nana challenged her. "Don't you remember not to venture into the officials' area on your own? You're breaking our rules."

Heat burned her cheeks. "Our agreement shouldn't include Ying Jie. I was with him alone on the prairie during the past months."

"I think you have special feelings for him." Nana chuckled and wagged a finger at her.

May-May hid her face in her hands. Nana was right. Somehow, Jie filled her mind day in and day out, and memories of her previous years and her friends back in Beijing grew faint.

Then a letter from Old Zhang reached them. Nana broke the news to her. "Yao was killed in the Pearl River when he tried to flee from China."

May-May's body grew cold and hot by turns, moisture gathering behind her eyelids. She didn't go to Ying Jie's office that day.

As they began preparing potatoes and pickled cabbage the next morning, Nana spoke. "Ying Jie stopped by earlier. He asked me why you didn't make snacks for him yesterday. I told him about Yao, and he simply said to let you be."

A week passed in a foggy gloom. As the dull sun reached the other side of their room and stray rays of light illuminated the window, something in May-May's soul warmed again. *I've crossed a threshold. A door has closed.* She stared at the fading sunlight, tears rushing down her cheeks. *I can only move forward. There's no turning back.*

She wiped her face and lifted a prayer. "Lord, thank You for keeping me and Nana safe. I don't know about tomorrow, but I know You're with us here today."

Big Sister Liu stopped by on Saturday. She and Nana went out together for a long discussion.

After lunch, Nana sat May-May down. "Ying Jie has followed our Chinese tradition and implored Big Sister Liu to send his proposal of marriage. My darling girl, will you take this step?"

Heat rushed to May-May's face. She couldn't help lowering her head, yet she managed to answer clearly. "I do."

Nana let out an audible sigh. "I hope you're not marrying him because you know I'm always worried about your safety. Do you care for him?"

"I've considered many factors." May-May twisted her fingers together. "You want me to go to college. The reality is clear. We'll never leave Inner Mongolia. Jie is the best choice we have in the current circumstances."

"I've given my consent. We're not in a position to refuse."

When Nana sighed again, May-May lifted her gaze. "Will you be unhappy if I say I love him as much as I love you?"

A smile crinkled up Nana's face. "I believe the Lord has special blessings for you. With your temperament, you'll benefit from a husband who encourages you to venture out of your comfort zone. Jie is a natural-born leader. And he adores you. I only pray he'll soon accept Christ as his personal Savior. I'm so thankful. Now, we must prepare for your marriage."

Just like other couples in the area, May-May didn't expect to have a wedding ceremony. They simply completed the registration procedures. But Mei-Hua brought over a portrait of Jie and May-May together as a gift. "You're the envy of all of us. Lucky girl. You deserve it. You're always so kind and generous toward everyone."

The evening before her marriage, Nana pulled her aside to a corner in the kitchen. "I'm not worried about your domestic skills. The part I'm more concerned about is your duty in the bedroom."

Why did Nana hesitate? May-May's heart skipped a beat at an embarrassing situation. She feigned a smile. "What duty, Nana?"

"Remember the book of Song of Songs in the Bible? Many Chinese Christians avoid that book because they think sex is a dirty subject. It isn't." Nana brought a palm to her heart. "In Genesis, God created everything, including sex. The Bible said all His creation was good. We also learn from the New Testament that, in the metaphor of marriage, the union between a man and his wife symbolizes the permanent union between Christ and the church. It should be sacred and beautiful." Nana tapped her fingers on the wooden table. "Do you recall what the Bible says about Adam and Eve?"

Heat spread from May-May's cheeks to her ears. "'The man and his wife were both naked, and they felt no shame.'"

"Good." Nana gave her arm a gentle squeeze. "Within the covenant of marriage, sex is beautiful. Jie loves you very much. Let yourself go and love him back."

On the selected day, May-May moved her belongings into Jie's room and offered him an object. "This is from my mama's grandma. The only valuable thing we still have. I want you to have it now."

His large hand took hold of hers, and the warmth of his touch sparked a flaming sensation on her face.

"You..." He fixed his gaze on the jade pendant. When he spoke again, his tone was more gentle than usual. "We'll give it to our daughter in the future."

Because of Jie's special status, Big Sister Liu and the officials organized a dinner party for them. Following the feast, after Nana left with the other guests, May-May entered the unfamiliar spacious room, unsure of what to do next. Jie approached her from behind, hugging her.

"Are you tired?" He nuzzled into her hair.

She shook her head. A mixture of spicy soap and earthy grass, the scent of her husband, filled her nostrils. He turned her around and kissed her forehead. His lips glided down onto her nose and neck, then up to claim her mouth.

"May-May, my lovely bride," he murmured. "You have an alluring little mole on the end of your left eyebrow."

She nodded, a symphony of emotions in her heart—love, joy, excitement, and anticipation mingled with unease. She closed her eyes and let the moment wash over her like a tender melody.

He lifted her and laid her on their bed. His touch felt like a soft breeze as he unwrapped her garment. He spoke in a husky voice, "Your every curve is as smooth as a moonlit stream."

His fingers traced a path down to her core, setting off a cascade of delightful sensations that curled through her being. Her hands grasped the sheet, her moans a song unfamiliar yet pure.

He whispered, "Don't be alarmed if you experience some discomfort. A wondrous journey awaits us."

In that sacred joining, their souls intertwined, and the two became one flesh.

Chapter Twenty-Three

"What does love look like? It has the hands to help others. It has the feet to hasten to the poor and needy. It has eyes to see misery and want. It has the ears to hear the sighs and sorrows of men. That is what love looks like."

Saint Augustine (354–430)

A bullet hit Yao's left thigh. With its impact, he dived into the water.

Deep, deeper.

The water closed over him, embraced him. He opened his eyes. A mass of extended seaweed whipped around, stretching out its strange tentacles to crush him, choke him.

He kicked his legs hard to propel his body toward the glinting surface, away from the marine plant's death grip. His heart raced. His lungs threatened to burst.

Air. Please.

At last, his head emerged from the water.

He inhaled hard and fast, each puff bringing new energy.

Still too close to the shore. I must get farther away.

He took a deep breath and dived once more. After he surfaced again, the guards' shouts vanished.

Good. His wound hurt, yet he forced himself to swim.

A piece of wood bumped into him, and he grabbed it.

Night fell. He and the log floated together in utter blackness.

Something brushed against his arm. *Oh no.* With a free hand, he fished out the jade pendant necklace to whip the surrounding water. *It's useless. Please, let it not be sharks.*

When nothing bit him, he let out a breath of relief.

In the unsettling murkiness that swallowed everything, a feeble twinkle gleamed in the far distance. He let go of the log and swam toward the light. The water became shallower. His feet soon touched the bottom. Under the cover of darkness, he dragged his injured body forward. Soon he passed the riverbank. His body buckled down to the sandy beach, and he drifted off to sleep. When he stirred awake, golden rays from the morning sun rippled across the water's surface, beaming into his eyes. An almost electric jolt surged through him.

"I'm still alive," he blurted out. Yet... what was life for? Pa was dead.

"Meaningless! Senseless!" Unable to contain his tangled emotions, he stretched out his hands toward the sky. "Wrong, all wrong, awfully wrong."

He yelled until hoarse. Then his voice dropped to a whisper. "This water be my witness—I'll never set foot on that cursed land, ever."

Would he see May-May again?

A burst of warmth emerged in his heart.

Once he made enough money, he'd get her out of that horrid place.

The loud ringing of a bell jarred him. In the distance stood a white building with a cross. He pushed against the ground to stand up. Shuffling forward one foot at a time, he reached its door and passed out.

As muffled sounds echoed in the hollowness of his mind, Yao fluttered his eyelids. Shadowy figures shifted before him. A woman spoke in poor Mandarin. "You're awake."

He focused on the three concerned faces. The same woman said, "You bled a lot. How do you feel?"

He nodded. She tucked the blanket around him. "You're lucky we have a doctor here." She pointed to the man next to her. "Dr. Sun has removed the bullet from your leg."

Dr. Sun stepped closer to examine him. "Your wound is serious. The bullet injured a joint. I'm afraid you won't be able to recover fully. You may walk with a limp."

Yao opened his mouth, his voice fading to a soft murmur. "Where am I?"

"You're in Macau," the other man spoke. "You must have just escaped from the mainland. We call people like you freedom swimmers. What's your name?"

"Chen Yao." He struggled to sit up, but a sharp pain overwhelmed him.

"Don't move." The doctor patted Yao's arm. "Give it a few more days."

"Are you hungry? Let me get some porridge." The woman hurried away and returned with a bowl. After propping him up, she fed him one spoonful at a time.

Dr. Sun told him that the couple was Pastor Yang and his wife and they were at the parsonage.

Under their care, Yao soon grew strong enough to get up. Once his wound healed, Pastor Yang came to talk to him. "Macau isn't safe for you. You'll need to go to Hong Kong. The government there is more tolerant toward freedom swimmers."

Yao jerked up his head. "How do I get to Hong Kong?"

"Don't worry. This is familiar territory for us. I've already informed our contact. Someone will take you to Hong Kong tomorrow."

Moisture gathered behind his eyelids. He blinked and choked back his tears. "Pastor Yang, I don't know how to thank you. Mrs. Yang and you are extremely kind to me, even though I can never pay you back."

"You don't need to thank me. Our heavenly Father loves us so much. We have no way to ever repay Him for the blessings bestowed on us. We can only pay forward. It's an honor to serve Him in some small ways." Pastor Yang sat by him. "After you get to Hong Kong, you'll find a land full of opportunities for ambitious young men like you. Watch out for alluring traps that come with prosperity.

Sometimes a person can get lost in the shadiness of glorious riches. Do you mind if I say a prayer for you?"

Without waiting for an answer, he stood, placed a hand on Yao's head, and asked for God's protection over him.

That night, for the first time since his arrival in Macau, May-May and his pa entered his dream. The three of them went swimming. The river drifted slowly, lazily. They paddled their feet at leisure. When a school of fish passed by, the water accelerated. Turbulent currents swallowed up May-May and his pa. He tried to grab them. Yet within a blink of an eye, they were gone.

"No..." He awoke with the protest lingering on his lips.

***

Three months after May-May got married, Nana pulled her to a corner in the kitchen. "You look good. No, not only good. Your whole person radiates a lovely glow."

May-May shifted from one foot to the other, a burning flush spreading from her neck to her cheeks. "You can tell?"

"I've seen many young brides. The happy ones often beam." Nana patted her arm. "Jie treats you well in the bedroom?"

May-May touched her hot cheeks, pleasure mingling with her embarrassment. "He's very patient with me. It's just..."

"Yes?"

"He wants to do it every night, often more than once. Is it normal?" At the thought of their creative bedroom activities, heat crawled up to her ears.

Nana chuckled. "Do you like it?"

May-May nodded again.

"Ah." Eyes twinkling, Nana caught her close in a hug, then whispered in her ear. "As long as you both enjoy it, nothing is abnormal between a newly married couple."

Yeah. I'm a newlywed.

As May-May strolled away, she couldn't help but marvel at life's fluxes. Before leaving Beijing, she never thought about marriage. It hadn't even been two years. "Lord, thank You for Jie. I pray that Your amazing grace will soon touch his heart so he gets to know You as his personal Savior."

Back in their room, Jie was reading a battered old book. She walked over to take a peek. It was in a foreign language. "What are you reading?"

"Come sit by me." He motioned for her to come closer. "This is the Bible my mother gave me on my tenth birthday."

She flipped through the pages. "What language is it in? Is it in Russian?"

"Yes." He pulled her onto his lap.

"I didn't know you read Russian." She touched his face, tenderness swelling up in her chest.

He kissed her ear. "My mother taught me to read, write, and speak Russian."

May-May giggled. "You're tickling me."

Chuckling, he put her down on the floor. "Enough reading for today. The weather is warm. Will you go horse riding with me?"

Unlike before, she didn't ride Orange, but they rode the black stallion together. On the hilltop, they got off and sat on the grass.

Had it been a year since he first took her riding? Spring had arrived again. A profusion of wildflowers on the grassland unfurled their petals. He gathered her into his arms and brushed her cheek with his fingertips. She closed her eyes, relishing his touch, sucking in the scent of her husband. As the songs of prairie birds rang in her ears, her heart expanded with gentle sweetness.

A faint murmur of protest escaped her lips when Jie broke their embrace. He stood to pace, then came back to sit by her.

Smiling, she plucked a pink wildflower, its vibrant hue mirroring the buoyant joy inside of her. "What's bothering you?"

He raked through his hair. "During the past weeks, I went back to reread the Bible. The Old Testament is a compilation of various Jewish writings. I found it difficult to understand the connection between the different books."

She grasped his hand. "If you don't have a larger scope, it's easy to become disoriented. Nana taught me to keep one theme in mind while reading the Old Testament—the preparation for the coming of the Messiah."

"Why so?"

"The central theme of the Old Testament is consistent. God called Abraham from the beginning with one clear goal. In the future, all nations and people would receive God's blessings through Abraham's one offspring." She placed the flower in his palm.

He closed his fingers over it. "Different books also record other events, including the Jews' rebellion."

"Yes." She nodded. "Even so, the entire Old Testament, in essence, revolves around this important message. A descendant of Abraham will bring salvation to anyone who believes in Him."

"Hmm." He tucked the flower behind her ear. "I have to go back and read the Old Testament from this perspective."

She grinned and pulled him down on her. *Lord, thank You. Sharing my life with Jie is a dream come true.*

The next morning, May-May stepped into the kitchen, and a wave of nausea surged through her. After taking deep breaths and still not feeling better, she dashed for the sink.

Nana came over and rubbed her back. "Are you all right?"

Straightening her hunched-over stance, May-May shook her head.

As Nana examined her, her mouth crinkled up into an enormous smile, and tears shimmered in her eyes. She guided May-May toward a chair. "You're going to be a mother."

A baby is growing inside me? May-May sat, a sensation of elation engulfing her. "Don't worry. I feel better already."

Nana gave her hair a gentle touch. "This child will bring you and Jie even closer. The only thing left in my daily prayers for him is his salvation. By now, he must know we're Christians. Has he ever spoken to you about spiritual matters?"

"He's been reading his Bible. We even discussed the theme of the Old Testament." She grinned. "From time to time, he sings hymns to me. Last night, he sang me another hymn, 'Jesus Loves Me This I know.' He learned it from his mother."

Nana hugged her tight, pressing the warm words to May-May's ear. "Let's continue to pray for his soul."

***

The man who came to Macau for Yao wore a cap covering half of his face. He introduced himself as Brother Ma. Yao followed him into an old speedboat. Along the way across the open sea, anxiety, excitement, hope, and sorrow all mingled in his heart. *I'm determined to make a fortune in Hong Kong.*

Upon arrival, Brother Ma brought him to Kowloon. As the tall buildings towered over him, Yao's lips curled up. *I'll get May-May out of Inner Mongolia soon.*

After entering an apartment, Brother Ma pointed to a large woman with a kind face. "Yao, this is Mrs. Wong Kam-Chu. You can stay with her until you find a job."

"Welcome to Hong Kong," she spoke Mandarin with a heavy accent. "Oh, ignore Brother Ma. You can stay here as long as you want."

Brother Ma took leave, and she led Yao to his room. "Make yourself comfortable. I'll go cook dinner now."

He went to the bathroom to freshen up. On the way back, he passed a group of pictures on the wall and nearly tripped as one stopped him—a teenage girl with shoulder-length hair standing next to a woman.

He rushed to the kitchen, his voice trembling. "I recognized two faces on the wall."

Kam-Chu gave him a questioning glance. He drew her to the living room. "I know the girl and the woman in this photo. They're Lee Ann-Ann and her mother, Wang Leesan."

"How do you—" She clamped a hand over her mouth, then grabbed his arms and jostled him. "You're Chen Yao, the one May-May talked about all the time in her letters. Oh my. Why didn't it occur to me that this Chen Yao and that Chen Yao are the same person?"

Warmth crept into his core. "Auntie Kam-Chu, don't blame yourself too much. Chen Yao is a common name among the Chinese."

"Well, well." Her eyes sparkling, she rushed to the phone. "This is huge. I must call Leesan right away. She lives nearby and will come over in no time."

Twenty minutes later, Yao came face-to-face with a woman who seemed so familiar, yet was a stranger. Without hesitation, Leesan pulled him into her arms. "Yao, my May-May grew up with you. She mentioned you in every one of her letters."

After their emotions dissipated, Leesan grasped his hand and tugged him to the sofa. "Are they still in Beijing? What happened? How come they didn't write anymore?"

"Yao must be exhausted. He just came here from Macau this afternoon." Kam-Chu waved. "We have plenty of time. Let me get dinner ready. We can talk as we eat."

While eating, Leesan mentioned she lived alone. Ann-Ann had gone to California. He told them the latest information about May-May, her nana, and Uncle Duan. When he came to his own story, he broke off in mid-sentence at the mention of his father's murder. Moisture blurred his vision. Although anguish flooded him, he squelched his tears.

"Oh, poor child." Both aunties came to hug him.

He shook his head hard. "Thank you. I'm okay."

An eerie hush followed. Then Leesan broke the stillness and asked him about May-May's new address. He jotted it down and added, "Please don't send them letters. Mail from outside continues to be confiscated. They cause trouble for the recipients. It's been like this since the beginning of the current political turmoil."

"Tell me more about May-May." Leesan stood and sat back down.

"She's sweet and timid, maybe too timid." He described how May-May as a child got tormented at school.

The two aunties dabbed their eyes.

"But she's become strong and capable. In spite of the rigor of her work, like managing her kitchen, garden, and chickens, her manner remains genteel. She always speaks in her usual mellow tone that mirrors Lee Nana's. I dare say many people in our circle like her a lot."

Both aunties beamed.

The more he talked about May-May, the more energetic he became. "Her nana has taught her well. They're kind to everyone in our division. Every time they received supplies from you, they shared food with all the families in our courtyard. I believe one reason why Lee Nana didn't suffer too many abuses during her denunciation meetings was that people remembered her kindness."

"I almost forgot." He reached into his shirt to pull out an object—the jade ox pendant on a silk cord. "May-May gave this to me the night before she went to Inner Mongolia. She said I might see you first since I remained in Beijing."

"Whose pendant is this?" Leesan took it into her hand.

"May-May told me it belonged to Uncle Duan. Before he left for Yunnan, Lee Nana went to see him. He asked her to give it to you if there's a chance."

Tears trickled down Leesan's cheeks, and her fingers fisted over the pendant.

In the following days, he left Kam-Chu's apartment early every morning to look for potential employment. Pastor Yang was right. Wealth and opulence were visible all across Hong Kong. The booming economy propelled the construction industry into full gear. Everywhere, old buildings were being torn down. Newer, taller skyscrapers shot up like bamboo shoots.

Each night, Leesan came to talk to him more about May-May, Nana, and their lives in Beijing. One evening after dinner, she gave him an envelope. "From Kam-Chu and me."

Yao pulled it open to expose a wad of cash. "Oh, Auntie."

"Not much. Just a few hundred dollars. Go buy something nice for yourself." Kam-Chu gave his arm a gentle pat.

With money, Yao treated himself to a decent lunch. Next to the restaurant, at a site with a vast reclamation project to claim more land from the sea, he found a job as a construction worker, even though he walked with a slight limp.

On Sunday, Kam-Chu asked him to go to worship together. At the mention of the word *church*, his pa's death swept across his mind. Anguish pierced his heart, and he lowered his head. "New freedom swimmers are arriving soon. I plan to move out today. I've found a job and will start tomorrow." He gave her hand a shake. "Thank you so much for taking care of me. Here's my new address. I don't have a phone. Please tell Auntie Leesan for me."

Kam-Chu hugged him. "Take good care of yourself. Call us once you get a phone."

Chapter Twenty-Four

"Do not let your heart turn to her ways or stray into her paths. Many are the victims she has brought down."

Proverbs 7:25–26

Yao stretched his eyes wide at the chaotic scene. Bricks, timber frames, felt, metal sheets, stone, and concrete were stacked in scattered piles across the muddy field. He trod around an enormous cement cylinder to enter the makeshift office.

"Chen Yao?" Mr. Lam, the construction site supervisor, looked at his application form and then at him. "Do you have your ID with you?"

Should I lie? Yao's chest twinged. "I don't have one," He replied in Mandarin. "I just arrived in Hong Kong a week ago."

"I see." Mr. Lam nodded with obvious sympathy. "Do you understand what this project is about?"

Yao bobbed his head. "We're to create new land from the sea for the expansion of Kai-Tak Airport."

"Good." Mr. Lam put down the piece of paper. "I'll introduce you to Moi Fabian. He speaks better Mandarin than I do."

Yao exhaled his pent-up breath.

Fabian came and introduced Yao to his coworkers. Most of them were locals. They smiled and talked to him in Mandarin laced with a heavy accent.

During the lunch break, he didn't follow the others to the nearby restaurant but stayed in the break room to draw May-May in his notebook.

May-May, are you well? Have you any idea how much I long for you?

After Fabian returned, he peeked at Yao's drawings. "Wow, you're gifted. She's gorgeous. Is she your girlfriend?"

Yao grinned but didn't answer. He liked his new friend right away, partially because Fabian spoke Mandarin and partially because of his happy-go-lucky personality. When Yao asked why his Mandarin was so good, Fabian scratched his head. "I love Mandarin pop songs. Want me to sing you one?"

Without waiting for a reply, he crooned. "'Cannot forget, I cannot forget your care, I cannot forget your love...'"

Yao couldn't help but laugh at Fabian's offbeat style.

As their friendship deepened, Fabian often invited him to go horse racing and shopping.

Should he? Or should he not?

The amount of money in Yao's bank account brought no comfort, and he declined.

On this Saturday, Fabian treated him to dinner. "My mother's birthday is coming up. I must buy her a present. This time, you ought to come with me. I need your advice. I bought her a kitchen knife last year, and she scolded me nonstop for an entire week. Maybe you know better what a woman wants." He chuckled. "Don't you have a girlfriend back in China? Show me her portraits again."

Fabian took the pocket notebook, then flipped through the pages. "She's lovely. Have you kissed her?"

At the thought of the one time he placed his lips on May-May's forehead, a tender warmth swelled Yao's heart, and his mouth quirked into a grin.

"Ah, you have. What else have you done with her?"

While he remained quiet, Fabian poked him in the chest. "Don't be shy. You've gone all the way with her, right?"

"Ouch." Yao feigned a look of pain. No. Fabian wouldn't understand his special relationship with May-May. He loved her too much to do anything against her beliefs.

After supper, they strolled to an area in Mongkok. Yao's jaw slackened at the hawkers everywhere. The street became a narrow passage only wide enough for a single file of people. The vendors offered anything and everything from clothes to food like fish balls on a skewer.

As they reached the other end of the alley, he surveyed the numerous carts. "How do those folks get their supplies?"

"No clue." Fabian bit into a fish ball. "Why do you ask?"

"I'm curious." Yao couldn't take his gaze away from the phenomenal sight. "I've been thinking about how to make more money in the evening. This looks promising."

"You have too much energy." Fabian tossed aside the bamboo stick. "Usually, I'm dead tired after a day's work. All I can think of at night is to visit Meow-Meow or play mahjong." He gave Yao a wink at the mention of Meow-Meow, a cheap nightclub in Mongkok.

When Yao didn't reply, Fabian threw a teasing punch at his shoulder. "Guess why I idolize you? You're the opposite of me— the kind of person I wish I were." His tone turned serious. "I know somebody in our housing complex who operates a cart in this area. If you're interested, I'll introduce you to her."

The next day, Fabian took him to the government-owned residential complex in Tung Tau Tsuen. He waved. "Wait here. I'll go fetch Susie."

Yao scanned the two-room unit, envy intruding. Like most young people in Hong Kong, Fabian couldn't afford his own place and lived with his parents and a sister.

Since the influx of refugees from the mainland, Hong Kong's population grew from about six hundred thousand to more than two million in a mere few years. Although the government tried to alleviate the housing shortage by providing homes for low-income residents, it was far from adequate. After Yao moved out of Kam-Chu's flat, he could only afford a cot that offered barely enough space for him to lie down. The sole separation between his bunk and the next was a pile of old newspapers.

Fabian returned with a tall girl. A pair of large eyes gleamed from her heart-shaped face. "This is Han Susie, the prettiest girl in our neighborhood."

The two of them spoke in rapid Cantonese, glancing at Yao from time to time. Then Fabian slapped his back. "Susie will let you help her tonight. Come at three thirty. She leaves at four to set up her cart before five."

That night, Yao stood behind mounds of cheap women's clothes, learning to be a street vendor. With his new friend's help, he operated a cart in the same area within a month, selling scarves, blouses, and skirts to a constant stream of people who ambled through the narrow passage.

Susie also introduced him to her brother, Han Shawn, a giant bulging with muscles. Shawn shook a finger at him. "Are you aware of the different triad forces in Mongkok? Vendors and minibuses must pay monthly protection fees. Since you're Susie's friend, I'll take you under my wing."

"Oh, thank you so much." Yao grinned.

Through the Han siblings, he became acquainted with several suppliers. One of them was Mr. Kong, a mainlander who came to Hong Kong in 1950.

Mr. Kong treated him like his own son. "We're one of the lucky few. We sold our property early and brought gold bars to Hong Kong. Otherwise, we wouldn't have the money to set up our factory here." He retrieved a picture portraying Mongkok's busy streets. "Look at all the carts. They sell the same stuff, garments that fail inspection or have gone out of fashion. The competition is fierce."

Such valuable information! Yao leaned forward. "What happens to the good clothes in fashion?"

Mr. Kong pointed to a beautiful dress on the wall. "Most of the factories either own their own designs or make designer clothes under contract for export. Factories that sell the garments locally have their stores. If someone can come up with distinct designs for us suppliers to make cheaply, that person will make a fortune."

Determination tautening his muscles, Yao pressed his lips together. He went to the local library to collect fashion ideas from European countries and later showed his drawings to Mr. Kong.

Mr. Kong flipped through the pages. "You amaze me. I never thought a young man of your age could be so capable." He draped an arm over Yao's shoulders, jostling him. "You probably already know how to conduct business. As an example, to ensure I make clothes solely for you, you need to sign an exclusivity contract with me."

Yao blinked, his chest swelling. "Mr. Kong, you're so kind."

"My only child is in the States. You're like my son here." Mr. Kong pulled out two chairs for them. "Apart from operating your cart, will you come to my factory to help out? Can we add one additional clause in our agreement to allow me to sell the outfits you design in my store?"

"Of course." Yao's jaw dropped at the news. "I must terminate my contract at the construction site. Is it okay if I work part-time? Maybe three to four hours a day?"

Under Mr. Kong's guidance, Yao sold the newest fashion at the cheapest possible price, and his business picked up. He saved enough money to buy a studio apartment. After moving in, he called Auntie Leesan.

Her gentle voice floated into his ears. "Kam-Chu and I usually dine together at least once a week. Will you come to dinner with us this Wednesday?"

"Sorry. I can't." He told her about his new business. "I have to work every night."

"I suppose you young people don't want to hang out with ancient folks like us," Leesan said. "Take good care of yourself. Don't work too hard."

An image of May-May floated into his mind. He would love to have dinner with Leesan to talk about his dream girl. But he needed to make more money to get May-May out of China.

Later in the evening, Susie stopped by his cart. "Tell me where you get your garments."

"From Mr. Kong." As anxiety tightened his chest, he shifted his stance. "But they're my design. I have an agreement with him. He can't give them to others."

"This is beautiful." She held up a pink blouse. "You need to make an exception for me. Remember who helped you set up your cart and who protects you from other gangs? It's payback time."

Ignoring him when he scowled at her, she grabbed a scarf to wrap around her neck.

He let out a hard breath. "Okay. I'll give you part of my supplies if you sign an agreement with me. You must promise not to give any of them to others."

After she left, Pastor Yang's words about payback and pay-forward intruded Yao's thoughts. Was there a difference between Christians and non-Christians?

I ought to spend time with Auntie Leesan and Kam-Chu.

He invited the two aunties to lunch the next week. "Auntie Leesan, have you received any news from May-May?"

A shade dimmed Leesan's eyes. "No, not at all. The situation in China isn't improving."

"Leesan and I pray for them often." Kam-Chu set down her chopsticks. "Let's set this aside for now. Yao, give us an update on what you have been up to."

After he showed them his notebook with various design sketches, Leesan patted his arm. "You're gifted. I have no doubt you'll become very successful."

"Success may bring happiness but also misery." Kam-Chu gave him a meaningful gaze. "Yao, you ought to set aside time to attend worship."

The mention of spiritual matters brought a shudder to his body. He stifled a sigh at the grievous memory of Pa's death. "Sunday isn't convenient because we open our cart earlier. Maybe when I have more time, I'll go to church."

Before they parted, Auntie Leesan asked, "Should I send May-May a letter?"

He shook his head. "Don't do it. You'll cause them trouble. Wait until the political situation eases in China."

The days rolled on. As his birthday loomed closer, loneliness weighed on him. *Maybe I ought to buy something for myself.* He checked his bank account and let out a low whistle. Not bad, but still insufficient. *After May-May joins me, we can celebrate together.*

On his birthday, Fabian stopped by. "Since you moved on from the construction site, we don't hang out together like we used to. Today is your special day. Why don't we close your cart early tonight? I'll give you a treat."

Yao grinned, basking in the warmth of friendship. "You don't have to work tomorrow?"

"Nope, I'm off." Fabian gave him an answering chuckle.

At two o'clock in the morning, they stowed his cart away. Fabian tugged at his sleeve. "Let's go eat dumplings."

Many shops around Mongkok opened all night. Most of the late diners were people like him who had to work in the wee hours.

Fabian halted at a dingy little restaurant. "This place is famous for dumplings."

The food came. Yao sampled it and had to agree it was excellent.

One corner of Fabian's mouth crooked up. "I'm glad you like it. Are you done? Let's go to the Concubine. My treat."

A plethora of considerations overwhelmed Yao. *Does Fabian know I've never been with a woman?* Should he go? Was everyone doing it?

They strolled to a nearby nightclub. Yao slowed down. "I thought you favored Meow-Meow."

"This one is even better." Fabian guided him to the door.

Yao's steps faltered. "I–I—" He bit his lip, heat spreading to his cheeks.

Fabian chuckled and slapped his back. "You've never been to a clubhouse before? Don't worry. It's straightforward." He pointed toward the woman at the counter. "You pay her, and she'll give you a key with a number on it. Enter your room. A girl is waiting for you to do whatever you want with her."

"Do..." Yao's voice wavered. "Do we get to choose?"

"You have to pay extra. I usually don't care who she is."

Yao entered and found a woman perching on the edge of the only bed inside the room. She wore heavy makeup and a see-through robe. He couldn't even guess how old she was.

The woman walked up to him without a word. She stripped off his clothes and ran her hands up and down his nakedness. With a pounding heart, he followed her to bed. As he shut his eyes, May-May's face flashed across his mind. He lost his virginity.

On the way back to his apartment, he could barely breathe past the competing ideas racing through his head. *What have I done? If May-May finds out, what will she say?*

A tight lump lodged in his throat. He swallowed hard and murmured, "No, May-May won't know."

It'll be okay. A man needs to sow his wild oats before marriage.

Six days later, he followed Fabian to the Concubine again. This time, Yao paid for himself. After that, they met almost every week and set off to different nightclubs in Mongkok.

One Saturday, Fabian called, "I won't make it tonight. Why don't you go by yourself?"

At two a.m., Yao locked up his cart and went to Meow-Meow alone.

Chapter Twenty-Five

"Success is not final, failure is not fatal: it is the courage to continue that counts."

Winston Churchill (1874–1965)

Hong Kong
Spring 1969

As Yao entered the factory, Mr. Kong stopped him at the door. "I'm leaving Hong Kong. My son's application for us to go to the States got through."

Yao gaped at Mr. Kong, his chest tightening. "How about your factory?"

"We plan to shut it down."

"But—"

"I'm sorry." Mr. Kong waved. "Maybe you can line up with other suppliers. Your designs are so clever. You'll do well, no matter whom you go with."

Yao rubbed his temples but couldn't push away the thought pulsing there. "Is it possible for me to take over your factory?"

A distressing silence stretched across the room. Yao waited, his ribcage constricting further. Then Mr. Kong spoke, "Right. Why didn't I think of it?" He strolled to his desk to go through a pile of paper. "I've already approached several people to sell my setup to them. Will you have money to purchase my equipment?"

Yao's heart sank. He didn't have the money.

"Don't be discouraged." Mr. Kong dropped the paper back in place. "Tell you what. I'll introduce you to a banker. You have such an outstanding track record. No doubt he'll give you a loan."

After their deal went through, Yao huffed out a rush of breath. To show his appreciation, on the night before Mr. Kong's departure, Yao invited him and his wife to a Korean restaurant for dinner.

Mrs. Kong picked up a piece of ginseng chicken from the clay pot. "I often told my husband to extend his business beyond Hong Kong. He said he didn't need to work so hard because of his age. You're young. You shall try to expand. I heard you're proficient in English. I suggest you also learn Japanese. The Japanese market isn't much smaller than the US."

Such a brilliant idea! Yao nodded, a jolt of energy coursing through his veins. Heeding her advice, he hired a Japanese private tutor and added yet another activity to his already hectic lifestyle.

On a sunny morning, as he finished crunching the numbers for the week at his factory, Susie stopped by. Her jaw slackened at all his newest designs. "You should give up your cart in Mongkok and focus on designing new fashions for me. Have I told you? My sales have tripled since you furnished me with your goods."

Sweet. But for her alone? Why not involve other hawkers?

Following Susie's suggestion, he sold his cart to another vendor and took up the mantle as the primary distributor of the women's apparel heaped on the street carts. He ensured everyone signed an agreement with him.

A three-bedroom flat in his apartment building came up for sale, and he grabbed it.

The Mid-Autumn Festival arrived. He held a party in his new home with Kam-Chu and Leesan as his only guests. After he told them about his business development, Auntie Kam-Chu wagged a finger at him. "You're moving at light speed. Beware of the success trap. Don't let it lead you down the path of spiritual blindness."

Yao kept his silence. *After May-May joins me, I'll go to church with her.*

"If May-May knew you're doing so well, she would be very happy for you." Leesan gave out a long breath. "Too bad the situation in China remains bleak. We still can't exchange letters."

While he served them steamed crabs, he stilled at an idea. "I have vacancies in my company. Do you know any young people in your church who may be interested?"

The two aunties looked at each other, and Kam-Chu spoke. "Our church has job-seeking college graduates who are accountable and mature. I'll introduce them to you."

He turned to Leesan. "Your parents live in Taiwan, right? I plan to source materials of better quality to make clothes for boutiques. Do you think they can help?"

She nodded. "I'll write to my father for you."

Auntie Leesan acted fast. In less than two months, Yao imported fabrics from Taiwan for his company to make and export high-quality garments to Japan and the United States.

Nice, but I need to diversify. Real estate seemed an achievable investment project.

As usual, Fabian stopped by his flat one Saturday. "Wow, look at all the high-end furniture. You're truly a big boss. Let's try a luxurious clubhouse in Tsim Sha Tsui tonight."

In the hallway, Yao couldn't help asking, "Do you plan to be a construction worker all your life?"

Fabian gave him a sharp glance. "What's wrong with being a construction worker all my life, Big Boss?"

"Sorry. I didn't mean to intrude on your privacy." Yao patted his friend's arm. "Seriously, what will you do once you can't work at the construction site anymore?"

"I have no clue." Fabian scratched his head. "When the right thing comes along, I'm sure I'll recognize it."

"How about coming to work for me?" Yao eyed his friend, his heartbeat escalating. "I need someone to coordinate between my factory and the vendors. The new hires, all college graduates, have no clue how to deal with hawkers."

Fabian halted. "I know myself well. The coordination job is too monotonous. I can't do it. But Susie would be an outstanding candidate."

"Excellent idea." Yao grinned. "With her brother's connections, it's perfect for her."

After Yao welcomed Susie into his clothing business, he discussed his interest in real estate with Fabian. "The recent riots have scared a lot of people away. Many believe China will liberate Hong Kong soon. Housing prices have been falling. I plan to buy an old flat. Maybe you can assemble a team to renovate it for me?"

Fabian clapped. "Ah, this is definitely my thing. I'll call my friends today. We can start anytime you want."

Through Fabian's efforts, Yao racked up twenty old flats in Kowloon to revamp. He sold some and kept those with good locations as rentals.

One Friday morning, he dialed Fabian's phone number, excitement pulsing through his body. "Yesterday, you mentioned the Dat-Fu Building in Waterloo is for sale. Do you know who owns it?"

"Are you serious? You want to buy the entire building?"

Yao smiled. "Why not?"

"Okay. I'll ask around. But Dat-Fu is quite run-down. The building has been neglected for many years. The renovation will cost a lot of money."

He straightened his shoulders, his chest swelling. "Dat-Fu's location is great. We can take care of the rest."

While he added Dat-Fu to his assets, Fabian warned him. "I'm concerned about your debt. You took out a hefty mortgage for the purchase."

"Don't worry. It'll be all right." Yao gave his friend's arm a firm squeeze. "Trust my judgment. Once the work is done, it'll have forty units. The rental income can cover the mortgage and provide a steady stream of profits."

Two weeks after Yao signed the deal, his phone buzzed when he affixed a new Chinese painting to the wall in his apartment.

"Mr. Chen Yao? My name is Alan Chiu. I'm an attorney based in Vancouver, Canada. I represent Mr. Ed Kwong."

"I'm sorry." He pinned the receiver between his shoulder and his ear while adjusting the crooked painting. "I don't know any Mr. Ed Kwong. You must have dialed the wrong number."

Perfect. Yao stepped back to admire the delicate blossoms depicted on the canvas.

"Mr. Chen, Ed Kwong is Mr. C. P. Kwong's son. I'm sure you know Mr. C. P. Kwong. You recently bought Dat-Fu from him."

Yao's mouth went dry. His hands and feet grew cold.

"Mr. C. P. Kwong passed away last week. My client has a mortgage note in his possession. According to the contract, he's obligated to give you ninety days' notice. We wanted to notify you with a courtesy call first. My law firm will send you an official letter...."

The rest of the attorney's words became blurred in Yao's mind. After the call, he reviewed Dat-Fu's sales contract, then plopped down onto the sofa and stayed in the same position for a long while.

Outside the window, the subtropical sun shone, casting geometric patterns on the street. An image of the riverbank in Macau from times ago floated into his mind. He'd vowed to make money to bring May-May out of China. Wasn't he on the brink of realizing his dream? But now...

He stood up and dialed Fabian's number. "I'm doomed. There's no way out."

"What happened?"

"A certain Ed Kwong holds a lien on Dat-Fu." Yao relayed the news, apprehension throbbing in his gut. "He's Mr. C. P. Kwong's son."

"Is it legit?"

He heaved a hard breath. "I've scrutinized the contract. The lawyer is correct. If I don't pay, Ed Kwong has the right to seize the property. I'm still responsible for the mortgage I took out."

"Can you get another loan?"

"I don't think so. I've borrowed to the maximum." He tapped his foot on the floor, a chaotic storm of feelings leaving him woozy. "I should have been more careful. Greed has blinded me. I'm doomed."

"Yao, take courage. It can't be that bad."

"Nasty, extremely brutal." He sat back down and slapped the sofa arm, trying to release his pent-up emotions.

"Did you say you have ninety days?"

He blinked. "Useless. I can't borrow that amount of money within ninety days."

"No, you can't." Fabian went silent, then let out a whistle. "You may be able to fix Dat-Fu in time for a quick sale."

"What do you..." Whoa! Yao jerked upright in his seat. "Excellent idea. It's not in my original plan, but I have no choice. How many people do we need? Can we start today?"

"I'll take care of it."

Fabian assembled seventy-three workers in one day. They worked around the clock. By the end of the third week, Yao couldn't believe the gorgeous structure was the same Dat-Fu he'd bought.

"We did it." He high-fived Fabian. "Now all I need is a buyer who will pay me top dollar for it."

Dat-Fu's prime location did its magic. Yao sold the building within a month. After he signed the papers, he took his friend to a French restaurant. "Order the most expensive item on the menu. You deserve it."

Fabian grinned. "You made a decent profit. What's next? I'm ready for whatever you have in mind."

"Okay. Come to work for me." Yao shook his friend's hand.

Fabian proved good at what he did. They bought old buildings throughout Hong Kong Island, Kowloon, and the New Territories for flipping.

At a dinner to celebrate another big sale, Yao ordered three lobsters for the two of them. "The tide is turning. With the interest of Western countries in the Orient, Hong Kong is now an important meeting point between the East and the West. We must get into the hotel industry."

"Big Boss." Fabian raised a hand to his right temple and saluted. "Whatever you say, I'll do."

***

Hong Kong
Summer 1970

Leesan glanced at her watch. *I'd better hurry. Kam-Chu is waiting.*

As she entered the dim sum restaurant, Kam-Chu greeted her with a question. "Have you got hold of Ann-Ann?"

"She called this morning and told me she was in Europe." Leesan squinted, then huffed to loosen the tightness in her chest. "How did she get enough money to go to London?"

"Maybe she went with other college kids. Many students travel around Europe with backpacks. It doesn't cost much." Kam-Chu handed her the menu. "How about May-May? Any news from her?"

"Still nothing about May-May." As Leesan's chest further constricted, she heaved a deep sigh. "With each passing day, Ann-Ann seems to grow more distant. I should go see her."

Kam-Chu patted her arm. "Tell you what. I've always wanted to visit the States. Let's go together."

Three weeks later, they arrived in San Francisco. Ann-Ann had booked their hotel and set up a guided tour to Yellowstone National Park. The three of them enjoyed a fantastic time.

Leesan breathed out her relief. "Ann-Ann looks happy with her new life in California."

"There's so much to do and see here." Kam-Chu nodded. "Let's come again next summer."

The next year turned out differently. At the airport, her girl's short hairdo prompted Leesan to blurt out, "How come you cut your hair?"

A muscle in Ann-Ann's jaw twitched. She didn't respond but took them to the hotel where they had stayed before.

"Why can't we stay in your apartment? That way, we can save money." Irked by her daughter's attitude, Leesan threw her purse on the bed.

Ann-Ann rolled her eyes. "Mama, didn't you ask the same question last year? I have the same answer for you. My roommate would object."

Kam-Chu flipped through the travel magazine on the desk. "Will we join a tour?"

"I've signed you up to visit the Canadian Rockies. I can't go, though." Ann-Ann's expression softened. "I have to work."

A tour guide came to the hotel to pick them up the following morning. Leesan settled in her seat on the bus and slapped her thigh. "We came all the way from Hong Kong to see her. How could she give us this terrible treatment?"

"Maybe she's busy." Kam-Chu patted her hand. "It's useless to get angry. I heard Canada's national parks are gorgeous. Let's put away our troubles and have some fun."

The tour bus traveled for hours. Kam-Chu took out a bag of sunflower seeds to share. "Years ago, when Yao gave you the jade ox pendant from Liang Duan, I saw tears in your eyes. What was on your mind back then?"

Her friend's unexpected question brought heat to her cheeks, leaving Leesan tongue-tied.

Kam-Chu nudged her. "It looks like you have a special feeling for him."

Leesan grabbed a handful of sunflower seeds to hide her blush. "Liang Duan's parents passed away when he was a baby. His grandmother brought him up and gave him the jade pendant." She cracked open a seed. "Yes, I understand the meaning of his gesture, although I never suspected anything before receiving the gift. I suppose he considered it improper to express an interest in me. After all, I was his best friend's wife."

"He's a decent gentleman. An indecent man would have taken advantage of you at your most vulnerable moment."

Did Kam-Chu think of Danny? Leesan let out a soft breath. "I don't want to think much about it. We're at different places in our lives. Duan isn't a Christian. I won't consider marriage again unless a suitable Christian man comes along. As we've discussed, even great sex fades into a boring routine. Life is full of turmoil. If a couple doesn't have the same values based on a commitment toward a larger purpose beyond self, the two will drift apart, especially amid difficulties."

"I agree." Kam-Chu sighed. "That's why a marriage needs to have a solid foundation based on the Christian faith. Too bad you and Brother Hsieh didn't work out. You put Ann-Ann's happiness above your own. Now she's all grown up. Brother Hsieh has married someone else."

"I'm happy for him. Otherwise, with Ann-Ann's constant interference, I can't imagine how miserable our life would become." Leesan cracked open another seed. "Looking back, I don't think Brother Hsieh and I were compatible. Yes, we're both Christians, but that's not enough. Our love for each other was too shallow. That's why it fell apart when challenges arose."

When she lapsed into silence again, Kam-Chu looked into her eyes. "If Duan becomes a Christian and comes to Hong Kong, he'd be an ideal match for you. It's not easy to find another man who loves you as much as he does."

Leesan didn't respond, and they talked no more about Liang Duan during the rest of their trip.

Back in the Bay Area, Ann-Ann took one week off to accompany them to some nearby tourist attractions. After a pleasant time together, as they waited for their flight at the San Francisco airport, Ann-Ann surprised her by asking, "Have you received news from May-May and Nana?"

A weight pressed down on Leesan's whole body. "No, not at all." Moisture blurred her vision. "Haven't I told you about Chen Yao, the boy who grew up with May-May? He said May-May and Nana went to a remote area in Inner Mongolia. He warned me not to write because letters from outside often cause trouble for the recipients. That's the last piece of information I have about them."

While tears stung Leesan's cheeks, Ann-Ann gave her a stern glance. "Mama, here you go again. You always care more about her."

"Ann-Ann." Leesan gasped. "How could you say that? May-May is your sister. We have no idea how she is now. She might even be..." Choked with emotions, her voice broke off before she could say the word *dead*.

"I know! May-May needs this. She needs that. She'll benefit from—" Ann-Ann shouted with fire flashing in her gaze, her breath fast and shallow. "Since I was a child, you've been saying the same thing. I'm sick and tired of your May-May. Fine, if you want to track her down, stay in Hong Kong. Don't bother to come to see me anymore. I'm living a good life here."

Leesan's shoulders slumped. She'd failed both daughters miserably. She waited for Ann-Ann to stop her tantrum and forced herself to speak in a calm tone. "I spent lots of money and time to come all the way to see you. If that's not love, what's it? I love you very much."

A scowl slashed across Ann-Ann's face. She stomped her foot. "Maybe so. But you love her even more. All your tears are for her. Don't come to California next summer. I'll be busy with my job." She ran out of the airport.

On the plane, Leesan kept weeping. Kam-Chu gave her arm a gentle pat. "Ann-Ann has concealed resentment in her heart. She let it all out today. When you talk to her in the future, be more careful. Don't let her think you favor her sister."

The cabin lights dimmed. After Kam-Chu dozed off, Leesan's mind drifted toward the past years. As she aged, men no longer paid her attention. She didn't care. Her life fell into a routine of writing, church, friends, and visiting Yao.

Her lips twisted upwards into a semi-smile at the thought of Yao. At least he was doing well.

Before they left for San Francisco, he'd told her he was in the process of buying a house at Mid-Levels on the Hong Kong Island side. "Auntie Leesan, I'll invite you and Auntie Kam-Chu to my new house later. If you hear anything from May-May, please call me right away."

I need to get in touch with May-May and find a way to get her out of China. She sighed and drifted off to sleep.

Following a lengthy plane ride and a disheartening journey, the familiarity of the homely routine brought Leesan solace. Upon the arrival of the Mid-Autumn Festival, she and Kam-Chu hailed a taxi to Yao's mansion. While the car turned into Bowen Road overlooking Victoria Harbour, Leesan couldn't help thinking of her first trip to this area with Danny. *Such a long time ago. Kam-Chu said his oldest son is in college.*

Yao awaited them by the gate.

As they stepped into the foyer, Kam-Chu's eyes opened wide. "Wow, this place is gorgeous. How many bedrooms do you have?"

Yao grinned. "Only three. In this area, this house is considered quite modest."

Leesan nodded. When she'd visited Mr. Tang, his mansion with a private road looked like a castle. "It's already very nice. But I know what you mean. Sometimes I'm shocked by how rich people live their lives here."

Yao led them to sit at the table underneath the magnificent chandelier, and a servant placed a crab on each of their plates. "For sure, we need to have steamed crabs at this time of the year."

He leaned back in his chair. "Recently, I set up a holding company, Chang-Ji, to manage my business."

Leesan flashed a smile. "With your hotels, rentals, factories, exports, and boutiques, you do need a holding company. Chang-Ji signifies a lasting foundation, an awe-inspiring name."

"We watched you realize the Hong Kong dream in a few years." Kam-Chu pointed a finger at him. "Watch out. Money often drives people further away from God."

Yao didn't respond and pulled his crab apart. "Auntie Leesan, how is Ann-Ann doing?"

"She's doing well, just very busy." She didn't want to talk about her unpleasant experience in California.

"Ah, yes, every one of us is busy." He tilted his head to the side. "Have you heard anything from May-May?"

She lowered her eyes. "Still nothing. I heeded your advice and didn't send her letters."

Yao let out a long breath. "I hope the situation in China improves soon."

"Yes," Kam-Chu interjected. "We pray for Su-Ann and May-May every day. God willing, things may turn around in a blink."

Chapter Twenty-Six

"Unless I go away, the Counselor will not come to you... When he comes, he will convict the world of guilt in regard to sin and righteousness and judgment."

John 16:7–8

Inner Mongolia, China
Spring 1970

As May-May contemplated the baby within her, elation surged through her being. When she met Jie in their room, she wrapped her arms around his neck and whispered, "I threw up this morning. Nana said I'm pregnant. Don't be concerned. I felt better right away and have been feeling well all day."

He took one step back to stroke her belly, beaming with a special brightness in his eyes. "Our boy is right here. I can't wait to take him horseback riding with us."

"Why are you so sure it's a *he*?" She giggled.

He gave out a loud, hearty laugh. "Okay. I can't wait to take her horseback riding." Then his tone lowered. "Will you consider using a midwife? If you want to go to the hospital in the nearby city, we'll need to send in our request today or tomorrow."

"Nana also talked to me about it." She tilted back her head with confidence. "Since I'm young and strong, she believes I shall do well with a midwife."

He pulled her closer and, in a slow descent, kissed her lips down to her neck.

She leaned against his chest, anticipation mingled with a trace of anxiety. "Does this pose a risk to the fetus? Maybe we shouldn't do it anymore."

He licked her below her ear. "I'm sure the baby will be fine. If you're worried..."

She didn't answer and unbuttoned his shirt. Afterward, she lay in his arms, a content smile spreading across her face. "Jie, I love you very much."

"I love you too. Last night in my dream, I told my mother about you." His fingers brushed her bare shoulder. "I haven't dreamed of her for a long time. Somehow, she came to take me to a beautiful place and told me she lived there."

May-May caressed his face in silence, tenderness flooding her heart.

He glanced at her. "Do you believe in ghosts?"

She sat up from him and flashed an affectionate grin. "I do believe in spiritual beings. The Bible teaches about them. But the belief in our folk religion that dead people turn into ghosts may not have any merit."

He also sat up. "What do you mean?"

"Nana mentioned my papa, an atheist, experienced great distress involving ghosts and dead people when he got seriously ill. After he received Christ as his Savior on his deathbed, the evil spirits stopped bothering him." A chill crept up her spine. She snuggled closer to him, taking solace in his comforting embrace. "Satan and many evil spirits under him exist in the spiritual realm. They have the ability to appear as our deceased relatives to disturb us. By the power of the Holy Spirit, we can rebuff them."

Jie drew her to lie down. "Who's the Holy Spirit? How does He work?"

She'd often discussed the Trinity with Nana. Still... "It's difficult to describe my interaction with Him. How do you tell someone the taste of a special drink if the person has never tried it? I can just tell you the outcome. In the presence of the Holy Spirit, we still have peace, even at the darkest moment in our lives."

She shared how she suffered the ordeal, the fear, and the hopelessness from the nonstop political campaigns. Tears trickled down her cheeks. "But even during those difficult moments, the Holy Spirit's assuring presence never left me."

"Oh, May-May, my darling." Jie gathered her into his arms once more.

"I'm fine." She forced a smile. "You also asked me about the work of the Holy Spirit?"

He nodded.

Is the Almighty Spirit working on Jie? She wiped her face with the back of her hand. "The most important work of the Holy Spirit is to let us recognize our sins. I regard myself as a good person. But when the Holy Spirit enters my heart, I begin to see all the darkness within me."

"Maybe it's a form of autosuggestion?"

"No." She shook her head. "In autosuggestion, we try to tap into our strength to become more confident. The work of the Holy Spirit is the opposite. He points out sins hidden in us. And all Christians share the same experience."

"Isn't it bad to acknowledge I'm a sinner? Most of us would rather believe we're good people."

"You raise a great question." She drew her brows together. *Lord, please give me Your wisdom.*

Jie touched her forehead. "Even frowning, you're adorable."

"Wait. I got it." She grasped his arm. "Whenever I refuse to confess my sins, I get stuck in a self-seeking, sinful state, which blocks me from receiving God's grace. Once I admit I'm a sinner, my soul opens up to receive Jesus Christ and His wonderful salvation. I'm born again. Self-centeredness becomes Christ-centeredness. I start to view and love others from the Lord's perspective."

"Wow, what a deep discussion between husband and wife." He chuckled. "Come. Let's go to sleep. I'm exhausted."

A trace of disappointment crept into May-May's heart. *Lord, will Jie get to know You soon?*

The next two months blended into a cycle of blissful moments and captivating conversations between Jie and her. On this night, May-May grimaced at her reflection in their bedroom mirror. "My belly has grown so much."

Jie kissed her ear from behind. "What are you looking at? Come. It's time for our evening chitchat."

Her lips curled into a smile. *Jie still desires me every night.* "Don't you think I'm fat and ugly?"

"By no means." He let out a throaty laugh. "You're more attractive every day. I'm utterly bewitched."

He pulled her to sit on his lap, his tone turning serious. "When I applied to join the Party in high school, I studied the Party constitution carefully. I felt I was well qualified. After rereading the New Testament, I don't think I deserve to be a Christian."

May-May brushed her fingertips across her darling's cheek. "What makes you say so?"

"I guess you've already known from our first night together. Unlike you, I'm not..."

She dipped her head to kiss him.

"I always strive to be a disciplined guy. Still, if lovely girls threw themselves at me, I..."

"Shush." She touched his lips with a finger. "Say no more of your past. Think of the robber who was crucified with Jesus and consider Mary Magdalene, who was probably a prostitute before following Jesus. They were saved. The Bible tells us everyone has sinned. By God's grace, we're justified freely because of Jesus."

Jie nuzzled her neck. "I'm sure you haven't sinned."

"You would be shocked if you could see what's on my mind." Her touch lingered on his jaw. "Nana told me many times that due to my temperament, I may not sin by commission, but I often sin by omission."

"What does that mean?" He ran his fingers through her hair and lightly down her face.

She gave his shoulder a gentle rub. "I may not do things that displease God. I often don't do things that please Him, which is equally bad. We've all sinned against God because we're self-centered. Salvation is free. You don't need to pre-qualify to receive it."

His eyes became moist.

Gasping, she stood up to gather him into her bosom.

He spoke again, his voice choked. "As far as I can remember, my dad never spoke a word of encouragement to me. He let me think he would love me only if I brought him honor. All my life, I've been trying to make him proud. Since my mother died, before I met you and Nana, I didn't think true love existed. I thought there's always a hidden agenda, a string attached."

"Jie, I love you very much." She placed her lips on his forehead.

He regained his composure. "I'd never dreamed I would find a girl like you who loves me for who I am. When I first laid my eyes on you, your beauty intrigued me. But despite my position and"— he hesitated—"good looks, you just wanted to stay away from me. You became a challenge, and I made a plan to seduce you. One step was to move you from the yurt to my area. Soon I found myself conquered by your goodness. For the first time in my life, I was hopelessly in love." He raised his gaze to her. "Even then, you didn't want to have anything to do with me. What made you change?"

She shook her head. "I don't know. It came upon me slowly."

"Remember that I tried to kiss you on the prairie? You stiffened and became like a piece of wood."

"I was terrified." Heat flushed her cheeks. "We heard so many horrid stories about how officials take advantage of young girls under their supervision. I feared you would do something bad."

"Yeah, it's unfortunate. Indeed, many terrible things happened." He sighed. "Did you think better of me after I let you go?"

"You rode away and left me alone on the prairie. I cried for a long while. It was my first kiss."

"So, maybe my strategy worked." He laughed with mist in his eyes.

She couldn't help hugging him tight, an intense tenderness engulfing her.

He leaned into her arms. "May-May, you pray every night. Can I join you tonight?"

They held hands and poured out their hearts before God. *Lord, thank you for answering my prayers.* Now she and Jie truly became one—body, mind, and soul.

As soon as Jie left for his office in the morning, she hurried to the kitchen to share the news with her nana.

With tears in her eyes, Nana grinned. "You're blessed. Seldom has a woman felt what you experienced last night."

Four months after Jie accepted Christ as his personal Savior, May-May gave birth to a healthy baby boy. As Nana had predicted, it was an easy delivery. She held her son in her bosom, joy and love flooding her soul. "Jie, even now I can tell he'll grow up like you, with wavy black hair and beautiful eyes."

Her beloved husband brushed a finger over the baby's soft cheek. "He'll be as kindhearted as his mother."

At Jie's request, Nana named her great-grandson Nian-Rong—in remembrance of Rong.

A year later, May-May gave birth to a second son. This time, Nana named him Si-Rong, also as a tribute to Rong.

Chapter Twenty-Seven

"One day Naomi her mother-in-law said to her, 'My daughter, should I not try to find a home for you, where you will be well provided for?'"

Ruth 3:1

Hong Kong
Spring 1973

When the situation in China improved following President Nixon's visit, Leesan received a letter from May-May, the first since 1966.

She told Yao right away. Because of the time zone difference, she called Ann-Ann in the evening. "I've finally got in touch with May-May. She's married with two little boys. Their family and Nana are coming to Hong Kong, although I don't know the exact date yet. Her husband will start his graduate study at the University of Hong Kong in the fall. You ought to come home this summer."

"I don't want to go back to Hong Kong. My memories there are too painful."

Her chest constricting, Leesan drew her eyebrows together. "Ann-Ann, you've not seen your twin sister for almost twenty years."

"May-May, May-May, it's always May-May. Mama, when are you going to put me first?"

"Ann-Ann." As she stifled the urge to scream, to shout out that she left China with her, not May-May, she dug her nails into her cheek, then pulled in a long, heavy breath. "You graduate in May, right? Auntie Kam-Chu said she'd go to California with me to attend your graduation ceremony. How about we join a tour afterward and then return to Hong Kong together?"

A strained silence descended. At last, Ann-Ann broke it. "Okay, just for one month. I've already lined up a job. I'll start on August sixth."

***

Inner Mongolia, China
Spring 1973

On the day May-May noticed a tooth in her second son's mouth, Jie received a letter from Beijing. Her father-in-law had been restored to his original position.

Jie's eyes sparkled. "May-May, my dad urges me to return to Beijing. He wants to see you and his two grandsons. What do you think?"

She nestled Si-Rong into his crib. "Let's seek God's guidance. I'll also ask Nana to pray for it."

Yet they remained in Inner Mongolia because of Nana's advice. The timing wasn't right, and they ought to wait until the political outlook became clearer.

Then, Jie received another letter from his father, informing them that the Ministry of Foreign Affairs planned to dispatch students with a college degree to foreign universities for graduate studies. He asked whether Jie might be interested in going to the University of Hong Kong.

"Hong Kong? I'll finally see my mama and Ann-Ann. I haven't had contact with them since I was in high school." May-May perked up but shook her head right away. "I can't leave Nana here all by herself. It won't do."

"The political situation seems to ease. Since US President Nixon's visit last year, we've normalized our relations with many countries and sent out students to a few places." Jie gave her cheek a gentle peck. "Dad has the power to make special arrangements. Let's pray with Nana to seek God's guidance."

This time, her nana urged them to leave. "Soon, the two boys will need to attend school. You shall take this opportunity to go to Hong Kong regardless of me. My journey in this world is coming to an end, anyway."

May-May rushed over to hold Nana's hand. "Oh, please don't say that."

"Let's pray you can go with us." Jie smiled. "Through my dad's connections, I feel hopeful. We can send a letter to your mama right away."

Their application went through. In the spring of 1973, May-May met her father-in-law for the first time. Her chest warmed as the weighty, serious soldier doted on his two grandsons like any ordinary grandfather.

Jie chuckled. "I never knew this side of my dad."

Two weeks after they arrived in Beijing, her nana shared the gospel with General Ying and led him to the Lord. At Nana's request, they prayed together.

Afterward, Jie stepped forward to hug his father. "Dad, I love you very much."

At the sight of tears welling up in her father-in-law's eyes, May-May couldn't help but cup a hand on her mouth, her heart swelling.

They stayed in Beijing until early summer and left China for Hong Kong. On the train, she lifted a silent prayer. "Lord, great is Your faithfulness. I once thought Nana and I would never get out of Inner Mongolia. Now we're on our way to Hong Kong. Oh, Lord, I can't wait to meet Mama and Ann-Ann face-to-face."

***

Hong Kong
Spring 1973

On Chinese New Year's Eve, Yao switched on the TV. The news anchor replayed a snippet from President Nixon's visit to China last year and commented that China was opening up to outsiders.

He grinned, elation sweetening his heart. *Soon I can get May-May out to Hong Kong.*

Then, his thoughts shifted toward his recent health issue. *Not sure why I experience pain during urination.*

Two months later, he noticed an abnormal greenish-yellow discharge and visited a doctor. Shocked to the core, he sprang from his chair after the doctor disclosed he'd contracted multiple sexually transmitted diseases.

May-May's image haunted him. Would he pass the disease to her once they were married? He chewed the inside of his cheek. Why didn't he think of this terrible outcome before?

The doctor looked at him with sympathy. "Antibiotics will take care of the bacteria, but we still can't treat the virus."

Back at home, he clutched a bottle of whisky and holed up in his bedroom for the weekend, drinking to numb himself. Still, the relentless nausea in his stomach clung to him like a foul odor.

As he poured more liquor into his glass, the phone rang.

"Yao!" Auntie Leesan gushed on the other end. "I've received a letter from May-May!"

"I'll be right over." He dropped his glass and rushed to her apartment. On her coffee table lay a picture of three adults and two boys.

"I can't believe it. She's married with children. Look at her smile. She must be happy." Leesan waved in excitement. "Her husband is so handsome. My mother-in-law looks good too."

Yao gaped at the picture. The bottom fell out of his world. A drape of blackness covered him as if someone had snuffed out the only flickering flame in his heart.

The aunties didn't seem to notice his silence. Kam-Chu tapped the table. "They're coming to Hong Kong soon. May-May's husband will be a graduate student at the University of Hong Kong in the fall."

Auntie Leesan beamed. "Most likely, they'll come in the summer. I'm waiting to confirm their arrival date. Yao, will you go to Kowloon Station with us?"

"I–I have a business trip. I won't be here." He gritted his teeth and stared at his feet. "I'm sorry. I need to go now."

As soon as the door clicked behind him, he leaned against the wall next to the elevator, tears wetting his cheeks. He hadn't cried since he learned about his pa's death.

Don't be ridiculous. What do you expect?

He shook his head hard.

You have other women. Why can't she marry another man? Look at yourself. Even if she were still single, what could you offer her beyond money?

In the evening, he didn't fall asleep until three in the morning. The same dream visited him. May-May and he swam in the clear stream. They splashed water on each other, playing, giggling. His father appeared with an anguished expression. Pa shouted at them in an attempt to convey something, yet he couldn't hear a word. As he watched, a wave hit May-May. In an instant, she was gone.

"May-May." He woke up and shivered. *At least I don't need to worry about infecting her with herpes.*

***

Hong Kong
Summer 1973

At Kowloon Station, much to the relief of people waiting, the train pulled into the shed.

Leesan craned her neck for the appearance of Su-Ann, May-May, and her family. "I'm so blessed, so happy."

Her mouth crinkled up into a broad smile over the arrangements she'd made for her daughter's family. Since Jie's dorm wouldn't be available until late August, her best friend had offered the spare room in her apartment for May-May and her family.

"Here they are." Leesan rushed toward a young woman holding a toddler. "Oh, May-May, Si-Rong." She gathered her daughter and grandson into her bosom.

May-May's eyes shimmered. "Mama."

Uncle Su-Nong and his wife, Shu-Fang, stepped forward, their faces also full of tears. "Su-Ann."

Her mother-in-law covered her mouth. Leesan couldn't help moving over to embrace her. "Mother."

May-May clutched Ann-Ann's hand. "You're more beautiful than your pictures." She reached to pull forward the man behind her. "This is Jie, my husband."

Leesan strode over to hug him and the boy in his arms. "Jie, Nian-Rong."

Si-Rong touched May-May's hair with his finger. "Mommy." He pointed at Ann-Ann and called again, "Mommy."

Following his brother, Nian-Rong scrunched his nose. "Daddy, why is there another Mommy?"

The adults burst out laughing.

Leesan dabbed her cheeks with a handkerchief. *Tears mingle with laughter. What a precious moment.*

"No." Jie patted Nian-Rong's head. "She's Auntie Ann-Ann. She looks like Mommy, doesn't she?"

Kam-Chu stepped up and spoke in a loud voice. "Okay, we'd better leave. We're blocking people's way here. Let's go to my flat. My place is the largest."

They ambled out of the station to the busy street. May-May twined her arm with Leesan's. "Mama, a while back you mentioned in your letters that Yao lives in Hong Kong. Nana and I were so delighted to learn he was alive! I thought he would come today. Is he not in town?"

Leesan hugged her daughter, struggling to believe this wasn't another dream to be awakened from. "He's in California. He travels a lot for his business."

A woman by the road was selling magnolia flowers. As the sweet fragrance drifted into Leesan's nostrils, she yelled with joy in her heart, "Taxi!"

Back at Kam-Chu's flat, Leesan asked Su-Nong, "Uncle, are Ming-Ming and Tong-Tong coming over for dinner?"

Su-Nong shook his head. "I told them not to come since Kam-Chu's flat is too cramped for so many people."

While everyone was busy chatting, Kam-Chu stood up. "I'd better start cooking."

May-May raised her gaze. "Auntie Kam-Chu, please let me do it tonight. I've wanted to cook for my mama for a long time."

Kam-Chu waved. "But you've just arrived."

"Let her do it." Jie grinned. "She's been wanting to cook for Mama since the day we decided to move to Hong Kong."

Leesan watched her daughter cook, pride buoying her. With ingredients Kam-Chu had prepared earlier, May-May whipped up dishes worthy of a banquet. She steamed fish with thinly shredded green onion plus young ginger and cooked shrimp with garlic, rice wine, together with lots of tender basil. Fried chicken and pork chops were juicy inside and crispy outside. Even stir-fried snow peas were scrumptious.

"Jie, you're a lucky man." Uncle Su-Nong reached for another piece of fried chicken.

"Yeah." Jie wrapped his arm around May-May's shoulder. "I'm truly blessed. Marrying her is the best decision I've ever made."

"Ann-Ann, you ought to learn from May-May—" Oops. Leesan shut up as Ann-Ann's grin faded.

May-May set down her chopsticks. "Mama, unlike me, Ann-Ann is a college graduate. The only thing I'm good at is cooking."

At May-May's words, Ann-Ann smiled again.

Leesan couldn't resist taking May-May's hand into hers. "Maybe it's too early to ask. Have you considered going back to school?"

Kam-Chu chimed in. "The Hong Kong government is in the process of implementing the Touch Base Policy. Anyone who applies to the Registry can stay legally." She described the details. "You ought to look into it. Once you obtain your legal residency status, you can get more benefits. The local economy is still booming, with lots of opportunities. Look at your old friend Yao. In a short period, he went from a freedom swimmer to a successful big boss."

"I don't know yet." May-May glanced at Jie. He inclined his head slightly, and her eyes sparkled. "Mama, I will if the opportunity arises."

After dinner, Leesan took Su-Ann to her flat. Ann-Ann went straight to her room, leaving them alone in the living room.

"You're still so young and beautiful. Time seems not to affect you." Su-Ann patted Leesan's arm.

She touched her forehead. "See my wrinkles? I'm no longer young."

"In my eyes, you still look youthful." Su-Ann chuckled. "May-May mentioned she gave Yao an ox jade pendant to pass on to you. Did you receive it?"

"I did." Her cheeks burning, Leesan reached into her blouse to pull out the pendant.

"It's Duan's gift from his grandma. He was born in the Year of the Ox." Su-Ann cleared her throat. "You must have guessed its meaning."

"I–I..." Tongue-tied, Leesan ducked her head and fidgeted. "We wrote to each other regularly until I lost all communications with the mainland. His letters were always about you and May-May and sometimes about the situation in China. When Yao gave me Duan's pendant, I got its meaning right away."

"I dared not mention it in my letters for fear of causing Duan trouble. He accepted Christ and is a dear brother in God's family." Su-Ann described her conversation with him. "He loves you very much."

"Oh, Mother." Leesan brought a hand to her eyes, unsteady with the different emotions stirring her.

Su-Ann tapped the table. "I think he remains in Yunnan. Didn't Kam-Chu say the Touch Base Policy may go into effect soon? Jie's father is quite powerful. He probably can get Duan out of China to Hong Kong."

Leesan stood and sat back down, unsure of what was going through her mind. "Mother, do you pretend to be Naomi to marry off her daughter-in-law?"

"What's wrong with that?" Her mother-in-law laughed. "Let's go to bed. I'm exhausted."

Leesan led her to the bedroom they would share until Ann-Ann returned to San Francisco. But who could sleep tonight? She remained still, listening to the soft breathing beside her. At last, May-May's gentle smile and beautiful sons eased her somnolence.

Before the sun rose, the bed moved, and her mother-in-law padded from the room. Smiling, Leesan also rose and tip-toed into the kitchen so as not to disturb Su-Ann, who kneeled by the living room window.

During breakfast, Leesan commented, "Mother, you're still doing your No B No B every day."

"Yes, No Bible No Breakfast." Su-Ann dipped her head. "And you? I heard you reading in the kitchen."

"I'm following in your footsteps." Leesan curled up her lips. "Let's finish breakfast. Kam-Chu is waiting for us."

Ann-Ann rolled her eyes and said she had to run some errands and wouldn't go with them.

Too happy an occasion to get upset over trivial matters, Leesan stifled a sigh to subdue her annoyance and strolled with Su-Ann to

Kam-Chu's apartment. As they entered the living room, May-May and Jie pulled her aside.

"Nana told us about Uncle Duan. Somehow, I've never associated the ox pendant with..." May-May's voice trailed off, and her cheeks flared with crimson. "Uncle Duan was so kind to us. Nana often said that, if not because of him, our situation would be much worse during the numerous campaigns. Mama, I'm so happy for you." She winked at her husband. "It's all up to you. Please ask Dad to find Uncle Duan as soon as possible."

Jie flashed a tender smile. "My dear wife, your wish is my command."

When Leesan entered the kitchen, Kam-Chu moved over and whispered, "Your son-in-law is an accomplished young man. May-May mentioned he speaks Mandarin, English, and Russian."

"He certainly is quite capable. More importantly, he's kind to May-May and the boys."

Kam-Chu leaned toward her. "I've never seen a couple so in love. Last night, they held family worship in their room. I heard them sing 'All the Way My Savior Leads Me,' she in Mandarin and he in English. They also recited Bible verses and prayed together."

"It's wonderful, isn't it?" Her chest warming, Leesan pressed a palm to her heart. "They not only adore each other but also share the same faith and values."

"A beautiful sight to behold." Kam-Chu hugged her. "Su-Ann did an excellent job with May-May. She's so gentle and sweet and takes no pride in her appearance or ability."

"My mother-in-law taught May-May always to look to the Lord for guidance in whatever she does. I'm so relieved. After all the turmoil, May-May found true happiness." Leesan scratched her cheek. "I just wish Ann-Ann will be as blessed."

"Have you spoken to Ann-Ann about marriage?"

"She became angry and shouted, 'Mama, not this again. I've said it repeatedly. You'll be the first to know if I find someone.'" Leesan sighed. "I often asked myself what I did wrong with Ann-Ann. Since she was a child, I've tried to teach her biblical principles. They're identical twins, yet their lives have taken such divergent paths."

Kam-Chu reassured her with a gentle pat. "Their temperaments are distinct and so are their surroundings. A prosperous environment has its many traps, sometimes even more treacherous than persecution. You've tried your best. If there's any omission, it's not just by you, but by the entire church. We fail to alert our youngsters to be vigilant against the deceptions in this world. Her first boyfriend was a playboy. Before him, Ann-Ann had never been deliberately deceived. The abortion left a permanent mark on her soul. By God's mercy, the Lord may heal her one day."

Leesan let out a long breath. "At least she goes to Sunday worship."

"Yeah. I remember she often skipped worship while in Hong Kong. I wonder what propelled her change. We can only pray for her." Kam-Chu cast her an uncertain glance. "Su-Ann mentioned Liang Duan accepted Christ as his Savior a few years ago. Back when we talked about him, you didn't want to think about it too much because he wasn't a brother in Christ. Now that concern seems no longer valid."

"Yes." Leesan shifted her feet. "I told you we were at different places in our lives."

"I often say a happy marriage is that the husband and wife are in harmony in body, mind, and soul. I'm so glad to witness this kind of relationship between Jie and May-May. You and Duan..." Kam-Chu waved and brought up a different subject. "Before Duan left Beijing, he must have fallen into despair at the thought of never seeing you again. He took the best step he could think of at that time."

"My mother-in-law also said so." Leesan forced a tentative smile.

"If the Cultural Revolution had any merit, this might be it. He wouldn't have expressed his love for you if not because of his being sent down to Yunnan." Kam-Chu slipped her arm around Leesan's waist. "Do you have a way to get in touch with him again?"

"Jie's father may be able to help." With heat rushing to her cheeks again, she described her earlier conversation with Jie and May-May.

Kam-Chu laughed. "Wow, I hear wedding bells ringing already."

Chapter Twenty-Eight

"If anyone thinks he is Christian and yet is indifferent toward his being a Christian, then he really is not one at all."

Søren Kierkegaard (1813–1855)

Bay Area, California
December 1973

Ann-Ann followed her colleagues into the banquet hall. A seven-foot-tall pine tree decorated with beautiful Christmas ornaments gave the illusion the hotel ballroom had shrunken. Food, drinks, and presents burdened the table in a corner.

"Hi." Susan, a coworker, stopped next to her. "Did you see those gifts? They're all expensive stuff. Mr. Chen Yao will draw for us later."

A wisp of hair fell into Ann-Ann's face. She brushed it aside. "Yeah, someone said there's a Chanel bag."

Susan tilted her head back. "I suppose it's your first time meeting Mr. Chen tonight? Didn't you come in August?"

"You're right." Ann-Ann smoothed down her blue silk dress. "You joined when the subsidiary started?"

Susan nodded. "I met Mr. Chen in May. I was shocked to learn he's not yet thirty. And he didn't even graduate from high school." She lowered her voice. "Who cares? He's single, the most eligible bachelor in my acquaintance."

"I heard he's lame." Ann-Ann touched her newly permed curls.

"Oh, that." With a wave, Susan chuckled. "He's lame because he got shot by a gangster in one of his fortune-hunting adventures. It didn't slow him down a bit. He's a rising star in the Bay Area's Chinese community."

Susan's comments brought back a conversation between JT and Ann-Ann. She could still hear him mentioning that one of his friends planned to start a subsidiary in the Bay Area. He even asked if she'd be interested as if that should appease her. She'd pursed her lips, bitterness souring her. "How about my position at your company?"

"Ann-Ann." JT drew her into his lap. "In May, you'll graduate. It'll be time for us to part."

She rested her head on his shoulder. "I love you. I don't want to leave you."

"In the beginning, we never considered the messy subject of love." He let out a long breath. "Deep in my heart, I desire to maintain our current relationship. But I love you too much to drag you along like this. You deserve to be the wife of a good man, not just a mistress."

"Can't you get a divorce?" She knew the answer. Even so, she had to ask once more.

"I wish I could. We both know it's not possible." He exhaled again. "This friend of mine, Chen Yao, is rich and single. He'd be an excellent match for you."

She slid off his knees. "Is he as rich as you?"

"Not quite." JT drew her back to sit by him. "He has an advantage over me. He's young. From the way his business is going, he may become richer than I am when he reaches my age."

JT's leaving me for good.

The dreadful void inside of her ballooned again, and she covered her face with her hands.

"My baby, don't cry." He kissed her below her ear. "I'll leave at the end of April. Tell me what you want for your graduation. I'll get it for you before I leave."

She wiped away her tears. "I want a string of pearls. One of my friends in Hong Kong has a necklace. Each bead is about ten millimeters. I used to envy her so much. Buy me a pearl necklace. Make sure each pearl is larger than twelve millimeters."

At the end, JT not only gave her a string of pearls but also another apartment. "Chen Yao's subsidiary is in Palo Alto. This is my parting gift. You can practically walk to work from this place." As he spoke, his eyes misted over. "I consider myself lucky. At least from you, I learned why people say love is the most powerful force in this world."

Lost in reverie over those sweet moments with JT, Ann-Ann pressed her lips into a firm, straight line. How she missed him. Then her thoughts drifted to her days in Hong Kong following her twin's arrival. Mama had taken them shopping every day. Whenever anything caught May-May's eye, even before she uttered a word, Mama retrieved her wallet and bought for her.

No matter. May-May's hands became so rough from too much housework, and her ear-length straight hair made her look rather plain.

That hunky husband of hers, however...

He and May-May always glanced at each other. Whenever Jie said something, her twin's giggles lilted through the air. All of them could tell May-May's every pore oozed happiness.

Watching them together... hurt.

But he's just a poor graduate student. I'm sure I'll do better.

"Mr. Chen is here." Susan's voice pulled her back to the present.

Ann-Ann directed her gaze toward the entrance. Their manager, David Chow, strolled in with a tall, well-built man. Perhaps because of his confident expression, Mr. Chen Yao looked older than his supposed twenty-six or twenty-seven years of age. An air of dignity shrouded him. Apart from that, he appeared quite ordinary.

Disappointment slithered through her heart. *Don't be silly. He's a businessman, not a movie star.*

As he walked toward the lectern, he limped. At least that part was correct. He was lame.

Mr. Chen thanked the employees for their hard work and wished everybody a merry Christmas. He spoke English well, with a slight accent.

She asked Susan in a low voice. "Where did he learn to speak such good English? I thought he didn't even graduate from high school."

"Yeah, mysterious, right? David said he also speaks fluent Japanese." Susan whispered back.

After his speech, the party began.

***

Yao ambled around and shook hands with people he knew.

What a cheerful occasion.

His gaze fell on a familiar figure across the room. She hadn't changed much—the same oval face, almond-shaped eyes, and a high straight nose. Her hairstyle changed. Thick black hair, instead of straight and ear-length, was permed into a wild curly mane. Under the chandelier's lustrous light, her skin looked fairer. The rest was the same.

The surrounding chatter faded, leaving him and her in the center. He gaped at her, a peculiar agitation pulsing through his body. RUN! The voice of his mind shouted, yet his heart yearned to talk to her.

"Don't be ridiculous," he muttered under his breath. "This can't be May-May. May-May's married. She and her family are in Hong Kong. This is Ann-Ann, May-May's twin."

"Did you say something?" David Chow patted his arm.

"Nothing important." Yao swallowed hard. "I thought I'd seen somebody from my past."

Still, he couldn't turn his eyes away from her. "Excuse me, David. I need to see someone right now. Let's meet at the entrance in fifteen minutes."

He strode across the room and bit his teeth against the pain in his leg, trying to appear normal.

"Are you Lee Ann-Ann?" He stared at her familiar face, his hands and feet trembling.

She gave him a questioning glance. "Yes? Mr. Chen?"

He forced a smile. "I'm Chen Yao. You have a twin sister named May-May, don't you? I grew up with her in Beijing."

"You're *that* Chen Yao?" Her jaw dropped. "The boy May-May talked about all the time in her letters? What a surprise. Somehow, I've never associated you with him."

Unlike May-May's soft-spoken voice, her tone was modulated, strong. He calmed down and spoke in his usual manner. "Don't be too hard on yourself. Thousands of Chinese men are named Chen Yao."

She clutched a fist to her chest, her eyes flashing and lips curving. "What a coincidence. We need to get together."

Without hesitation, he jotted down her phone number.

In the evening, he didn't sleep well. The same dream, in an altered format, visited again. Pa and he swam in a river. He moved toward Pa, but the torrent pushed him away. He yelled for help, and May-May jumped into the current. In an instant, both of them disappeared. "Pa, May-May..."

He woke up in a cold sweat.

During the following week, he spent hours going over documents each day and dining with his managers every evening. When all data indicated the subsidiary had an excellent start, he breathed out his relief.

Yet happiness eluded him. No matter how hard he tried, he couldn't purge the desolate darkness consuming his heart. *Chen Yao, accept the fact. Didn't the doctor say you suffer from a mild form of depression?*

***

On New Year's Day, Ann-Ann received a call from Yao. "I've not had a chance to see San Francisco. Will you be my guide?"

She'd been waiting for his call since the Christmas party. "Sure. It's my honor. Do you want me to drive?"

"No. I'll pick you up."

Putting down the phone, she examined herself in the mirror. "No, this doesn't look right. I need something more alluring."

She went to her closet and rummaged for that special outfit. The green silk pantsuit with a low-cut neckline would do. As JT wished, she'd make Mr. Chen fall in love with her.

From her apartment, they went straight to the Golden Gate Bridge. Even though it was the rainy season, the day turned out beautiful with the Bay Area's signature blue sky.

Yao pointed at the magnificent span linking the San Francisco Peninsula to Marin County. "This structure was once called 'the bridge that couldn't be built.'"

"Yeah, it's considered one of the great wonders in the world." Ann-Ann ducked her head to hide a smile. She'd seen it too many times to be amazed. "Let me take a picture of you."

After receiving the camera back, he checked his watch. "What's next?"

She tilted toward him, increasing the visibility of the plunging neckline. "How about Fisherman's Wharf?"

A quick drive brought them to the waterfront. As they strolled along the pedestrian walkway, she shot him a teasing glance. "How's life in Hong Kong?"

He grinned. "It's a rather general question. What do you want to know? The life of the general public? Or mine?"

"Yours." She donned her glasses to hide her mischievous smirk. "Tell me about your personal life."

"I live by myself in a house on the Hong Kong Island side." He blinked. "No, I don't live alone. I have a few servants."

She brushed her fingers against her chin, a wave of anticipation spreading through her. "Tell me what you do for your pastime."

"Hmm..." He put a hand in his pocket. "I don't have a lot of free time. I work ten to twelve hours most days. Occasionally, I hang out with friends. That's all." He huffed a dramatic sigh and shook his head. "What are you doing? Interrogating me? How about you? Have you been in the Bay Area for long? How's your life here?"

She smoothed her hair behind her ears. "My life is quite simple. I'll answer your questions later. First, I need to clarify a few myths. People in the office circulate many wild tales about you. I'm sure some of them are totally untrue."

He raised an eyebrow. "Such as?"

"Like you got shot by a gangster during one of your fortune-hunting expeditions." She couldn't stop giggling. Even what she'd said sounded funny, unreal.

"What if it's true?" He chuckled along with her.

The more she knew him, the more she liked him. In the beginning, she thought him weighty, too serious. Yet he was witty, clever. She examined her nails. "Maybe. Tell me."

"You guessed it right. I got shot. More a life-and-death situation, not a fortune-hunting expedition." He told her about his escape from China to Hong Kong.

"Wow, sounds like it would make an awesome novel." She patted his arm. "What was your life like in Beijing?"

Sadness came into his eyes. "My mother died when I was four years old. My pa did his best to take care of me. Pa was a good father.

He taught me many Bible stories. I often recited Bible verses with him."

Warmth seeped into Ann-Ann's heart. "How did he become a Christian?"

A fleeting smile softened his mouth. "Your grandma, Lee Nana, shared the gospel with him. He accepted Jesus as his Savior." His expression turned somber again. "After our pastor was put in prison, the church building got shut down, but we continued to meet in small groups. Just in case the government confiscated our Bible, Mrs. Fu, our pastor's wife, assigned different books in the Bible for each of us to memorize. I believe, eventually, everyone memorized most books in the New Testament."

Her jaw dropped. "I'm impressed. Do you still remember them?"

"Yes." His steps slowed. "Try me."

"Revelation twenty-one verse two."

"'I saw the Holy City, the new Jerusalem, coming down out of heaven from God, prepared as a bride beautifully dressed for her husband.'"

"Acts seventeen verse twenty-eight."

"'For in him we live and move and have our being.' As some of your own poets have said, 'We are his offspring.'"

She picked two more verses at random. He recited them verbatim.

"Incredible. You've indeed memorized most of the New Testament. So, you're a Christian?" She brushed her hair with one hand again, a surge of joy buoying her heart. *Mama will be thrilled if I marry a Christian.*

Yao didn't answer. Instead, he asked, "Do you go to church?"

"I've been attending church since I was a child." She glanced at him sideways over the thought of how she'd skipped Sunday worship during her high school years. "I can recite quite a few verses."

He resumed his pace. "Which church do you go to? Is it a Chinese church?"

"I don't like Chinese churches. We have a small Chinese community in the Bay Area. Too much gossip. I attend an American church in Berkeley." She pointed a finger at him. "Let's get back to your life in China. Tell me more."

"Our situations turned rather destitute. Everybody suffered from a lack of food. Even so, I was happy because—" He swallowed hard.

She raised her gaze to him. "Yes?"

"I was happy because I had my father and..." He sucked in a deep breath. "Your nana was very kind to us. She taught me and May-May English." He paused again. "We experienced nonstop political movements. One winter, I went away from home, and my pa died. A Red Guard killed him in a denunciation meeting." He pinched his lips tight, his face a ghastly white.

After not hearing any words from him for a few minutes, she gave his arm a gentle squeeze. "You poor thing."

He shifted one step away, his expression cold and distant.

Didn't I sound sincere? Why was this sudden change? "I'm sorry. I didn't mean any harm."

He blew out a long breath. "It's okay."

She flashed a smile and tried to lighten up their conversation. "Did you leave anything out?"

"No, that's all." He held up a hand. "Now it's your turn to answer my questions. Why don't you go back to Hong Kong?"

She moistened her lips, unease creeping in. "My mama asked me the same question. I'm used to living alone. Besides, my grandparents are in the process of moving from Taiwan to Hong Kong. My grandpa has retired." She stepped up closer to him. "Most likely they'll end up staying with my mama. Her flat is quite small. If I go back to Hong Kong, I'll need to rent an apartment by myself, anyway."

An awkward silence descended. As she prepared to break the stillness, Yao spoke. "Your mother is always kind to me. I've been to her place. She told me you attended UC Berkeley and worked to put yourself through college."

"Yes, I worked part-time in college." *Oh no. I'm edging toward a dangerous topic.*

Whew, he didn't ask about her temporary job.

The sun dipped low on the horizon with lingering rays in the western sky. She stowed the sunglasses in her bag. "When are you leaving San Fran?"

"I'm scheduled to leave tomorrow." He touched his eyebrows. "I plan to change my ticket to stay for a few more days. Will you be available for dinner tomorrow?"

***

241

Yao turned his Mercedes-Benz off the road from Ann-Ann's apartment and glanced at her in the passenger seat. *My last night with her.* He'd take her to his favorite French restaurant.

For the occasion, she wore a red jacket. After they sat at their table, she peeled away her blazer to reveal a simple black dress with double straps.

Illuminated by the flicker of the candlelight, her smooth shoulders glowed like polished white jade. As a tingle of heat crept up to his belly, a muttering sound emerged in his mind. "May-May wouldn't wear such clothes."

Following dinner, he drove her back to his house in Palo Alto. He'd bought the ranch in a large lot equipped with a koi pond when he established his subsidiary in the Bay Area. But he'd never invited a woman over before.

Inside the garage, a flurry of questions filled his head. *Why did I bring her here? What do I want?*

With no easy answers in sight, he made martinis, and they sipped their drinks overlooking the yard. In the dark garden, the lampposts around the pond cast mystifying shadows from the nearby trees.

She set her glass down on the end table and shuffled over to his side. Her hand went up to remove his drink. He stood still with a half-smile. She cupped his face and licked his lips.

As an accomplished equal, his skillful tongue ventured down her neck. In response, her body twitched. They shifted toward the white leather sofa and fell together. With a fluid gesture, she unclasped the dress straps. The garment cascaded off her body, revealing nothing underneath.

He goggled at the beautiful female form in front of him and froze. While the fire in his loins grew into a flame of hunger, he couldn't help thinking of May-May. *She wouldn't do this.*

Instead of launching forward, he stood up from her.

"What's the matter?" Ann-Ann straightened her chest, her eyes narrowing.

He grabbed his glass, tossed down a long swallow of the drink, and remained silent.

She put her dress back on. "Don't tell me you're gay."

His lips pressed together as though his words were struggling to stay within. But no. He should just let them out. "I have herpes."

An angry glower tightened up Ann-Ann's face. She spoke with clenched teeth. "So, you sleep around a lot, right? Didn't you say you're a Christian?"

He shook his head. "I've never told you I'm a Christian."

She stood up. "You're not? You memorized the entire New Testament."

"That doesn't make me one." He took a step back. "You're not a Christian either."

"What?" Her body shook as if she were the center of a massive earthquake. "Don't be ridiculous. Certainly, I am."

"A Christian doesn't do"—he slashed a hand toward the sofa—"what you just did."

Her nostrils flared. "What do you mean? Did I do anything wrong? I've received my baptism, and I believe in Christianity. If I'm not one, then what's a Christian?"

He shifted farther away. "I can't tell you what a Christian is. I can tell you what a Christian isn't. A Christian isn't someone who receives baptism, attends church regularly, or serves as a pastor in the church. A Christian isn't someone who reads the Bible often or even memorizes the entire Bible. If it's that simple, all the Pharisees at Jesus' time would be Christians."

She bared her teeth and scoffed. "How dare you teach me what a Christian is or is not? You're an insufferable, stinky jerk!"

An urge to slap her engulfed him, but he forced himself to stay motionless. "I'll call you a taxi."

The next day, he left for Hong Kong. Ann-Ann didn't see him off at the airport.

Chapter Twenty-Nine

"When I kept silent, my bones wasted away through my groaning all day long."

Psalms 32:3

Hong Kong
February 1974

Yao and his two business partners ambled down a narrow street in Tsim Sha Tsui off Nathan Road, hemmed in by men with similar shady smiles.

They strolled by a place named Pussy Cat. His two companions slowed to survey the photographs of naked bodies displayed inside a covered glass case. A tall lad with a cigarette dangling at a corner of his mouth stood in the doorway and shouted, "Come on in. Young chicks. Very beautiful."

One of his friends, the one with thin tufts of a mustache on his upper lip, gave him a questioning glance. Yao shook his head and spoke in Japanese. "Kawai-san, we'll go to Sweet Memory tonight. Mama-san there told me they've just recruited a few gorgeous ladies in their early twenties."

They strolled into the nightclub, and a middle-aged woman with heavy makeup came over to meet them. "Mr. Chen, long time no see. I'm glad I called you yesterday. Otherwise, who knows when you'd come to visit us again? Do you want me to make the picks for you?"

He gave her a nod with a slight smile. She yelled to several misses nearby. "Lily, Nancy, Elaine, the guests are here. Table five."

Three females in high heels shifted toward them. Tight red *qipao* dresses highlighted their every curve. "Welcome to our club." The girls greeted them in Japanese in unison.

They entered a room with a table situated behind an embroidered silk screen. The women guided them to their seats and carried on small talk in poor Japanese. The two Japanese men didn't seem to mind. Kawai-san grasped Nancy's hand and placed it on his thigh. In response, she giggled and urged him to drink more.

Out of intuition, Yao sensed Lily, who sat by Tokuyama-san, kept peeking at him.

I hope it's not a sign of trouble.

Sometimes club girls competed for certain guests. Other times, patrons vied for the same woman. No matter what, it often caused problems.

Lily and Elaine spoke to each other in Mandarin. As he suspected, they asked for a seat adjustment. After Lily took the seat next to him, she whispered in Mandarin. "You're Chen Yao, are you not?"

Yao stretched his eyes wide and stared at her heavily made-up face. Recognition slammed into him—his former neighbor, Shao Li.

Maybe alarmed by his stupefied expression? The guests around the table paused their eating and drinking. Lily murmured again, still in Mandarin. "Calm down, Yao."

His years of business experience didn't fail him. He pulled himself together, and everything returned to normal. When the wine bottles emptied, the other two couples went upstairs. He remained at the table with Lily.

She spoke in a teasing tone. "Shouldn't we go to my assigned room like them?"

He stood up. "You're joking."

"What happened to your legs?" She must have noticed his wobble.

"I'll answer your question later." He peered around. "Let's find a place where we can chat. I don't suppose you live nearby, do you?"

"I do." A grin widened her mouth. "I've never taken my client back to my flat, though."

"Let's go to your apartment. I live on the Hong Kong Island side. Going there tonight isn't convenient. I'll invite you over soon." He led the way out.

Lily directed him to her studio apartment in Waterloo. Once inside, she mixed a drink for him. "How did you learn to speak such good Japanese?"

"Lots of practice, plus an excellent teacher." He told her about his life as a construction laborer, street hawker, and entrepreneur.

She leaned against the wall. "So, you've made it, as the Hong Kong people love to say, right?"

He sipped the Bloody Mary. "It all depends. This city moves too fast. Nobody can claim to have made it. Once you relax, you'll be replaced." He set his glass down on the coffee table. "I consider myself lucky. From a tranquil fishing outpost to a booming financial mecca, this place witnessed a remarkable makeover in the span of a few short years. I caught the boom of Hong Kong."

She drew him to sit together on the sofa. "I wish I were here earlier. It's still not too late. At least I caught the end of the boom."

They talked about the present but focused more on the past. Yao told her how he got hit during his escape from Guangdong to Macau.

"My story is similar, except I'm more fortunate. I wasn't shot. My sister and I went to a small village in Guangdong to be retrained. Hui married a local cadre. I became a freedom swimmer." Shao Li picked up her glass from the coffee table.

Yao fixed his gaze on his glass. "How are your parents? Is Mrs. Dong still there?"

"They're all doing well. Believe it or not. Mrs. Dong turned into someone like May-May's nana. She tries her best to help everyone in the courtyard." Shao Li smiled. "Have you heard from May-May? You used to like her a lot."

Upon hearing that special name, he frowned. The memories of Pa and his past crashed over him, his emotion plunging into turmoil.

Shao Li sipped her drink. "She's so kind and gentle. I always favored her even more than my own sister. I hope she's well in Inner Mongolia."

He let out a silent sigh. "She's in Hong Kong. Her husband is a graduate student at the University of Hong Kong, studying law. They have two boys."

"My, I'm in shock. She's married? Has two sons?" She raised her eyebrows. "Have you met them?"

"Yes."

"Is she still as beautiful as before?"

Yao touched his chin. "She... She hasn't changed."

Yet May-May didn't look the same. His visit with her family following his return from California remained vivid.

The Lees had reserved two tables at a Shanghainese restaurant in Tsim Sha Tsui. When he arrived, everyone was already seated. May-May and her husband stood to greet him, each holding a child.

"Jie, this is Chen Yao, my good friend whom I grew up with." She used her free hand to point at him. After he and Ying Jie exchanged polite words, she spoke to her children. "Say hello to Uncle Chen."

The two boys obeyed, and he sat across from her at the round table. Although they busily took care of their kids and chatted with other family members, Jie and May-May exchanged subtle nonverbal cues from time to time.

Bitter envy engrossed Yao's heart. Only a few years ago, he'd been the recipient of her glances and smiles. Now they were for another man.

And another aspect of her changed. In addition to trust, her whole person oozed desire and seduction toward her husband, something he'd never seen in her before.

Shao Li tugged at his sleeve. "Does she still blush easily?"

"Yes."

He recalled every detail of that gathering. At one point, Ying Jie whispered to May-May. Her cheeks flamed crimson, but she giggled and gave him a playful pinch.

Shao Li waved to catch his attention. "Does she know you have a gigantic business?"

"I don't think she's interested." At Auntie Kam-Chu's request during lunch, he'd given them a brief report of his newest deals, and May-May congratulated him with a sweet grin.

Shao Li gave his arm another gentle touch. "Have you seen her again afterward?"

"No."

As his answers became shorter, their conversation died down. They lapsed into silence and listened to the street sounds on an ordinary Hong Kong evening.

When he regained control of his emotion, he stretched his legs and stood. "I'd better leave now. Hope Mr. Tokuyama and Mr. Kawai have a wonderful time. Are Elaine and Nancy good?"

Shao Li winked. "You don't have to worry. Everyone in my clubhouse is superb."

During his drive home, perplexing questions raced through his mind. "Why can't I be happy? What's wrong with me? If I were offered the opportunity to give up my wealth in exchange for being with May-May, would I do it?"

He had no answer.

On Shao Li's next day off, he went to pick her up. Back at his house, after he parked his Mercedes-Benz inside the main gate, she got out and sauntered to the garden to examine various bushes with yellow, orange, red, and golden blossoms.

"How large is the lot?"

Yao trailed behind her. "About a quarter of an acre."

She glanced at him, her long hair sweeping over her face. "It's still winter. How do you get these flowers to bloom at the same time?"

"Simple. Hire a gardener." He chuckled. "Hong Kong's winter isn't too cold."

In the foyer, she pointed at the light green floor. "Is this marble?"

"Yes."

Walking into the living room, she slapped a hand on her cheek. "I know you're successful. I didn't realize you're this rich."

"I'm just doing okay." He walked around her to stand in front of a Chinese painting depicting the countryside. "In this city, a few hundred million Hong Kong dollars are nothing in some people's eyes."

Shao Li waved toward the other rooms. "Could you show me around your house?"

"Sure, it's my pleasure. Please follow me." He led the way out past the more understated dining room with its grand crystal chandelier as its focal point. From there, they strolled to the family room.

She peeked through the French doors. "Is that an Olympic-size swimming pool?"

Nodding, he guided her back to the dining table. Soon, two maids brought in food and drinks. He dipped his chopsticks into the roasted duck. "Will you consider working for me?"

"What kind of job do you have in mind?" She took a sip of cabernet Sauvignon. "And the pay?"

He placed a piece of duck breast on his plate. "It depends on your abilities. The most suitable job may be as a PR person for one of my hotels. The pay is pretty decent, two thousand Hong Kong dollars a month."

"Public Relations?" She wrinkled her eyebrows. "It won't do. Sometimes I make more than that in one night."

Yao halted his chopsticks in mid-air. "It's different. You don't—"

She raised her index finger. "Let me tell you one simple fact. In this society, if you're poor, you get laughed at. If you have money, no matter how you acquire it, your friends respect you. I'm aware of how risky my job is. Many go astray. I must be careful to avoid drugs and gangsters. So far, I'm okay."

He heard similar tales from other girls, but the story conjured up a distinct meaning when told by someone from his past, a past that still haunted him. He resumed eating and took time to enjoy the juicy meat. "I'm sorry. I don't mean to judge you. Tell me your thoughts. I assume you don't plan to do this for the rest of your life?"

"Of course not. Nobody can do this for long. Once I save enough money, I'll open a boutique to become my own boss." Articulating her idea, she gestured with excitement. "I'm always interested in fashion. I'll do well."

Impressive. She wasn't the kid back in the Beijing courtyard anymore. "How much do you have now? How much more do you need?"

She gave him a number. He did a quick mental calculation. "How about if I give you a loan to start your business right away?" He stared at her without blinking. "I own several boutiques myself. I'll introduce you to Han Susie, my manager in this sector."

Shao Li dropped her chopsticks. "What do you want in exchange?"

"We can strike a deal. I'll be your partner and share your profits. I'll ask my lawyer to draw up a contract."

True to his words, he arranged for Shao Li to meet Susie in his Chang-Ji office. With Susie's help, Shao Li set up a boutique in Tsim Sha Tsui within two weeks. Yao's factory provided all her supplies. She proved capable, and her business took off.

In early April, he stopped by Shao Li's shop. "Chang-Ji will set up a new hotel named Teaton on the Hong Kong Island side. Do you want to run another shop in the new hotel?"

"Of course." She clapped her hands together.

After the second boutique opened its door, she called him. "I bought a flat with a harbor view. Please come to my housewarming party tomorrow at six."

Yao brought a two-year-old Merlot. He stepped into her apartment but didn't see any other guests. Shao Li prepared an array of food, including his favorite—tender bamboo shoots stir-fried with fresh soybeans and baby carrots.

She poured him a glass of red wine. "Why do you like this simple dish so much?"

He didn't answer. Tonight, he didn't want the past to disturb his emotion. "Li, show me the harbor view."

They sipped wine in silence, soaking up the enticing Hong Kong evening.

Then she put down her glass and sighed. "I love this city."

She strolled toward him, dipped one middle finger into his wine, and moistened his lips. He shut his eyes, letting her kiss away the liquid. She whispered, "Everything in my bedroom is new, new pillows, new silk sheets. You ought to look."

He turned away. "Li, I have herpes."

"No need to say more." She clasped his arm. "A little raincoat will work wonders. Come, the night is still young."

On his way home in the morning, he couldn't help wondering aloud. "Why can't I resist temptation? Sex with Li will complicate our business deal. Why do I keep doing things that I don't want to do?"

With no definite answer in sight, he entered the living room.

The phone rang. Auntie Leesan's voice sounded. "Yao, are you available tonight? Have dinner with us. Everybody will be there."

He plopped down on the sofa. Should he go? *No. Seeing May-May smile at her husband will only bring more misery.* "Thank you very much. Sorry I can't. I have a conflict."

"You're always so busy."

He dropped the phone and sighed. After working alone in his home office for a few hours, he went to his favorite nightclub, Sweet Memory, by himself.

The following Friday, Fabian and Susie stopped by together at Yao's Chang-Ji office. An enormous grin sprawled across Fabian's face. "Susie and I just got engaged. We want you to be the first to know."

Yao's mouth dropped open. No wonder his friend hadn't asked him to go to nightclubs for the past few months. He shook hands with them. "Congratulations. When is the wedding?"

"The first Saturday in September." Fabian pulled out two chairs for him and Susie. "Yao, you're our dear friend. We worry about you. The faster your business grows, the more your mental health deteriorates." He spread his hands to encompass the enormous office around them. "Lee May-May's marriage dealt you a heavy blow. It's tough. We hope you'll forget the past and find someone new."

Touched by Fabian's deep concern, Yao blinked as moisture clouded his eyes. He blurted out the hidden thought in his mind, "Easier said than done. Where will I find a girl who loves me instead of my money?"

Susie exchanged a glance with Fabian. "Finding a suitable match in your current situation won't be easy. We wish Lee May-May were still single."

The darkness in Yao's soul expanded to gobble him up. He squeezed out a few words. "I... I'm glad May-May is happily married."

"Yao, you're worthy of our praises." Fabian let out a long breath. "You'll be a good husband. Whoever becomes your wife is a lucky woman."

Once his friends left, Yao sat alone in his seat for a long time. Hours later, he headed to Shao Li's flat.

After sex, he lay in bed with his arms under his head.

She tickled his neck. "You appeared melancholy during our lovemaking."

He stared at her exposed white shoulder.

"Yao, why are you so miserable?" She drew her hand back. "I asked you the question before. You've never answered me."

She looks lovely. He averted his gaze. *But under her feminine façade, she has great ambition.*

When he remained quiet, she hit her fist against the silk blanket. "I seldom see you smile. What can I do to make you happy?"

Keeping his composure, he waited for her to continue.

"Forget May-May." She sat up, baring her upper body. "Don't dwell in the past, especially now she's married to a wonderful husband and has two little boys."

How did Shao Li read him so well? He frowned and rolled away from her. She said it effortlessly. *Could she help me sever the twisted threads that weave me with Pa and May-May into an inextricable bond?*

"Yao?" She jabbed at his back. "Say something, please."

"My life has become too complicated." He glowered her way. "I'd better go."

After brooding through the weekend, he entered Teaton Hotel, determined to work and put the past behind him, but somebody came forward to greet him. "Yao."

Why was May-May's nana here? He bent to hug her. "Lee Nana, what a surprise. Are you here by yourself?"

"Yes." She bobbed her head, white hair ruffling about her thin cheeks. "Jie is busy with his studies. May-May took her sons to visit her mother. I heard this hotel belongs to you and decided to stop by."

He guided her toward his office. "What a coincidence. I don't come here every day. It so happens that today I need to process some paperwork for them."

Lee Nana waved a finger at him. "Nothing in the Lord is by chance. This morning, during my devotion, the Holy Spirit urged me to come to Teaton. Here we are."

He pulled a chair for her. She was just like before, always talking about her faith.

She settled into her seat. "We consider you a member of our family. Since our arrival in Hong Kong, we've been dining together every week. Leesan told me she calls you often to invite you. You're usually occupied with your business." Her eyes bored into his. "I've been praying for you. I sense you're under a heavy yoke. Will you tell me about it?"

He clasped his hands in his lap and frowned at his custom-made leather shoes. "No, Lee Nana, nothing."

"You look miserable." She reached forward to touch his arm. "You're no longer that carefree boy back in Beijing."

When he kept silent, she let out a sigh. "I brought you something. It's the last letter I received from your father. He asked me to share a message with you."

She laid a piece of paper on his desk and directed his attention to one paragraph.

Yao is on his way to visit you and May-May. When you see him, please tell him, no matter what befalls me, I'm prepared to face it. Recently, I've received words from Him, 'Be faithful, even to the point of death, and I will give you the crown of life.' I consider it a blessing. Death is our doorway to the promised land.

At the sight of his pa's handwriting, he could no longer contain himself. A slow letting go of unstoppable tears trickled down his cheeks. Lee Nana didn't say much but looked at him with deep concern.

Following an uncomfortable silence, he spoke. "Revelation two, verse ten."

"You still remember the Bible verses?"

He nodded.

"We'd been extremely careful not to mention God, Jesus, or any religious terms in our letters. It's unfortunate your..."

As moisture glinted in her eyes, she pulled out a handkerchief to dab her face. "Your father must have had a special relationship with the Lord. Remember what Paul said in Second Timothy? 'I have fought the good fight, I have finished the race, I have kept the faith. Now there is in store for me the crown of righteousness.'"

"Second Timothy four, verses six to eight," he whispered.

She inclined her head. "I've found something rather astonishing. Those who walk closely with the Lord always learn in advance when their journey on earth is ending. Your father was a beloved child of God. He wanted you to know it."

Fresh tears stung his cheeks. His thoughts drifted in and out of focus, along with memories of Pa and his days back in Beijing. His weeping turned into howling.

Lee Nana came over to hug him, her arms warm around him, her voice soft in its crooning.

At last, he raised his head and gazed at her wrinkled face. "Since my pa's death, I've sinned..." Between sobs, he revealed his innermost thoughts—the hatred he harbored deep, the anger toward God, his futile love for May-May, his frequent visits to the nightclubs, his sexually transmitted infections, his encounter with Ann-Ann in California, and his recent liaison with Shao Li.

Lee Nana patted his back. "Yao, do you remember the parable that Jesus taught about the father and his two sons? Our heavenly Father is waiting for your return. He does care about you. Otherwise, I wouldn't be here today. I believe He has sent me to bring you back to Him. Will you come home?"

While crying, he fell to his knees with her. After he said his prayer, by some means he didn't fully comprehend, the darkness entwined in his heart drifted away, thread after thread.

Chapter Thirty

"Pass me not O gentle Savior, Hear my humble cry. While on others
Thou art calling, Do not pass me by."

Fanny Crosby (1820–1915), "Pass Me Not, O Gentle Savior"

May-May stood with Nana outside the church sanctuary and
directed her gaze at the main entrance, eager to see her other family
members. "I wonder why they're not here yet. We have ten minutes
left before worship starts."

"Maybe they're stuck in traffic." Nana patted her arm. "Did Jie
take the boys downstairs to the children's Sunday school?"

"Yes. He'll be up soon." At the mere mention of her husband,
elated sweetness flooded her heart.

An hour ago, after she'd changed into a dress in their bedroom,
Jie hugged her from behind and whispered, "You look magnificent."

She turned around to give him a long kiss, oblivious to the time
until Nana yelled from the living room. "May-May, we need to get
going."

Only then did she rush out of their room with Jie.

Nana tugged on her sleeve, drawing her back to the present. "Is
your granduncle's family here?"

"Yeah, they've already gone in."

Her thoughts floated along with memories of their first week in Hong Kong. Mama had treated them to a shopping spree. She seemed determined to purchase all the suitable clothes from the Wing-On store for them.

"Leesan, enough," Nana had grumbled while grinning. "At my age, how can I wear so many clothes?"

Her mother didn't listen. Instead, she took them to jewelry stores to buy gold necklaces, bracelets, and rings, almost like she wanted to compensate for her lost opportunity of sending them supplies during the past years.

May-May crinkled up her mouth into a smile. How blessed to be around her loved ones again—her mother, grandparents, and Auntie Kam-Chu.

All of them constantly begged to babysit the boys. Yet Jie set aside every Saturday for their family. No matter how busy he was, he took the four of them to the countryside. They didn't own a car. By bus and ferry, they traveled around outlying islands.

The elders didn't give up and compiled a schedule to take turns babysitting the children. Her weekdays became free. She planned to attend a school to expand her culinary skills but couldn't afford it. Her mother learned of her plight and gave her a large sum of money.

When Jie contended that it wasn't right to take money from Mama, Nana sat them down for a talk. She gripped his strong hand and looked into his eyes. "It's okay to accept the gift. Just remember to pay it forward and extend God's grace to others."

Jie had given in. No one could resist Nana.

May-May smiled and tilted her face to the sun filtering through the stained glass. *God's mercy is great.*

At the sight of four familiar figures and their companion, she stretched her eyes wide and gasped. "Yao?"

Nana stepped forward to greet him. "You came all the way to Kowloon? There are churches on the Hong Kong Island side."

Yao scratched his forehead. "Lee Nana, it's not too troublesome to drive over. I don't know anyone in other churches."

Mama took Yao's arm. "Mother, he called me this morning and came to pick us up. After worship, he'll have lunch with us."

As Jie came up the stairs, Auntie Kam-Chu walked toward the sanctuary. "Jie is here. Hurry! Let's go in. Worship is about to start."

Lord, thank You for Yao. Please bring him closer to You.

May-May's prayers paid off to a certain degree. Yao started joining their family gatherings, although he still kept himself off to the side, not quite the dear brother and friend from her youth. Still, she cherished her childhood friend's presence in her life again—and for his return to God's kingdom.

And her boys loved their uncle.

With them at her sides, she couldn't help grinning as she read them a familiar storybook about the prodigal son. Somehow, Yao had found copies of the books Mama sent them all those years ago.

The phone rang. She handed the book to four-year-old Nian-Rong to continue "reading" with his brother while she answered it.

"What a surprise, Shao Li." She tightened her grip on the receiver, the air whooshing from her lungs and her mouth sliding open. Her gaze jerked to the book, a copy of the one Shao Hui helped her fix after they'd torn it. "When did you come to Hong Kong? How did you get my number?"

"I have my connections." Shao Li laughed. "Are you free? Can I come to see you this afternoon?"

"Of course. I have time. My mother is coming soon to take my boys to dim sun with her and my grandparents." She provided directions to their apartment at the University of Hong Kong.

After the phone clicked, Nana approached. "Did Shao Li just call you?"

"Yes." May-May tugged her to the sofa. "Nana, you knew Shao Li was in Hong Kong, right? How come you didn't tell me before?"

"I learned about it recently. I meant to tell you. Somehow, I forgot." Nana touched her forehead. "My mind isn't sharp anymore. My days have become too busy. I go out almost every day with your grandma and others."

May-May made a face with rolling eyes to tease Nana. "You're not complaining, are you?"

"Me? Complaining? No way. I praise our good Lord nonstop." Nana grasped May-May's hand. "Now your grandpa and grandma are in Hong Kong, life can't be any better. Everybody tells me they love to see you and Jie together. In his presence, you always radiate a special glow."

Her face burned. "They said that?"

"Yes." Nana patted her cheek. "All the time, your mama says she's so thankful you and Jie share the same values rooted in the Christian faith. She only wishes Ann-Ann will be as blessed as you." At the mention of Ann-Ann, Nana sighed.

May-May didn't respond but gave Nana a bear hug.

"Your mama said Ann-Ann changed her job again. I hope she can come back to Hong Kong." Nana's eyebrows contracted. "I've been praying for her. Last year when I saw her, I sensed something buried deep inside of her. Later, your mama told us about her abortion."

May-May let out a hard breath. "Quite disturbing."

"Let's continue to pray for her." Nana walked toward the bathroom.

Someone knocked, and Mama rushed in. "Have you packed the boys' clothes? We'd better hurry. Your grandpa and grandma are already in the restaurant."

May-May sauntered to check on her boys, who were busy playing woodblocks. "Okay. Time to go to dim sum."

The boys jumped up and ran toward Mama. After they left, Nana strolled back to the living room. "Your mama stopped by already? That was fast." She moved to their coffee table to flip through a pile of envelopes. "Has Jie confirmed that your uncle Duan is arriving this week?"

May-May put the toys into a storage bin. "Jie said everything is going well. Uncle Duan will come to us this Sunday. I can't wait to see him. I haven't seen him for so long."

Nana's lips curled up. "Me too. Duan is like my second son. I miss him so much."

A second son... May-May's mind drifted toward her childhood friend. "I'm glad Yao has been coming to church these past weeks. Since our arrival, we met him once. Then he disappeared for almost an entire year. I wonder what made him change."

"God works in mysterious ways, but His timing is always perfect." Nana brushed the hair away from May-May's temple and cupped her cheek the way she had when she was little. "Be prepared, my darling girl. I have a hunch Shao Li's visit this afternoon will be about Yao." She lowered her arm. "What time does your mama bring back Nian-Rong and Si-Rong?"

Heat crept up to her face again. "Mama wants to keep them with her tonight. She told me I ought to have a kids-free date night with Jie."

"I guess she wants a granddaughter badly." Nana smiled. "Let's have lunch early today. Our guest is coming soon."

At two, they welcomed Shao Li into the small living room. May-May stepped forward to embrace her old neighbor. "Li, you're all grown up."

"You're even more beautiful than before." Shao Li handed her a box of chocolate. "Lee Nana, you look well."

After May-May poured their tea, her visitor took one sip, set the cup aside, and scooted to the edge of her chair. "Have you seen Yao recently?"

"Yes." May-May sat by Shao Li. "We see him at church. He also comes to our family gatherings."

"I..." Shao Li described her relationship with Yao. "He's avoiding me. I called him every day but couldn't reach him. I went to his office at Teaton. He wasn't there. They informed me he stays at his Chang-Ji office nowadays. I don't have the employee badge and can't go there."

May-May raked her fingertips across her cheek, at a loss for what to say.

Shao Li waved. "I suspect he's seeing someone else."

Nana came over to sit by them. "I can assure you Yao isn't seeing any other woman. He's in a new relationship, though."

"What do you mean?" Shao Li clutched her purse to her chest. "Is he dating a man? I had no idea he's—"

Nana shook her head. "No, it's not that. Yao has told me..." She recounted their recent conversation. "He's finally established a personal connection with God through Jesus Christ. He's trying hard to please the Lord in whatever he does."

Frowning, Shao Li blinked. "I don't understand."

"We believe in God, who created us because of His love. Although our sin prevents us from knowing Him, He still loves us." Nana gazed into Shao Li's eyes. "God wants to connect with each of us. Since He's holy, He needs to deal with sin and let Jesus Christ die on the cross to pay for the price of our sins. If we're willing to repent and accept Jesus Christ into our hearts, we can establish a connection with God. The Holy Spirit will begin to live in us."

Nana gave Shao Li's arm a gentle pat. "Although Yao cares very much about you, he needs time alone to sort out the issues in his soul, since he's now a member of God's family."

Shao Li stroked her neck. "Do you think so? If he cares about me, he shouldn't avoid me like this."

Nana's mouth crinkled up. "You're an attractive girl. I can appreciate why he wants to avoid you until he becomes sure of himself. In time, you'll hear from him."

Shao Li's face dropped. "I often observed he wasn't happy even..." Tears welled up in her eyes. "I've tried to talk to him. He never responded. Sometimes he just stood up and took leave. I didn't know he thought what we did was bad." She dabbed her cheeks with a handkerchief. "Is there anything I can do to get in touch with him?"

"You have to wait. When the right moment comes, he will reach out to you." Nana put her hands together. "Li, do you want me to pray for you?"

Shao Li pursed her lips. "All these things about God are new to me. I need to think about it."

"I understand." Nana nodded. "No problem. We can wait until you're ready."

Compelled by a tender emotion, May-May embraced her friend. "Maybe you can come to our church on Sunday?"

Shao Li lowered her chin. "What's the use? If Lee Nana is correct, my presence will only vex him."

May-May's heart ached for her. "Not to see Yao but to learn more about the Bible."

"I'll try." Shao Li retrieved a notebook from her purse. "What's the name and address of your church?"

On Sunday, Shao Li came into the sanctuary before the worship started, sat in the last row, and left as soon as Pastor Mang gave his benediction.

Following worship, the family went to their favorite Shanghainese restaurant like before. While Granduncle chewed on a piece of steamed dumpling, he turned to Yao. "May-May's dumpling is so much better than this."

Yao grinned. "I agree. She should open a restaurant of her own."

Overhearing their conversation, May-May couldn't help saying, "Granduncle, here you go again."

"May-May, seriously." Mama smiled at her. "Many of us wait for our turn to babysit your two boys. Maybe you ought to consider doing something interesting."

Uncle Ming-Ming licked his lips to tease her. "At least we'll get to eat our free lunch."

Yao directed his gaze toward her. "Chang-Ji has built another hotel on the Hong Kong Island side. We want to set up a restaurant there. If you're interested, please let me know."

She exchanged a glance with Jie and sensed affirmation in his eyes. "Let's pray about it. If the Lord wants me to do it, I will."

Nana stood up after they emptied the plates. "It's about time. Let's go to Kowloon Station together."

May-May followed the others out, her husband's hand on the small of her back and her family's words in her heart. Perhaps she would open a restaurant. When she peeped up at him, Jie winked back.

At the station waiting for Uncle Duan's arrival, her mother was unusually quiet.

"Are you nervous?" She grasped Mama's hand, her fingers icy cold to the touch. "Don't worry. You and Uncle Duan will work out well as a couple."

Mama nodded. "Yes. It's just—" She touched her forehead. "I've not seen him since I left Beijing some twenty years ago, even though we kept up by letters."

Nana interrupted them. "He's here."

A familiar tall figure stepped off the train.

"Uncle Duan." May-May ran to him and wrapped her arms around his neck. "You've not changed much, except more tanned. You still look so handsome." Laughing, she tugged him toward Mama.

"Hi, Leesan." Uncle Duan smiled.

Color spread over her mother's cheeks.

While everyone wept and laughed simultaneously, Kam-Chu spoke in a loud voice. "We'd better leave. We're blocking people's way. Let's go to Yao's place. His house is the most spacious."

***

A few days after Duan settled into Yao's house, Leesan answered her phone to May-May's chirrupy voice. "Mama, tonight we plan to

261

dine with you and Uncle Duan in our apartment. He'll drive Yao's car to pick you up."

Leesan let out a soft sigh. "Aren't you busy preparing for your new restaurant in Mindeng Hotel? How do you find time to cook for us?"

"It's okay. Please just come."

May-May cooked all Duan's favorite dishes, and they chitchatted late into the night.

The next morning, another call from May-May came through for Leesan. "Mama, Uncle Duan is new here. Someone should show him around town. You're familiar with Hong Kong. Could you be his guide?"

Heat rushed to Leesan's cheeks. But she heeded her daughter's request and took him to a few hiking trails in the New Territories. At first, awkwardness flooded her. After a few dates, she looked forward to their outings.

On this day, they traveled by ferry to an outlying island, Cheung Chau. Leesan led him toward a natural cave where the famous Guangdong pirate Cheung Po Tsai was said to keep his treasures. Sitting side by side on a rock, they watched the waves crawling to the shore.

Duan grasped her hand. "How did you find your way back to God's family?"

Without hesitation, she confessed everything. Tears of sorrow flooded her eyes at the memories of her previous unbearable humiliation.

He drew her into his arms and whispered, "It's so difficult for a young widow. I thank God you've established a close relationship with Him."

She rested her head on his chest. "Rong's mother told me how you came into God's family. Those years were oppressive. If it weren't for you, May-May and Nana would have suffered more."

He smoothed down her hair. "Our lives are in God's hands. Born in China during this era, I don't know if it's a blessing or a curse."

She listened to his even heartbeat with a content grin. As he ran his fingers down her arm, a familiar sensation zipped through her body. The passion that had laid docile for years flared up.

Then his baritone voice caressed her ears. "Yao has asked me to join his company. What do you think?"

She played with the buttons of his shirt. "That's great. How about you? Do you like it?"

Duan chuckled. "I was a farmer in Yunnan for quite some time. I suppose I can do anything. Yao also said after we get married, he has a newly renovated rental ready for us to move in."

"Married?" She raised her head to look at him.

He sported a broad smile, his usual melancholy expression gone. "Everyone is waiting for our wedding bells. I don't have money to buy a ring. If it's okay with you, I'll propose right now. Will you marry me?"

Her head grew dizzy. "I–I..." She nodded.

"You're still as beautiful as when I first met you." He cupped her face and placed his lips on hers.

Amidst the sound of waves smashing against the rocks, she hugged him and kissed him back.

Following that outing, she called Ann-Ann. "Remember that I told you Uncle Duan came to Hong Kong? I plan to marry him."

The other end of the line went quiet.

"Hello? Ann-Ann?"

"I'm still here." Her daughter's tone chilled Leesan. "Mama, how old are you? Aren't you ashamed of being an old bride? Haven't you any fears of being ridiculed?"

"You—"

A *click* reached her ears. Ann-Ann had hung up.

After staring at the dead phone, Leesan headed to her friend's flat and shared her daughter's response. "It seems she still doesn't want me to remarry. I don't know what to do."

Kam-Chu patted her shoulder. "Don't forget, another daughter is by your side, anxiously waiting for you to marry Liang Duan. You can't please everybody. I don't think you should consider your daughters' opinions this time. Pray and just follow the guidance of the Holy Spirit."

For days, Leesan made more calls to the Bay Area. Finally, Ann-Ann said, "Okay, go ahead if you're so determined to marry him."

Leesan let out a long breath after her stubborn daughter promised to be a bridesmaid.

Once they began, the wedding arrangements took less than a month. Much easier than she thought.

This momentous morning, as she opened her eyes, the darkness in her room startled her. She glanced at the alarm clock. "Only four forty? No wonder it's so dark."

It had been a long time since she dreamed of Rong. Yet he came to her last night, in a fragmented dream full of different incidents. He still looked so youthful. She leaned to kiss him, and the reality of her age hit her. No, she was no longer his young, vibrant bride, but a middle-aged woman, old enough to be his mother. When her lips almost touched his face, she ducked her head, full of shame. Then Duan approached and asked her in a low voice, "Why are you leaving Beijing?"

We were both in our twenties when Duan asked me that question.

Time fled. She stifled a sigh, mixed emotions stirring inside of her.

Noises from the living room reached her ears. She glanced at the clock again. Not even six o'clock. Why had her parents awakened so early today? Maybe they also experienced a myriad of feelings on her wedding day? After all, they hadn't been there for her first one.

Ugh, I'd better get up now.

She turned on the light and strolled to the closet to take out the white bridal gown. Admiring the lace dress, she hummed, "While on others Thou art calling, do not pass me by."

Chapter Thirty-One

"Amazing grace, How sweet the sound, That saved a wretch like me,
I once was lost, But now I'm found, Was blind, but now I see."

John Newton (1725–1807), "Amazing Grace"

Hong Kong
March 1975

After the wedding ceremony, Su-Ann led Su-Nong's family into Yao's mansion at Mid-Levels on the Hong Kong Island side. She tilted her head toward her sister-in-law. "Praise the Lord. The weather forecast said it would rain, but God gave us a beautiful sunny day, perfect for a wedding."

Shu-Fang nodded. "Yes, it's so nice. The Lord's mercy is amazing."

Two gigantic flower vases stood by the entrance, welcoming guests to a place well decorated for this grand occasion. Hydrangeas in glass jugs graced the bride and groom's table. The words *Wishing Liang Duan and Wang Leesan lots of love and happiness* gleamed from a red banner on the wall.

"Nana." In a light-green gown as enchanting as a fairy, May-May came forward to greet her.

Su-Ann touched her granddaughter's bare shoulder. "How long have you been here?"

"Yao drove Jie and me here straight from church." May-May adjusted the flower on her dress for her. "This qipao suits you well."

"You're adorable too." Su-Ann couldn't help smiling. "Where's your mama?"

"I talked to her minutes ago. Where did she go?" May-May craned around. "She and Uncle Duan are in the corner."

Her gaze followed May-May's index finger. Leesan, with her new husband by her side, was conversing with the editor from her publisher.

Su-Ann squinted at the couple. "Your mama is still gorgeous."

"Yeah, she and Uncle Duan look great together." A grin widened May-May's mouth. "Jie said if there were a beauty pageant for the mothers-in-law, my mama would be crowned the champion."

"That husband of yours is a sweet talker." Su-Ann curved up her lips again. "Where is he?"

"Over there." May-May pointed in the other direction at Jie and Yao standing together.

"How about the boys?"

"Don't worry." May-May patted her arm. "Nian-Rong and Si-Rong are with Yao's servants. Since food is catered from my restaurant today, they have time to supervise all the children for everyone."

"Excellent." Su-Ann surveyed the guests in the spacious room. "Is Ann-Ann here yet?"

"She arrived with Auntie Kam-Chu a while ago. I don't know where she's now." May-May cast her eyes around. "Yao's house is huge. You can disappear out of sight easily."

As they chatted, May-May's restaurant manager rushed over. "The kitchen needs you."

May-May brushed aside a stray wisp of hair. "Nana, I have to go. I'll be back soon."

"No problem. Don't worry about me."

Su-Ann scanned the area. Where was her brother?

A few steps away, Wang Jia-Ting, Wang May, and Kam-Chu waved at her. She strolled over.

"The red flowers fit well with your silver-gray traditional qipao dress." Kam-Chu touched the small bouquet of roses on Su-Ann's dress. "Don't forget, you're the groom's family representative. You'll say grace for our dinner at six thirty."

She glanced at the corsage. "I'm thankful Duan wants me to represent his family. In a way, he's like my other son." She turned to Wang Jia-Ting. "The moment you and Leesan walked into the sanctuary, I wept."

"I wept too. We didn't attend Leesan and Rong's wedding. I never expected..." Wang May pulled out a handkerchief to dab her face.

"My dear sister Wang, don't cry. It's a joyful occasion." Kam-Chu patted Wang May's shoulder. "Leesan's bridal gown was simple yet elegant. Originally, she didn't want to wear a white dress. She worried others would sneer at her since she's an old bride. I told her not to mind what others think. She didn't get to wear a bridal gown when she married Rong and shouldn't miss the opportunity this time."

Su-Ann nodded. "The bright-red dress she's wearing now also fits her perfectly."

"I dare say everything is outstanding. The pastor's sermon touched me very much. Pastor Mang has always preached well. Today it's especially good." Kam-Chu swung her arms. "I loved the way he quoted the book of Ruth and used the jade ox as his prop. During his talk about how Duan gave the jade to Su-Ann, several people nearby wiped their tears. When he described how Jie and May-May helped locate Duan, they laughed out loud."

Wang Jia-Ting smiled in his daughter's direction. "The newlyweds will go to Lantau Island tomorrow for their honeymoon. They don't want to leave Hong Kong since Duan is still waiting for his permanent resident card."

"I'm so thankful." Wang May's eyes sparkled. "The two ring bearers did well. Si-Rong is too young to understand what's going on, but he followed his older brother and did an excellent job."

"After two identical bridesmaids, one in green and the other in blue, entered the sanctuary, I heard people whispering. Some guests probably didn't know about Leesan's twin daughters." Kam-Chu grinned. "May-May walked in and kept staring at Ying Jie. Her affectionate expression cheered up everyone's heart."

"Jie's appearance made me laugh." Su-Ann chuckled. "With a smug expression, he acted like the groom waiting for his bride to go to him."

"They're an enviable pair. In comparison, Yao stood next to Jie with a serious countenance." Kam-Chu directed her gaze at Chen Yao. "Ann-Ann didn't smile either."

"We have to pray for them." Su-Ann let out a long breath. "Excuse me. I have to speak to someone. I'll be back shortly."

She'd visited this house many times. As she strolled toward the study, she breathed out deep, savoring the moment's contentment.

The children God put into her care turned out well at last. May-May's restaurant at Mingden Hotel became a popular hangout for young professionals. Her granddaughter had also set up a soup kitchen at church to provide free meals to low-income families. And Yao? He'd contacted Shao Li but made it clear he couldn't continue his liaison with her. Despite appearing dispirited, Li still came to church on Sundays. Maybe one day, she'd come to know God.

At the study, Su-Ann pushed open its ajar door. Ann-Ann sat by the desk, tears streaking her face. As she approached, Ann-Ann cried out, "Even Mama is married now. I'm left alone all by myself."

"Oh, my dear girl." Su-Ann stepped forward to hug her.

Sniffling, Ann-Ann wiped her eyes. "Everyone looks so happy today. Why do I feel miserable? I should be excited for Mama. Uncle Duan is a great guy. I..." She buried her face in her hands.

Su-Ann gave her back a gentle pat. "Is there a hole in your heart that makes you feel upset?"

"You know?" Ann-Ann lifted her face.

How fragile her granddaughter looked. Su-Ann rubbed the ache in her chest. "Nana has been there."

"You also had an—" Ann-Ann cupped a hand over her mouth.

"Your mama has told me quite a few things about you. No, I've never had an abortion." The poor child. What had been the magnitude of her anguish? Su-Ann raised her gaze toward the ceiling, searching for the right words. "After my husband's death, I plunged into despair. My life lost focus. Our family was well-to-do. Maids took care of my son, your papa. I grew addicted to playing mahjong and often played late into the night until morning."

Ann-Ann's tears stopped. "And then what happened?"

"We moved to Chungking during the war against the Japanese and became neighbors with your grandpa and grandma. Your grandma invited me to Sunday worship. I declined at first. She didn't give up. Later, I went with her to be polite." Su-Ann's hand returned to her granddaughter's back. "Jesus caught my attention, and I accepted Christ as my Savior. The void in my heart disappeared."

Ann-Ann's face crumpling up, she unfolded a handkerchief to wipe her cheeks. "I'm also a Christian. How come I still experience a hole deep inside of me?"

Su-Ann clasped her hand. "Do you think you know God personally?"

Frowning, Ann-Ann fisted the handkerchief. "I don't understand what you mean."

With a deep breath, Su-Ann sank to her knees before the girl, grasped her chin, and peered up into a face she knew so well, yet eyes she didn't know at all. Tired eyes. Lost eyes. "Do you have a confidante? Think about how you interact with your good friend."

Something—hesitation?—flashed across Ann-Ann's face. "I once knew a person who understood me well. I felt secure with him. When he left me, the void returned right away."

"Interacting with God is just like you and your pal. It's even better. People will leave us. God won't. We may fail Him, but God will never abandon us." Su-Ann released her granddaughter's chin and cupped the side of the girl's face. "Do you have a normal relationship with God?"

Ann-Ann wrinkled her eyebrows.

Pushing herself up from the floor, Su-Ann pulled out a chair and sat. "A Christian is a person who has established a link with God through Christ. If someone has no connection with God, then he's not a Christian."

Ann-Ann's mouth curved downward. "I've been to church since I was young. I'm familiar with the Bible and consider myself a Christian."

"Many kids from Christian families often think if they attend church and read the Bible, then they're Christians. If that were the case, the Pharisees in Jesus' time would be considered believers." Su-Ann tapped the table with her fingertips. "The Lord told them they had nothing to do with the kingdom of God. To become a member of God's family, you must interact with Him on a deeply personal level."

"Nana?" Ann-Ann gave a choked sound. "Do you know God personally? What does it feel like?"

"I do." Su-Ann stopped her fingers. "Knowing Him brings transformation to my person and renews my life perspective every day. In the most fearful moment, I sense a unique peace in my heart...." She described her persecution during the Cultural Revolution.

Ann-Ann heaved an audible breath. "I had no idea your situation was so bad. I always thought Mama loved May-May more than me." She spilled out her heart, including how she harbored intense jealousy toward her twin since childhood. "How do I connect with God?"

Her chest warming, Su-Ann patted Ann-Ann's arm. "What do you think? What does the Bible say?"

"Repent of your sins..." The girl wept again.

Su-Ann remained quiet.

At last, Ann-Ann regained her composure. "All the time, I've tried to justify to myself. The abortion wasn't my fault, and living together with my boyfriend was a good decision." She blinked. "Deep in my heart, I admit those things aren't pleasing to God. They're sin."

"God is holy. You can't know Him with sin inside you. If you repent and receive Jesus' redemption, the Holy Spirit will help you establish a personal relationship with God." Su-Ann gave her granddaughter's shoulder a gentle squeeze. "Do you want to confess your sin to the Lord today?"

"I do."

They knelt together and prayed. Afterward, Su-Ann lifted her gaze, and Yao was leaning against the doorframe. "Yao, we have a new member in the family today."

Ann-Ann's face shone with a new peaceful glow.

Yao stretched out a hand. "Lee Nana, the guests are waiting for you to say grace."

"Really? What time is it?" She twisted her watch into view. "Six forty already? Dinner was scheduled to start at half past six. Look at me, so demented."

"Nana, you're not demented at all." Ann-Ann grinned. "Don't let the guests wait. You and Yao go first. I'll patch up my makeup and join you right away."

Su-Ann took Yao's arm. As they entered the ballroom, the live band started to play her favorite hymn, "Amazing Grace."

At the sight of Leesan, May-May, and their husbands standing together, Su-Ann raised her voice to sing. "'I once was lost, but now I'm found. Was blind, but now I see.'"

The End

Curious about Yao and Ann-Ann's future? Dive into *Detour to Agape* https://www.amazon.com/dp/B0CD9P29GJ, an atypical sequel to *Blazing China*.

A Note from the Author

Hello and thank you for sharing this journey with me. Writing this book was a special and emotional experience, and I cannot say how honored I am that you joined me through these pages. If you like the book and have a moment to spare, I would appreciate a short review. Thank you for your help.

About the author

Although I grew up in Hong Kong and Taiwan, my family members live in different parts of the world, a common phenomenon for most Chinese my age because of political conflicts.

I work for a small biotech company and have published 120+ scientific books and papers (under my legal name).

While I am relatively new to the realm of creative writing, I am honored that the Anoka County Library in Minnesota chose me as a 2025 Featured Author and the Suffolk Virginia Authors Festival selected me as a 2025 featured author.

My book, *Echoes over Stormy Sea*, has won several awards, including being recently chosen by readers as a winner in the HOLT Medallion Contest.

Amazon Best Sellers
Our most popular products based on sales. Updated frequently.

I currently live in the Midwest with my husband, a retired pastor. We served together at three churches from 1987 to 2020. Our grown son works in a nearby city.

Check out my other books.

The Way We Forgive (Women's fiction): https://www.amazon.com/dp/B0BQ5LNLNB
Blazing China (family saga): https://www.amazon.com/dp/B0CD9P49HW
Detour to Agape (sequel to *Blazing China*; contemporary romance): https://www.amazon.com/dp/B0CD9P29GJ
Prestige of Hearts (contemporary romance): https://www.amazon.com/dp/B0CV4FL3CH
Center of Enigma (Paradise PA Mystery Book 1; mystery/suspense/thriller): https://www.amazon.com/dp/B0D9R2M134
Essence of Illusion (Paradise PA Mystery Book 2; mystery/suspense/thriller): https://www.amazon.com/dp/B0DFVPKW3N
Allure of Elegance (Paradise PA Mystery Book 3; mystery/suspense/thriller): **https://www.amazon.com/dp/B0FCP1BV32**
Series Page: https://www.amazon.com/dp/B0DFNXPSGW
Love Under Holy Skies (contemporary romance): https://www.amazon.com/dp/B0F362Q7T8

Echoes over Stormy Sea (Action/Adventure; Dual-time Odyssey Book 1): https://www.amazon.com/dp/B0DPGQ6TZP

Thunders over Idle Land (Action/Adventure; Dual-time Odyssey Book 2): https://www.amazon.com/dp/B0F49GFHW6

Fire Between Two Skies (Action/Adventure; Dual-time Odyssey Book 3): https://www.amazon.com/dp/B0G2YZZ8LG

Series Page: https://www.amazon.com/dp/B0F4LKXS2W

Nonfiction (under Ruth Wuwong):

Are your health and finances linked? A Christian Entrepreneur's Quest:
https://www.amazon.com/dp/B0BQ5JXFYY

Wander Or Not: https://www.amazon.com/dp/B0CXJ79MWF

To connect with me, please go to www.ruthforchrist.com.

Follow me on social media:

Amazon: https://www.amazon.com/author/love.respect.grace
Goodreads:
https://www.goodreads.com/author/show/42632055.R_F_Whong
Bookbub: https://www.bookbub.com/authors/r-f-whong
Twitter/X: https://twitter.com/RWuwong
Instagram: https://www.instagram.com/ruthwuwong
Facebook: https://m.facebook.com/ruth.wuwong